Quiet jog, g... ...evening

merely a question of holding that suddenly
required break, which had I left it later
till every one else was going to move I
could never have gained. The fight would
have been sterner and closer. It was as
usual a case of getting first break on the field,
catching them napping, and for all practical
purposes the race was over 300 up
from home. I had merely to keep steady pace
down the back straight, coast round the
bottom bend & then at the beginning of the
front straight put in another little effort
as a second response to dishearten and
choke off a further attack. I finished in
wonderful form, relaxed & comfortable, and
jogged on another half lap.

It was undoubtedly the most beautifully
executed race of my career, a true climax!
to 8 years steady work, an artistic creation

Later felt a little weary but v. fit.

(P.J.Q.)

LOVELOCK

LOVELOCK

James McNeish

"How could anyone stop a man doing what he did
in his dreams?"

SIEGFRIED LENZ
The German Lesson

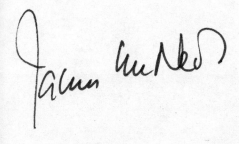

HODDER AND STOUGHTON
LONDON SYDNEY AUCKLAND TORONTO

For James Bertram

in gratitude

British Library Cataloguing in Publication Data
McNeish, James
  Lovelock.
  I. Title
  823[F]   PR9639.3.M23

ISBN 0 340 36430 0

Hodder and Stoughton Editorial Office: 47 Bedford Square, London WC1B 3DP.

CONTENTS

MAPS

Page 210

Plan of the Olympic Stadium, Berlin 1936

Page 212

Plan of the Olympic Village, Berlin 1936

AUTHOR'S ACKNOWLEDGMENTS

I record first my grateful thanks to members of Dr Lovelock's family, principally his sister, Mrs Olive Butler, his daughters, Mary Lovelock and Janet Baer, and his nephew, Dr M. J. Butler. Among survivors of the Berlin Olympics I am especially indebted to A. G. K. Brown, J. F. Cornes, Glenn Cunningham, Hans Fritsch, Gisela Mauermayer, Friedrich Schaumburg, Siegfried Schulz and Sydney Wooderson. Also to two other former athletes, Anthony Leach and Aubrey Reeves, for their many letters containing a wealth of detailed reminiscences. In Berlin, Professor Richard Löwenthal first alerted me to the activities of the anti-Nazi underground during the 1936 Games; Dr Felix Escher and Gerhard Obermüller gave freely of their knowledge, their libraries and many other kindnesses; similarly Dr Jürgen Wetzel of the Landesarchiv Berlin and his staff, and Eva Orbanz and Werner Sudendorf of the Berlin Filmarchiv, went out of their way to smooth my path. In New Zealand the Rector of Timaru Boys' High School, Mr Ian Sawers, provided access to the Lovelock Collection; the Winston Churchill Memorial Trust gave generous support. In Oxford, the Warden of Rhodes House, Dr Robin Fletcher, opened files and, at Exeter College, Mr Walter Eltis provided introductions and hospitality and made a suggestion which brought a flood of correspondence from old Exonians. Research in Germany was conducted while I was a guest of the DAAD Berliner Künstler-program and I acknowledge the help of this remarkable institution. I am indebted to Anthony Stones and particularly Janet Wilson for some outstanding research after I left England. I thank my London agent, George Greenfield, for his enthusiastic support – this project could not have begun without him. Nor would it have proceeded so happily without such a wise and sympathetic editor as John Bright-Holmes.

I plead guilty to omitting an important Lovelock victory

(Empire Games, 1934): a comprehensive record of Lovelock's sporting career will be found in Norman Harris' *The Legend of Lovelock* (London, 1965), Nelson & Quercetani's *Runners & Races* (California, 1973) and C. Tobin's *Lovelock* (Dunedin, 1985).

Several people have read the typescript in whole or part before publication, among them Mr J. F. Cornes, Dr Dermot Manning and the Lord Porritt, while Stan Greenberg has cheerfully kept my statistics in order. Their suggestions have rescued me from a number of pitfalls and I thank them warmly. I am indebted in addition to people in many places, especially New Zealand, who have provided information and help, and answered queries. To record all the names would require a fresh chapter. I hope they will accept my gratitude and the spirit of this narrative in return for their kindness and pardon me if I list only the following:

Dr E. Peter Allen, Neil Allen, Mrs M. R. Bainbridge, W. D. Baragwanath, Dame Josephine Barnes, Professor Richard Barrer, Mrs John Begg, Mrs Jane Bonthron, Mrs Werner Böttcher, Bill Charteris, Basil Chubb, Mrs J. F. Cornes, Sir Lance Cross, Robert Dahl, Mr and Mrs Dan Davin, Professor Liselott Diem, Sandy Duncan, Sir Jack Eccles, Hugh Elliot, Dr and Mrs A. W. Frankland, Professor Russell Fraser, Hans-Joachim Funke, The Hon. David Geddes, Sir Arthur Gold, R. St G. T. Harper, Norman Harris, Mrs W. Hawkesworth, Charles K. Heaton, Mrs W. E. Henley, the late Dr C. J. G. Hodson, Dr Peter Hubrich, Dr A. H. James, R. Ossie Johnson, Dr T. A. Kemp, Maj. Leslie Lambert, Dr A. W. Lewis, John Lockwood, Dr D. Ludbrook, Mr Edward McCullough, D. B. G. McLean, Professor J. W. McLean, Terry McLean, Norris McWhirter, Dr J. B. Maddicott, Emeritus Professor J. C. Mahoney, Mr W. M. Manchester, Cecil Matthews, Yogi Mayer, Ekkehard zur Megede, Gerlinde Metz, Wolfgang Mönninghoff, Professor G. E. Moloney, Wilfred Morgan, Dr Hendrik Muller, Dr N. North, James N. Oliver, Ron Palenski, Robert Parienté, Brian Pheasey, Bill Pullar, J. Railton, Dr A. M. Rutherford, S. P. Salek, Dr John Saxby, Hans Senftleben, Professor J. D. Sinclair, Maisie Smith, Sir John Stallworthy, Dorothy Stevens, Mr Neville Stidolph, R. E. Tongue, Major-General P. G. Turpin, Walter Volle,

Mrs G. W. Washbourn, Dr J. C. Watt, Charles Wenden, Sir Edgar Williams, Professor Charles Wynne, Florence Winter, Professor Dr Wolfgang Wippermann.

Acknowledgment is made to Mr Anthony Abrahams, chief executor to the will of Harold Abrahams, for various matters including copyright; Mr Abrahams also read the typescript. I thank the *Guardian* for the quotation by Evelyn Montague on pages 382–3. And, for granting access to records: BBC Sound Archives; Radio NZ Archives; Bodleian Library, Oxford; Bundesarchiv (Film Dept.), Koblenz; Ullsteinarchiv, Berlin; Mr Keith Lockyer, Secretary, St Mary's Hospital Medical School; Janet Foster, Archivist, St Bartholomew's Hospital; Tay Wilson, NZ Olympic Association.

Acknowledgment is also made to Methuen London Ltd for permission to quote (on page 380) six lines of Noel Coward's "Lie in the Dark and Listen" from his *Collected Verse*.

I thank my typist, Sylvia Lawton, for a great deal, including many hours of overtime. And finally my wife, Helen, who interpreted and translated for me in Berlin, for everything.

April 1986   J.McN.

AUTHOR'S PREFACE

One cannot travel far in the mountains of Olympic conquest without encountering Lovelock. With some exceptions the fame of sportsmen is notoriously short-lived and it is not often that an athlete who is remembered for only one race continues to dominate a landscape after the passing of half a century. Fifty years after Lovelock's victory in the 1500 metres at the 1936 Olympic Games a mystique remains; an aura surrounding a small wraith-like figure in black continues to stir the imagination of people who have no other interest in sport. Indeed Pindar's Olympian odes, which raised the champions of 2500 years ago to a divine order of beings, might have been written for someone like Lovelock.

Still, now that words like glory are out of date, it is not enough to say he was the man who ran "like a god": who hypnotised his opponents from the back: who caused the Berlin Stadium to erupt in a tumult: the man whom, so the legend has it, Hitler was moved to crown with a laurel wreath. More compelling, to me at any rate, is the disguise Lovelock adopted to overcome an inherited handicap; and his view of himself. John Edward Lovelock (1910–49) was born in an obscure mining town on the west coast of southern New Zealand, an empty corner at the ends of the earth; he came to Oxford as a Rhodes Scholar in 1931; five years later he was an international celebrity and household name. At Oxford he read Physiology and treated his body as a human laboratory. His unexpected victory in 1936 against the greatest field of milers ever assembled has about it all the hallmarks of a great discovery.

What seems to have happened in the last fifty years is that writers on both sides of the Atlantic have lifted this athlete from the field of sport and placed him in another sphere, that of art. Where once his name was coupled with Nurmi's, now it is as likely to be placed alongside Nijinsky's. Lovelock has become

11

to middle-distance running what Nijinsky is to ballet or Caruso to opera. This is partly – but only partly, I suspect – because of the manner of his death.

Despite the millions of words that have been written about Lovelock, his death in New York at the age of thirty-nine has never been explained. In diaries and journals Lovelock analysed himself as no runner had ever done before and – he has been called the first modern athlete – here lies his significance for sportsmen: he changed a climate of thinking and anticipated the four-minute mile. Otherwise his life is a resounding blank. Lovelock covered his traces as adroitly as he ran; he was at pains to hide his private life and in my case might have succeeded had not his daughter Mary written to me at Oxford early in 1984. I was then at the end of my European researches. Shortly afterwards when I visited her in New England, Mary Lovelock presented me with a small pocket diary belonging to her father which had been travelling about in luggage items and drawers, overlooked, since his death in 1949. It was this diary for 1936, revealing among other things the depth of his obsession, that provided a clue to her father's death and gave me the courage to write the sort of book that this has become.

It is not the book Lovelock would have written. Rather, as an attempt to explore an obsession, it is the diary that he never wrote. After the Berlin race, letters and other documentary evidence fall away. The diaries and journals, copious as they are, are remarkable chiefly for what they do not say and when I began my research important witnesses, including Lovelock's widow, were dead. A strictly factual biography was ruled out. Where facts are known, I have included them; elsewhere I have followed the novelist's craft, the only one I know, and the convention of using the recollection of contemporaries as a basis for dramatic interpretation. Fiction is tidier than real life and there are inherent dangers in a fictional diary approach such as I have adopted, but there is one advantage: the view from inside the subject's head is restricted and this has forced me to curb the novelist's tendency to embroider. I have tried not to indulge in myth-making.

Several people in the book are still alive and my thanks to them as well as to many others who have helped me at various stages are recorded on pages 7–9. I interviewed sixty

12

contemporaries in five countries: England, Germany, New Zealand, Switzerland and the United States. Many travelled long distances to see me and at the time this response surprised me; I realise now that it has to do with an ingredient in a man's personality quite outside running, some touchstone or human frailty common to genius that evokes a response in us all. In the book names are unchanged; conversations are invented, as are the letters by Lovelock in Chapters 6, 10 and 17. Although I have sometimes quoted from Lovelock's actual journals, the "diary" extracts are substantively fiction. But unless my interpretation is badly astray, the narrative essentially corresponds to Jack Lovelock's real life.

Part One

1932

"Now! Now!" cried the Queen. "Faster! Faster!"

LEWIS CARROLL
Through the Looking-Glass

I had been up at Oxford for nearly six months when I made my blunder. Until then I had, like the dutiful Rhodes Scholar I was, done everything right, everything correct, I thought. My college had accepted me. Because of my disability – I have trouble in sleeping at night, a failing that runs in my family – Exeter College had given me its quietest rooms over the Fellows' Garden at the top of the dons' staircase, an unexpected privilege. I was determined to honour it. Oxford puts you under a microscope and if you are a Rhodes Scholar from one of the colonies you are all the time conscious of being different. Almost the first thing I did when I arrived was to buy an umbrella at Walter's in the Turl and a pair of Oxford bags. I joined several clubs; I was boxing for my college; I was secretary of the Oxford University Athletic Club and I had been elected to Vincent's, the most select club in Oxford, to which only Blues and Half-Blues are admitted. I was working well in Physiology. I flattered myself that I had not put a foot wrong. I was even losing my New Zealand accent. As my identity merged with the spirit of the place, I felt I was catching the manner of Oxford perfectly.

Then, the day before my race at Iffley Road, I met Janie.

It was 1932. The year of "Stormy Weather". The year of the Benzedrine Inhaler, of the first Zippo cigarette lighter, the year that Franklin D. Roosevelt was elected President of the United States. It was the year Schmeling lost the world heavyweight boxing title to Jack Sharkey in New York, the year they put a new bridge over the Thames at Lambeth, and Greta Garbo came to Oxford in the movie *Grand Hotel*. Half the male undergraduate population of Oxford seemed to be talking about Garbo that year – and all the rest, about Janie Van den Bosch. She was Dutch – Dutch-American. She was very rich, they said. Her people owned a castle. She was "it". I knew all about her. The odd thing was that although she was right on my beat, as it were, we had never met. I had been running through the University Parks past the door of her college and past the courts where she played tennis, running almost in her lap. I had been doing this for six months, but until that afternoon in 1932 – it was during Eights Week, the summer Eights at the end of May – we had never met. Michael Albery, another Exeter man, introduced us at a river party.

"Hullo. You're the New Zealander, aren't you?" she said. "The dark horse."

I was flattered. "You're at Lady Margaret Hall?" I said. "Yes."

She had dark acorn eyes. She was hatless in a light summer dress and her thick brown hair shone nut-brown, parted on one side. We were standing amid a crush of people on the Exeter barge below Folly Bridge. Punts, decked with streamers, were crossing from the bank. Three boats were approaching in the distance. People were drinking pink champagne or eating from cups of strawberries and cream, crowding gently to one side of the barge. Even in that gathering, she took the eye.

"I'm sorry. I didn't catch your name. Miss — ?"

"Van den Bosch. Please call me Janie." She held a glass of champagne with the little finger crooked round the stem. "You know, Michael," she said, as her eyes looked straight at me over the rim of the glass, "he's blond, he's not dark. And he doesn't look like a New Zealander."

"No? Oh, Jack's one of us."

"That's what I mean. He looks a born Englishman."

"Absolutely. To the manner born."

Michael Albery, also an athlete, was junior to me on the track and also younger than me, but socially at ease, a good mixer, and in other ways very much my senior. He was in his final year reading law. I had the feeling amid the hidden language of Oxford which comes naturally to Public Schools men like Michael that in his diffident amusing way he was setting me up. I felt my poise slipping. Just then an older, splendidly attired woman appeared, one of the dons' wives, I think, or somebody's mother. "Oh. Mrs Bidwell — " Michael introduced us.

"Who?" she said. "Love-lock? What a charming name." She extended her hand and stepped back. "You must be one of those Rhodes Scholars from America."

Crushed. Utterly deflated.

Michael and Janie exchanged amused glances. Today, although I am still painfully shy, I can look back on the incident and laugh at myself, but at the time I couldn't. Janie said, "Why aren't you in training?" I was too off-balance to speak for a moment. I said, "I am," and held up my empty champagne glass. It had been empty all afternoon, most of the week in fact. I had been spending the week watching the Eights and attending river parties, keeping away from the track at Iffley Road, trying to distract myself to be fresh for the race next day. I had been trying hard not to think of the race.

"Jack doesn't need to train," Michael said. "He runs like a poem."

"Michael says that you're both running tomorrow."

"Yes. In the mile." Michael and I and another freshman, Tony Leach, had been picked to run the mile for Oxford against the AAA, the Amateur Athletic Association of England. "It's just the annual match," I said, playing it down.

"Will you win?" Janie said.

"What does Michael say?"

"Michael says — " She was interrupted by cries from the bank " — Come on the House. You're going up!" A group of freshmen charged along the towpath shrieking encouragement. Hooters sounded. Yells of "House, House, House" came from a neighbouring barge. The boats swept by, each trying to sink the one in front, and everyone craned forward to watch. Janie kept her eyes on mine over the rim of the glass.

"Michael says that you run like a poem."

She must have been all of eighteen. How can anyone be so poised, so assured, so utterly Oxford, I wondered, at eighteen? I wanted to kick her. Presently, producing my best smile, I excused myself. As they turned away, back to the party and the chatter of the barges I heard Michael say, "There, what did I tell you? Isn't it amazing?"

And Janie: "You're right, it goes all the way. When he does that, it goes all the way."

19

They were discussing my smile. I can't help it if I have the biggest mouth in Oxford.

I don't know if it was then or the next day, the day of the race, that a feeling of mutiny began to grow in me. I only know that that night I didn't sleep. My father, when he was alive, had a saying: Lovelocks eat, Lovelocks sleep, Lovelocks win. I never understood what he meant, because in our family everyone pecked at their meals, nobody slept properly and until I came along and won a Rhodes Scholarship, nobody had Ever Won Anything. People said after my father died that he was a born loser, but they never understood that his health was to blame. My mother's health is rather worse, she suffers from chronic insomnia. "Well, Jack," she said, when I left New Zealand, "if I've given you nothing else to take home to the English, I've given you my insomnia." We used to joke about it. Sometimes when I am depressed and can't sleep I think that the virus I have inherited from her isn't just insomnia.

I lay full length on the bed in my rooms and tried to relax. That's all you can do when you can't sleep, lie back with your elbows cupped behind your head and try to relax. I watched the shadows of the chestnut tree overhanging Brasenose Lane flicker on the ceiling of my garret; I heard Great Tom in Tom Tower strike nine, and all the neighbouring clocks of Oxford join in. I loved the clocks of Oxford, almost as much as I loved the bells. When Great Tom stopped, I heard the college gate close – first the wicket, then the gate itself. I waited for the bar to drop with a clang. I liked that feeling too, the feeling of being safe in college behind a locked and barred porch. I heard Tom strike nine, then ten, then eleven. When the street noises had gone and the college was asleep, I got up, put on my warms and went downstairs into the Fellows' Garden. It was quite cold. There was no moon. A single lamp burning in one of the upper rooms of the Bodleian Library cast a glow over the raised walk at one end of the garden and the big horse chestnut overhanging the lane. As I climbed up beside the pond and sat on the wall, something moved under the chestnut tree.

"Hullo Walter," I said. Walter was the college tortoise, named after the Bishop of Exeter, Walter de Stapledon, who founded Exeter College. Walter lived in the garden. "Walter. If you'd won a Rhodes — ?" I put the question to Walter which had been troubling me ever since I came up. "If you'd won a Rhodes scholarship to study medicine but all you wanted to do was run, what would you do?" I climbed up the raised walk and sat on the wall looking into Radcliffe Square; I sat in the seat of old Oxford with the Radcliffe Camera in front of me and the Bodleian Library at my back and an hour later, hearing the midnight chimes of Great Tom echoing through the night, the question was still there, unanswered. As usual, I couldn't make up my mind.

I was reading Physiology. In New Zealand my Rhodes Scholarship had interrupted my medical course in the middle, but in New Zealand there had been no clash – Oxford, not running, was the goal.

"I'm only using my running, Mother, to get to Oxford," I said. She believed it; I half-believed it. My mother had sacrificed everything, including her health, to get me to Oxford. My sister too. I owed it to them, I felt, to try for a good degree, even a First. I had talked it over with my tutor when I arrived. "Better a running Blue and a Second-class degree, Jack, than a First and no Blue." That was what my Physiology tutor had said. Now I had my Blue and already my running and my medical studies were starting to clash head-on.

Something would have to go.

Just before leaving New Zealand I had met a German runner, a teacher and doctor of philosophy, quite unlike anyone I had ever met before. In Germany – in the old Grunewald stadium in Berlin – he had become a national hero: he had beaten the great Nurmi. His name was Peltzer. When he visited New Zealand I skipped lectures and travelled two hundred miles hoping to meet him. I saw him run. He ran like a man in torment. We only met briefly, but the meeting had a strange effect on me – I became fired with the idea of running at the Olympic Games in Berlin in 1936. Since coming to Oxford the idea had grown on me. The Berlin Olympics were still four years away.

The more I thought of Berlin, the more excited I became, and the more excited I became the more horribly I ran and the more hopeless it all seemed.

My running had improved at Oxford. People said nice things about my style, the way I pattered along keeping close to the

21

ground. But our club president, Jerry Cornes, could still give me a start of nearly twenty yards in a mile and run me down. The only reason I had gained my Blue, running in the sports against Cambridge, was because Jerry had waited for me in the final straight. We had crossed the line together in a dead-heat. "Congratulations," Jerry said. "You've got your Blue." But I knew he had waited for me to catch up.

My last race, just a day or so before the start of Eights Week, had been a fiasco. I don't know what happened. In the straight Jerry shot by me on one side and a runner I'd never heard of on the other. I simply stopped. I fell over the line floundering in third place. And I didn't care, that was the odd thing about it. I simply didn't care!

With part of my brain I told myself that I didn't care about tomorrow's race either. Then why was I sitting here on top of a wall at one o'clock in the morning still thinking about it?

From beyond the square, from the direction of Parks Road, the lights of an approaching vehicle were cutting through the blackness; the lights swung into the Broad, illuminating for a moment the dome of the Radcliffe Camera. So much learning, I thought. So many hopes concentrated around me . . .

"*Will you win?*" she had said.

I stood up and walked along the top of the wall to its lowest point, where it joined the shadow of the Bodleian; peering across the stones of ancient quadrangles and silhouettes, I could see openings in the night leading to Wadham and the Parks where a moment before the car had been. I found I was trembling. I had a mad desire to leap into the square, break bounds; run pell-mell through the enveloping night down the avenue of acacias beside Wadham and Keble, through the Parks and up to the door of her college, crying out, "Yes. Yes, I will win!"

What stopped me?

People will tell you that there are no rules at Oxford, that you can do as you please. But there are rules. Even in a race there are rules. There are the hidden rules. When the trembling ceased, I came down from the wall and went back to my rooms. I took down a textbook, Mountcastle's *Medical Physiology*, for I still had my weekly essay to write. Later when I had swallowed a sleeping draught I continued to tell myself that the race didn't matter. I would do my best. I would run the race as planned, the way our coach, Bill Thomas, wanted; if I failed I would fail gracefully, the way Oxford wanted. I fell asleep just before my scout woke me, as the railway yards were starting up, with the sound of shunting in my ears.

"Half past seven, sir. Lovely day. New College boat just going by."

I don't know why my scout wakes me like that. He has been doing it for nearly six months. His patter never varies.

"Thank you, Charlie. What sort of day is it?"

"Bit nippy, sir. Very still. Not a breath of wind."

No wind? Good. The track at Iffley was exposed to the wind on all sides.

"Breakfasting in Hall, sir? Or shall I bring up the usual?"

"The usual, Charlie."

"Mr Thomas rang up. He'd like to see you and Mr Albery and the gentleman from Balliol, Mr Leach, at the track at one thirty."

Bill Thomas was the university trainer.

"Good luck, sir. We're all coming."

After roll-call, I breakfasted in my rooms. Cheese, an apple, four biscuits: my usual pre-race meal. I sent round a note to Tony Leach at Balliol and worked until lunch-time, examining and writing up specimens in the Physiology Department. Coming down the stairs on my way to the track, I almost cannoned into the Sub-Rector, Dacre Balsdon, whose rooms were on the corkscrew landing immediately below mine. Dacre taught Ancient History. Dacre wore a lilac-blue tie and smelled of Morning Glory; as I corkscrewed down, he drew back to let me past. "Dear boy," he said, emitting a sharp laugh. "In pursuit already?" It was Dacre who in his understanding way had granted special permission for me to take meals in my rooms. Dacre seemed to approve of my running, yet, although I lived above him, I was conscious of the fact that I was firmly under his wing.

His teasing high-pitched laugh accompanied me all the way to Iffley Road.

I arrived early and warmed up on the rugby field alongside the track. I walked; I strode; I ended with a gentle 660 yards as

23

the first coaches bringing the AAA team and their supporters from London pulled into Jackdaw Lane by Whitefriars Church. I remember thinking as I walked back to the pavilion: the church looks the same, the grandstand looks the same, the track looks the same: there is nothing in the air to give this day a sense of occasion: yet I feel different. Not tired, not apprehensive. Just – different. I showered and changed, decided not to have a preliminary rub-down, pulled on two sweaters, spoke with Bill Thomas, and with Michael and Tony – we had agreed on a plan for the mile – and went upstairs to sit on the balcony on top of the grandstand. The mile was due to start at 2.30. Presently Jerry Cornes joined me.

"How does it look?"

"A bit dead," I said. "The inside lane needs raking again."

Jerry's owlish face broke into an explosive laugh not unlike the Sub-Rector's. His eyebrows shook. "My dear fellow. All arranged."

I nodded. I was watching the visitors warm up on the track below. "Which is Harris?"

Jerry pointed him out. They had put Aubrey Harris against me.

"Don't worry about Harris. Aubrey's a broken reed."

Aubrey Harris was one of the best milers in England. He was a twenty-year-old soldier star, a trooper in the Seventh Hussars. The previous year he had won the British army title and had topped that run sharing in a world's record performance at Cologne, running for England in a relay match against Germany, a landmark victory. I watched Harris test the cinders below the pavilion, short, canny, a bit of a card. He was casually knee-tapping and not so casually eyeing the long front straight. It was said he wanted to break the Iffley course record set by Jerry of 4 mins. 17 secs. My best time in England was only 4 mins. 23. Jerry himself wasn't running in the mile event, thank God, but in the half-mile – he faced Tommy Hampson, who ran in spectacles, one of England's great hopes for the Olympic Games at Los Angeles that year. But Jerry, whom Bill Thomas had been quietly preparing for two years, was an almost equal Olympic hope.

Jerry said, "Tommy Hampson looks fit! Poor Tommy can't see a foot without his glasses. Now let me tell you something about Harris . . ."

24

It was typical of Jerry Cornes that he tried to forget his own fears in order to help me reduce mine. He was an inspiration towards modesty and achievement without glory; the perfect English amateur; an enormous man. He ran, he celebrated; he sometimes overdid it. He had once been sent down for hurling potatoes in Corpus Hall during guest night. Once after a relay match against Cambridge, after the customary celebration dinner, he had started smashing lamp-posts, resisted four policemen and spent the night in clink. Yet he continued to run and break records. Jerry held all the records at Oxford. He was unbeaten on the Iffley track. How can a man be that determined, I wondered, and not show it?

"Another thing about Aubrey Harris," Jerry was saying. "He doesn't like this track. That should please you."

It did. The Iffley track at Oxford is one of the strangest in England. Not only is it right-handed, that is to say back-to-front, with three laps to a mile instead of the customary four laps, but it has a slight dip along the back straight which continues and deepens into the top camber, with the result that in the final straight, an uncomfortably long straight, you seem to be running uphill. It is an illusion, of course, but it is the sort of illusion that distresses outsiders who don't run here every day. *Outsiders?*

"Jerry. I've just realised something."

"What's that?"

Already the grandstand below us was filling; motors were still pulling in to the entrance by Jackdaw Lane. On the river the bumping races, a far greater attraction, were at their height, yet even rowing fans were coming here – I recognised the blazers and scarves coming off the Iffley Road by the Church of St John the Evangelist and spilling down the slope at the western end. At the other end, knots of college servants were gathered by a dumped railway carriage. All our servants were here. Among the newspaper correspondents I recognised the prowling birdlike figure of Harold Abrahams. Harold was talking to Sam Mussabini and Joe Binks, one of the British Olympic selectors. Half the Olympic selection panel appeared to have come up from London.

"What's that, dear boy?"

"I've just realised, Jerry. This will be my first race, I mean my first race against outside competition."

25

"Oh, Jack, Jack!" Jerry's eyebrows shook with his laughter.

Yet it was true. All my previous races had been small events, gentlemanly university affairs between Oxford and Cambridge or similar clubs, the tactics and the results often predictable, almost pre-determined by the commonly accepted practice of "stringing". This was different. This was like running against England.

Jerry said, "Just remember, keep to the plan. Don't punish yourself, don't lead." I nodded: "Here are your corks – you forgot them."

They were still raking the inside lane when I came to the start. Bill Thomas was standing with the officials; he was one of the timekeepers. He frowned when he saw my corks. Running corks were worn by sprinters; you gripped them in the palm of the hand for fortitude, like biting a bullet after being wounded on the field of battle; they were supposed to summon endurance. I had adopted them as a fad. Bill didn't say anything. He moved his legs up and down.

"Clip-clop, sir," his legs said. "Nice and steady now."

That was Bill. Dark-suited, bowler-hatted Bill. A formula man. Wanted me to conserve energy, not spend it. I know I'm small and frail, but I'm not that frail. Mother hen Bill.

Bill Thomas never said much but what he said seemed to work. I don't think he knew why. We all respected him.

We shook hands. Aubrey Harris had drawn the inside lane, Michael Albery and Tony Leach were in two and three; I was on the outside next to the other two London runners. Six of us. Michael, my third string, was to act as the "hare". He was to go into the lead and stay there as long as he could, then Tony with his fast stride would take over. I was to lie back, aiming to run four evenly paced quarters of 65 secs. each, making a final time of 4 mins. 20 secs. That was the plan. Secretly I was hoping for a time of 4 mins. 18. I had posted friends with watches to give me the lap times. If Harris came through, I was to hold myself back and try to outsprint him over the last sixty yards.

Michael broke, first time. The starter called us back.

As I walked back, I looked across to the pavilion and saw Janie standing there with Jerry and Jerry's girlfriend, Ray Addis. Ray and Janie Van den Bosch were chatting like old friends. It flashed through my mind that Ray and Janie were in residence at the same college and that, although I saw Jerry and Ray all the time and we had entertained each other to tea in our rooms, they had never once mentioned Janie to me or introduced me. Subconsciously, I believe, I had already decided to run the race in my own way, but it was as if until that moment I had not taken hold of the idea properly and swallowed it. Something uncorked inside me. To hell with the lot of you, I thought; I'm going for a record. I just had time to pull Tony aside and tell him what I was going to do, and we were off. I ran straight into the lead.

I sprinted the first 150 yards, then waited for Michael to pass me. "Now go," I said, as he shot past. "Go!"

He led down the whole of the back straight, round the top bend and into the front. The pace was stupid, much too fast; yet I felt at half-throttle. I wanted more. I was running up Michael's legs.

"Go!" I yelled.

Jerry said later that I could be heard shouting all over the ground.

"Go, Michael!" I hounded him through the first lap. I wanted Michael to hold the lead for a full lap and then half a lap more almost to the halfway point, so that Tony Leach could take over along the back where the slight fall would give him a lift. I glanced round. I couldn't see Harris. Tony was still there.

Past the pavilion, Michael began to wobble. "Faster!" I called, ranging alongside. Poor Michael. Halfway round the bottom bend he threw me a look and blew up. Rivulets of mucus were streaming from his nose. I prayed for Tony to come. I seemed to wait for ages. I had no plan now, just speed. Only speed. I was running on air. I had never felt like this before. Behind me, the cinders crunched. I *prayed* it was Tony, not Aubrey Harris, and moved wide on the curve to let him through; but Tony for some reason went wider still, losing valuable time, going round me so slowly I seemed to be back-pedalling. "Now go," I hissed at him. "Go till you drop." Tony Leach was tall, thin as a knife. He was all arms and hair. But he had zest, and he went. He came off the bend and went past me into the back straight like a startled rabbit. He took me down the back and almost another full circuit before he stopped. As I remember – I am writing this from notes in a journal made long ago – that was when the pain should have started. But it didn't. There was no pain at all until the last 300 yards, only the wind in my ears and the cold air rushing by and the sensation of being wrapped in a cocoon, moving freely and rhythmically and insubstantially inside a bubble, inviolable. It was like being wrapped in the hollow of a wave. It was like riding my bicycle again down the one asphalt road in town. There was just the one strip of asphalt in the town where I grew up as a boy – all the rest was stones and cobbles. I remembered that marvellous feeling of coming off the cobbles on to the asphalt. It was like that now, only I wanted more speed. I craved speed.

If the timekeepers I had posted called out the sectional times, I didn't hear them. In the dip passing the railway carriage I saw one of the servants open his mouth and shout something. I heard nothing. At 300 yards I began to sway. At 200 yards I knew I had only to stand up to win. All my instincts and training told me that now was the time to pause, to regain my balance and form and stride gently on to the tape. I couldn't do it. I wouldn't. The desire for speed had overwhelmed all thought of caution. At 75 yards the pain ceased, and I came off the cobbles for a second time. I went at the tape like a bull and jumped it. I had read somewhere that that was how the American sprinter Charles Paddock won his races.

I had never tried a Charles Paddock dive before. I won't do it again. As I jumped, my tongue hit the roof of my throat. I nearly swallowed it.

I felt scarcely blown. I continued trotting round the bend and stopped, looking up at the row of Victorian houses in the Iffley Road and the square tower of the Church of St John the Evangelist. I remember thinking, that tower isn't square, it's round. The houses on either side were falling down. Everything had changed. What I couldn't understand was the silence. One of the runners was just finishing, the others appeared to be frozen in their tracks. Tony Leach was retching. There was a small crowd standing by the finishing line. As I walked across, Michael said, "What's happening?"

"I don't know," I said.

I stood on the edge of the circle surrounding the timekeepers, trying to hear what was said. I heard someone say I had won by

50 yards. I heard the word "record". I couldn't see Bill Thomas at all. I heard Bill's voice say, "One second off."

Just my luck, I thought, and turned away, for I had been thinking that I might have been close to the course record of 4 mins. 17 secs. I had missed it by a second apparently.

A shout made me turn. Bill Thomas had appeared, looking fierce. He had removed his bowler hat. Everyone was talking. Bill was gabbling words without making any sense. He seemed to be accusing me of something. Then I saw that there were tears in his eyes.

"I'm telling you, sir, you've done it. You've done it."

"Got the course record, you mean?"

"No, sir, not the course record. You've broke the British record." He held the bowler hat in one hand and waved the stop-watch in the other.

"See for yourself. You've done it."

"One and two fifths seconds off. Congratulations." Little Joe Binks was pumping my hand.

The watch said 4 mins. 12 secs. "I don't believe it," I said. "It's a mistake, Bill. It must be a mistake."

"No mistake, sir. All the watches agree. You've done it, that's what you've done. You've done it."

People, Joe Binks, Harold Abrahams and others who were there, say that I sat down on the ground and grinned weakly. As if I had suffered a kind of catatonic attack or mild fit. I don't know. I don't remember. It wasn't until the next day when Harold came to see me that I understood properly what I had done. I do remember, however, sitting up later in the afternoon when Jerry's voice suddenly crackled over the ground. Jerry had seized a loud hailer from one of the officials and was saying in an exasperated tone:

"Ladies and gentlemen, you do not appear to *realise* what has happened. History has been made on this track today. Mr J. E. Lovelock, formerly of Otago University, New Zealand, and now of Exeter College, has run a mile in a time which is a new meeting and track record and which, subject to ratification, will be a new English, British National and British Empire record. His time of four minutes TWELVE seconds is also — " Cheering drowned out the rest of his words.

Jerry appeared to be still smarting with dissatisfaction at the crowd when I went up to thank him. I still regard him, with David Burghley, as the greatest sportsman in England. Even as he made the announcement, a gesture that was to begin my international career, Jerry must have believed that his own hopes for Olympic selection had suffered. Only moments before, he had been beaten in the half-mile by the bespectacled Tommy Hampson.

The remaining events of the day passed in a daze. The only other thing I remember is Bill Thomas coming out from beneath the pavilion at the end of the afternoon, when everyone else had gone, stripped to his runners. Black shorts, striped vest, striped socks – he looked like a bumblebee. He walked past me on to the track, muttering to himself, and began to trot. I knew Bill was old. I knew that he still ran, that wet or fine he came to the track and ran five miles every day to a strict schedule, carrying a stop-watch. But I had never seen him do it before in a hat. He had forgotten to remove his bowler hat.

As he ran, he bounced up and down. He looked so determined and so comical beneath the hat that I couldn't resist running up behind him. "Nice and easy, sir," I mimicked, matching steps with his bouncing form. "Clip-clop, clip-clop, keep it steady now. Keep to the schedule."

He stopped dead. He turned and said:

"I hear you, sir. I hear your little joke. Don't think an old rubber like Bill Thomas can't take a joke now and then, don't think I can't. Bit chesty, are we today, sir? Bit full of ourselves? I can understand that, after the way you ran. I'm proud of you, yes. Oh yes. If you was my own son, I couldn't be more proud of you. But like a lot of gentlemen round this place that's been to school, you're still green. Do you realise — "

He wiped his chin and put his face close to mine. The corners of his mouth were dripping saliva.

"Do you realise how close you came today to the world record? Do you realise what you might have done, if only you'd kept to one of my even-lap schedules? *Do* you?"

"Begging your pardon, sir," he added, after a moment.

He turned and trotted away. The force of his hurt was so total and so unexpected that I stood there watching him, unable to speak, with a silly grin pasted to my mouth, the way I used to grin at home when my father flew into one of his rages in the kitchen. Later, when I knew Bill better, I was sorry for my cheap jibe, but at the time I didn't even consider how much I had humiliated him or even that I might apologise. Apologise, what for? I was immune to anger, Bill's or anyone's; I was still floating on air.

I went to bed that night and dreamed of rooks coming home to roost, diving down with a sense of apartness on a long smooth descent, no joggles, no wind-changes, no resistance, just a smooth uniform dreaming motion, like going down the one asphalt road in town. The blow came next morning.

2

"Ten to eight, sir. Lovely day. New College boat just gone by."

Oh my God. "Charlie — ?"

"I'm a bit late this morning, sir, but if you're quick you'll still get down for rollers."

"Charlie, what's that smell?"

"Ten minutes to roll-call, sir. Your shaving water's ready."

He was in the sitting room, moving things about. I had been lying there listening to the scouts talking below the stairs, hearing Charlie come and go, take up the ashes and light the fire, wondering at the smell of Lysol entering my bedroom from the sitting room. I had a disturbed taste in my mouth, as though I were getting the 'flu. The sitting room appeared wreathed in smoke.

"Who opened the windows?" I stumbled out. A thick mist was pouring in over the parapet.

"I'll close them now, sir. Just opened the windows to let some of the odours out."

"What odours?" I went to the door, half-remembering something, and peered down over the landing giving on to the Sub-Rector's rooms. Lysol again. But the stairs were spotless. I had a memory of clambering upstairs on all fours, being sick –

31

"Charlie. Did I run yesterday?"

"Yes, sir. It's in all the papers. There's a heap of telegrams come for you."

"And then what?"

"Well, sir. Seeing you wasn't in Hall for dinner, Bill Stones and me come up to congratulate you. Bill thought you might like a rub-down after your big effort – Bill's an old rubber. That was about half-nine. The outer door was shut. We thought you must have retired early."

"But — ?" Oh God. As I shaved, I remembered. After I'd gone to bed Reggie Tongue and half a dozen others had burst in singing that ghastly tune "Little Man, You've Had a Busy Day" and carried me off in my pyjamas to a celebration party. But to whose rooms? Reggie's? Ken Conibear's? Montagu Scott's? There was beer and sherry and a gramophone playing and a faded Vermeer print on the wall, *Head of a Girl*, the same print that had hung in our dining-room in New Zealand. The eyes used to follow me about the house. I turned the faded print face in to the wall and began throwing sardines at it. Everyone joined in. Then we made sardines on toast. At one point Ken Conibear disappeared and came back with a pimply scholar in spectacles called Purling Minor and we had a wonderful butter fight. I remember thinking, as I plastered his spectacles and rubbed butter into his hair, how can anyone have so many pimples and be called Purling Minor? Basil performed a war dance. Basil Chubb —

I said, "Charlie. Was I sick in here?"

"Well, sir — "

"Very sick? On the landing too? *Dacre's* landing? Oh God. And in here as well?"

Basil Chubb had led us outside in a crocodile war-whooping across the back quad, past Palmer's Tower and into the Rector's garden. We finished up underneath Paul Petrocokino's window listening to him playing Handel. "Hark," Basil said. "That is Handel. Paul is playing Handel." That was when someone performed a Maori war dance. It couldn't have been Basil. It must have been me. After that we went to someone else's rooms and drank champers. I don't know who brought the champagne.

"We must have woken up the whole college, Charlie?"

"I did hear, sir, from one of the other scouts that the Rector's wife had a broken night. Oh, and the Rector's compliments. He would like to see you after breakfast."

"Dr Marett?"

"At nine fifteen sir, if that will be convenient."

I scrambled down in time for roll-call. I said to Basil and Ken after rollers, "I'm for it. The Rector wants to see me."

"About last night? I shouldn't worry, Jack."

"It will just be a fine, the usual thing. Stick it on your battels."

So far I had not been aware that the Rector, Dr Marett, a noted anthropologist, had even noticed me. I had never spoken to him. He was a mystery to me, as much as the Latin inscription on the floor of the Gothic chapel we attended every Sunday or the life of the college founder, Bishop Stapledon, who had been torn to pieces in 1326 by a London mob, or so Basil said, "for one, lechery, and two, heresy. In that order." Occasionally in Hall when an undergraduate committed some indiscretion the Rector would surprise us with a lightning stare, his glance travelling down the long polished tables to one of the gruesome paintings of past Rectors that hung about us. The Rector would make a quip, and we would laugh at his sally. Otherwise his gowned presence at high table, like the Bishop's mitred portrait which gazed upon us from behind his back, was a source of awe and dignity beyond my comprehension.

The Rector's house was behind the chapel.

"Ah, Mr Lovelock. Come in, come in – thank you for coming." He waved me to a comfortable chair.

"Too early I suppose for a sherry, C.K.?"

There were two others present in the Rector's study. Carleton Kemp Allen, the Warden of Rhodes House, known as "C.K.", and the Sub-Rector, Dacre Balsdon.

C.K. said, "I think Jack is teetotal, Rector. He keeps his internal combustion strictly for the running track."

"Of course."

A slight pause. The Rector smiled. "Mr Lovelock – well done! I think congratulations are in order."

Handshakes. Genial nods all round. Dacre sniffed the sprig of Morning Glory in his buttonhole. The Rector touched a fat envelope on the desk before him. My name was on it, and it contained a wad of unopened telegrams. So *that* was the reason for the summons. It had nothing to do with last night's escapade. Perhaps there would be a presentation?

"Exeter College, Mr Lovelock, is proud of you. Only last night I was dining with the Warden of New College, and the subject of your race came up. I said to him, 'Your loss is Exeter's gain.' I am right, am I not, in thinking that New College was your first choice at Oxford?"

"Yes, sir."

"And your second choice was Merton? Quite. Exeter was but third in line. And we nearly didn't take you, did you know? It was a close-run thing, if you will excuse the pun. Happy Exeter! Poor New College, poor Merton. We are a small college, as you know, but you have come to the right place. The Sub-Rector has reminded me that the first athletic gathering since the Olympic Games of classical times was mounted by this college, in – when was it, Dacre, 1850? Yes, 1850. An Exeter man thought it up over his wine after Hall; next day a sports meeting was inaugurated on Port Meadow, some flat races, even a mile, I'm told. It was vulgarly called a 'College Grind'. After that the idea of foot-racing spread through England like wildfire. It began here. You are not of Irish extraction, I hope?"

"Irish? No, sir. My father was from Gloucestershire."

"Good. Because the Irish, I'm told, sometimes claim priority, maintaining that a sports gathering was held in Dublin as early as 1846. It was probably a sweepstake. Undoubtedly Exeter was first. The Exeter Athletic Club is the oldest in the world. That is why I say you have come to the right place."

Any moment, I thought, champagne will appear, served on a salver.

"And what are your plans now, Mr Lovelock?"

"Plans?"

"You are the first Exeter man to break a British record."

"I shall continue with my medical studies, sir."

"Yes."

"Dr Eccles thinks that I might manage a Second in Physiology."

"Yes. And your running?"

"I shall continue to run, sir, and train of course."

"For Los Angeles? Of course it is premature to talk of the

34

Olympic Games this year, and I am being frightfully rude to take up your time this morning when you must be bursting to read your telegrams. There are more by the way at the lodge. These are only some of what has come for you. But, you see, there is a slight problem." The Rector got up whisking his gown round his ankles and moved to a seat in an alcove, smoothing down a tuft of hair and gazing across at C.K. Allen as if lost in thought. C.K. tapped the ash from his cigarette. Dacre, slumped in his chair, touched his bow-tie and rubbed the pouches under his eyes. Nobody spoke.

C.K. said, "The letter, Rector."

"Ah, the letter. Thank you, C.K. We – that is, the Warden of Rhodes House – has received a letter from New Zealand, from someone who is a close friend of your family. It concerns your mother. You are very close to your mother, I understand."

"My mother has not been well for some time, sir."

"And your sister. You have an older sister?"

"One year older, sir, Olive. My sister's health is not good either. Ever since my father died, Olive . . ."

"Quite. The letter refers to her engagement being broken off recently, dreadful business, and the effect this has had upon your mother. It is a distressing business all round. You know about the engagement?"

I nodded.

"And the reason for its being broken off? Then you know to what I am alluding. Nothing more needs to be said. Our concern – this is in the strictest confidentiality, you understand, entirely *entre nous*. Nothing, I do assure you, will go beyond these walls. C.K. has told me of one or two talks you have had with him at Rhodes House; he has formed a great affection for you; he thought it proper to discuss the matter with me and your moral tutor, Mr Balsdon, to see if there was some way in which we might help. If you think we are interfering, if this upsets you in any way, you must say. Our concern — "

"Do you think I should go back to New Zealand, sir?"

"Back to *New Zealand*? No, no."

"Heaven forbid." Dacre's squeaky laugh sounded. "We've only just *got* you."

"I don't understand, sir."

"Of course not. Heredity is something about which we know

35

very little. Similarly the question of human endurance. When a young man of your sensibility pushes himself to the very limit of human endurance, then – I don't quite know how to put it to you. I see you are still puzzled."

"Question of approach and general balance, Jack. Of staying the course." C.K. tapped out his cigarette and lit another. "The English athletic world is stunned by your performance yesterday, breathtaking, absolutely breathtaking. I saw the race. It is the very brilliance of that performance that disturbs the Rector. But 'disturbs' is too strong a word. I think what the Rector is saying is that in view of your studies, and not just your studies – Oxford life puts peculiar strains and pressures on its new men. This is your first year, after all. In view of this, and the other things we have been talking about just now, he thinks you should perhaps give some thought to husbanding your energies for the future. A great career lies ahead of you."

"Not overdo the running, you mean?" I spoke directly to the Rector.

"Please don't think this is a criticism of any kind, Mr Lovelock. No criticism is intended. The college rejoices in your running. We want you to go on running. We want you to win races for your college — "

"I have always tried in my races, sir, to beat the man rather than the stop-watch."

There was a moment's silence. On the mantelshelf a clock chimed. The Rector adjusted his gown and appeared to frown into his lap. Then his expression changed.

"Ah! Good. You have seized the point. That is the very point I wanted to make. You understand me completely." He jumped up. "C.K.? Mr Balsdon? Nothing to add? Thank you so much for coming, Mr Lovelock. We shall leave you to enjoy your feast of telegrams. I see that one is addressed to you, 'Apollo of Exeter'. Not bad, eh, C.K.? Ah, Dacre, you are going too. Once again, Mr Lovelock, my very warmest congratulations."

Dacre escorted me out into the sunshine. The mist was beginning to clear. Outside I found myself gulping down the spring air in great draughts and stepping gingerly on to the gravel path as if I was about to overbalance. What had gone wrong? Taking my arm, Dacre piloted me through the Rector's garden, past the library and into the main garden, where he paused with his back to Kennicot's fig tree, chuckling with pleasure at the roses along the south wall and pointing out to me the new buds on the Morning Glory he had made climb to his balcony.

"I was thinking, Jack," he said, squeezing my arm, his eyes merry, kindly, encouraging. "If I were you and I'd nothing better to do, a stroll through the Meadows down to the river on a day like this might be quite soothing."

I collected the remaining telegrams from the porter at the lodge and headed north through Jericho. I crossed the canal, went through a gate on to Port Meadow. The lower meadow was still sheeted in ground mist. At the river, another gate. Then I began to run. Horses stumbled by out of the mist. Another gate, made of iron; a rattling bridge, made of planks, the river clearing now on either side. Boatyards, a faint smell of bacon cooking, the river now on my right. Pleasure craft with pennants flying churned towards Binsey, a rowing eight slid by in the other direction, the coxswain barking in time to the stroke. I ran past Binsey, then left the rutted path and flung myself down on a grassy slope opposite a herd of cows and took out my telegrams. I read them hungrily, watched by the cows on the opposite bank. The telegrams were nearly all from New Zealand and they both excited and confused me, for my mind kept leaping back to what the Rector had said and that confused me even more. The only sense I could make of the interview was that something important had not been said. I appeared to have committed a blunder, an error of some magnitude. The presence of three busy and senior university officials was enough to underline that. Ought I to be quaking? Yet in an obscure way the silly side of me wanted to laugh. On the one hand the interview had terrified me. On the other – I saw myself sitting there, growing calmer by the minute, while they mouthed polite phrases unable to say what they meant – I couldn't take it seriously. The whole thing appeared ludicrous. Yet it couldn't be ludicrous, I reasoned, it was dead serious, since my blunder – whatever it was – had been too terrible for them to mention. I didn't know what to think.

On the bank nearby a fisherman in waders was mending a

wicker creel. I sat for a long time watching him mend the basket. I read the telegrams a second time without taking them in. Then I stuffed them back into my pocket and set off running steadily along the line of willows that led to Godstow. As I ran, my head began to clear. I slowed to a walk and kept on walking. Dacre Balsdon was right. At that moment there was nothing more I wanted than to be alone.

When I was four years old I was taken to a birthday party by my sister Olive. I sat under a table, watching a handsome cock that had strayed in from the verandah. I chased it out into an oleander bush and then I chased it round the garden. It flew on to the road. I ran into the road and continued to chase it. Every time the cock flew into a ditch or tried to take refuge in a bush I chased it out. I didn't know that domestic animals are untrained, that because of a fatty layer around the heart they can easily die of exhaustion. I chased the cock down the long road to Crushington and when I caught it I carried it back and laid it proudly on the verandah with its legs sticking up. By then it was dead. My father beat me afterwards, but even then I think I knew that he wasn't punishing me for killing the cock but because I hadn't run fast enough. If I had been faster, I would have overtaken it sooner, I told myself. It wouldn't have died. Even then I had the strange feeling that things would always be all right if only I could learn to run a bit faster.

The first time I saw a pony, I chased it. This was later, on a wild plain, when we came to live in the mountains. I remember the pony's tail floating in the wind, thinking to myself as I ran after it, that tail is perfect. Why can't I run like that? Afterwards when I told my father about chasing the pony all he said was, "Did you catch it?"

"No," I said. "I wasn't fast enough."

I was seven or eight at the time. I ran my first race proper when I was ten, at a boy scouts' camp. It was a mile and I won by five yards. My father was pleased, but not as pleased as all that. "If you'd trained a bit harder," he said, "you could have won by fifty yards." I was sick after that race. I was in bed for two days, vomiting. You'll have to do better than this, Jack-o, I told myself, if you're going to please your father. I never did.

My father died when I was thirteen, in my first year at boarding school.

At boarding school I borrowed a stop-watch and began to train in secret, like Nurmi. Nurmi was my first hero. One day I read in a newspaper that in Paris, France, Paavo Nurmi had won three Gold Medals and broken three world records in the space of a single day, two of them in the space of an hour. I decided that if I could grow up to win an Olympic medal like Nurmi, that would please my father. The last race I ran before my father died was in the school steeplechase, although I must still have been a junior. It was run over the golf course. Halfway round the course, I was so far in front that I knew I would break the record. Then someone called out that I had missed a marker and I had to go back. By the time I had run back and gone round the marker, I had lost two hundred yards and the field was in front of me. I set off after them. I caught the front-runner and passed him just before the tape was reached. I won. But I hadn't broken the record.

"What happened?" my father asked.

"I missed a marker. I missed a marker and had to go back."

"You made a mistake, Jack."

"But I missed a marker, Dad!"

It was no use. I could tell by the expression in his eyes, a sort of blankness that came over them, that he was disappointed in me. My father had absolute standards – not just in running but in everything. Yet it was the running that seemed to matter most, even though running was not in his blood. Or mine. My father was employed by a mining company. My mother is a piano teacher. There is nothing in the family to account for me. I have probably made my father sound a bit of an ogre, but, strangely enough, as I grew older I came to agree with him and adopt his standards. At school in my final year I won so many honours the Rector took the unusual step of announcing to all the parents that I would one day win a Rhodes – as indeed a few years later I did. My father would have wept to hear the Rector say that. My father taught me. I feared him, and have remained grateful to him. He taught me to strive. To do the right thing. I don't mean by that that he still haunts me, and yet there always seems to be someone watching at my elbow or looking over my shoulder, like this morning. This morning's interview is a good example. It has always been like this. Every time I manage to come alight, to catch fire or lose my inhibitions, just at the point when I am reaching out to grasp the pony's tail, I seem to make a mistake and come down with a thump. Something always happens to spoil the vision.

It was almost noon when I reached Godstow and went into the riverside pub there, the Trout. I got a snack at the bar and took it on to the terrace, still thinking about the interview.

The letter they had spoken of: there was nothing new in that letter. The letter had arrived over a week ago. It spoke of my mother's "depressions", but there was nothing new in that either. I had talked it over with C.K. and he had advised that the best way to help my mother would be to write home regularly, every week. I was already doing that. I didn't believe that my mother's condition had anything to do with my leaving New Zealand, on the contrary – she had moved heaven and earth to help me win the Scholarship to Oxford. There was nothing ominous about the letter. It wasn't as if my mother was having a breakdown. There was a story, never spoken of openly, that someone in the family on Mother's side had had a "turn", I assumed some form of breakdown, but I didn't believe that this had anything to do with my sister's engagement being broken off.

The more I thought about the interview, the more unreal it seemed, and the more unreal it became the less I was convinced that my mother's health – and certainly not *my* health – had anything to do with it. Then what?

On the terrace tables were being set for luncheon. I could tell by the hoots of laughter coming from the public rooms that an undergraduate luncheon party had just arrived. Presently they trooped out on to the terrace, followed by waiters with trays and magnums of champagne. I moved nearer the river and pretended to amuse myself feeding the swans. There were several couples in the party; they were younger than I was; they were enjoying themselves.

"Charles. Bring the gramophone over here!"

"Oh Patience, *please*. Not 'Stormy Weather'. Not again."

I longed to join them. I knew I didn't fit. What fascinated me was the way they swanked in like lords and occupied a place as if it was theirs by right. I loved their style, the way they ragged and flirted with one another. I hated their voices. Soon, I thought, they will begin cutting up. Someone will be chucked in the river.

But that was all right.

It is all right, I thought, to be chucked in the river. It is all right to cut capers, cut lectures, cut down to London by the 6.15 and sleep with a prostitute in Soho, as I knew some of the "hearties" did, and return by the "Flying Fornicator" at midnight and knock up the porter to get in – that is expected. That is the form. All you do is pay a fine. "Stick it on your battels, Jack." It is all right to go on a spree in your pyjamas, wake up the Rector's wife and spew your guts out at two in the morning all over the Sub-Rector's landing. Nobody turns a hair.

Then what?

"Stormy Weather" had finished. The gramophone was now playing "If You Knew Suzie". They were dancing between the tables, their hooting laughter drowning out Paul Whiteman's band.

"Swanky stuff."

"Patience, you look divine. Show a leg."

"Bee-bop."

"Absolutely positively electrifyingly divine!"

They flirted beautifully.

Suddenly I put my finger on it. I knew what I had done wrong. It was the race, of course. I had failed to flirt with it. I had run the race as if my life depended on it and in doing so had let it be known how I felt. That was the enormity – not that I had cared, but that I had been *seen* to care.

And that was all?

Sensation. That was all!

Well, I may make blunders but I'm not completely brainless. And I had the solution now. It was so obvious and presented itself so cunningly that I turned to the undergraduates and announced it with a grin, making them sit up and notice. My grin is like that, it is my most redeeming defect. Without it, so my sister says, I might have been pretty. It is quite startling. It isn't a normal grin. It starts in the pit of the stomach and comes out at both ears; all my scrawniness vanishes, the gaps in my teeth show and my ears change shape. Whenever I get excited

41

or find a solution to a problem, out it comes. It is quite involuntary, independent of the brain. I don't even have to think about it. My grin does the thinking for me.

I don't know how long I stayed there feeding my grin to the swans and the undergraduates hooting on the terrace. When I thought they had had enough, I put it away and ran back to Oxford.

"Visitor for you, Mr Lovelock."

"Thank you, Charlie."

For an instant I thought that it might be Janie, and paused on the dark little stair going up to my garret. No. Almost certainly she would be preparing to go on the river for the last day of the Eights. Half Oxford would be on the river this afternoon. Anyway, women didn't visit men's rooms unchaperoned. And we had barely been introduced. It wasn't Janie, it was Harold Abrahams.

"Harold!"

He was crouched in the semi-dark at one end of the sitting room, bending over something, like a stork. I recognised the wingbat ears and the rumpled Achilles Club blazer. Harold was now the correspondent of the *Sunday Times*, in his thirties, to me a legendary figure. He said without turning round, "Hullo, Jack. I had hoped to be able to greet you with a small Olympic flame, but I can't get this colonial contraption of yours to light. What is it?"

"It's a meths burner. It makes tea."

He darted up, his head grazing the low ceiling. While I lit the burner and found cups, he subsided into my only armchair, folded his long twiglike knees up to the chin and produced a notebook. "Nice little view you have here, Jack. Now. When you have finished playing tea-ladies, sit down and listen. I haven't much time. Now. I am composing something for Sunday's paper about a chap called Lovelock. I have a question. Is it true that in New Zealand you never won a major race?"

"Quite true."

"You never won a national title?"

"No. I came third once."

Harold looked at me. He nodded.

"All right. What was your fastest time in New Zealand?"

"For the mile? Four twenty-six, just under."

"Say four twenty-six. I thought so, I wasn't sure. When was that?"

"Couple of years ago."

"So. Two years ago 4 minutes 26 seconds, this year 4 minutes 12 seconds. Yesterday you ran 4 minutes 12. That is an improvement of 14 seconds."

"My lap times were all over the place. Bill Thomas says — "

"Bill? I know what old Bill says – usually before he says it himself. Don't listen to Bill. Bill's an old rubber. He may be the doyen of athletic coaches in England, but he knows nothing about people like you and me who run on their nerves. He makes no allowance for the personality. Please don't interrupt. I'm catching the 2.10 to Paddington. Time is of the essence . . ." Harold's long face creased into a smile. "Especially in this equation. Look here. I have worked it out. The English mile is 5280 feet or 1760 yards, as you know. Your performance yesterday represents an improvement on your New Zealand peak of nearly one hundred yards – ninety-eight yards, to be precise. That is equivalent to running twenty-five yards a lap faster than ever before. It is like – imagine yourself if you can to be a long jumper. It is like leaping two feet further than anyone has ever done. Do you follow?"

"I hadn't thought of it quite like that."

Harold nodded. "That's because it hasn't sunk in yet. It happened to me after I ran those ten seconds in Paris. Ten point six, actually. It didn't sink in for days what I had done. Only two men have run a mile faster than you did yesterday, Nurmi and Ladoumègue."

"I know." I had already done a graph in my journal, comparing my times with theirs. The Frenchman, Jules Ladoumègue, was the world record-holder. I was only three seconds away from Ladoumègue.

"Nurmi is past his best. He has only one ambition now, he says, to win the marathon at Los Angeles in August. Ladoumègue has just been disqualified for life for taking money under the counter. Beautiful runner, you say? Don't feel sorry for Jules, be glad for yourself. Ladoumègue now earns a living, I'm told, in Variété, chasing artificial hares round a revolving stage in Paris. He won't run again. Nurmi is finished. Ladoumègue is eliminated. That leaves you. The question is, my dear Jack, what are you going to do with yourself?"

"Well, I had rather thought of trying for the Olympics."

Harold said nothing. His large liquid eyes seemed to be taking in a problem I couldn't see. He said, putting away his notebook:

"How serious are you?"

"Do I have to answer that?"

"You already have." He made a wry face. "What do you mean, you had *thought* of trying for the Olympics? Is there any doubt after yesterday that you won't be nominated to represent your country?"

"It's all been so quick, Harold. I mean, I've hardly thought about it. It all seems a bit premature . . ."

"There isn't much time, I admit. What does Uncle Bill say?"

"We haven't really discussed it." I said, "Do you — You don't mean *this* year? Los Angeles?"

"What else? What did you think I meant?"

I had been thinking all the time of Berlin, four years away.

"Of course, Los Angeles would be wonderful, wonderful," I said. "A marvellous experience."

"Don't you want to go?"

"It isn't that."

"You're not taking Schools this year. No problems with your college, are there?"

"No." I hesitated. "No," I said.

"Funny smell, Jack." He leaned over the chair, sniffing a patch of worn carpet. He said, "I'm not boring you, am I?"

"No, no. But I think it's already too late for Los Angeles. I had a telegram. It's in this envelope somewhere." I gave him some of the telegrams from New Zealand.

"'CONGRATULATIONS. NEXT STOP CALIFOR-NIA . . .' Well, what's wrong with that?"

"No, it's another one. That's from a friend. It's another one, signed Amos."

"'REGRET LOS ANGELES GAMES TEAM SELEC-TION ALREADY MADE AMOS . . .' That the one?"

"Yes. Amos is the secretary of the New Zealand Olympic Committee."

44

"*Regret?* Don't they read the papers?"

"I don't think there's very much I can do at this stage."

"Jack. Evelyn Montague in the *Manchester Guardian* has just called you the most exciting thing for British athletics since Arnold Strode-Jackson went to Stockholm in 1912, and all they can say for you back home is 'We regret'. Regret! What do they mean, *regret*? Surely they can reopen the selection?"

I explained about the New Zealand Olympic Committee. How small it was. How small the country was. That the Committee went cap-in-hand for everything. That it could only afford to send a small team. That once a team had been selected, unless you could pay for yourself, and I couldn't, that was the end of it. Anyway, I said, I hadn't been building any hopes on Los Angeles . . . Harold seemed to have lost interest. He got up with a shrug and stood at the window, arms folded, body hunched, looking over the balcony at the vista of grey turrets and gables beyond the Bodleian.

"Oxford is an amazing place," he said after a pause. "It offers dreams, liberty, the prizes of Empire, and every summer the roses bloom. Yet it is – stuffy. I speak as a Trinity man, you understand, from the Other Place. Cambridge. Now Cambridge is less stuffy than Oxford. Yet it is always Oxford that ends up surprising me, why? What is it? Oxford transforms people. What is it in the air? It can't be the damp. What is it in the atmosphere, do you suppose, that can transform a common chrysalis in the space of a few months and make it flower into a butterfly?"

"I'm not a butterfly," I laughed.

"No. But Oxford is a hothouse. Don't let it stifle you."

"Why do you say that?"

"I don't know. Does it matter? Yes, I do know, actually. The first time we met, at an Achilles dinner, I remember you saying it was a point of honour in your family to buy British shoes, even though you lived in New Zealand. I thought it touching – that just because it was British, it was considered best. I also thought you rather naïve, oh yes. You hadn't long arrived in England. We spoke of the Rhodes Scholarship idea and the Empire. You were terribly concerned about not letting the side down or your college down, I forget which. Arthur Porritt introduced us, I think. Also – you were wearing a borrowed

45

dinner jacket and it didn't fit, you were very concerned about that. You were very naïve, very earnest, very sincere in your desire to do the right thing. This man, I thought to myself, is tailormade for Oxford. He will kill himself rather than do anything to disturb the prevailing ethos. No, wait, wait. But yesterday, at Iffley, you did precisely that. It was a bit cheeky what you did, you know – all the shouting and that swanky dive at the finish. Some people didn't like it. They considered it boasting. No, no, don't misunderstand. I liked it. It seemed to me you were going out of your way to thumb your nose at them; it seemed to me a point in your favour."

This Abrahams, I thought – although I called him Harold, we had only met a couple of times before – knows all about you, Jack-o. He sees right into you.

"Interesting, you see, Jack, because when I compare that with the young man I'd met only a few months before, I seemed to be seeing a different person. Sure I'm not boring you?"

"No, no. I like it." I was sitting on the edge of my chair, drinking in his words.

"It made me wonder, that's all. If you're dead set as I think you are on winning an Olympic prize, you are going to have to tread a very fine line. Oxford changes people. It also exacts a price. My own case won't console you — "

"It might," I said. "You'll miss your train."

"I have already missed it. Sooner or later, Jack, if it hasn't happened already, this place is going to try and stamp you, make of you its own creature. You will be quite powerless to stop it. Is that what you want? It sometimes helps to know first what you are. Are you an Oxford man? Or your own man? In my own case – well. I come from a distinguished Jewish family – originally refugees. We needn't go into that. My uncle Solomon was long-jump champion of England. All my brothers achieved renown. I was the youngest, the skinniest – almost as skinny as you are – the least spectacular. Now. When I won the hundred metres at the Olympic Games in 1924, people said, 'Aha, you see? Abrahams. Nephew of Solly Abrahams, a Jew. Another Jew. He *had* to win.' That's what they said. They thought I was trying to prove something, and so I was, but not about being Jewish. Not a bit of it! I ran those ten seconds in Paris not for my Cambridge college, not for my country and not even for my family, I ran to show my brothers and uncles I was as good as they were. I ran for myself."

He turned from the window. "Were you by any chance about to offer me some tea? The kettle, old chap."

The kettle was boiling. I jumped up.

"By the way," he said, "do you mind if I take that telegram with me, the one from the New Zealand Olympic Committee? I'll have a word with Arthur Porritt in London. Arthur might be able to do something."

"About Los Angeles?"

I filled the teapot and ran downstairs to the scouts' pantry in search of milk, my mind whirling from all the things he had been saying. A year before, half a year before, half an hour before only, my mind had been tuned to a single fixed idea, a recurring dream of Berlin. Through doubts and uncertainties, an image called "Berlin 1936" had flickered and glowed like an Aladdin's lamp. Now in some magical way another light had appeared on the horizon. Presto. Like a conjuring trick. Los Angeles? Already I could feel an Atlantic boat ticket in my pocket. At the same time a voice inside me was saying, "Wait, it's too soon. Think about it. It's too soon!", but I paid no heed. I found the milk and raced back up the stairs. As I reached the top, Harold emerged from my rooms on to the landing, his overcoat over one arm.

"Aren't you staying to tea?" I said.

"No. No, thank you, Jack. Please don't trouble on my account. Thank you very much. I only dropped in to ask a question." He was gone.

3

Two weeks later I came to London and made certain that I would go to Los Angeles. On a perfect spring day, with six teaspoons of glucose in my stomach and a line of handicapped runners that stretched almost halfway round the track in front of me, I ran three laps at the Stamford Bridge track and then, as my friend Arthur Porritt so nicely put it, "dropped my guts" into his best handkerchief. Three-quarters of a mile is a terrible distance to compete over. There are no pauses, no penultimate lap as in the mile where you can range craftily alongside an opponent to test his staying power, no psychological incentive of any kind – it is like running up a moving staircase that's going the other way, at best you only appear to be standing still. I had never competed over a three-quarter-mile distance before. After the first lap I was boxed in. I told myself, this will never do. In the second, I began to move. I ran the third lap nearly blind, the tears welling in my eyes from the wind. After the race "Doc" Porritt appeared in the dressing-room. He is the New Zealand surgeon who ran third against Harold Abrahams and Jackson Scholz in Paris in 1924, winning a bronze medal. "Well, Jack," Arthur said, and quickly gave me the handkerchief from his breast pocket. When I had finished being ill, vomiting the glucose my stomach had refused to digest into his handkerchief, Arthur tried again. "Well, Jack. The New Zealand selectors will have to send you now, won't they?" I thought so too. I had just broken a world record.

Looking back on that year of 1932, those few weeks that led me to the Los Angeles Olympics, I am still surprised and bewildered – bewildered at the speed with which I seem to have made the decision; surprised at the way I allowed myself to believe, simply because I had broken a couple of records in England, that I could succeed against an Olympic field. I didn't know that an Olympic mile is a nightmare, a trauma, a spiritual battlefield where untried men are discarded and left out to die in the rain. But what else could I have done? After the race at Iffley, after Harold's visit, my head was completely turned by the English sports writers. "MILER WHO MAY BEAT THE WHOLE WORLD", was one headline. "NEW OLYMPIC HOPE", another. Since Arnold Strode-Jackson's victory at Stockholm in 1912, English middle-distance athletes had fallen by the wayside, their places taken by the Finns or the French. If it wasn't the Finns and the French, it was the Americans. I was something of a catch. Cartoonists featured my smile. Photographers came to my rooms. Undergraduates and dons I didn't know stopped me in the High. I was asked to parties and dances and, triumph of social triumphs, I was invited to join that exclusive club, the Adelphi. Members wore a special waistcoat of yellow silk with blue lapels; on the buttons was the picture of a bird, symbol of the Adelphi. Membership was restricted to twelve. I felt like the Duke in *Zuleika Dobson*, or like Byron. Byron, it is said, awoke one day to find he was famous at the age of twenty-four. I was twenty-two.

In New Zealand I had attended a boarding school in the South Island town of Timaru. In winter my job as a fag was to go round the lavatories and warm the seats for the prefects by sitting on them. I had come a long way from Timaru – and further still from the little mining town of Crushington, where I chased my first cock, and my father bicycled through the puddles and potholes to his job in the Keep-it-Dark mine. There were two mines in Crushington, the Wealth of Nations and the Keep-it-Dark. I was born in Crushington. I was born on a rainy summer's morning in January 1910 and an old nurse told me later I was so small I could have fitted into a quart milk bottle – but that may have been my younger brother, Jim. Jim was sickly too. My sister Olive developed an obscure ailment and was taken by my mother to eighteen doctors in three years. Perhaps that was when my mother's depressions started, I don't know. Later, after we moved to the mountains, my father ran a motor garage. By then my mother had developed tuberculosis. We always seemed to be moving about the island, from one town to another, in search of health. My father had come out from England with an older woman, a companion, who died I think of tuberculosis. We were all sickly or delicate in some way. My father had left England in search of sunshine. He had had pleurisy. One of my earliest memories is of him rising in the dark, and my mother saying, "What sort of day is it, dear?" And my father, standing at the window, saying, "Raining, Ivy. It's always raining." Crushington has one of the highest rainfalls in New Zealand. I don't know why he chose Crushington.

The week after I broke the British record at Iffley, I was interviewed for the *Isis* in Oxford. "We're splashing you," the editor said. When he asked for details of my background and my father's profession, I thought of my father ending his Antipodean days in a garage filled with old motor buses, having begun them in an open-cast mine called the Keep-it-Dark – and I kept it dark. Instead of saying what he really was, a kind of glorified mechanic, I promoted him to Superintendent of Mines. I thought the article in the *Isis* read rather well.

The article was headed.

ISIS IDOL
J.E. Lovelock (Exeter)

and it began, "Unlike André Maurois, Emil Ludwig and other well-known biographers, I will not begin our Idol's story with an account of his illustrious forebears . . ." I cut the *Isis* article out and pasted into my scrapbook, a journal I had already begun to keep in New Zealand containing accounts of all my races. I regarded the article and the favourable press attention as sweet revenge upon the establishment, making up for an omission when I had run my first races at Oxford as a freshman. At these sports an Australian friend, Jim Mahoney, and I had made up an "Anzac" stable and caused some comment by winning four races between us. My journal, I see, doesn't mention the omission, but Jim noted in his diary at the time:

November 3, 1931. Freshman's Sports:
The Etonian, Lord John Hope, the Public Schools record holder for the half-mile, had come up to Oxford with a great reputation and was the centre of interest for the Press. I overheard two Press photographers discussing their work. One said to the other – "Well, you've got the Hurdles and you've got Lord John Hope, what more do you want?" This morning's London illustrated dailies show: "Lord John Hope dead-heating with Maxwell-Hyslop in the Oxford University Freshman's Half Mile." The picture looks very effective, but the caption omits to make it clear that some 25 yards ahead and well out of range is one Lovelock.

That spring everything was conspiring to make me smug, to revel in my new-found popularity and put an Atlantic boat ticket in my pocket. Even my Physiology tutor, J. C. Eccles, conspired. Instead of his normal discourses on the nerve impulses and spinal reflexes at my weekly tutorial, Dr Eccles

50

ran tests on my circulation and pulse rate. Before the race at Stamford Bridge, we did a plot, distances against speed. The plot got lower and lower, ending up with a smooth curve. "It's below the line," he said. We looked at it. We discussed it endlessly. Dr Eccles said, "Here's your chance to break a world record." Jack Eccles was a neuro-physiologist and a junior Fellow at Exeter, brilliant, dynamic – and Australian. He was the one who got me into Exeter when the other colleges wouldn't have me. I think he looked on me as a sort of family mascot in his battle for superiority over the Brits.

And then, there was Janie.

We met for the second time at a dance at the Randolph Hotel. I sat upstairs in the gallery at first, afraid to approach her. She looked unbelievably select. There were about two hundred guests and most of the women, someone said, had been imported from London. They floated like potato crisps, all in white, with puff sleeves and gold flowers in their hair, except for Janie. She was sleeveless in turquoise, something long and fine that flared from the hip, and she wore long pendant earrings that caught the light and yet seemed not to move as she was passed from one admirer to another. The band was starting a Viennese waltz. I was feeling self-conscious in my hired tails, debating with myself whether to break into her circle, when she saw me and came straight across. She said in her American-flavoured voice:

"Mr Lovelock, everyone is talking about your hair. I have been sent to ask. Is it permed?"

"No." I was annoyed. Out of the corner of my eye I saw the circle she had left dissolve among the dancers, and three men waiting. They were watching us. I expected her to return to them. She didn't return. The band played. One hand went to the opening at her throat, where a tiny locket hung on a chain, and I saw that beneath the thick eyebrows and the small flared nose one lip was quivering. She was as shy as I was. Her eyes went up, then down, they were a deep acorn brown, deeper than I remembered them, and clear, very clear. Like clear water.

"Miss Van den Bosch (I had been rehearsing the name to myself) – I have a question too. How long are you staying at Oxford?"

"Three years."

"So am I."

That broke the ice. She blinked, and curtsied. I threw out a glove, and bowed. Then we stopped putting on airs and danced and talked until it was time for her to be back in college. After that, we saw each other almost every day. She was old for her years, a combination of old-world polish and bouts of American exuberance which hit me like a breeze coming off the Atlantic. She was in everything, debates, lacrosse, tennis, secretary of the Spanish Club – she moved round Oxford in a bubble of nervous energy and came to me, I think, to recuperate. She said I calmed her down.

"You'll have to come and stay with us in the States," she said.

"What? What? Who?"

"My stepmother is American. We have a nice place on Rhode Island. Won't you be running at Princeton next year?"

She seemed to have lived in half the capitals of Europe. She brought them close. She made me realise how little I knew of the enormous world beyond.

"I don't understand," she said, "why you don't want to go back to New Zealand." I said I didn't understand why she wanted to marry an American.

"Americans don't lisp."

Surrounded as I was on all sides by English Public Schools men who spoke out of the sides of their mouths, I had been desperately trying to imitate them in front of a mirror.

"I promith not to lithp," I said.

"If you do, I shall call you Jackie." She called me Jackie just the same.

We walked all over Oxford that spring. There were cowslips and bluebells in Christ Church Meadows, fine skies at evening with the tower of Magdalen showing behind the elms, and anemones growing through the lush grass where I ran at twilight beside the Broad Walk while Janie was at the Spanish Club. We studied together and read Chesterton together. We lay in a punt and listened to the razor-stropping sound of swans crossing from one river to another. Janie wore a flounced dress and showed me the Dodo from *Alice in Wonderland* in the University Museum. I showed her Mesopotamia by Dame's Delight and the Alice-in-Wonderland gate. Everywhere we walked, looking through gates into college gardens, there were crocuses out, saffron and purple, and ladybirds in the branches of the almond trees coming into bloom. Spring was late that year. I don't know if we were in love with each other or simply intoxicated with Oxford – it was my first English spring after all – but I remember a long walk past Hinksey, coming back in the early evening over Boar's Hill and looking down on the spires below. Janie had gone on ahead of me. I remember pausing to drink in the view. I seemed to be seeing it for the first time. Gosh! I thought, Oxford. Where the toffs go. Everything was drenched in a soft milky glow at evening. And again: Gosh, Oxford. My garret is down there somewhere. I'm there too! And then sitting down in the grass at the side of the road and hugging myself in a sort of quiet ecstasy.

We never talked about Berlin. I think Janie took it for granted, like Jerry Cornes and everyone else, that Los Angeles was the goal. I had already begun, after the interview with the Rector, to put into operation a secret plan for Berlin. My father used to say, quoting one of his favourite stories by Chesterton, "There are only two ways to succeed: one is by doing very good work, the other is by cheating" – and I suppose from the point of view of the college what I was doing was a form of cheating. Yet secrecy seemed the only way. Once, coming back from a party, I almost gave myself away.

It was after Jerry's final Schools. Jerry, already a Civil Service probationer and expecting to be posted abroad, had thrown a going-down party in the middle of the Iffley Road running track. Returning to Oxford late at night, we came into the Broad arm-in-arm, about a dozen of us, and passed the row of emperors' heads outside the Sheldonian Theatre and the Old Ashmolean Museum, heading for the little pub beside Blackwell's bookshop. Half the party dived into the pub; Janie and I elected to stay outside and keep watch for the proctors; Jerry went into the pub, then reappeared saying, "I have to say goodbye to someone." He disappeared across the road. We found him minutes later saying goodbye to one of the bearded figures outside the Sheldonian.

"Bye-bye, old chap." Jerry reached up and patted the stone headpiece on its pedestal. I must have sniggered because he said, "I suppose you think I'm being sentimental?"

"No, no," I said. "But the stone's a bit soft on that one."

"Look," Janie said, pointing up in the moonlight. "That one's lost his nose. It's broken off."

"Broken right off," Jerry said. "Hooligans." He inspected it. "Downright hooliganism."

I said, "That's old John Dory. The stone's completely rotten on him."

"I'm sure the nose was there last week, Jackie."

"Probably. But he's no good either." I knew these mouldering old heads, one of the glories of Oxford, intimately. I passed them every day on my way to the Physiology labs.

"No good for what? And why John Dory?"

"Just a name," I said. "John Dory's a fish."

"Jackie, you philistine," Janie said.

"He is, isn't he?" Jerry was looking truculent. We were all a bit tipsy.

"No, really," I said. "The John Dory is a fish in New Zealand. It's got a black thumb-print on it. The Maoris say that it's the thumb-print of God. If you look closer," I said, trying to hoist her up on to a railing, "you'll see that in place of the old boy's nose, where the stone has crumbled, there is a distinct thumb-mark."

I heaved, but Janie refused to budge. "Philistine!"

Jerry was peering up at the disfigured head beneath its delicately sculpted crown. "What absolute nonsense. There's no mark there. I don't see any thumb-mark. You know, Jack," he said, towering over me, "a chap might almost think you were the one responsible for this barbaric act."

As it happens, I was. I had already discovered that the carved heads outside the Sheldonian made excellent footholds. The back of Exeter abutted on to the Sheldonian. Beyond the heads a railed-off enclosure led to a series of flat roofs beside the Rector's lodgings, and from there one dropped down over the bathrooms into the back quad of Exeter. It was not the easiest way to climb into college, but it was the most interesting. The night before, climbing in, I had slipped and, reaching up wildly for support, had fallen, bringing down a nose with me.

"Oh, come on," I said, dragging them back across the road. "Let's get the others and go for a swim in the river."

Later, walking back to Lady Margaret Hall, Janie said: "What do you do at night when you can't sleep? You've never told me."

"Oh, there's lots to do."

"Where? In your rooms? You can't sleep, you say."

I grinned, and changed the subject.

I still trained by day at the Iffley track, going there twice a week to run with Jerry or Jim Mahoney, my Australian friend. We ran middle distances against Bill Thomas' clock or worked out lightly over a longer distance, varied with bursts of striding. At night after the college had gone to sleep I climbed over the wall and ran as I pleased. I waited until midnight, until the college had settled, dropped down over the wall at the end of the Fellows' Garden by the Bodleian and returned in the small hours by scaling the heads outside the Sheldonian. Running by night, I told myself, was a way to cope with my insomnia and to help me relax, but in reality it began as a way to spike the Rector. Why shouldn't I run as I pleased? Keep faith with my dreams? And what was that about "not staying the course"? I wasn't ailing or unwell; I just didn't sleep. That was all. My granny used to say, "You don't get enough sleep, Jack." But I reckon I didn't sleep less than anyone else – I just didn't take so long to do it.

Oddly enough my night running didn't help the insomnia – if anything my sleeplessness grew worse. Later, as the habit grew on me and my body adjusted to the rhythm of night running, other things began to happen. I made a disturbing discovery. But that was later. What was it Harold Abrahams had said – about there being a price or a choice? About being an Oxford man? Or one's own man? Well, I had thought about that too.

Why couldn't I be both?

The first night I went out, I expected to be nabbed getting back in. And the second. At morning roll-call I held my breath, searching the faces of the other undergraduates to see who had discovered my secret. But nobody had. On the morning after the third night when Dacre Balsdon stopped me on the stairs with, "Oh Jack. One moment . . ." I stiffened, thinking, I'm going to be sent down. This is it. I entered Dacre's rooms like a

55

condemned man. But all he wanted was to show me a quotation from one of Pindar's Olympian odes:

> *A man born with great gifts*
> *May be sharpened and sped*
> *To an excellent weight of glory*
> *If a God be on his side.*

I borrowed his copy of Pindar and copied the passage into my journal. At the time it gave me quite a turn, wondering if the Sub-Rector knew. Dacre never said. And nothing happened.

I still didn't know about Los Angeles, whether or not I had gained a place in the New Zealand team. Yet I *knew*. More and more everything contrived to help me. Spring blossomed into summer and that summer, with the lushness of Oxford all round me – and Janie – even my failures melted into triumphs. In June for example when the press had trumpeted my "world-breaking" three-quarter-mile run at Stamford Bridge so loudly, it was as if my time of 3 mins. 02.2 secs. had already been ratified as a world's record. Yet it wasn't really a record at all. That small southern Frenchman, Jules Ladoumègue, the first man to better 3 mins. 50 secs. for the 1500 metres and 4 mins. 10 secs. for the mile, had already run the three-quarter-mile distance in three minutes flat. But when our recorded times were tabled at a meeting of the International Amateur Athletic Federation, Ladoumègue's time was not allowed. Mine, almost two seconds slower, was ratified as the world record.

After the Stamford Bridge race, I slackened off. Trinity Term ended. Marquees appeared in the quadrangles of Jesus College and Oriel and in Tom Quad at Christ Church, ushering in Commemoration Week, my first Commem. ball, and Commemoration ushered in my first taste of international competition – a race across the Channel at Antwerp with the Achilles Club.

Bill Thomas had warned me about Continental manners – barging and elbowing at the start – and when we lined up in Antwerp I was dismayed to find I had drawn the outside lane of seventeen runners. Then a huge Belgian runner, a giant of a man who had drawn the inside lane, ambled over, waving his arms. I thought he was crossing himself and inviting me to do the same, but in fact he was offering to exchange places with me. I declined, thanking him profusely. He extended a paw, we shook hands. The race started. It was my first attempt over the Olympic distance of 1500 metres, yet I couldn't lose. Two nights before, after a ball and champagne breakfast at Christ Church that ended at 5 a.m., I had staggered through Carfax and down the Cornmarket barely able to reach my rooms and crawl into bed. Yet I couldn't lose! At Antwerp I romped home.

When I returned to Oxford there was an international telegram waiting. "CONGRATULATIONS," it said. "YOU ARE IN REPEAT IN STOP GOD AND STARTER'S GUN GO WITH YOU." I stared at the words. Arthur's done it, I thought. I'm in the team! I knew Arthur Porritt had been trying to intervene on my behalf. As it happened I was wrong. Arthur's intervention, I learned, had cut little ice with the New Zealand selectors; the selectors had reopened the list, only to close it again, leaving me out a second time. The only reason I was going, I heard later, was because pupils of my old school and a group of friends in my university town had passed the hat round and collected my fare, forcing the Olympic Committee to include me.

I grabbed the telegram and rushed into the Turl, heading for LMH to give Janie the news – I was going to Los Angeles! And then stopped, realising I had turned the wrong way. I remembered that Janie had already gone down for the Long Vac., back to Holland. I walked on and stopped again, hearing music from an upstairs window. I was grinning to myself – not only telegrams were calling. I began to dance and jig in the street in time to the music. The music was coming from a wind-up gramophone in Lincoln College. The gramophone was playing, "California, Here I Come".

4

Unknown to me at that time an Italian runner, who trained on a diet of pasta, onions and red wine, had been preparing himself for the Olympic mile at Los Angeles since 1926, when I was still at school wearing short pants. He came of a poor family. He had emerged in Milan in 1926; had appeared briefly at the Amsterdam Olympics in 1928; then dropped out of sight for some years until, in 1932, shortly before we sailed for the Los Angeles Games, he had run an astonishing 1500 metres in Italy, returning a time of 3 mins. 52.2 secs., which was like running a mile in 4:11 or 4:10, very near to the world's best. I read a short press report about the race in England, and I showed it to Jerry. "Interesting," Jerry said. "Italy's never had a miler before." His name was Luigi Beccali. That was all we knew.

We sailed from Southampton on *The Empress of Britain* on 14 July, 1932. As soon as I went on board I began asking members of the British team about Beccali. Nobody, I discovered, seemed to know any more about him than I did. Then on the second morning, exercising on deck with Jerry, we almost collided with the half-miler Tom Hampson. Tommy Hampson was a danger on that ship. He had just become engaged; he was so much in love he ran round the deck in a dream, bumping into people and saying "Sorry!" I had already noticed him in the ship's pool. Tommy lay on his back singing, staring up at the sky from behind wire spectacles, goofy-eyed. Later, in the massage room, he put his bespectacled head round the door, gave me a nod and a quick smile, and went out again. I think he must have overheard me asking about Beccali because after lunch he came to my cabin and smoked a cigarette and told me he'd run against the Italian.

"You know the song, Jack – 'My Old Man Works on the Railways'? That's your Luigi. His father drives a railway engine. But Beccali's chief claim to fame is that he was born in the same year I was, 1907." Tommy smiled shyly and took off his glasses. He was very short-sighted. Without the glasses he looked like a shy and impoverished schoolteacher, which in fact is what he was.

"They call him Nini, happy-go-lucky Nini. Kiss-kiss, on both cheeks: you know how these Continentals are. I quite liked him, even if he has got PRO PATRIA stitched in big letters across the front of his chest. Enormous chest. You'll see him coming. He's good. Sorry! Don't want to scare you, Jack. My God, you'll probably smell him too, if you get through to the final."

"How's that?" I said.

"Hair oil. It sounds silly, but that's how I beat him at Stamford Bridge last year. Beccali has sleek black hair that stands up when he runs and it's plastered with the stuff. Some wop brilliantine that he uses. Lovely stink. You weren't in England last year?"

"No. I didn't arrive till October."

"I didn't know Beccali was even in the race until the last ten yards. I was floating home, well home. You know the feeling? I was ready to kiss the tape. Suddenly I felt this hot scent in my right nostril, like a hot wind. It was Beccali. I just managed to scramble home. I *smelled* him coming."

"That was a half-mile?"

"Yes. But I think Beccali is a genuine miler. He almost never runs outside Italy. Oh, no need for you to run scared. I should say Beccali is a danger in your event, but not a threat. There's a big American called Venzke, another late starter. Friend of Cunningham's. Venzke is supposed to be faster than Beccali."

"Yes, Venzke ran 4:10. But indoors."

"Was it?"

"I think it was an indoor race. I don't know anything about the Americans, Tommy."

"It's the same in my event. Times are relative anyway, or so I tell myself. Jerry is saying that every record that ever was will be broken in California."

"Harold doesn't. Harold is saying these Games will be the greatest financial disaster in athletic history."

"We just don't know, do we? It's going to be a lovely surprise. Cigarette?"

"No thanks."

"You should smoke one occasionally. We've got five days at sea, then another week on a train – we shall arrive looking like dish-rags. The Yanks will be gloating. Interesting thing about Beccali, though. He seems to have come up after a long period of failures, bit like me. It isn't good, Jack, to face a long winter preceding an Olympic Games with the knowledge that you've gone off. I had a rotten season last year. At one point I became quite indifferent to running. Now, suddenly, I am the favourite for the 800 metres. That annoys me. You know, in three successive Olympics, 1920, 1924 and 1928, an Englishman has

59

won the 800 title and in two weeks' time I am expected to do the same. I feel I'm beaten before I start."

I hadn't realised until then what this gentle, very precise, very quiet-spoken, phlegmatic Englishman was driving at. He was attempting to calm his fears by talking, the way one talks to a cat or to a stranger in a bus. Tommy was an Oxford man. His rise, like mine, had been meteoric. At Oxford he hadn't even won a full Blue. The week before we sailed, in the British Championships at White City, he had run a curious last race.

"You don't seem nervous," I said.

"Nor do you. And we're both terrified. It's the mask that counts. Have a cigarette. Go on, do." I accepted. Tommy perched on the edge of the wash-basin. I lay on the bunk in the cabin. The sea rose and fell out of the porthole. Tommy's voice, merging with the throb of the engines and the smoke from our cigarettes, had the effect of a drug. "I couldn't run at all if I didn't have the luxury of knowing a cigarette was there when I wanted it. This whole psychological business is very strange. 'Why do you run, sir?' one of my pupils said to me at school the other day. It's a good question. 'The important thing about the Olympic Games, Latimer,' I said to him, 'is not the victory but the struggle, not the winning but the taking part.' I was quoting Coubertin, of course. But that isn't why we run. Why do we run? Is it a basic principle to compete? Or do we run to gain social approval? Now I overheard you, Jack, telling a reporter at Waterloo when we boarded the train that you were running for New Zealand. Did you mean it?"

"I shan't have PRO PATRIA written on my singlet at Los Angeles."

"No, but you'll have the Silver Fernleaf on your vest, just as I'll have the Union Jack on mine. I must remember to sew it on before we land, and that reminds me. Can I borrow a needle? Jerry says you're terribly organised. But it's strange. The hardest thing, I find, is having to live up to something. If you don't, the critics will drop you. You, for example, must be thinking at this moment of that 4:12 performance of yours at Iffley in the spring?"

"I wasn't, actually." I had in fact been thinking of my last race in the British Championships just a few days before, when I had lost to Jerry. The critics were saying I was losing form.

"That race at Iffley doesn't bother you?"

"Not really."

"I am not sure I quite believe you. You were above yourself that day, almost manic. These things come back to haunt us, believe me, usually when you least expect them — Can I live up to that performance? Can I do it again? Anyway for the sake of argument, that is your burden. But at least in your event you're not a hot favourite. That's my burden. I don't know which is the worst, Jack. We're like snakes, trying to shed our skins. Sometimes I think that that's why we run, to get rid of our burdens."

"You're lucky," I said. "You're in love."

"Oh yes, head over heels. Winnie's wonderful. If I didn't have Winnie back there to write to, to keep me going, I wouldn't be able to run at all. Oh, sorry!"

There was a crack. Tommy had just broken the wash-basin, sitting on it. In the days that followed he was to become even more absent-minded, thinking about his Winnie.

Saturday, 16 July:

Third day at sea. Fog. Occasionally an iceberg looms through the saloon window – great excitement. The movement of the ship makes it hard to run, even though they have laid special matting on deck for us. Calf and thigh muscles hard, like ropes – like it was the first time I tried cinder tracks in England after I arrived. Still wobbly after my defeat by Jerry last Saturday, my second poor showing in two weeks. Am I stale? I am hoping like hell I won't have to run my heat and a final on successive days in Los Angeles. Jerry's in top spirits. He discounts the Italian, Beccali. Is worried only about Harri Larva, the defending 1500 metre champion, and the other Finn, Purje.

Everyone skips or relaxes at the flicks (today we saw *The Flying Fool*) or speculates about the Americans. We still don't know who the Americans are putting up in the 1500, apart from Gene Venzke. Venzke seems certain to be in. Their final try-outs are taking place in California now, while we are at sea. There's going to be a rush to see the results in the papers when we dock in Quebec.

Later: Tommy returned my needle and helped me to sew the Silver Fern on my vest. He showed me his running shorts.

They're pure silk, not the standard cotton issue. The only other man in the British team who has silk is Lord Burghley. Tommy's fiancée Winifred got them for him. "If Lady Burghley can get silk shorts, so can I," Winnie said. They cost £1.

I feel very green alongside the English athletes, half-awed, half-exhilarated. I've put a photograph of Janie on top of my dresser. Her eyes peek out at me from under dark lashes, actually they match my colours. Alongside Janie are my black running shorts. They come to below the knees. My mother made them. I haven't worn them yet – I don't see how I can. They stand up on top of the dresser by themselves, like boards.

Sunday, 17 July:
Slept well, for the first time since coming on board. The vibrations of the ship help, I think. Wrote to Janie:

"Mr Baldwin the Prime Minister is on board (going to a conference in Ottawa). I'm on C deck, next to Tommy Hampson. He's 408, I'm 410. Tommy is a wonderful companion. He inspires confidences. He's taught me to smoke, calming me down, they way you say I do with you. He claims we're two of a kind, like Knight Errant of old going to the Crusades, for God, for love of country, for love of our lady . . ."

The difference is though, that though we're both loners, both painfully shy, Tommy seems to know exactly where he is going, what lies ahead: a home, a family, a career. Do I?

Weight, 9st. 9lb. I've gained two pounds. I *must* get my weight down. I've started masticating my food, counting the chews, twenty-five chews before I swallow – a sure sign of stage fright. Jerry is gaining weight too. We ran an obstacle race with Tommy today between decks – over rails, up stairs, under life-boats – showing off to the other passengers. Mr Baldwin much amused. Afterwards, skipping, sun-bathing, a warm scented sea-bath. I wish some of the New Zealanders were here.

Another name to conjure with, Cunningham. Another tough American. Somebody mentioned it. He sounds big, Herculean. His nickname is the Camel. Cunningham has run 4:11, the third fastest mile ever, although Jerry doesn't rate him, just as he doesn't rate Beccali. He calls Cunningham a second-class American.

Monday, 18 July:
After breakfast a flying boat came over. Now, as we approach Quebec, there are small boats buzzing round us, sirens, and crowds of people on the Heights of Abraham, waving. It's interesting how the atmosphere changes. Earlier, when we were fog-bound in the St Lawrence, everyone dropped their voices, began complaining of imaginary aches. You could feel the tension among the athletes. Now suddenly the decks are bursting with anticipation; Dr Pat O'Callaghan, the Irish hammer thrower, is turning cartwheels; I'm so happy, for two pins I'd dive off and swim to shore.

We are late arriving. We berth tonight and transfer to our "Olympic Special" train. Tommy says the tracks in California will be harder even than the decks on board ship. He's got thigh pains.

Evening: Extraordinary news! The American team for the 1500 metres reads: Cunningham, Pen Hallowell, Frank Crowley. Gene Venzke, the favourite, is out. He didn't qualify. I don't know what to think. It looks like anybody's race. Tommy is delirious. His arch rival, Ben Eastman, isn't in the 800 metres either.

We pounced on the newsboys when they came aboard so quickly that the P.M. and the other delegates to the Ottawa Conference didn't get a newspaper. Tommy said, "Well, we're ambassadors too." For the first time I am feeling proud to be a New Zealander, to know what I'm doing here.

Thursday, 21 July:
Toronto: We lurched into our hotel here two days ago, punch-drunk from the boat and train, quite groggy. I lay in a bath. Spent part of the second day on a track, wobbling about. My legs still feel rubbery, but the days at sea have done us good. Now we are off again – it's nearly midnight – with 3000 miles still to go. The train is humid, unbearably hot. Tommy says, "I'm glad I don't have to run the marathon when I arrive." This journey is becoming a marathon. I try to read a story by Chesterton about a man in a tree, but people keep bumping into the compartment as the train sways, and I have to put it aside. They're training in the corridors.

They won't stop running. I'm not the only one who can't sleep.

Friday:
The Canadian team came on board at Hamilton in the small hours. They greeted us with cheers and a brass band. Now we are in Chicago. An even greater crowd was waiting for us on the platform, including tiny Mary Pickford, the film actress. She's coming to Los Angeles too. We have been driven to a lake-side club track to exercise in the sun. I stretched out with Jerry, who is running beautifully, and afterwards swam in the lake. A man came up and said, "Hi, Jack. They told me you were a pigmy." I found myself looking up to a gangling negro from British Guiana, my Canadian opposite number, Phil Edwards. Phil pumped my hand, all smiles. "Old Rabbit", they call him (these are his second Olympics), though Phil is still at university. Like me, he is studying medicine. We talked about the oxygen-debt theory and he told me something about Cunningham. Phil has interesting theories. He makes me realise how pampered we are at Oxford and how much tougher and better prepared these North Americans are – they eat more, train more, think more, run more. But why are they all so *tall*?

It isn't going to be easy!

In February the European critics were picking four major contenders for the 1500 metres title at Los Angeles: Ladoumègue, the world record holder; Reggie Thomas, the British record holder; Venzke, who had run the world's second-fastest mile; and Larva, the inheritor of Nurmi's crown. On the eve of the Games, Ladoumègue is out (disqualified in March), Thomas is out (with a split tendon), and Venzke is out (fails to qualify). Only the Finn, Harri Larvi, is left. It is the most astonishing reversal.

Later: I had to break off my journal to get back on the train. Now we are swaying towards Kansas City and I am trying to work out the probabilities for the final.

Jerry Cornes, who must now be a favourite, fears Larva. But the other Finn, Purje, has equalled Ladoumègue's world-record time for a three-quarter-mile distance, which is superior

64

to anything Jerry or I have done. And there are four new-comers – the Americans Cunningham and Hallowell, the Swede Erik Ny, and Luigi Beccali – all of whom have appeared since May, like sudden flowers. Now it becomes interesting, Jack-o.

The American critics are picking Jerry (or me, funnily enough). But we are both slower than Ladoumègue – I am using Ladoumègue, who has five world records, as a yardstick. Now. Harri Larva has outsmarted Ladoumègue on more than one occasion, yet Purje is faster than Larva. And so is the Harvard American, Pen Hallowell. Hallowell, Purje and Larva are given only a "slim chance" by the critics, Cunningham and the Swede Ny, who have no consistent form whatsoever, are considered "threats", while Beccali, who has run a faster 1500 metres than anybody in these pre-Olympic weeks, is hardly mentioned. All very puzzling.

Tommy Hampson has borrowed a book and fallen asleep with *The Madonna of the Sleeping Car*. I am wide awake staring out at the blurred face of America as we rattle on through the night.

Sunday, 24 July:
Horrible, horrible train. Snatches of sleep only. Chicago – Emporia – Dodge City – on and on. Desertlands, Nebraska, Colorado, . . . Wrote to Janie:

"Everyone is suffering. Temperature in train, 118° Fahrenheit. Whenever the train stops we pour off in shorts and singlets and run up and down in single file, like geese; at Emporia we found a fountain, stripped and fell in, watched by curious townsfolk and hordes of autograph-hunters. Tommy almost missed the train. At Dodge City he wandered off, then reappeared, surprised and bespectacled, at a hand-gallop, as the train was steaming out of the station. Everyone yelled, 'Jump!' He jumped, and we pulled him back on board."

Pray God I run as hard for New Zealand in the race as Tommy did for the train.

We have taken on six more teams and our "Olympic Special" is now more than five hundred yards long. At last it's cold. We are climbing, in mountains, somewhere near the Grand

Canyon. I can see a solitary peak rising from the plateau. For a moment I imagine myself back in New Zealand, a ten-year-old coming home from school, smelling the snow tussocks and searching the horizon for the outline of Mount Cook piercing the top of the Two Thumb Range. I can still see in my mind's eye a schoolboy with skinny legs and matchstick arms running over that wild and empty landscape.

Please God, don't worry too much about New Zealand, just give me a hole to get through in the race. Even a little hole. I have a terrible fear of being boxed in.

The Games open in a week. We reach Los Angeles tomorrow.

5

It was four days before the reaction set in. I had settled into the Olympic Village with the New Zealanders, was relishing their company and the warm Californian air, warm and soft and dry like wine, and had begun training on a nearby school track with Jerry and Tommy. The track was made of baked clay. It felt hard, like asphalt. We had all lost weight on the train journey and were frightened of losing more. My training times were not spectacular, but adequate. I noticed how rapidly the sweat evaporates from the pores in the dry air and drank liquid by the gallon and advised anyone who complained of muscle-cramp to do the same. It is important, I said, to restore the moisture lost from evaporation.

Then on the fourth day, two days before the Games were due to open, I woke with a sickening pain in my neck and limbs so sore that at first I couldn't get out of bed. I knew at once what it was, or so I thought – muscle-jarring from the hard clay tracks. They have none of the elasticity of cinders we use in England. I had been told that the track at the Coliseum would be just as hard and decided that my spikes were far too long. What I needed, if my muscles weren't to seize up altogether, was a pair with short spikes and like a fool I rushed straight into town to find a sports shop. Had I stopped and talked to Tommy, he would have sent me to the British masseur, a wonderful Irishman who at that moment was putting Dr O'Callaghan, the hammer thrower, into a bath and rubbing him with a mixture of oil and potheen – O'Callaghan had woken that morning with sharp pains in his back. Half the British team, I discovered later, were having similar reactions. Some put it down to the climate whose exhilarating effect, after the first few days, induced feelings of torpor, stiffness, weight loss, aches of all kinds – even in one case, the 400-metre hurdler Robert Tisdall, total collapse. It wasn't the climate and it wasn't the hard tracks, it was due to nerves, just nerves, and Tisdall, an old campaigner, had the sense to realise it. He took to his bed and stayed there fifteen hours a day. On the day of his race he came out, wonderfully restored, and won a Gold Medal. The only mistake he made was to hit the last hurdle. Even then he created a world record.

Nerves! I traipsed about Los Angeles from one sports shop to another. The first had sold out of short spikes, so had the second. By the time I had been to four shops I knew it was hopeless. There had been a run on the sports shops. I decided to try one more store. I entered the fifth shop in a state of anxiety bordering on panic. There were four other athletes at the counter when I entered. One of them, a tall angular man with veined hands and impatient gestures, was calling the proprietor an idiot. "Sie Vollidiot," I heard him say in precise clear German. He seemed almost as agitated as I was. Apparently the tall man had reserved a pair of short spikes the day before; now, returning with the money to buy them, he discovered that the proprietor had in the meantime sold them to a Swede. It was the last pair. "Zum Teufel mit Ihnen!" I heard him mutter, and as he turned from the counter I recognised him. It was the German athlete I had met in New Zealand, Otto Peltzer. "Ich werde es selbst machen," he told the shop owner. "I'll file the points down myself," I understood.

Peltzer left the shop without seeing me. I thought of running after him but didn't. I didn't need to. He had already solved my

67

problem. That evening, back in the village, I borrowed a hand file and began grinding down the spikes on my shoes.

I sat up most of the night, filing till my arms ached, and next day took the file to the Los Angeles high school track and continued to grind the points. Later when I put on the shoes, the stiffness in my joints was still there but it seemed to be easing. I began to eat again, recovering some of the weight I had lost. At the track-side I watched Cunningham and Beccali work out, noting their rhythms with less awe than when I had first seen them in action. I sat in the shade and continued to whittle down the spikes. The very act of holding something in my hands, of drawing one piece of metal across another, had a soothing effect. Travelling across America I had had a recurring dream of failure, of jagged patterns that refused to mesh and come together. As soon as I came to the Olympic Village I searched the post for a letter from Janie (there was none); I searched the programme when the draw for the heats was announced; I read my allotted number, 216, forwards and backwards to see if it would bring me luck – I was looking for a sign, I realised, some omen. Now finally it came. It seemed a tiny miracle – that chance, which had so often favoured a course of action in the past, should rescue me now in the shape of an eight-inch piece of metal suggested by an enigmatic German with grey eyes and a small moustache whose name was Otto Peltzer. In New Zealand Dr Peltzer had helped me once. Now, unknowingly, he had done so again.

Cunningham, I noticed, had a sharp transfixed stare in the eyes when he ran. I understood now why he was nicknamed the Camel – he ran leaning slightly forwards. Beccali took very short strides, shorter than anyone's. He bounded up and down, a noisy energetic runner with an odd tension in the angle of his head. Both men had powerful chests. Compared with these two the other runners, except for Jerry Cornes, seemed lightweights. My eyes were on the runners as I rubbed with the file, but my mind kept returning to the German, Peltzer. Otto Peltzer had not appeared on the track at all. Yet he was entered for two events, Tommy Hampson's race, the 800 metres which was early in the programme, and mine. Tommy had told me he knew Peltzer, once the conqueror of Douglas Lowe and

68

Nurmi; that he respected his reputation, but considered him, at thirty-three, "washed up". Tommy thought him opinionated and arrogant. But I remembered sitting at Peltzer's feet two years earlier in 1930 in New Zealand, when his name was a byword, asking him questions late into the night. I hadn't liked him at first either, yet when we parted that night a strange intimacy had grown between us. Before the meeting I had gone to the library and devoured everything I could find on Peltzer, discovering that in youth he had been stricken with poliomyelitis and at the age of twelve was still confined in plaster casts to a wheelchair. A solitary boy. A boy who had one day torn off the plaster supporting his legs and taught himself to run by running. No doubt I identified with the puny German lad, lonely and insecure, derided by his schoolmates for his weakness. Like the Sac and Fox Indian athlete, Jim Thorpe, Peltzer had first tested himself against deer and fox, running through the hills and valleys of Schleswig-Holstein.

Reading about Peltzer in New Zealand, I seemed to be reading about myself. That night in the hotel he had talked to me about self-reliance. He said, "You must discover the body's secrets. Alone you must find them. Then teach the body to run at changing speeds."

It was a hot night, the middle of summer, yet he had lit a fire in the hotel room and wrapped himself in a coat and two blankets. At one point he lay down on the floor and went to sleep. Ten minutes later he sat up, refreshed, and we continued talking. I was impressed by his self-discipline and by the power of his self-education. Earlier in the day, watching him run at Lancaster Park, Christchurch, displaying the insignia of his Prussian club, I was aware of a fanatical quality in him. He seemed to subject himself to the worst kind of body-abuse, to defy everything the experts of the time were saying. But he told me that he had taught his body to run at varying speeds to the point of exhaustion, and then to answer a summons and run three hundred metres more. That was how in 1926 he had conquered Britain's double Olympic champion, Lowe, and a few weeks later in Berlin he had overpowered Nurmi. Whether or not Peltzer's reasoning was correct, whether or not that was how he had set those two world records in 1926, I left his hotel

69

that night feeling I had imbibed a secret wisdom. Somewhere inside my body, independent of all theory, all medical logic and all accepted practice, was a mysterious and delicately balanced inner clock waiting to be wound and tripped. If I was going to run at the Olympics and win a Gold Medal, I had but to seek and find the key. But only *I* could do it, I alone. I, Lovelock.

How much nearer was I now, I wondered, as I sat there working the file, to penetrating the mystery?

Cunningham had finished training and was talking to his American coach. Beccali had already left the ground, going off in a jaunty beret arm-in-arm with his team-mates. Erik Ny was out there now, jogging quietly by himself, watched by Jerry and Tommy Hampson. Tommy was chatting to Douglas Fairbanks. Fairbanks, a Tommy Hampson fan, had driven out from the Olympic Village. Tommy was due to run in the heats already on the first day. I walked over and joined them. Tommy said, "Come on. Let's strut our stuff." He took us round an easy quarter in 65 secs., then Jerry and I ran two laps more. The baked surface felt surprisingly easy. The shortened spikes, I told myself, had made a difference. There was no jarring to the legs. The stiffness in the thigh and neck muscles had quite gone.

The Games opened on the last day of July, a Saturday. We stood at the centre of the Coliseum, unfolding like a nutshell at the foot of a city whose millions seemed to have been poured in around us in such hundreds and thousands as I had never before imagined; we heard a short oration by the American Vice-President, Mr Charles Curtis; I raised my right arm with two thousand other athletes to take the Olympic oath and as I did so, looking up to the orange flame burning over the rim of the stadium, I thought, Yes, this is how it is. This is how it was. This is how it always will be. For in the Village the night before we had discussed this very thing, the spirit of comradeship launched by Baron de Coubertin, the founder of the modern Olympics. Somebody at the next table, I forget who, had scoffed, saying that the Ancient Games of Greece had never been like this, that young men like us would always go to war, that Coubertin's notions of fair play and sportsmanship were

70

so much hogwash – and at this point I stood up and began shouting at him. I forget what I said. I shouted across the tables in the dining-room, using words I'd never thought of before, defending Coubertin's ideal and the nobility of the Games. I ended, "Whatever you think, success is glorious only when nobly achieved!" I was very noisy. Little Billy Savidan, our long-distance runner, and the other New Zealanders at the table were embarrassed. But now at the ceremony, standing below the peristyle in the Coliseum taking the sacred oath, I knew I was right. As I joined in the Olympic Hymn,

> *Now sing of virile Games*
> *By which the body's beauty*
> *Is made to live once more,*

I felt a heaving sensation in my breast and I knew that what I had said the night before was right. I was right. Baron de Coubertin was right. The Ancients were right. The Age of Pericles was not dead.

But I was also ashamed.

I was watching the British standard-bearer, David Burghley. Lord Burghley stood a little way off, gripping a heavy flagpole fixed to a socket at the waist, sweating hard, motionless in the broiling sun – knowing that next day he had to defend his title in the 400-metre low hurdles against the American Morgan Taylor. When Burghley discovered that Morgan Taylor had been named flagbearer to the United States contingent, he had immediately volunteered to carry the Union Jack, because otherwise, David Burghley said, he would have an unfair advantage over his rival. A few days before, I had been asked to carry the flag for New Zealand. I was flattered, but not so flattered that I failed to see how this might affect my chances. The reward for practising the manoeuvres involved, and then holding aloft a heavy flag in the sun for two hours, would be to lower my strength and ruin my chances of success, I reasoned. So I made an excuse and declined to carry my country's flag. Now, watching David Burghley, I felt ashamed. Then and there I vowed to myself that if I survived Los Angeles and got to Berlin, I would carry the New Zealand flag if it killed me.

71

Neither David Burghley nor Morgan Taylor, the two flag-bearers, won the hurdles next day.

Tommy Hampson won his heat of the 800 metres.

Two days later, on the eve of our 1500 heats, Jerry and I sat in the competitors' stand, transfixed by Tommy's final.

"He's too far back," Jerry said.

Phil Edwards, the British Guianese running in the colours of Canada, had opened a huge lead and at the halfway mark was increasing it. Tommy was in fifth place, over twenty yards behind.

"He's giving it away, Jack."

"No, he's not."

"He's almost last. Get up, you ass. Tommy, you'll never make it!"

But Tommy had confided to me how he intended to run this race. He intended to run two dead-level laps, regardless of what the rest of the field did.

Stay there, Tommy. I willed him to stay back, knowing the danger and anguish of a big gap opening in front of you, while your intelligence fought against the instinct to move too soon and undo months and months of planning.

"He'll never make it," Jerry said.

Tommy began to move only when he reached the back straight. He caught one man, then another. I tugged Jerry up. We began to shout incoherently. Then there was a hush. Phil Edwards had faded, his place taken by a Canadian team-mate, Alex Wilson. Eighty yards from the tape, Tommy began to gain on Wilson, the rims of his glasses reflecting little stabs of sunlight with the forward movement of his body. The entire stadium was hushed, caught up in the drama of that final sprint as the Englishman and the Canadian duelled stride for stride over the last fifty. Tommy won by a foot in the world-record time of 1 min. 49.8 secs., having become the first man to beat 1 min. 50 secs. and achieve what Harold Abrahams and other sports writers next day called the seemingly impossible. So many people rushed out on to the track to congratulate Tommy – he told us he was thumped on the back "in seventeen languages" – that they smashed his glasses.

So many records broken. I have forgotten the count of those first days. Tommy's inspired finish overshadowed everything. I was still thinking of it the next day as we emerged from the cool dark tunnel beneath the stadium and sat on the heat benches for the 1500. The track was a rich chocolate-brown, made of a fine peaty clay. It looked inviting, not hard at all. Beccali, I noticed, hadn't filed his spikes down, nor had Ny. Only Peltzer and I seemed to have done this. We still hadn't spoken, Peltzer and I. The Swede, Ny, was smiling at me. He wore white shoes, white shorts, white vest, even the eyebrows were white – Erik Ny smiled and pointed out that my number had slipped. I was so grateful I jumped up and shook his hand, forgetting we were not running in the same heat. Peltzer was in Ny's heat, with Beccali. I watched Peltzer stand in his heat lane and test the track. He looked haggard. He hadn't shaved. He ran a few paces and paused, examining his spikes. He seemed unbalanced. Now he was speaking in German to the starter, Franz Miller, pointing to his shoes. Paavo Nurmi, who had materialised from the tunnel and had been sitting with his compatriot, Purje, went across. Nurmi and the starter appeared to be reasoning with Peltzer. Peltzer sat on the track and began unlacing his shoes. My God, I thought, he's going to run in bare feet. This is his last chance (the day before, in the final of the 800, Peltzer had come in last) – this is probably his last chance in the Olympics and he's going to throw it away. The starter was shaking his head. Peltzer grunted something and stood up. I saw that he had discarded the spikes for a pair of gym shoes. He made two false starts. When the heat finally began, he shot out wildly, almost reeling. Even so he would have qualified easily, I thought, but 300 metres from the end, running in third place, he dropped out. I was puzzled. For the surface he was running on – I had by this time already run my heat – was like silk: ploughed, watered and rolled to an almost satin texture. It would be four years before I saw Peltzer again and asked him what had happened.

Altogether the heats were puzzling.

Cunningham won the first heat, I won the second, Beccali the third. Jerry qualified, so did both the other Americans, Hallowell and Crowley, the two Finns, Larva and Purje, and the Swede, Ny. But our heat times were so slow on a track which was so fast that afterwards I was no nearer solving the problem of who was the man to watch in the final next day.

Still, I had learned something. I could run in extreme heat. The heat hadn't bothered me at all. More interesting was the discovery that I had developed a sixth sense for anticipating trouble. I appeared to have the faculty of "scenting". Two hundred metres from home, seconds before it actually happened, I sensed the field at my back preparing to engulf me, as everyone tightened for the run in to qualify. So that when a moment later I was enveloped and boxed in, I remained calm. I saw a hole, and shot through. I bumped one runner. He in turn bumped another man who swerved off the track on to the grass, so Jerry told me afterwards. Jerry said, "There might be a protest." But there was no protest against me. My luck seemed to be holding.

Yet I wasn't running well. I had drawn the easiest of the three heats. I had felt sluggish. And I didn't know why.

That night I had no dream, no premonition of failure; nothing occurred to upset me. After a light meal I walked through the Village, enjoying the soft night, listening to the crackle of cicadas mingling with snatches of music and laughter coming from the athletes sitting outside their wooden chalets, responding to shouted greetings – "Good luck, Kiwi" . . . "A demain". It felt good to be alive. But when I got back to my cabin and sat on the little verandah looking out over Beverly Hills to Hollywood, I was unaccountably depressed. I couldn't get Otto Peltzer out of my mind. Why had he given up like that? Why?

Peltzer had dropped out on a curve with 300 metres to go. He wasn't labouring. He was in third place behind Beccali and Ny, running well within himself. It happened just as he was passing the starter, Franz Miller. I had the impression that Miller had ordered him off the track, for, as Peltzer drew abreast on the curve, Miller shouted something and appeared to wave him down. I saw Peltzer look round and stop dead, as if replying to a command. When he left the field, there were tears in his eyes.

I slept well. I woke to a blue sky, ate an underdone egg with dry toast and tea, and about eleven o'clock lay down in the cabin feeling faintly nauseous and oppressed, as if invisible spiders were making cobwebs in the air that I breathed. Not even the arrival of a messenger bringing a telegram from

Janie could shake me out of myself; nor the sight of John Watt, a New Zealand friend from Oxford, who walked in out of the blue. He arrived unannounced and presented me with a lifesize stuffed kiwi that he'd found in London for luck. John, bless him, a Rhodes Scholar like myself, had saved the fare and come all the way from Oxford to see me run in the final. When he had gone, I laid out my kit and was sick into the hand-basin. Some time later Tommy came in and told me to stop pacing.

"I didn't realise I was pacing," I said.

"Up and down, up and down," Tommy said. "At least you're visible. Jerry is hiding in the lavatory and won't come out and Erik Ny has vanished altogether. Ny's manager is having kittens. I've been doing the rounds with Harold Abrahams. Pen Hallowell is having a haircut, Phil Edwards is playing the guitar, the Finns are complaining it's too hot and Cunningham says his legs are cold. Cunningham's got a sore throat. Oh. And Beccali is lying in a hammock under a mosquito net practising the Fascist salute. As for you — "

"I think it's anybody's race, Tommy."

"Yes. Well if I was your headmaster, I'd keep you all in after school. You've got stage fright, that's all. Come on," he said. "They've advanced the time of the final by twenty minutes. Pack up the gear or you'll miss the bus."

On the bus I couldn't sit still. Tommy wished me luck. At the competitors' door leading to the dressing-room he said: "Two things to remember, Jack – Lot's wife and Ray Watson."

I grinned vaguely. "Lot's wife" we had talked about before. That referred to Amsterdam, 1928, and the Frenchman Ladoumègue. Halfway round the last bend with victory and a Gold Medal in sight, Ladoumègue had made the mistake of looking back, and that glance had cost him the Olympic title.

"OK, Tommy. I won't look round. But what on earth did Ray Watson do?"

"Against Nurmi, remember? Paris, 1924. Nurmi raced out from the gun to see if he could kill off the opposition, just as Phil Edwards did against me on Tuesday – and just as Phil will probably try and do against you and Jerry today. It wouldn't surprise me. Either Phil, the old rabbit, will try and kill you off, or Cunningham will, I'm sure of it. Anyway in Paris against

75

Nurmi, Ray Watson made the fatal mistake of trying to keep up with Nurmi. He finished seventh. So don't — "

"OK. Message received and understood. I won't try and emulate Ray Watson." Such was my mental state, however, that when the race started that was exactly what I did do.

6

"Somebody," I heard Jerry say as we lined up for the starter, "is going to learn a lesson today."

The start was on a bend: eleven runners. Jerry was two or three away from me; Cunningham right inside by the pole-line; I was second from the outside furthest from the pole. We were in a half-crouch, waiting. Cunningham stood up and walked back. He took three sharp breaths and drew his knees up to his chest, one at a time. The backs of his legs were livid scar tissue, a bright ruby colour. I remembered being told he had once been in a fire, almost burned alive. A loudspeaker crackled. The starter, Franz Miller, lowered his pistol. "Sorry," Cunningham said, as he rejoined us. We crouched again. "Get set!" Then Beccali, buried in the middle of the line, broke and ran twenty yards. "Damn that. That sort of thing riles me," Jerry said.

We stood up again. The starter waited impassively. He wore a long white coat like a surgeon's coat. This is just like going for an operation, I thought. We are all patients waiting for the jab of the needle. The needle is quicker, that's all. Beccali trotted back gaily, gesturing, palms outstretched. Nobody spoke. I got a whiff of Beccali's hair oil. As we went to our marks for the third time, I heard a bell strike three times and for a moment had the impression I was back at Iffley Road under the belltower of St John the Evangelist. I was unnaturally calm. I even saw myself in a mirror-image from the side of the track,

76

wiggling my back foot into the earth for the "Set" position, so calmly that when a runner on my left moved slightly I anticipated the whistle for a recall and prepared to stand up. The pistol went. I was so flummoxed that I recoiled like a jack-in-the-box and in a few yards had crashed into the lead. That was my first mistake.

Charlie Paddock, the American, later claimed that the lead changed hands, or legs, seven times in the first lap. Hallowell had it once, then Ny, I had it twice, then Phil Edwards, Hallowell again; then Cunningham, elbows out, his eyes glassy and transfixed, rushed up and displaced Hallowell, seeming to come from nowhere. At one point, lunging forward before Ny relieved me, a loudspeaker overhead bawled in my ear, "Lovelock leads!" The next minute I was trailing in fourth place. I seemed to be either too far ahead or too far back. My brain cleared and I made a snap decision to stick with Cunningham, resolved to follow the flat of his head; but I felt bustled. The blare of the speaker had thrown me, upsetting the rhythm of my stride. Now we were bunched together. We seemed to be crawling. I had the absurd notion we were spider-walking up a wall like soldiers on fatigues, one inching forward and then another and each reluctant to top the rise for fear of being picked off. I had the even more absurd notion I should be pausing and bowing to the others, saying "After you". Without warning Phil Edwards catapulted himself out of the bunch, followed by Cunningham, exactly as Tommy had predicted, opening up a gap of ten metres. I raced after Cunningham, my second mistake, and then unable to hold him found myself back with the bunch, labouring, as the gap widened to 20 metres. 25 metres. I felt awful. Nobody moved to close with the leaders. It was uncanny how we let them go – Phil Edwards, a novice at the 1500 distance, and Cunningham bustling at his elbow, trying to become the first American to win the race since Mel Sheppard in 1908. Now I was convinced that everyone else had been talking to Tommy and studying "Ray Watson's mistake". The bell sounded for the last lap and still the gap widened. It was totally quiet. The only sound was Beccali, inside me. He was grunting. My breathing and Beccali's grunts came together. Now Jerry appeared. He came and went. When Jerry moved, I moved. Beccali followed. We

77

made a trio. We scuttled down the back straight, three rabbits after two hares. Then there were only two rabbits. On the last bend I was in fourth place behind Jerry and then he was gone. He simply left me, and the field began to sweep by. First Beccali absolutely shot past me, and past Jerry. Then Hallowell. Then Erik Ny. They ran me down. I tied up completely. Beccali won by four yards from Jerry, breaking the tape by catching it in both hands and tearing it in two – Luigi Beccali, a former cyclist from Milan, the man who had returned the fastest time in European racing that year and "the man everyone forgot".

Beccali one, Cornes two, Edwards three, Cunningham four, Ny five, Hallowell six. I came in seventh. Like Ray Watson.

San Francisco
Sunday, 14 August 1932:
I am sitting in an air-conditioned hotel room with Jerry, drying out. Last night we de-segregated ourselves and broke bread with the women athletes at one of the hotels in Los Angeles where they have been staying. End-of-Games celebration. Wild. I was put to bed by a schoolgirl prodigy from Germany, pretty good. A fencer. Not quite my first experience of sex, but v. satisfactory for us both. Afterwards I slept like the proverbial top for five hours. Uninterrupted! Something I have never been able to do before while in training. Usually the most I can get is two or three hours' sleep a night.

Jerry says: "How on earth can you compete after going to bed with a woman?" I don't know. I'll find out today.

Presently we go out to run for GB and the Empire against the USA. It will be my second meeting with Cunningham in ten days. I don't really care what happens. Jerry says he doesn't either. He is still smarting from his defeat by Beccali. I tell Jerry he ran the race of his life. He is furious with the English sports writers – they say he "lacked judgment". I say, "What do they know, who only sit and write?" Jerry says, "Whatever happens, Jack, you must not chuck running." For I had been saying after my débâcle, that today would probably be my last race. I can't console Jerry and he fails to console me. We're like a couple of old soldiers licking their wounds in the trenches. I pick up one of my spikes and fling it across the room.

Jerry socks me with a pillow. We fall about the room, socking each other, and end up breaking a chair. "*At least,*" Jerry says, "we participated. We took part. We won't end up like Jim Thorpe."

Poor Jim Thorpe. We saw him two days ago. He was one of Jerry's heroes. King Gustav V of Sweden once said to him, in 1912, "Sir, you are the greatest athlete in the world." That was at Stockholm where Thorpe completed an epic double, winning both the pentathlon and decathlon events. Shortly afterwards an American paper revealed that as a boy Thorpe had once played professional baseball and as a result he was stripped of his amateur status and ordered to give back his Olympic medals. I wish we'd never seen Thorpe. It happened on the last day but one of the Games while we were talking with Paavo Nurmi. A group of us had descended on Nurmi in the stand, some pumping him for information, some wanting autographs. Nurmi sat there holding his big hands – he looks like a farmer – not saying much, occasionally smiling, hiding his feelings, hiding his bitterness, for he too was suffering. Nurmi had come to Los Angeles intending to close his career with a victory in the marathon, only to be told when he arrived that he couldn't run. I don't know the details, but it seems to be some sordid feud between the Finnish and the French officials going back to the disqualification of Ladoumègue in February or March. Nurmi found on arrival that he had been suspended by the IAAF for accepting payment over and above expenses during an exhibition tour. Until the last moment Nurmi fought the rejection and even continued training for the marathon each day, but it was no use. Anyway, he just sat there with his farmer's hands and his phantom smile, signing programmes for us. Then he said, looking across to a man in a straw hat sitting not far off, Nurmi said – and I shall never forget it. He said, "Water which doesn't run, goes sour."

Somebody said, "My God, that's Jim Thorpe. That's Big Jim Thorpe."

Jim Thorpe was sitting idle on the stone steps of the stadium about twenty yards away. He had a broom in his hands; his face partly hidden by the straw hat. I wanted to go up to him, but Jerry stopped me. It seems that in 1924, after his Gold Medals were taken away from him, Thorpe had a complete breakdown. He gave up athletics and sank into oblivion. Just before the Los Angeles Games, however, he was discovered wielding a pick and shovel on a nearby construction site – discovered and rescued. And here he was, the most famous of all American Indian athletes, employed by the Games administration as an attendant to sweep up the discarded programmes and the litter.

Monday, 15 August 1932:
On a train, heading east. Another train over five hundred yards long. It is hot, unbearably hot. Every two or three hundred miles we tumble out in shorts and singlets and run up and down in file like geese, watched by the local population and crowds of autograph seekers. Somebody says, "Haven't we done all this before . . . ?"
We are going home.

29 August 1932
Empress of Britain, at sea
en route England

Mrs Ivy Lovelock
38 Warden Street
Opoho, Dunedin
New Zealand

Dearest Mother,
    Thank you so very much for your cablegram which arrived in the Olympic Village two days before my race. I have sent postcards from every stopping point as we trudged back across America, knowing I wouldn't find the peace to write properly until we rejoined the "floating gym", as we have christened this ship. Also I was too depressed, even though I have run twice since Los Angeles, once in San Francisco and once in Vancouver, and even though I managed at S.F. to settle my score with Cunningham. He really is a man of courage, a lion. I don't know why Cunningham should still be there – or here – in my thoughts, when all the honours

were the Italian Beccali's. Luigi is like a sun child. At the Victory ceremony he gave the Mussolini Fascist salute, then embraced and kissed everyone on both cheeks, including the Olympic officials. Can you beat it? I didn't know what glory meant until I happened to walk past his cabin next morning. All his team-mates were waiting there. They were calling, "Luigi! Luigi!" He appeared in the doorway to find the pathway laid with a carpet of rugs they had brought from their rooms. They had lined the path with wicker chairs and piled the chairs up with flowers. Beccali just stood there, speechless, choking with emotion. About the race: I don't understand it. There was nothing wrong with me. When I think that Glenn Cunningham ran with tonsillitis and abscessed teeth, Pen Hallowell with a migraine and Phil Edwards (who had never run the distance before) was having his fourth race in as many days – and all three of these minor place-getters left Yours Truly, Jack-o, staggering in their wake, I am, as Father would have said, "disappointed in you, son". That is my one consolation, that Father wasn't there to see it. I have been thinking: Is there something in the Lovelock blood that stops us rising to a great occasion? Something bad? Forgive me, dear. I don't want to depress you more than you must be already, having to smile and make excuses to all the people who sent messages of support and were counting on me. Tell them I am truly sorry and I feel a fraud. I feel I have let you all down. Ossie Johnson, Jim Barnes, Bill Pullar, Noel North . . . when I write their names down I can see the hills over Dunedin and the colour of the broom, the pine trees along the ridge and the blue gums hanging over Anderson's Bay, reminding me of those lovely Saturdays and Sundays with Noel running over the Peninsula. (I can still taste the mustard in your sandwiches!) But it seems like all that happiness and all those dreams have gone for nothing.

Give my love to Olive and brother Jim. I hope little Jim didn't put his shirt on me. Somebody who owns a betting shop in Dunedin thinks I threw in the towel – he sent a telegram calling me a "Typical New Zealand cream-puff". He sounds disgusted with me. He isn't nearly as disgusted as I am with myself.

Now it's back to Oxford and Pharmacology Schools (Bugs & Drugs to you). Jerry is off to Africa to be a Big White Chief in the Colonial Service. He says we shall meet in Berlin. But I don't know. Pain is good, Father said. Striving is good. And failure is not all bad. I have learned a lot this past month. But I don't seem to be cut out somehow for the Big Stuff. I don't seem to have the push, the inner strength, to cope with heats and finals on successive days which is what first-class racing demands.

Do you remember the little volume of Chesterton you gave me? I read it on the train. Unfortunately the first story I opened was one about a man who went mad and danced in the garden because he'd invented a new language. Well, I'm not dancing and I haven't invented a new language of running, but sometimes with all this worry of trying to screw myself up to make a supreme effort, I do wonder at my mental state . . . I'm joking, dear. By the way, I sent you a new drug that has come on to the market in the States, try it, dear. It will help you to sleep . . .

Your loving son,
Jack

"May I come in?"
"Who's that?"
"Janie."
"What are you doing here?"
"Looking for a man called Jackie. It's very dark in here."
"How did you find me?"
"I'll draw back the curtains, shall I? There. It's a beautiful November day."
"For God's sake, close them. Close them!"
"All right. I've closed them. Is that what you want?"
"Yes."
"You want to be alone in the dark?"
"Yes."
"Are you all right?"
"Yes. How did you find me?"
"By asking."
"Did Dacre send you?"
"No. But he's worried about you. You've been gone nearly

82

a week. Jackie, you didn't tell me you have relations here in Oxford."

"I haven't."

"Oh. I'm sorry. But the woman who let me in, Mrs Knox — ?"

"Captain and Mrs Knox are looking after me. I met them last term."

"She calls you John. She's very English. At first she didn't want to let me in and said something about you stopping running. She's very protective about you. I went to Rhodes House looking for you. The Warden's wife, Mrs Allen, said you might be here in Park Town. Wow, you're secretive. I've never been to Park Town before – it's like going into the country, isn't it, all these trees and gardens, hidden away. Little crescents, big houses, right in the middle of Oxford. Real Regency. You sure do pick your hideouts, Jackie."

"I must say, you've got an awful cheek."

"Mrs Allen thought it might be helpful if I dropped in. I thought you'd be pleased to see me."

"It's very sweet of you to come."

"So is it true then?"

"Is what true? I'm not having a breakdown, if that's what you think."

"Ray and I wondered what had happened. You just disappeared. Ray's heard from Jerry, by the way – he's in Nigeria. No. I meant, true that you're giving up running?"

"I was dreaming just now. I was in a tree, like the man in the story who got away and lived in a hole at the top of an elm-tree."

"Which story?"

"I don't remember."

"Jackie, listen. Jerry says in his letter there was nothing wrong with you in Los Angeles, except nerves."

"Nerves, nerves. Of course it wasn't nerves!"

"Jerry is in northern Nigeria, Ray says, at a place called Kamo. Or Kano. Lots of mud huts and chickens running about. Jerry's an ADO."

"It's a nice feeling being in an elm-tree, like floating on a calm sea. Forwards and back, backwards and forwards, without direction, without plans. Without clocks."

"The Emir put on a race when Jerry arrived. They had to run eight miles round the mud walls of the city, and everyone turned out to see the great Cornes. But then a schoolboy came along and passed him. Jerry can't run in the heat, he says."

"Tell Janie — "

"What?"

"Tell Janie I'm not having a breakdown. I can't sleep, that's all."

"Jackie. *I'm* Janie. I'm here. I have to go now. Mrs Knox said five minutes only. Listen, Jerry says he may get leave to run in England next year."

"Jerry? Jerry's in Africa."

"But he's coming home next year, silly. You're not listening. Jerry and Ray might be getting married. Anyway even if he doesn't get leave, Jerry's got a date with you in Berlin, he says. He sent a message. That's the message.

"Aren't you interested?"

"I'm not going to Berlin."

"What shall I tell Dacre? And Bill Thomas?"

"Nothing."

"They're worried about you."

"It's none of their business. I have to work this out for myself."

"I have to go. Funny, I didn't know you even wanted to run at Berlin. You never told me. You are coming back, aren't you?"

"Back?"

"To college. You've got to sit B.M. examinations next month – Oh, Mrs Knox. I'm just going. Thank you for letting me see him. The Sub-Rector asked me to remind Jackie about the examinations next month, and the relays too. You've got the Relay Match against Cambridge next month."

"I'm not running in the relays."

"I'll tell them that. Goodbye."

I lie here in my darkened room and watch the light coming through the curtains. The light comes in through the chinks. Somewhere I can hear a train shunting. I like trains. I think of trains with affection. On a train you are going somewhere. I'm not going anywhere. I'm frightened to go back to college.

I am the man in the tree who won't come down. The man who has fallen off the ladder and won't go up. I am the parachutist who stays in the plane because he doesn't believe the parachute will open. But is it only fear?

"She seems a nice girl, John."

"Yes."

"Nicely brought up, I mean."

"I didn't know she was coming, Mother."

"You must ask her to tea some time. John, I thought of running over to Eynsham in the car. I have to pay one of my guinea-pig calls. Would you like to come?"

"No. No, I think I'll stay, if you don't mind."

"Howard brought the post at lunch-time. I've put it in the hall."

"I'll have to think about going back to college."

"Ah. Your young lady has done you some good. But you know you can stay here as long as you like. Howard and I love having you. Is she American?"

"No, not really. She had an English governess. Her step-mother's American. Janie says she wants to graduate a happy Third and then get married."

"To you?"

"I don't think so. No, no. I don't think I shall ever marry, Mother."

"Well, time enough for that when you've passed your examinations and qualified. First you get your foot back on the pavement, as Captain Knox says. You'll make a good doctor, John."

"I was thinking, I might try psychiatry after I've done my clinical work. That will be in three or four years' time, if I can get into a London hospital. Arthur Porritt thinks I should do my clinical work at St Mary's. I can always keep up my athletics on the side."

"Yes. You needn't give it up altogether."

"I don't know. I was thinking, Mother. If I don't run in the relays, that will be it. An end to running."

"You *have* been doing some thinking, son."

"My mind's a bit clearer."

"One step at a time. You don't have to decide now."

"I think I've decided."

I am small. I am five feet seven inches high and I weigh less than ten stone. I have small feet, good arches and none of the toes are missing. My muscles are co-ordinated. Even my hair is co-ordinated. My hair is either blond or tow-coloured, depending on the light, parted on the left side, and wavy. Whatever I do to it, it settles in crinkled waves. It fits me like a woolly cap. My grin – well, you know about my famous grin. My centre of gravity is handily placed. It is low to the ground. My pulse rate is also low. It is below 40. Under stress my pulse returns to rest so quickly that the scientists are puzzled. I know this because when the Physiology Department lends me to the Radcliffe Infirmary or some other hospital for, say, an experiment in basal metabolic rates and I am made to run up and down stairs against a group of control patients, my resting pulse starts at 39, rises to 70, and then when I have stopped running returns to 39 within two minutes; whereas my "control" usually begins at 70, goes up to 160 and takes half an hour to return to 70! My teeth are sound. I have clear vision. Basically there is nothing wrong with my body. One way and another I know quite a lot about it. The only thing I don't know is what triggered the power failure that led to my collapse after I returned from Los Angeles.

When I got back in September I stayed with the Knoxes in Park Town off the Banbury Road, while I waited for the new term to begin. Captain Howard and Nesta Knox live at No. 30 Park Terrace, Park Town. They have no children of their own. I had met them the previous term at Rhodes House – they were friends of C.K. and his wife who only arrived in 1931. I was the first Rhodes Scholar they welcomed; and when Nesta Knox began her Sundays At Home for Rhodes Scholars I was the first one she invited to tea and crumpets. The Knox house was warm and undemanding; I came and kept coming; I fixed Nesta's clumpy old car which was always breaking down, made friends with Besta the dog, plundered the larder – and also their affections. Before I went to the Games they had already adopted me as a son.

Oxford, when I returned from Los Angeles, seemed to have softened and languished in my absence. It was a familiar place, both cheerful and wheezy, like the clocks. Oxford in mist, with leaves on the ground and dripping trees, matching Janie's dripping hem-line, wherever we walked. I bought a long winding scarf, hung up my running shoes, told myself I could easily afford to buy a new pair from Law's the shoemaker in London, but when my scholarship money came through I blew a hole in it throwing an elegant dinner party in my rooms. I joined two more clubs and engaged in a bout of social and physical pursuits that lasted for three weeks. I should have been training for the relays, instead I boxed and dabbled at fencing, went up to London for dancing lessons, played a bit of rugby, attended "Informal Smokers" and I don't know what, anything to take my mind off the track. I sent a note to Bill Thomas to say I was studying. If I saw Bill and his bowler hat coming, I dived into a shop. I kept off the track altogether. I told myself, I am studying to be a doctor. I attended lectures on anatomy and dissection, I looked at children's tibias in bottles, I wrote about the periostal changes in the ends of bone, but sometimes looking at the other nineteen-year-old youths working devotedly away in the demonstration room I seemed to be the stupidest member of the class. Instead of commenting on a microscopic slide showing a rare condition of the brain, I found myself writing down: "I don't understand which mechanism in the brain triggers and rejects the impulse to succeed." I shall never make a decent dissection, I told myself. I have no feeling for the tissues. I shall never prepare a good slide! At night I raged at myself in my journal. I lay in my frowsty twelve-by-eight bedroom smelling of formalin and tried to recapture what the lecturer had said in the afternoon. All that came to me was the crackle of cinders flying like shrapnel and the roar of the crowd mounting in slow waves, as if someone were moving heavy furniture across a distant part of the brain. Jerry had gone down, Jim Mahoney, my Australian friend, had gone down. I had made no new friends. I couldn't discuss running with Janie. I seemed to be filling my days in a race against time leading nowhere.

One night I turned back the pages of my journal and forced myself to read an account I had written in May:

After the race [I had written] I felt scarcely tired or blown, but later on in the afternoon I felt a little weary . . .

Underneath that, at the end of the account, I had written out the following comparative table of times:

	Ladoumègue World record 1931	*Nurmi* World record 1923	*Lovelock* 1932
	Secs.	Secs.	Secs.
1st lap	60.8	58.6	57.4
2nd lap	63.4	63.2	64.6
3rd lap	63.8	64.9	71.0
4th lap	61.2	63.7	59.0
Time at			
¼ mile	60.8	58.6	57.4
½ mile	2: 4.2	2: 1.8	2: 2.0
¾ mile	3: 8.0	3: 6.7	3:13.0
1 mile	4: 9.2	4:10.4	4:12.0

On that windless spring day I had run a mile in 4 mins. 12 secs., when Jerry Cornes' best time was about 4:18. Three months later at Los Angeles Jerry had improved to run the equivalent of 4:12, while I had barely managed the equivalent of 4:18. What a sell!

Was I feeling humilated? No, not at all. I was indifferent to the figures. I might have been reading about a problem in mental arithmetic. There was no emotion. I stared at the figures before me as if I was reading a profit-and-loss account in a ledger belonging to a stranger. Somehow that performance in May had fallen to bits in my memory.

The next day in the Cornmarket I stepped off the kerb and walked in front of a bus. It was just before the evening rush hour. I had no intention of doing it. I had not been contemplating suicide. I saw the bus bearing down on me at speed and didn't move; I was deprived of the will-power to step back. It was more tempting somehow to stand still. What saved you, Jack-o? I'll never know. The bus didn't stop. After it had gone, I saw my umbrella lying on the roadway in fragments where the wheels had passed over it. I was so shaken I went into the nearest shop, which happened to be a bookshop, picked up a shilling shocker and walked out into the street without paying for it. In the street somebody caught my arm. It was Nesta Knox. She said, "John, you look awful!" She scooped me up and took me home to Park Town. It was there a few days later that Janie found me.

I lie here in my darkened room listening to the trains shunting and I tell myself, Tomorrow I am going back to college. First I have to convince the new president of the Athletic Club that he doesn't need me for the relays. Then I shall see my Physiology tutor. Then I shall shut myself in my rooms and work.

The afternoon sunlight creeps through the chinks in the tall curtains. Outside I imagine the trees a misty green. Sometimes I can hear a lark singing.

A door opens and closes. Captain Knox is home. He greets me from the hall and goes whistling into the bathroom. He whistles in the bath. I pull on my dressing gown, light the kettle in the kitchen and walk about the house. Glance at the post. I put the letters down unopened. Captain Knox appears, upright, towelled, elderly. We share a pot of tea in the sitting room. He says:

"I see Nurmi is retiring at last."

"Oh?"

"Yes. Strange fellow. There's an article in *The Times*. Nurmi says he will continue to run ten miles a day. He says if he doesn't run every day, he feels ill. Strange, that. Nesta get the car to go?"

"Yes. I cleaned the points. The distributor was falling off."

"Good show. You're looking better, son. Another week of Nesta's cooking and you might start to fatten up."

"I've gained three pounds already."

"That's the drill. The post's there by the way."

"Yes. Thanks, Father. I'll read it tomorrow."

"Tomorrow?"

"I'm going back to college tomorrow."

Cyril Mabey, the new club president, said: "Well that's a bit thick, I must say."

"You've got Pen Hallowell, Cyril. Pen's here from Harvard. You've got a strong relay team without me."

"You *are* secretary of the club, you know."

"You'll win the relays. I shall probably have to resign from the club."

"Next year you'll be the president. What! You can't resign."

"I'm sorry, Cyril. I really do have to work."

"If you were sick, I could understand it."

"I have to work. I'm way behind."

"You've gone off your head. What about Bill Thomas? Have you told Bill?"

"I was hoping you'd break the news to Bill for me, Cyril."

"Not bloody likely. All right, smile, Lovelock. Smile your head off. It's no joke. What about the sports next year, the Cambridge match?"

"What about it?"

"It's no joke! Where's your college spirit? What about your loyalty to the University?"

"Coffee, Cyril?"

"No thanks. For God's sake, stop smiling. I just don't understand you. I suppose next thing, you'll resign from Vincent's, buy a lavender shirt and become an Aesthete. We've got the Police Sports in May. You're supposed to be running in Antwerp with Achilles in June."

"I've got Pharmacology Schools in June."

"America in July, Princeton. You know there's a match with Harvard and Princeton on the cards for next year. Have you forgotten?"

"I've forgotten if you take sugar in your coffee, Cyril. It's only chicory, I'm afraid."

I had made chicory coffee on the methylated spirits burner in my rooms. Cyril took the mug I gave him, put it down and slammed out of the room. I closed my oak door and went back to work. I had surrounded myself with set books and was attempting to catch up for two weeks' missed tutorials. My first

B.M. examination was barely three weeks away. Half an hour later Cyril was back, his frame filling the doorway. He stood in the doorway, his flat harrier's profile even flatter than usual, looking desperate. He said:

"Saturday. Shotover. It's the cross-country."

"I know. I'm sorry, Cyril. I can't."

"You'll have to run, Jack. I've two men sick – I mean, really sick. I can't beat a team of London harriers solo."

"Oh, you win. All right."

So I turned out that Saturday in the cross-country against the South London Harriers. Bitter cold. We coated our bodies with oil against the cold and the mud, ghastly mud everywhere. Muddy track, muddy wood, muddy hair, muddy eyes, brambles. Legs torn to ribbons by brambles in the wood. The marsh rimed with frost, the water lying to the waist. At times we were nearly swimming. Three times through the wood, three times up the hill track called Shotover, high above the downs of Oxfordshire. Seven miles. We were blue at the start, frozen at the finish. In the wood I threw up. I didn't tell Cyril when it was over, after we'd trotted home together in first place a quarter of a mile clear of the other runners, how I was feeling. Cyril said he'd enjoyed it. I loved it.

That was Saturday. On the Sunday I was back again at the Knoxes in a state of nervous collapse.

Janie had said to me once, not long after we met:

"I don't understand. I don't understand why you run."

"It's a form of excitement. It's actually very difficult to think when you're running."

"You mean it empties the brain? Your brain is *empty*?"

"No, silly. I'm not brain-less!"

Even then I didn't see that there was a kink in me, a sort of virus or malady that has to be fed and cosseted or it will turn septic. Anyway, I'm not kinky. Is a steeplejack kinky? A tightrope-walker? Is a marathon runner kinky? I met a marathon runner at Los Angeles who was so fit he could run 26 miles in 2 hours 35 minutes, yet he couldn't jump over a twig or carry his bags on to a train for fear that he might put his back out. I was like the marathon runner: my talents had unfitted me for anything else. But I refused to accept this.

Now, in November 1932, Janie said to me:

"I don't understand why you want to stop running, just for medicine. When you say you've got no feeling for medicine."

"It's what I'm here for. It's my career. I have to study."

"But why? If it makes you miserable? You're so miserable."

I wasn't just miserable. I was falling apart emotionally. Sometimes when I saw my spikes hanging up in the bedroom I wanted to run away and cry. On one occasion I took down the spikes and tried to stand in them on the threadbare carpet and when I couldn't, I tried to tear the calfskin with my fingers; I flung the spikes against the wall making jagged tear marks down the wallpaper and began to sob. I thought, if I can just put them on – if I can put them on in here and wear them, I'll go out and run. I knelt down on the carpet again to tie the laces, and my fingers refused. They were not trembling. They were rigid. My fingers refused to lace the shoes. That was as near as I got to going out on to the track. There are names for my condition: Withdrawal Syndrome; Stress Factor; Depression prone; the Immobile Depression prone Athlete . . . *immobile*? I wasn't immobile. I was agitated! And what about the A-Syndrome (A for Anguish)? Anguish in the athlete, I know now, is a kind of phobia. Anguish lies in the conflict between the hope of achieving success and the fear of not realising it. That is why so many athletes, having risen above themselves and broken world records, fall out of the tree and sink into oblivion. They never make the Olympics. That's kinky too. We can't all be Nurmis. We didn't have these fancy names at Oxford then. My Physiology tutor, for example, just told me to lie down. I mean, here was Dr Eccles, my tutor, the coming man on nerves and neuro-transmission, the man who took on the President of the Royal Society, Sir Henry Dale, O.M., in a famous debate at the Physiological Society in Oxford and nearly made mincemeat of him, here was Eccles, a man who had once been an athlete himself, and all he could tell me was go away and lie down. "Lie down and relax," he said. "You shouldn't worry so much." Dr Eccles did say that I was "psychic". Otherwise there was no name at Oxford to describe a contradiction like me who was voluntarily sinking into oblivion. And so it went on through November. Days of fraud. Of malingering. Of hiding in my rooms. Of making excuses to myself. Fraud? It was fraud and double-fraud, for the weird part was that through it all I went on running. Not in spikes but in gym shoes. I went out every night, even at the Knoxes. I sneaked out at night after midnight like a footpad and ran round the Parks till my ears sang. Otherwise the craving would have become unbearable. The stupid part, the weird part, the really terrifying part was that the more I ran, the more inhibited and frightened I became of going on to the track. For it was fear. Straight fear. Subconsciously, I believe, it had begun to dawn on me after I turned back my journal and read the account of that race at Iffley Road. It was as if that performance at Iffley Road had subconsciously got frozen into the brain, had taken possession of the brain, as if it was holding a part of the brain hostage and then, returning in memory or sleep like a delayed-action fuse, had succeeded in immobilising the will to run. I had become, six months after it actually happened, frozen with fear at my own outstanding performance.

In the end I developed a kind of persecution complex.

A letter came, with a German stamp on the envelope. On the back of the envelope was the name Peltzer. I had not forgotten Otto Peltzer. A vision of the German athlete walking off the track at Los Angeles brushing the tears from his eyes had returned several times to trouble me. I read the postmark: Berlin. *Now* I knew, I thought. Something – no, not something, somebody, was trying to prevent me going to Berlin in 1936! I became convinced of this. That somebody was Otto Peltzer. Having thrown in the sponge himself, he wanted me to do the same. That was what was in the letter.

It was Sunday morning, shortly before chapel in college. The letter had come on the previous day. It lay under a pile of shirts on the dresser in my rooms, unopened. I had put on a clean collar. I poked the fire and stood at the window. In the quadrangle below, bare heads and long scarves were drifting towards the chapel. Dacre Balsdon appeared with a hymnal open as he walked. Dr Eccles appeared from his rooms shrugging on his gown, cutting diagonally across the lawn. Idly I wondered if the Physiology tutor would be invigilating the examination – my examination was on Saturday, six days off.

93

The examinations are on Saturday, I thought again, and the relays against Cambridge are *also* on Saturday. I added in the same moment, I'm going to run.

Then I returned to the fire and spoke into it aloud: "I don't care if my career is skidding. I'm going to win a Gold Medal in Berlin."

Part Two

1933–1936

"I'm a lean dog, a keen dog, a wild dog, and alone."
IRENE RUTHERFORD McLEOD
Lone Dog

7

I sat my examinations and I ran in the relays against Cambridge on the same day. The date, 3 December 1932. I ran once more cross-country in that year. The year ended. Suddenly it was the middle of 1933 – July 1933 – and I was on my way to Princeton.

Of course it didn't happen simply like that. But in my telescopic brain, that is exactly how it was. For I had a new timetable now. And I had more than a mere timetable. I had a master aim, a battle plan, a Napoleonic campaign stretching ahead four years to Berlin and 1936, with four staging posts picked out like stars to mariners. Of these staging posts "Princeton 1933" was to be the first.

This so-called "Mile of All Time" at Princeton's Palmer Stadium on Saturday 15 July 1933 was my American début and quite distinct from an invitation race I ran there two years later in 1935 which came to be known as "the Mile of the Century". There was a whole series of blue riband invitation meets at Princeton in the thirties styled Mile-of-the-Century. They were staged by a man called Asa Bushnell. The ballyhoo they generated was enormous. In English athletic circles pundits like Colonel Webster accused Bushnell of stunt-making and poured scorn on his meets, but Asa Bushnell, the young graduate athletics manager at Princeton University, knew what he was doing. Until Asa came along world athletics, especially miling, was centred on Oxford and Cambridge. After Asa, miling was no longer an English prerogative. England after all invented the mile, the noblest of all running distances, and the first authenticated recorded times for the mile in the 1860s were at Fenner's, Cambridge. Asa Bushnell's invitation meets put Princeton on the map. They changed the face of American miling. They changed the whole climate of thinking about the mile, giving it a cachet, and they put the word Golden

– as in the Golden Age of Milers – into the history books. The golden era dates from the middle thirties. Something else these Princeton meets did. They introduced the first serious mention of a concept called a Four-Minute Mile – which until Asa's day had hardly even been dreamed of. That's by the way. Where do I fit in? Asa Bushnell decided to stage his first Mile-of-the-Century at Princeton in 1934, after watching my race against Bill Bonthron in 1933. That's what gave him the idea. I started the ballyhoo, I am ashamed to say. I am responsible.

In 1933 Bonthron was a new star. Two years later in 1935 I faced Cunningham. In between, while I was racing in Europe and Scandinavia, these two very different men – one a language scholar who wrote a thesis on Dante, the other a bruising prairie-cropper who grew up in a covered wagon – were to electrify the American public in a series of duels culminating in a famous 1500-metre race at Milwaukee, Wisconsin, when they went across the tape almost glued together. Glenn Cunningham broke the world record on that occasion, and came in second. "It's a strange feeling," he said, "to break a world's record and still lose." I'm very glad I wasn't facing Bonthron on that day. By then I was having troubles of my own in England with a man called Wooderson.

Wooderson, Bonthron, Cunningham – and of course Beccali, lurking in the north of Italy and refusing save on rare occasions to come out of his lair – were to be my rivals, my bêtes noires on the road to Berlin, four of them. First four, then three, then two. Then the unexpected happened. I'm not going into that now. It isn't easy to face an Olympic prospect, as Tommy Hampson discovered before Los Angeles, with the knowledge of cold failure behind you. But what I was devising now was a simple strategy to overcome my faults. My fault at Los Angeles was this – I had made the mistake of training for just one big race. I forgot to prepare for the heat. I wouldn't make that mistake again.

But it was a necessary mistake – I was beginning to see this now. Without it, there would have been no master plan for Berlin, and no fumbling steps towards rebuilding my self-confidence which had begun that day in November 1932 after I received the letter from Otto Peltzer.

That Sunday, after chapel – after I'd got over my phobia as I thought and spoken so confidently into the fire – I went down to the track. Iffley Road was deserted under a grey sky. I was sweating. I put on my spikes and knelt down beside the track, unwilling to step on to the cinders. I hesitated. The phobia was still there. I offered up a prayer. I actually turned round on my knees and crawled on to the track, like a centipede, before I stood up. I had delayed so long, I half-expected my knees to buckle underneath me. Instead, as my feet touched the cinder crust and I began to run, I experienced a physical shock, half physical, half sexual, like a blade cutting through the flesh. I probably exaggerate, but in that moment I felt that a faith, a wavering faith in myself, had been reborn.

As soon as I returned to my rooms I opened Otto Peltzer's letter.

Berlin, Charlottenburg
24 October 1932

Mr Jack Lovelock
Oxford, England

Dear Mr Lovelock,

My friend. I greet you! I am here at the old Grunewald Stadium in Berlin with some of my pupils from Wickersdorf School to give a demonstration run. I was in Los Angeles this year, as you will know. I came to your cabin one day and was informed you were not well. I could see that, from the Lauf, the way that you ran – you were nerve-full and agitated. You ran in a pit of darkness. I could understand. I remembered from my visit to New Zealand how your dreams were all for Berlin, and that is why I came to you in Los Angeles, to explain about the movement in my country to try and stop the Games here. It is not enough that we have here street battles and political troubles between the Communists and the National Socialists. All the Deutsche Turnerbund, the movement of gymnastic sport, and many faculties of Physical Education in the colleges, are opposed to the English mode of sport that you and I love. They say this sport is un-German, a creeping poison. They demonstrate in public places against the 1936 Games. But do not dismay yourself if you read it in the newspapers. These heretics, the opponents of individual sport, they will not win. The Olympic sport is for all nations, all peoples of the world. The Games *will* take place in Berlin. That is my belief. It is also my belief that you will conquer, if you will do your country and mine the honour to compete.

My dear friend, I do not speak about your race in Los Angeles. You were not prepared. But I observed you on the training tracks, when you did not see me, and I see that you have the gift of few men. You have what we say in German, "hidden feet". You know to steal over the ground. When you watch our German runners of today, they are just running round and round in clogs. You are something shining. You are born to be a prince of runners. I said to you in New Zealand that the true contest for the runner is not on the track but the one that is inside himself. I tell you now something else. In Berlin you will face giants. You will be like a David against Goliaths without the sling. You have the speed. You can do anything what you want with speed. But where is the hidden sling that takes the opponent by surprise? You must first test yourself against the opponents you will meet in Berlin. A very great teacher and friend of mine, Dr Brustmann, once said to me, "You cannot judge a man until you have run in his moccasins." It is a saying from the Eskimo. Prepare well.

Auf Wiedersehen in Berlin.

Otto Peltzer

Peltzer's letter not only helped to restore my self-confidence, it acted on me as a clarion call. I read it with burning cheeks and that Christmas, which I spent alone at a small hotel in Devon, at a place called Chagford on the edge of Dartmoor, I took the letter with me. I knew already that I would have to prepare for Berlin, but so short was the English running season, so amateur the game, so hit-or-miss the whole attitude in England towards Olympic sport, I probably wouldn't get a peek at my rivals until I got there, unless by accident. Peltzer's letter decided me. I would have to go out and meet them as part of a concerted plan.

That was why I was going to Princeton. Officially I was a member of a Cambridge-Oxford universities team taking part in a series of friendly contests against American universities. Privately I was going only to meet Bill Bonthron. He was a first step, a staging post, my one goal for 1933. A strategy was forming in my mind. It was a strategy dictated by the negative certainty that with my constitution I could manage only one big test in a season. Prepare for that, Jack-o, I told myself. One hit, one season. All the rest is experience. It began to evolve in my mind at Chagford, walking over the moors. I told only one man, Bill Thomas, and he learned about it only gradually. Bill was my sole confidant. Harold Abrahams I think half-guessed. I was never sure about Harold, how much he knew, how much I should tell him. After Sydney Wooderson appeared and our duels began, I had the feeling that Harold was backing away from me. Wooderson was an Englishman. I was always the colonial, the invader. Even though I'd been to an OK university. I hadn't been to the right school. Wooderson had been to an OK English school, but not to Oxford or Cambridge. He wasn't quite kosher either. Poor Harold, it was a case of divided loyalties.

Harold was in a difficult position. In those duels Wooderson cleaned me up. The critics were baffled. I learned a lot from these sports writers, I learned that the last thing they want from their runners is intelligence. They want their runners to be quick, reliable, honest – and preferably first. But I always learned more about a man from the back than the front. I infuriated the critics. When I started losing races, many who'd been my friends dropped me altogether. That's when I learned the hard truth that today's rose is tomorrow's compost. Still, a rose always blooms again; a runner's self-esteem is more fragile than that. The only journalist who suspected that, as a doctor, I might be programming myself – and what for – the only one who understood my peculiar chemistry and put two and two together, was Evelyn Montague of the *Manchester Guardian*. Happily he didn't divulge what he knew until afterwards.

When I returned to Oxford from Dartmoor in January 1933 I went to the Bodleian Library and looked up everything I could find on past Olympic champions, going back to Athens 1896, the year of the first modern Olympics. I read up the mile, but I also studied the sprinters and long-distance men. I bought from Blackwell's half a dozen tenpenny exercise books with blue bindings and I began to fill them with notes, notes on diet, training, weather conditions, track surfaces. I even noted the personality traits and physical defects of the contestants. I pasted my rivals' performances into a scrapbook, bringing them up to date. I collected facts about my opponents until my brain was weak. Then I analysed them. I analysed myself too. I analysed everything. It became a routine, a way of living, and that was the pleasure – not the strategy itself but the slow painstaking evolving of it in between races. And the anticipation. Hence my excitement about Bonthron.

By the time I sailed for New York on the *Aquitania*, I felt I knew almost as much about Bill Bonthron as he did himself, although we had never met. I certainly knew something that Bonthron's trainer, Matty Geis, didn't know. Geis didn't even know that his star pupil had flat feet, for God's sakes. Quite a lot of intelligence about American runners was coming into Oxford at this time.

Bonthron incidentally had performed a remarkable double at the American inter-collegiate championships, winning both the 800 and 1500-metre events on the same afternoon. He had done this twice. He had never been beaten in college. His great weapon was a sort of amen charge, a potent finishing burst that was said to be invincible.

I prepared very carefully for Bonthron. In England between May and July I ran no race faster then 4 mins. 12 secs., and most considerably slower than that. I wasn't interested in speed – yet. Most of my energy went into swimming. I had learned to swim. After I had been swimming a month, travelling up and down to London for lessons, it occurred to me I might have hit on a new tool, a possible aid to relaxation – for the one thing I lacked was the ability to master my pre-race nerves. This was the hole in the strategy. I knew I could reach peak physically. I hoped I could perfect my pace judgment. I knew from my researches at the Bodleian that it was possible to assess an opponent in advance so one had a psychological edge on the day. Tactically, in the case of Bonthron, I was prepared.

But none of this helped my mental condition. My researches revealed there was a fourth element essential to any Olympic success. Call it luck, call it a state of mind, this ingredient was always there. It was elusive, illogical, unpredictable and usually invisible, yet it appeared to be a law. Not even Nurmi, who ran like a machine, was immune. In 1920 at Antwerp, for instance, Nurmi's fitness, pace judgment and tactics were impeccable, but mentally he was out of tune. As a result he was beaten in the 5000 metres by a tiny Frenchman, Joseph Guillemot, whose heart was on the wrong side of his chest. Similarly at Stockholm in 1912 when an unlikely Englishman, Strode-Jackson, won the 1500 metres in one of the greatest mass finishes in the history of the Games. Arnold Strode-Jackson hardly trained at all. But he knew how to ignite a spark that enabled him to peak on the day at exactly the right moment. This was the elusive factor, and my problem.

So on the ship sailing to New York I swam every day. I didn't run on deck at all. Evan Hunter, the team manager, was unhappy when he saw how much I was swimming. He didn't say anything. But he must have told Bill Thomas because Bill came to the pool, fuming, and ordered me out.

"I'm not drowning, Bill."

"Maybe not, sir. But I'm not going till you gets out."

"Don't be silly, Bill. I'm experimenting. Swimming helps my rhythm."

"And what about muscle tone? You'll lose your zest!"

"Haven't lost it yet, Bill. Didn't lose it at Antwerp last week, did I? Didn't lose it at the Police Sports last month, did I?"

"Just how long have you been swimming, sir, might I ask?"

"About six months."

"*How* long?"

"Six months. Since Christmas, Bill. I knew you wouldn't approve, so I didn't tell you."

Like all coaches of the day, Bill condemned swimming. It was said to develop the wrong muscles. It was considered the ultimate heresy.

"Talk to you later, Bill." I swam another four lengths and touched the rim. I looked up. Bill was still there.

"Oh come on, Bill. I'm enjoying myself. It's called 'dynamic relaxation'. I promise you, it'll be all right on the day."

"No, sir. It will not be right on the day. It will be all *wrong* on the day. Now, sir. You listen to me. I'm telling you now. Either you gets out from this pool double-quick this minute or you can look round for a new trainer."

"Bill. You're not serious."

This was unexpected. I was coming to rely on Bill. Bill was the Oxford trainer, he was not my personal trainer. But lately he had started coming to all my races, even accompanying me across the Channel at his own expense in order to watch me run. I needed him. I needed him emotionally. "Bill, it's only an experiment." I wheedled him. "Tell you what. If I lose the race against Bonthron, if it doesn't work, I'll chuck the swimming. How's that?"

Silence.

"Are you really serious, Bill?"

He wouldn't look at me.

People were sun-bathing round us on the deck, slipping in and out of the water under a cloudless sky. Bill stood at the edge, portly, erect, buttoned up in his perennial blue suit, looking fixedly across the pool at the funnel of the *Aquitania*. He fingered his moustache and said: "I am, sir."

He looked so lugubrious and pained, so mortally pained, I decided the risk was worth it. I ignored him and went on swimming.

Before the race at Princeton there was an outing at Harvard.

Saturday 8 July 1933   Oxford & Cambridge
                                     v. Harvard & Yale
                                     Harvard Stadium

One-Mile Run:
1. J. E. Lovelock (Oxford)
2. J. Turley, Jr (Yale)
3. F. Horan (Cambridge)
Won by 80 yards. Time: 4 mins. 12 ⅗ secs. (New meet record)

Boston Sunday Globe, 9 July
The fastest competitive mile ever raced within the vine-clad walls of Harvard Stadium was yesterday's choicest morsel when 3000 track lovers saw Jack Lovelock, the streamy-striding New Zealander from Oxford, win against ghostly competition. His time of 4 mins. 12 ⅗ secs. broke by almost two seconds the mark of the immortal John Paul Jones, unshaken for twenty years . . .

Morning Post, Cambridge, Mass. 10 July
The English universities team will leave by boat tonight for New York and go directly to Princeton to prepare for Saturday's meet. A great duel is expected between Lovelock and Princeton's inter-collegiate star, Bonthron . . .

To read the press over the next few days, one would have thought there was only one event on the programme at Princeton. The Oxford-Cambridge versus Princeton-Cornell match was made to seem quite incidental. I was delighted with the fuss and I silently thanked John Paul Jones, the Cornell "immortal" whose record I happened to beat at Harvard. It was Mr Jones who had helped me decide to meet Bonthron. I don't understand American legends and this is not the place to discuss the enduring legend of Mr Jones, but the connection is interesting. Jones was tall, nearly six feet. Most American milers are tall – Norman Taber, John Paul Jones, Fenske and Rideout were all tall men with long strides. So was Venzke. So was Bonthron. The reason I had decided on Bonthron when the first reports from America began coming in was that he was being compared favourably with John Paul Jones. Immediately he seemed to acquire a stature above lifesize and I seized on this fact. John Paul Jones by the way was only twenty when he set his first American record at Cambridge, Mass., in 1911. In 1933 when we met, Bonthron, a language student at Princeton University, was the same age.

8

His skull glistened. It was the first thing I noticed about him. The veins on the scalp stood out in small clumps in the evening light. His head was shaved, the black hair clipped so short it seemed to be painted on like a cap. We met the same evening I reached Princeton, a Wednesday.

I arrived two days late, in some trepidation, not knowing if I still had a trainer. The rest of the team had come on the Monday. I dropped my bags at the Elm Club in Prospect Road and went out to find Bill Thomas. He was in his hotel room, darning a sock. The wireless was on. "Sorry I'm late, Bill. Have I still got a trainer?" Bill grunted something and went on with what he was doing. I knew he would be angry with me. After the row over the swimming I had thought it best to keep out of his way. He had barely spoken to me at Harvard. Now he studiously avoided asking where I had been and I carefully avoided telling him I had been in the sea swimming. I had been at Rhode Island, staying with Janie and her parents. After three days lying up on a beach I was feeling marvellous. "Shall we go down to the stadium?" I said. Bill pulled on his sock, switched off the wireless, found his bowler and we went straight down. All he said when we got there, jerking his head towards a man wearing what appeared to be a skullcap, was, "That's Bonthron."

Bonthron had just finished running. He was standing beside a short chunky man in a fedora who resembled Jimmy "Schnozzle" Durante. I had recognised Bonthron at once – there is a tension great athletes have, that they project, although what Bonthron exuded wasn't so much tension as a naked tigerish aggression. Aggressive was the word commonly used to describe him.

The night was sultry, thunderstorm weather. The track seemed very red, the light harsh. About forty people were there.

106

I pulled off my sweater and began to jog around the bowl. The next minute Bonthron had appeared beside me in his sweat clothes. He introduced himself.

"Mind if I join you, Jack?"

"Not at all. Delighted."

We trotted together. After we had trotted a few yards he said: "We've got three things in common, matey."

"How's that?"

"Exeter, for one. You're an Exeter Oxford and I went to the other one, Phillips Exeter Academy, New Hampshire. Your first showing was at Exeter, matey. Right?"

"Right."

"So was mine. I ran my first big race at Exeter. Two, we both applied for a Rhodes. Only I flunked."

"What's the third thing?"

"Nicknames. Round here I'm called Bonny. At school they called you Bonny too. Right?"

"Actually – " I was laughing to myself. I wasn't the only one who'd been mugging up facts on my rivals. "Actually," I said, remembering how scrawny I had been at school, "it wasn't Bonny. It was Bony.

"Also Whitebait," I added, and imperceptibly speeded up. I was watching his feet. Bonthron's feet were enormous. If they were flat, it didn't seem to make a difference. "Nice track you have," I said, and continued to accelerate. His taped shoes lengthened stride slightly, that was all. His rhythm didn't change. I slowed down and accelerated again, this time abruptly. The same thing happened. His rhythm didn't alter.

We were trotting again. He said: "You always want to run, Jack?"

"Yes."

"I wanted to play football. Track coach Geis pulled me out one day, off the football pitch. Said to me, 'Bonthron, make up your mind. Make up your mind if you're gonna fish or cut bait.' So here I am, a runner. I'm a frustrated football player."

It was an interesting statement, I thought.

We trotted some more. I was just about to say, "Aren't we going a little slowly?" when there was a tearing sound in the air. It was the chunky little man in the hat, shouting at Bonthron to

107

stop. He appeared beside us and almost wrenched Bonthron off the track.

I jogged another lap, put on my sweater and rejoined Bill Thomas. I said, "Crikey. Am I glad I've got you, Bill."

"Are you now, sir?"

"That's Matty Geis? The trainer? That man is a dictator." Bonthron's just a fag, I thought. Geis' fag.

Bill nodded. "Now, sir – " He led me to a bench and took out a stop-watch. Put the stop-watch on the seat beside him. Removed his jacket, folded it on his lap, wiped his moustache, mopped his brow and adjusted the bowler on his head. I knew what was coming.

"Now, sir. Let's get it straight. The race is Saturday. Today is Wednesday. You were due here on Monday."

"I've been staying with friends, Bill. Didn't I tell you?"

"No, sir, you did not. Let's get it right, shall we? I need you. You needs me. I'm your trainer. I'm not a dictator but I've got my little ways, same as anyone. I don't take sugar in my tea and I don't like hanky-panky either. I tell you now, you're going to Berlin. Unless you breaks an arm and a leg, that's where you're going. I'll come too, if you wants me. But I want you punctual. No more hanky-panky. I want to know what you're at, where you are, what you're doing, before you does it. Do you follow, sir?"

"Yes. I'm sorry, Bill. It won't happen again." I added, "I'd like you to come to Berlin. It won't be the same without you."

He was still grumpy. He gave me a long stare, wiped the sweat from under the rim of his bowler and said, "Now I should like you to run me a little lap, nice and steady, sir, if you can manage it. How are you feeling?" "Amazing," I said. "Bit tired from travelling, that's all." "Good. I want 62 seconds, sir. Not 63 seconds and not 61 seconds but 62, dead on. If you can." I said I could. Bill picked up the watch and glanced across the track. "I think we shall just wait, sir, until the two gentlemen have departed. Mr Bonthron and Mr Geis." He put down the watch. "I should like you, sir, to keep off the track when they are here. They don't know you. Let's keep it that way. In fact, after tonight, I should like you to stay off the track altogether and just jog on the grass. I've found a quiet little possy I think you'll like. Nothing fancy but it's away from the press and you can be just by yourself. The gentlemen of the press is a pest, sir, a real pest. Now there is a masseur here by the name of Blake, a Mr Seymour Blake, a black man. Mr Blake has very kindly offered his services. I should take them, sir. I shouldn't swim. The papers, you'll see, are talking of a record for Saturday."

"What sort of record?"

"A world record, sir."

"Bill, let me tell you. I can tell you now." I told Bill something of the plan I was evolving. That I had come to meet Bonthron, not break records; that I wasn't interested in records any longer, only in beating the man. Bill listened. He didn't comment. I couldn't tell if he approved or disapproved.

"That's the ticket, sir. Now then, are you ready for that lap? Sixty-two, mind."

Pace judgment, about which Bill was fanatical, was one of my headaches. But I felt my judgment was improving. I ran a single lap. I aimed at 62 seconds.

"How was that?"

"No good, sir. I wanted a 62, you gave me a 59."

"Oh Lord."

I took a sleeping draught the night before the race. Apart from a cold-water swim stolen behind Bill's back, I had followed his instructions to the letter, working out gently away from the track on grass. I had never prepared so lightly or so comfortably immediately before a race. Bill, as I was to discover again and again, had an unerring instinct for sniffing out places that answered my need for privacy.

I got down to the track at four in the afternoon with Bill and Vicar Horan, my second string. Forbes Horan, known as the Vicar, was a theology student at Cambridge. The mile was the first event, timed to start at 4.30. In the dressing-room I laid out my kit, nodded to someone, found myself smiling. Usually I am sick with apprehension. I notice nothing. I never speak. Either there is horseplay and backchat, which I hate, or a yawning silence which can be terrible. Here there was a quick buzz of anticipation, like being in a Pullman carriage. Bill Thomas hung his hat on a peg. The Vicar lay with his head in a locker.

Somebody opened a newspaper. The rest of the team unpacked and spoke in undertones. Outside when we came on to the track it seemed to be night. A dark sky lowering, no breeze, and a faint acrid smell rising from the cinders. The crust of the track, a mixture of red clay and black Pennsylvania Railroad cinders, had a slight lift. The stadium appeared packed, the spectators piled steeply on open tiers rising from the edge of the cinders so they appeared to be sitting on top of us, yet it was not oppressive. No razz, no hooters, just a murmuring wave of grey and white flannels in shirtsleeves, packed solid. The loudest thing was Evan Hunter's red cricket hat. Bill had arranged for Evan to shout out the lap times. The crucial time was the three-quarter-mile distance. I was aiming, with the Vicar's help, to hit the three-quarters in 3 mins. 6 secs.

"You hit three-six, sir," Bill had said when we discussed it, "and you've got a chance." For the problem with Bonthron was his finish, powerful, sustained and unusually long. He had won all his races this way. I had a very short final sprint. Bill said, "The only way to nip him at the end is to sap him from the start. You wants a hot pace and a fast three-quarters. You must send Mr Horan out." I had agreed to this. The Vicar would lead.

One thing was certain, they wouldn't.

Bonthron was waiting at the start-line with his second string, a man called Hazen. They were to one side. Evan Hunter was walking about parading a blunderbuss which he was using to start the race. Somebody said, "Where's Bingham?" Hazen disappeared. Bonthron was adjusting a sash. He wore a diagonal orange sash and was tugging and twitching it at the neck. "What's the matter with him?" the Vicar said. "He'll throttle himself." I had never seen a man so nervous. Nerves were printed on his face. He's too nervous to shake hands, I thought, but when I went across and held out my hand to shake his, I missed and poked Bonthron in the chest. There was a loud click. We both jumped. It was Evan Hunter testing the blunderbuss. It wasn't loaded. Then Mr Bingham, the director of the meeting, arrived and the race started.

Bonthron flew into the lead. He ran from the outside position into the lead so quickly I thought it must be a mistake. You sweetie, I almost yelled, you absolute sweetie. Then Hazen, Bonthron's team-mate, ran to the front, absolutely haring, and I marvelled at my luck. Bill's last words had been "Mr Horan must lead, sir, they won't." But they were. They did. It was exactly what they were doing. The Vicar had slid in behind, understanding at once, and I lay back last. Oh beautiful, I thought. So beautiful. I was just settling into stride when, coming off the bottom bend, out of the corner of my eye I saw the groundsman. A man in overalls with a rake slung on his shoulder was walking diagonally across the field towards the track heading for Hazen and a small iron gate. He's sleepwalking, I thought. He'll see Hazen and he'll stop. Hazen the leader yelled out at him. But the man kept coming. When he had walked on to the track directly in front of Hazen he looked up, and Hazen hit him. The rake flew in the air. Bonthron hit Hazen, the Vicar glanced off Bonthron. I went round the outside. It was the weirdest thing. Afterwards nobody mentioned the incident and none of the papers reported it. We were all thrown off stride. Hazen still led. At one stage he gave the lead to Bonthron who immediately gave it back again. It must have seemed to the spectators that they were toying with us. I missed the first two lap times. In the third lap the Vicar led, then dropped away. The pace felt so warm that as we came down for the bell, towards Evan Hunter's red hat, I was guessing a time of three-six, what we had planned.

The bell sounded.

"Three-eight-a-half," Evan barked, over the bell.

Almost three seconds behind. I had misguessed.

Leaving the bell for the last lap Bonthron was five yards clear. I moved up on the bend and waited. The others had faded. One of Bonthron's shoe tapes had come loose. There is always a breaking-point in a race. Some people say it is when a man's shoulders tighten. Bonthron's shoulders, his upper body, were erect and flowing. Suddenly his neck jilted sideways and the veins in his neck expanded. With no more warning than that, and half the back straight before him, he surged. Hell. I shortened stride and tried to hang on. He was good. Too good, I thought. He's going away. Down the back straight he was going away from me. I remembered something Tommy Hampson had said – "When all else fails, lean. Lean over the tips." I leaned like the devil. I leaned out over the tips of my shoes until I felt I was choking. Gradually the gap between us lessened. On the last bend we were almost level. Only a stride separated us. That effort, Bonny, I thought, must have killed you. He had eased slightly on the bend. I gathered myself and moved to his shoulder, watching his neck. If you're that good, you'll go again, I thought. I half-expected him to force me wide. Only a gentleman won't force you wide on a corner. Bonthron was a gentleman. He didn't go wide. We had locked strides, oh boy. I didn't wait for his neck to roll over a second time. According to the *New York Times*, it was this moment I anticipated and "let fly". Never! It was the Palmer Stadium that let fly. The bowl of the stadium stood on its head howling. I couldn't see the tape. There was a tiny pink dot swimming in front of my eyes. The dot grew from a pinhead to a tomato to a raving red sunburst. The sun passed in a blur. It was Evan Hunter's red cricket hat. I had won.

There is a postscript to this race. In fact there are two. The first one shows what athletes are made of, how little people know about us. After the race I got all the praise, naturally. "Afterwards," the *New York Times* wrote, "Lovelock continued running. He jogged a full lap, unperturbed." Unperturbed? Over the last thirty yards my knees felt as though they were bending backwards. After the race I could barely walk. And what did Bonthron do? I wrote in my diary, "Athletes are like lovers. There are those who can do it all of the time and those only some of the time. I'm one of the latter. I'm not a Bonthron." An hour later, after the mile when I was still drained and trembling, Bonthron turned out again and won the half-mile against Oxford for Princeton. I couldn't have done that. Bonny's stamina was amazing but hardly anyone gave him credit for that. I loved that man and at a celebration team dinner afterwards, when Bonthron told me his feet *were* flat, we became good friends. Much later, after Berlin, I learned that he had been rejected for war service by the American Navy. The naval doctors looked at his feet and declared Bonthron "incapable of sustained physical exertion". They told him to go home and practise picking up marbles with his toes. It just shows you.

But Bill Bonthron was a gentleman. During that celebration dinner at Princeton on 15 July 1933 he did a wonderful thing – he stood up and presented me with a trophy. It was a blank shell-case from Evan Hunter's blunderbuss, the one that started the race. I've still got it.

It was this race that led the newspapers first to air and then to speculate about the limits of human endeavour. "The question on everyone's lips now is," said the *New York Times*, "will there be a Four-Minute Mile?" I admit that I ran a clever last lap (my last lap was timed at under 59 secs.). That I broke the world record. But so did Bonthron, four yards behind me. Bonthron broke Jules Ladoumègue's world mile record of 4 mins. 09.2 secs. by almost a second. I broke it by nearly two seconds. My time of 4 mins. 07.6 secs. was nearly three seconds faster than anything recorded by Nurmi, well ahead of Ladoumègue's disputed mark and also better than Cunningham's best. I forgot to say that Cunningham just before this, in June, had set an American record of 4 mins. 09.8 secs. But this was no excuse for the American newspapers to behave as they did. They lost all reason. I find in my scrapbook an unidentified American newspaper cutting which says, "Until his dramatic début, Lovelock, this beautiful British boy, was rated only a fair miler." The paper missed the point. It was not the miler who was rated only fair, but the mile. I have said this before and I shall now repeat it. Before Princeton, the mile was just another event. After Princeton, it became an all-consuming international topic, a household word. What happened? The American papers developed a fever. That's what happened. The papers developed a fever to promote records. They became dead nuts on records. They were besotted. First the newspapers were besotted, then the public, then the runners. We were all infected by this virus of chasing records. I wasn't, of course. Not I, Lovelock. I was immune. Promoters got the idea of putting de luxe "hares" out in front, on handicap, so the man on scratch would have to kill himself. For what? For the glory of defeating a clock? Cuckoo-clock racing, I called it. I could foresee a day that spelled an end to amateur sport, an end to the fun. This wasn't sport.

From America the bug spread to Canada, then to Scandinavia and Italy, even France. About this time in August, after I

113

returned to Oxford, I received an invitation from the French Amateur Athletic Federation to run in Paris against a stacked field in a specially staged attempt on Ladoumègue's outstanding world record for the 1500 metres.

"What do you think, Bill?" I discussed it with Bill Thomas at Iffley Road.

"Well, sir. It's a bit peculiar. Why should the Frogs want to help you beat their own man?"

"You're quite right. It's a silly stunt. I'd quite have liked to meet Ladoumègue, that's all."

That was an understatement. I was bursting to meet the banned Frenchman whom Charles Paddock had called the greatest 1500-metre man of all time, the gnome-in-the-wings I had heard so much about. The feats of Jules Ladoumègue had taken on an almost mythical quality in my mind.

"And what will it prove, sir? In Princeton you proved something to yourself. You shot your man, you got your priorities straight. In Paris – tell me, sir. Will Mr Ladoumègue be running?"

"You know he's not allowed to run, Bill. He's banned for life."

"Exactly, sir. You'd just be running against the clock. Against your own principles."

"You're absolutely right, Bill. It would be madness to go."

"There's your answer, sir."

So what did I do? I went to Paris.

"Monsieur Lovelock?"

"Yes. Oui."

"Monsieur Jacques Lovelock?"

"Oui."

"Ladoumègue, Jules."

"Lovelock, Jack."

"Enchanté."

"Do you speak English?"

"A little. You are libre, Monsieur Jacques?"

"Free? Oui."

"You have hunger?"

"Oui."

"Bon. Nous allons dîner ensemble."

It was a Sunday in September, the 17th. Paris in September, the chestnut trees beginning to turn, falling leaves, and crowds of Parisians eating out in the warm evenings in the restaurants of the Bois – although all I had seen since I arrived was the inside of stadiums, the Stade Rolande and the Stade Colombes where I had been training and, that Sunday afternoon, racing in a vain attempt to lower Ladoumègue's 1500-metre record. Now unexpectedly he had sought me out at a small hotel near the Odéon where I was staying.

He wore a beret and a smart leather jacket. He was more elegant than I had imagined and quite dark. He was twenty-six. He was I think a kind of orphan, like me. Outside the hotel he hailed a taxi and we crossed the Seine. The street lights were just coming on.

"A Calvados? A pastis, some white wine or red?"

In the restaurant everyone knew him. We were in the Montmartre district. He drank Calvados and ordered wine. He said:

"We cannot race together, Jacques."

"Oui. I know."

"We are together eating but we cannot be together running. Voilà. It is sad."

"I am sad too."

"I am disqualifié, Jacques."

"I know."

"I am disqualifié pour la vie."

"For life? Yes. I know."

"I am sad."

"We are both sad."

"My heart is very sad."

This is terrible, I thought. I had formed a picture in my mind of a small southern Frenchman, a little leaf-hopper man, a man of magic. Here he was, Jules Ladoumègue from Bastide near Bordeaux, the first man to put the Finns into eclipse, the man who had erected such a wall of records, the pivot around whom we had all been whirling, the man who had brought fame to France, and he made even the wine taste sad.

A photographer appeared at the table and took our photograph. Jules smiled, but on one side of the face only, not the other. His dark lustrous eyes grew more mournful as the meal progressed. Every few minutes he glanced towards the door. After the meal he ordered brandy.

"Jacques, I am disqualifié for receiving money."

"Yes."

"Do you know how much money I am paid?"

"No."

"I tell you. Salut."

"Salut."

"Mille cinq cents francs – 1500 francs."

"You were paid a franc a metre?"

"Un franc le mètre, voilà. Oui."

"Perhaps your mistake, Jules, was to become a middle-distance runner."

"Quoi?"

"You should have been a sprinter."

"Ah. Mais oui!" He laughed. For the first time he brightened. Then someone came in off the street and handed him a message and he grew melancholy again.

"Garçon."

A bottle of cognac appeared with two glasses. Steadily without lifting his eyes, except occasionally to fill my glass, he began to drink his way through the bottle. At length he said:

"You know Milan? The Arena?"

"No."

"It is where Napoleon parades son Armée. His Army. Vive la France." Then he showed me the message. It said:

"*Beccali. Milan Arena. 5 p.m. 3 – 49 – zéro.*"

The message meant that Ladoumègue's most precious world record had fallen. Beccali had finally done it.

"Jules, I'm sorry. Truly sorry." What else could I say?

A young woman approached our table. She bent over Jules, ruffled his hair and kissed him gently on the mouth. The patron appeared. Embraced him. I don't know how the news spread so fast. People were coming in from the street up to our table, offering condolences. Jules tried to smile. He was weeping openly, the tears sliding down his cheeks. I wondered if it had been like this on 15 July when the news had come from Princeton that I had robbed him of the mile. It was an education for me. I began to understand why the crowd had behaved as they did towards me that afternoon at the Stade Colombes. As soon as I appeared they began to shout, "Ladoumègue, Ladoumègue". Have you ever run against an invisible man? Against an opponent who is banned and has not the right to defend his own property? Ladoumègue wasn't there, he was seated in the stand. I was on the track. Yet he, I swear, ran the race – "Ladoumègue! Ladoumègue!" The spectators cheered him from the start. They cheered him every step of the way. It was an invisible man they were cheering. After the race when it was announced that I had failed by a big margin to lower his record, they cheered all the louder. That's mana for you. That's glory, if you like. Three of his five world records had now gone, the three-quarter-mile, the mile and the 1500 metres, and of these the most jealously guarded was the one that had first brought fame to France, the 1500. It was this mark of 3:49.2 that had survived attempt after attempt, including mine that afternoon. The week before, in Turin, it had survived an attempt by Beccali – Beccali had equalled but not beaten it. Now here we were, Jules and I, and here was the news that Beccali running on his home track in Milan at the very moment when I was running in Paris had made a fresh attempt and, by a fraction of a second, had succeeded.

I was suddenly moved to take off my Silver Fern, a tiny New Zealand mascot I wore inside my lapel, and pin it on Jules' chest. I did so. He stood up, smiling through the tears, and took my arm. "Allons-y." He threw some money on the table and we went out. At the first bar, he went in. We drank brandy. At the next, the same. It is not far from the rue Montmartre to the Place de la République, but there is a bar or a boîte on every street corner. We entered most of them. At some point after midnight I said to Jules, "Jules, I have a train to catch." "It is late, Jacques?" "No, early. Le train. Early." He said, "Bon. We hurry." He seemed to understand. Then we were in a cab together crossing Paris. "Where are we going?" I said. Jules had put his arm round me. We began to sing. We were very drunk. "Dépêche-toi!" he shouted. He kept telling the driver to hurry. The cab went in a circle with the traffic and stopped. "Plus loin, plus loin!" The cab rolled forward and stopped beneath an arch. I got out and saw it was the Arc de Triomphe.

117

Jules got out, paid the driver and began to undress, motioning me to do the same.

"You can see it, Jacques? Tu vois? L'obélisque?"

I could see an illuminated canyon stretching before me into the night. With street lamps and trees on both sides and vehicles moving in a double line. It took me a moment to understand. By then Jules had taken off his shirt and jacket, dropped his trousers and was moving off down the Elysées in his suspenders at a steady, or rather an unsteady trot. As he ran, he swayed. I stripped to my underpants and shoes and wobbled along beside him.

"Obelisk?" I said.

"Oui." He leaned against me and pointed. "L'obélisque. Place de la Concorde. It is at two hundred – non. Pardon. Two *thousand* and one hundred metres. Tout droit. Ça va?"

"Straight ahead?"

"Oui. One mile and one quarter. Ça va?"

I could see a needle. Beyond the Rond Point at the end of the Champs Elysées a tiny needle glimmered white in the distance. I could see it double. I nodded. We wobbled towards it, leaning against each other for support. I shut my eyes and thought, He wants a race. He's mad. What a lovely idea, straight down the Champs Elysées. No bends. Have you ever run down the Champs Elysées at night with your eyes shut? You have the feeling you have strayed into an extra hour not numbered among the twenty-four. The air is soft and reviving and full of silences without dimensions and all the time you are rolling over. It is like rolling off a mountain made of glass. A kind of ecstasy. Suddenly with a belch and a "Hop-là", Jules pinched my arm and we were off. We ran straight down the middle of the carriageway towards the Rond Point. Crossing the Point, I began to revive. A gendarme appeared. I had the impression that the policeman saluted us and that the traffic spinning round the intersection had ground to a halt. Jules missed a moving obstacle, rolled his eyes and sped on, looking neither left nor right. The Obelisk was in front. As we sped towards it, brakes sounded behind us. I heard the tinkle of falling glass. A taxi had appeared at Jules' elbow, cruising alongside. The driver leaned out. "Hé, Julot. Tu fais le sprint, quoi?" Jules nodded and hitched his underpants. Evidently the driver knew him. "Et va!" he shouted, and sounded his klaxon. Jules leered at me, glassy-eyed. His head went down and his tongue came out. I drew abreast. The driver kept us company, shouting encouragement at the top of his voice. Traffic banked up behind him. Horns blared. We ran the last four hundred metres full tilt at the head of a cavalcade of frenzied exhortations and blaring klaxons.

"Ça va, Jacques?"

"Oui."

I came to and sat up.

"Tu es content, Jacques?"

"Très content, Jules."

"Six minutes," he said.

Jules sat hugging his knees, smiling blissfully. I lolled against him. Tears of sweat ran down our faces. There was a fountain playing. We sat side by side, our bodies touching, saying nothing. I looked up at the Etoile where we had started. It had been, as someone said of Waterloo, a nice run thing. We had completed the course. We had killed nobody, caused only one traffic accident and collapsed on the steps of the Obelisk in the Place de la Concorde in a dead-heat. Jules was trying to read his watch. Just before I passed out again on his shoulder he said:

"Six minutes, Jacques. Un record."

He was weeping again. It was a warm night. There was a fountain playing. I forget the rest.

9

I should prefer to forget also, if I could, the whole of the following year, 1934. But since I am a creature of habit, quiet, neat, particular and, in the words of one of my admirers, insatiably curious about myself to the point of silliness, I can't skip it altogether. I'm curious about a dream I had. What's puzzling about it is that it came during a good year – I mean, 1933 had been a good year, but 1934 in many ways was better.

I sometimes wonder if Cunningham had dreams too. Cunningham also had a good season in 1933 – he ran thirty races in Europe without defeat. In 1934, better still. Bonthron too. Then there was Beccali. In 1934 we were all, so we thought, destined to be reunited in Berlin – I even wrote to Bonthron about it, making a joke of it and saying, "It's going to be a jolly little party." What none of us knew, and couldn't know, was that an unknown English schoolboy who spent his Sundays walking over the Kent countryside with an older brother was also planning to be at that party. In 1933 he was eighteen years of age. He was the sort of boy, actually a Londoner, for whom Billy Butlin invented the holiday camp. You wanted to take him home and feed him. He was only five foot six. His name was Sydney Wooderson. I found out later that he had been studying me from a distance, much as I had been spying from afar on Cunningham. Wooderson's father worked at Covent Garden in the markets. Had we both been living in New Zealand where there are no class barriers Wooderson and I would have trained together. In England this was impossible and I think he came to regard me and my Oxford-Achilles Club lot as toffee-nosed. He was probably right. I was becoming a snob. We never met socially. I beat Wooderson twice in that season and erased him from my mind. Blotted him out.

Did I? The psychiatrist says not. I think the psychiatrist is one reason I should prefer to skip this episode. He says that Sydney Wooderson was part of my trouble. The psychiatrist does not appear in my diary at all. Nor, for that matter, does the dream.

Briefly, for the record:

In 1934 I ran twenty-two races in England, Europe and Scandinavia. I ran against the Norwegian champion Lie, the Hungarian Szabo, the Swede Ny, all the top European runners – I kept to my plan. Only Beccali of the Europeans eluded me and, of the Americans, Cunningham. I was finessing. I wanted unfamiliar conditions and climates. I wanted to see, on the method of that strange German, Peltzer, if my body could run at changing speeds and then answer a summons. I wanted to see if Peltzer was right. Probably I overdid it. Halfway through the European tour I wrenched my Achilles tendon in Paris, quite badly. It was either in Paris running against Bonthron or in Amsterdam the week before. I didn't realise I'd done it till some time afterwards. In Paris Bonthron completely out-generalled me. Time to stop, I thought. I'm overdoing it. But I was travelling with an Achilles team and I couldn't drop out. In Strasbourg on 26 August I remember squeezing past dead and dying men, a horrible race, a sort of dog-fight, saying to myself, "This is nonsense. I'm too tired. I can't go on." But I hate funking – I hate funking as I hate cheating and bad manners and runners who swear at you on the corners and call you a shit or a *putano* or worse because you're getting the best ride and they can't get through. All the same I would have funked it and dropped out that day if someone hadn't spiked me. The sight of blood, even the thought of blood, makes me run better. But then three weeks later in Norway, when I was ready to be carried home on a stretcher, came a race when I caught fire.

It was at a place called Tönsberg, south of Oslo. A cold night, almost arctic, under floodlamps. At the end of three laps I was so fatigued I was beginning to hallucinate. Perhaps I was bored. I made a mistake and did a clown's act – I began to sprint long before I had intended to. I was just showing off. It was 300 yards from the tape. For some reason the crowd gasped. It was a peculiar thing, that gasp, it seemed to galvanise me like the flick of a whip and I ran the rest of the race in a tearing passion, almost in exaltation, to wild applause. But afterwards I couldn't remember what I had done, what it was that had produced that gasp that roused me. It was maddening not to remember. I had the feeling, if only I could remember what it was, that I had done something important. I was still thinking about this when the tour ended and I returned to London.

The tour ended on 23 September. I returned to digs in Bayswater (I had come down from Oxford in July) and in October entered the medical school at St Mary's Hospital, Paddington. My life changed dramatically.

In 1934 Mary's was probably the most dismal hospital in London. The corridors were of stone and the interior windows and skylights, obscured by grime from years of coal fires, were only slightly cleaner than the exterior façade, a tall flat-chested pile of red brick which reminded me more of a penitentiary than a healing institution. But this was no cause for alarm. Mary's was the teaching hospital of my choice. It had a brand new medical school alongside, a swimming pool in the basement and a staff that included Alexander Fleming, the discoverer of penicillin, who lectured us in bacteriology. Fleming, who was not yet famous, had made his discovery six years earlier in a corner room on the second floor just along the corridor from where I would be. The hospital was run by Dr Charles Wilson who was later to become almost equally famous – as Lord Moran, Churchill's doctor. Even then in 1934 Charles Wilson was much lionised and much criticised – his critics accused him of "making a rather mediocre medical school into a first-class rugby team", but this was sheer jealousy on the part of rival London hospitals. It was also fair comment, for in the twenties Charles Wilson had stolen a march on the other hospitals in London by going round the public schools and Oxford colleges and recruiting captains of cricket and rugby. He offered them scholarships in lieu of fees. Until Wilson came, Mary's had seldom won the Inter-Hospitals Rugby Cup. After Wilson, we never lost it. What Charles Wilson wanted, on the Cecil Rhodes model, was brilliant all-rounders. Mary's when I arrived was stacked with ex-Rhodes Scholars from the Dominions and sports fanatics like myself – in this sense my move was painless, like shifting from one prefects' common room to another, with the additional attraction of nurses on the side for play. What could be nicer? The psychiatrist agreed with me. The psychiatrist was also, I discovered, a sports fan. It was here at Mary's that I saw him.

He had a very thick neck. In 1934 I could have gone to see him at Uxbridge where he had a private clinic, but I preferred to see him at Mary's. It was safer. According to my Oxford records – there is a chit at Exeter in Dacre Balsdon's handwriting which reads, "J.E.L. – Dec. '33, Treatment in London for Sleeplessness" – I saw Dr O'Grady the psychiatrist nearly twelve months earlier at the end of 1933. I don't understand this, any more than I understand my dream. I saw Dr O'Grady in the autumn of '34 when I returned from my European tour. O'Grady was not his real name. It was just that he had appeared in a novel by André Maurois as the clever "Dr O'Grady" – so somebody told me – and I always called him that. The novel made him sound terribly clever and I put off going to see him for days. I was terrified he would ask about my mother or about my genes. I don't like these people who want you to bare the soul. It turned out he was old-fashioned and sane. For a psychiatrist he was very sane. I didn't read the book. In real life his name was Dr James.

"How long have you been having this dream?"

"It's been going on for nearly a year."

"With what result?"

"I wake up feeling violently ill, or with headaches. Then I vomit."

"Always?"

"Yes."

"Then what happens?"

"I can't study or do my hospital work. My head won't lie down. It ruins the day."

"Are your eyes inflamed when you wake?"

"No."

"The dream, I take it, is periodic."

"Yes. It comes and goes."

"Do you vomit at other times?"

"Only after races." I was vomiting now after almost every race. Aubrey Reeve, a young runner who had come out in England that year, told me that he was always sick *before* races – I used to see him at White City, ashen and unapproachable, crooped over the basin in the tunnel leading from the dressing-room out to the track. But I always vomited afterwards.

"After a race. Not before?"

"No, always afterwards. But that's usually a relief, a great relief. This other business is different. It leaves me feeling, I don't know – out of sorts."

"Out of sorts?"

"Well, dejected."

123

"Dejected? Or depressed?"

"I'm not sure." I answered as honestly as I could.

"I seem to remember you were coming to see me about a year ago."

"I couldn't come."

"I had a note from one of your tutors at Oxford. It was about insomnia. You were not sleeping, he said. He said you were run down."

"Yes. I'd been in hospital, having a cartilage removed."

"I remember. The papers were saying that you might never run again. It must have been a worry to you."

"Not really. I mean, the papers exaggerated. They wrote a lot of scare stuff. The knee came up with fluid after a relay match. It was just a cartilage. But I didn't come to see you about the other business because I decided I could live with it. I could manage it."

"The insomnia – do you mean? Or the dream?"

I still don't know how it started. It was a happy dream. It was a quite straightforward dream about a man going blind. It ended happily after an operation with the man's sight restored. There was nothing strange about it. The only odd thing was that I associated it in my mind with an undergraduate at Exeter whom I barely knew, Paul Petrocokino. Paul was a member of the Oxford Group – he was a follower of the American evangelist and do-gooder, Dr Frank Buchman – but until Paul was converted to Buchmanism and began hanging round the lodge at Exeter trying to bale up new recruits I had always assumed the movement was just another Oxford faith. Buchman said he wanted to reform evil and change the world and Paul the Buchmanite, who wore a leopard-skin waistcoat, became the butt of college humour. Question: What's the loudest thing in Oxford after Great Tom? Answer: Paul Petrocokino's waistcoat. I used to turn on him my most ravishing smile and flee. I had no particular religious conviction or guiding philosophy. Paul was a beautiful youth. He wore plus-fours, jade-green ties and was interested in cloud photography – I used to come upon his soulful aesthetic figure gazing through a lens from lonely riverbanks when I was out running. He was also a gifted musician and composer.

Buchman had a reputation for enrolling the better-heeled undergraduates and Paul Petrocokino, lonely, insecure and rich, was a natural target. When Buchmanism hit him, Paul took literally the exhortation to give away his surplus goods and handed out expensive cameras and his entire record collection of Handel. Some people did well out of it. I had no use for the gifts and refused them because I thought Paul was being silly. Yet I felt sorry for him and in a way that I can't explain half-envied him his certainty: his dedication to Buchman's idea of remaking the world.

What has this to do with my dream? Only this. After I returned from Princeton in '33, after breaking the world record, I found myself a celebrity. I too became a target. That summer Buchman was holding one of his annual "house parties" in Oxford. There were five thousand Buchmanites living in the colleges, his disciples were everywhere scalp-hunting and those who were sent to lay siege to me were without exception female, feminine and ravishingly pretty. They camped on my stair. I couldn't go down for a pee without being waylaid by one of them. I actually went to one of the meetings – not because, as my companion thought, I was ripe for persuasion and was in line for "a direct guidance from God", but because I was hoping to get her into bed with me afterwards. Paul was there. He – or she, I forget which – stressed to me the value of a "quiet time" in the morning – "Half an hour's listening to God each morning, Jack, is a basic minimum." I said, "But I am very busy." "In that case," she said, "a full hour is necessary." Paul was listening. They were not stupid, these people. Nor was the preacher. During the meeting when members of the audience were invited to make a public confession of guilt, some sin or wrongdoing they had committed, a man got up and said, "I once led an innocent girl astray." Whereupon another man stood up and said, "I once led two innocent girls astray." Then the preacher said, "Will anyone offer me *three* innocent girls?" I think Montagu Scott, another sceptic, might have been with me also that night. We were both laughing our jock-straps off. My female companion said, "I think you are both evil." Then she said an extraordinary thing. She said, "We in the movement thank God for the existence of a man like Hitler." "What rot," Montagu Scott murmured. "It isn't rot," Paul said. "It isn't rot at all if you're planning to change the world. We're going to do big things." "So am I," I heard myself saying. "You need a master aim for that, Jack." "Yes," I said. "And I already have one." Paul was looking at me in a pitying but not unkind way. Paul had changed. He was less flamboyant. He seemed more restrained, quieter and more sure of himself. He said, "I didn't mean running. Life isn't worth living, Jack, unless you have a master aim."

That was all. Berlin – the Olympics – Hitler – God – master aim, it was an odd association of ideas. But for some reason what Paul said to me stuck. Until then I had barely heard of Hitler. I thought it odd that Paul should use the same term "master aim" that I had conceived for my strategy for Berlin. I kept clear of Buchman's lot after that.

Shortly afterwards I entered hospital to have a cartilage removed from the left knee. I was in bed for two weeks. Janie came. She brought me aconites. Nesta Knox came, with the papers. Dacre Balsdon came. They were excessively cheerful. The more cheerful they were, the more despondent I became. I couldn't sleep. The knee kept me awake and I began to fear that the operation had been botched, and that what the papers were saying – that I would never run again – might be true. There was talk about Hitler and Germany in the papers. Captain Knox referred to it. Every day I read the sports pages. Then one day I noticed an article about Frank Buchman. The article quoted him as saying, "Thank God for the existence of Hitler", the same words the young woman had used at the meeting. I remembered what Paul Petrocokino had said to me that night. I found myself brooding on it. In January 1934 I went to Attlington in Dorset to spend a few days with Dacre Balsdon. It was there, convalescing after the operation, that the dream started.

"I don't see the connection, young man," the psychiatrist said.
"Neither do I."
"In the dream, you say, a young man who is born blind undergoes an operation. He is fearful of the result, terrified it won't work. He wakes from the operation and for the first time he can see – for the first time he sees a bird flying. He can see the afternoon sunlight through the window, the trees and the grass

outside. Presently shadows begin to form in front of his eyes. The darkness spreads around and the light fades. Oh well, he thinks, that's all the sight I'm getting. 'It hasn't worked,' he says to the surgeon. 'But it has worked,' the surgeon tells him with a laugh. 'It's only the twilight. It happens every day.' He is in fact cured."

"There's a bit more to it than that."

"But he is cured. It's a positive result. If I could wake up from a dream like that, I'd feel reborn. Yet you feel ill, you say."

"It's so frustrating!"

"What a complicated lot you runners are. You know, as we sit here I'm reminded of something, of a story. That dream is familiar. Are you sure it isn't a story that you've read somewhere?"

"Well, possibly. I was wondering. The Rector at my school in New Zealand used to read us stories on Sunday night after chapel. He would stand in the library at one end with his back to the fire, hogging it, and we'd be sitting in a group on hard chairs, all the boarders, listening to him read from the Bible and *John O'London's Weekly*. Spellbound, actually. Actually glued to what he was saying. He'd talk, you see."

"What did he talk about?"

"Oh, everything. Life – the usual stuff, life's purpose. Life's goal. And about what was in the stories he'd read to us. He used to talk about the School-beyond-the-gate. It was a favourite phrase of his, the School-beyond-the-gate. Dear old Bill. Bill Thomas. His name was Bill Thomas, same as my trainer. Another Bill Thomas."

"You seem to remember him with affection."

"Like anything, golly. He encouraged us. He had a sort of sixth sense for knowing what you could make of yourself. After my father died, when I'd be alone in the school, he used to take me home with him to a little place in the mountains. He was like a father to me. Some of them called him One-Testicle Bill because he didn't have children of his own, but he was an inspiration, he could make you achieve things that didn't seem possible. It's because of him I'm in England really."

"Yes?"

127

"He pushed me. I would never have applied for a Rhodes if it hadn't been for old Bill. He pushed me. I've remembered! I've got it – you're right. It was a story out of *John O'London's Weekly*."

"There you are. A man who influenced you at a critical period in your life read you a story. Ten years later it's come back to you as a dream. Clean as a whistle. Now that you've remembered, it will probably stop. Yes? Something is still bothering you. Is the light bothering you? Yes, draw the curtains if you want, not that it will make much difference. Pull them right across if it bothers you."

"It's just – well. Is there such a thing as a dream-within-a-dream? Lately the dream is interrupted, it stops halfway through. It won't end properly."

"You mean you wake up too soon?"

"No. Yes. I don't know. Lately I've begun to dream it in the daytime as well and it always cuts off. It cuts off after the operation, with the twilight closing in."

"Formulation without execution, eh. As a matter of interest, how long *do* you sleep at night?"

"Two, three hours. That was at Oxford," I said. "I don't think the dream has anything to do with my running."

"Why do you say that? Oh, I see, you mean because you've had a good season. You certainly seem to be on a winning streak."

"I've had a particularly good season, not only that. I've stopped running. I ran my last race in Norway more than a month ago."

"The running has stopped but the dream hasn't? I see. You've had a lot on your plate this year, haven't you? Knee operation, Empire Games, your final examinations, more races, the shift to Mary's – it's a difficult adjustment. Finals go all right?"

"Not really. I got a Third. I'd hoped for a Second."

"Bad luck. Does it worry you?"

"It doesn't please me."

"You know, I see a lot of young people from Oxford and Cambridge. I give them comfort, hope, reassurance, but I don't think you want that. I'm not sure that I know what it is you do want, apart from achieving your immediate goal of a Gold Medal in Berlin. Something wrong? You seem startled."

"Is it so obvious?"

"It isn't obvious to the general public, I dare say, but I notice whenever the subject is mentioned in the press the other English runners, Jerry Cornes, Reeve, young Wooderson, talk about Berlin quite openly, whereas you appear to skirt the subject. You play it down. Tactically it's a good ploy, but I suspect that Berlin is the only thing you really care about. Which is why a dream that you can't pin down might bother you. I'm interested you should say it has nothing to do with your running. I would have said that it has. Perhaps I'm wrong. I was thinking of Wooderson. You say that you've had a 'good' season – but also I suspect a very difficult season. Do you want me to look at the leg? You keep rubbing the left shin."

"It's nothing. Just a muscle twinge."

"I thought it might be the tendon troubling you."

"No. Just a muscle twinge. Well, it was a hard season. I lost races of course, minor races, but nothing to upset me. Wooderson didn't upset me. I lost to Bonthron in Paris. Wooderson nipped me once at Guildford. I'd forgotten about Guildford, quite forgotten."

"That was Wooderson's first race, wasn't it?"

"He's very young. I've beaten him twice since Guildford."

"Interesting how we forget and remember things. I'm surprised you should have forgotten that race. It is engraved on my mind partly because I lost a fiver on you. But I'm also curious about it. Speaking now as a spectator. I see I'll have to tell you, that I'm a devoted Lovelock fan. Charles Wilson is another, the Chief is quite dotty about your running, especially since you've joined Mary's – you're a Mary's man now. We rather pride ourselves on our sportsmen. Anyway I happened to be at Guildford that day when Wooderson made his début. Funny customer, I thought, with his little jellybag muscles going up and down. Nobody had heard of him before. Wooderson came in second, didn't he? Reeve won. Was it Reeve? But I was puzzled afterwards and so were the critics. They said you had thrown the race away."

"Not exactly. Hardly."

"Martyrdom has scant appeal, eh. Oh well, just a thought. A spectator's idle curiosity. Now it is my turn to remember something."

"What's that?"

"Doesn't Sydney Wooderson wear glasses?"

It isn't surprising I had forgotten the race at Guildford in which Wooderson made his début. My diary records:

Guildford, 30 June 1934
Southern Counties Championship
1 mile

Result: 1. A. Reeve
2. S. Wooderson
3. J.E. Lovelock
Time: 4 mins. 14.8 secs.

And that's about all it says. The entry for 30 June is sandwiched in between and swamped by more important events, chiefly by news from America. In Princeton Asa Bushnell was promoting his first invitation Mile-of-the-Century. Two things happened in quick succession. First Cunningham, running at Princeton, broke my 1933 world record for the mile by almost a full second. A few days later at the beginning of July came the news that Bonthron, in Milwaukee, had unexpectedly trounced Cunningham and at the same time lowered Beccali's world mark for the 1500 metres of September 1933, the one that had upset Ladoumègue in Paris.

My diary of 16 July 1934: "The names Cunningham and Bonthron are on everyone's lips. Electrifying news – but wretched. Bonthron's time of 3:48.8 for the 1500 coming on top of Cunningham's mile in 4:06.8 makes our English performances read like a freight schedule for a slow train on the Midlands loop line. Compare for example my winning time in the British AAA Mile against Wooderson and Jerry Cornes two days ago – 4:26.6! Slowest time for a British championship in twelve years. I've never known Harold Abrahams so taunting, so spitting angry with me after a race. I'm not surprised the critics jeered after this. Cunningham's 4:06.8 puts him thirty

130

yards clear of Nurmi in a mile at Nurmi's *best*. Who would have thought it? Harold thinks the bottom has dropped out of British miling; the whole emphasis he says seems to be shifting across the Atlantic and he doesn't like it. None of us does."

Jerry had come back from Nigeria that summer on leave. We had been running together. I was having diathermy for the knee almost daily. And missing Janie. Janie had gone down, back to Holland. I was looking for digs and preparing for a visit by Bonthron with a Princeton-Cornell team, chasing up and down to Oxford to make the arrangements. It isn't surprising with all this going on I had forgotten an isolated event on the County cricket ground at Guildford on the last day in June. Even now it doesn't seem important.

According to my diary, it was a beautifully warm day. The track was grass and "as usual, after the race I felt ill and vomited." I noted the performance of the winner, Aubrey Reeve – "Aubrey deserved the win and I wasn't particularly fit, because of the knee." The only other thing I noted was that the press had used the word "sensational", but this referred not to Reeve's win, nor to my being beaten into third place but to the size of the field. There were so many of us. We were lined up at the start in rows, like sheep. There were over forty entries.

After the race I turned to Aubrey Reeve and said, "Who was that?" On the tape a determined little man in black had appeared from nowhere and rushed past me like an express train.

"Sydney Wooderson," Aubrey said. "The Public Schools champion." He added, "Syd looks up to you, Jack. You're his hero." Aubrey knew him because they shared the same trainer.

I had read that a pupil from Sutton Valence in the Weald of Kent had become the first English schoolboy to run a mile in under four and a half minutes. This must be the chap, I thought. This is him, a year later, having his first big race out of school. I looked at Wooderson. His ears stuck out. Wooderson was smaller than I was. Wooderson was being congratulated by his trainer, Albert Hill. Beside me he seemed tiny although the difference was only an inch; beside Albert Hill he was a midget. He was pale and anaemic-looking, the colour of parchment. He was breathing hard, yet his chest wasn't expanding. He didn't seem to have a chest. It was hollow. There was something else that struck me. It was his ordinariness. He was so very ordinary.

I looked at this very ordinary little Englishman who didn't seem strong enough to carry a duster across the road and I went off to the dressing-room. I dismissed him from my mind.

"So at the time you didn't notice that Wooderson was wearing glasses?"

"I must have noticed. But it didn't register, I suppose. Of course. He's short-sighted like Tommy Hampson and Godfrey Brown. Lord knows how they run if they can't see without glasses. It must be a terrible handicap. So that's it. You think that's the connection with my dream? Wooderson?"

"Possibly. Oh, you can always find a connection. I shouldn't bother to chase connections any longer. Nothing wrong with your eyesight, is there?"

"Nothing."

"Had your eyes tested recently?"

"Yes, as a matter of fact. Vision twenty-twenty."

"Yes. And would you have gone to the trouble of having them tested if there had been no dream?"

"No. I suppose not."

"Yes. Yes, all right. You haven't mentioned drugs. Do you take anything to help you to sleep?"

"Bromides mostly. Just mild barbiturates."

"Nothing stronger?"

"Very occasionally, an opium derivative. I've tried veronal once or twice."

"Experimenting?"

"Yes."

"I should keep off veronal, if I were you. We don't want you hallucinating. I'm going to say something that you might not like. It's this. You're very, what I should call, tucked up. You're not a passionate person, you're actually a very modest person, yet you have a very deep passion inside you. It's smouldering away all the time. Nobody can see it except you. It's smouldering away now while you're sitting there smiling and relaxing, probably thinking about your dream when anyone

132

else of your youth would be thinking about that nurse who put her head in the door just now. Your passion is a form of will-power. There's an old saying that Charles Wilson likes to quote – a man's capital is his will-power. You've got that, I think. That's healthy, it will carry you through, dream or no dream. Most of us want something. Very few of us want something with a passion that is all-consuming. We couldn't live with it. You, apparently, can. Here you are, twenty-four, in the prime of life, sitting up smiling with your eyes crinkling at the edges when something amuses you – you are living with it. You quite enjoy living with it, despite the anxiety. It's a terrible anxiety you have over Berlin. It's the price of your passion. You hide it very well, probably too well. That may not be so healthy. You see, I can't help thinking that part of your trouble, your anxiety over a dream for instance, has to do with the fact that you set your standards too high. Anybody ever said that to you before?"

"My father used to say the opposite. He always said that my standards were too low."

"He must have been an interesting man, your father. Be that as it may. What I want to say is this. I think you are going to have to live with the dream. You're going to have to live with the insomnia too, brutal as that may sound."

"I thought you said that the dream would vanish."

"Possibly it will. I'm not prepared to speculate and I don't think you should either. You appear to want to get to the bottom of this dream, yet I'm not sure that you really do."

"I'm not hiding anything from you."

"Absolutely not! I'm sure that you're not hiding anything consciously. Let me put it another way. You're like Puck, you know. When you sit there with your legs crossed and your chin on your hands grinning like Puck, you appear to the casual observer just that – puckish and relaxed. The very picture of your picture in the papers. Not a care in the world. But inside you're really quite tense. Wait. Don't protest. I think you need that tension. You probably need the insomnia too. If I could cure the insomnia, which I'm glad to say I can't – "

"Glad?"

"Yes, strange as it may seem. Quite glad. I'm an old-fashioned physician. I'm pig stubborn, bull-necked and blunt.

Some people find me forbidding. I'm actually quite soft. I'm particularly soft on colonials – this hospital is full of colonials, which is why Mary's is such a happy place. I'm also full of selfish pleasures. One of my great pleasures – I told you that I'm prejudiced in your favour – is to see you run. My *greatest* pleasure will be, if I can get there, to see you run at the 1936 Olympics and lick the hides off that Nazi rabble in Berlin. Jack, if I cured your insomnia, the dreams might cease and you would possibly be more relaxed. But you would no longer be Jack Lovelock."

10

I never did get to the bottom of the dream.

That winter my whole timetable was upset. I did nothing but walk to the hospital each day, study, swim when I could, fight what seemed a losing battle against insomnia and worry about money. Asa Bushnell, the director of Athletics at Princeton, had written asking me to return the following summer, June 1935, and run in an invitation Mile-of-the-Century against Cunningham. Cunningham was now the top American miler. Luigi Beccali, Asa said, had also been invited. I knew how successful Asa's first invitation "spectacular" in 1934 had been and I badly wanted to accept, yet I felt that I couldn't. I told Bill this.

"An invitation like this, sir? You can't turn it down."

"I know it's important, Bill. But at this stage I can't accept."

"I'm disappointed in you, sir. You don't give me any reason."

I couldn't tell Bill the reason. It was money. I was living on thirty pounds, a sum I had put aside from my Rhodes Scholarship at Oxford. The scholarship had now stopped. I had no scholarship to pay the fees for my clinical studies at

St Mary's, and the hospital was my only anchor in England. When the thirty pounds ran out I would, short of a miracle, have to return to New Zealand. If I had taken a good degree, I realised, I might have won a clinical scholarship, but I had taken a Third. It wasn't even bad luck, it was bad management. I was lucky to have been accepted for Mary's at all – I was really just a passenger there. I was starting to panic. I wrote back to Asa Bushnell saying "presence doubtful" and in December moved from digs in Bayswater to a room at the hospital to save money. That way, I thought, I could probably last until April 1935. After April, I didn't know.

My digs in Bayswater just off Queensway had been noisy enough. Mary's was worse. My room was above Praed Street near Paddington Station. The station backed on to a line of warehouses by the Paddington Canal and the horse-drawn railway vans rattled over the cobbles with iron-shod wheels all night long; rumblings from the Underground passing beneath the hospital sent microscopes out of focus during the day and made cat-napping difficult. I don't know how many patients in the wards died from the din. After the quiet of Oxford I felt like a novitiate posted from a monastery to the lid of an active volcano. I tried sleeping tablets but they only left me feeling groggy afterwards and, in desperation, began going for night walks after lectures, sometimes taking a tube or a bus as far as Putney and walking back to the hospital. Still my head wouldn't lie down.

I'm not complaining. I put these night journeys to use. I was examined about this time by Adolphe Abrahams, the Olympic doctor and eldest brother of Harold Abrahams, and he declared my cardiac rate of 39 to the minute to be "the most infrequent I've ever encountered". That was my resting pulse.

"It goes even lower," I told Adolphe. "After violent exercise, it's lower than it was before."

We did some tests. Adolphe said, "That's peculiar." I thought so too. So I used the night journeys to carry out experiments. Before setting out I would check my pulse and I would continue to monitor the fluctuations at intermediate points, changing trains or on the tops of buses. I took hundreds of readings like this. It's amazing how you can enjoy your insomnia when there's something on your mind.

135

Of course the knee kept me awake. It resisted heat treatment. Massage brought no relief. Sometimes it appeared to be the tendon, inducing a swingeing pain between the shin and the knee and even in places where the textbooks said I didn't have any muscles. At one point when the throat was infected, then the eye, then the eye cleared up and the knee was bad again, I rigged a block and tackle and tried sleeping with one leg in the air. Mary's at this time had a medical giant, Sir Almoth Wright, the "father" of immunology, who was building up in the new Medical School the finest pathology laboratory in the world. And, just along the corridor from me, in a little room in the corner of the Clarence Wing, was Wright's protégé, the bacteriologist Alexander Fleming. Fleming's insatiable curiosity about microbes had led him to develop a theory about secondary sepsis and he was experimenting with antiseptics and vaccines that could have helped me, but I didn't know this. I have never talked about my ailments. It was strange to be in a place surrounded by so many doctors and not know what to do.

I was rescued fortuitously by an old remedy that was available in the male-dominated London hospitals of the period – I mean, sex. My room-mate, a lusty Canadian, kept a little black book and in a boastful moment told me how he used it to record the names of his girlfriends and the dates of their periods. With this encouragement and his inside knowledge, I began in my diary to do the same. I began visiting a Scottish night nurse who was free in the early afternoon. The nurses' quarters were in a far wing of the hospital, handily placed for diversions, and after the first shy encounters I found that making love in the afternoon was the best soporific; it induced a delicious combination of torpor and well-being enabling me to cat-nap at odd times during the day and so replace some of the energy I would have gained by resting at night. Eventually I learned to cat-nap between races, dropping off almost at will; meantime I was able by trial and error to adjust my training schedule to the new sport and return to a more or less regular routine of two to three hours' sleep at night, as at Oxford.

Obviously I never intended my diaries for publication; but, just in case, in my journals I disguised the new sport. I developed a clever code and that is why amid pages devoted to interval running, diet, weight, swimming, cardiac rates, blood-pressure counts, boxing and other training data there are certain references which I am pleased to say still puzzle students of athletics.

Cunningham throughout this period was never far from my thoughts. In December Asa Bushnell wrote again, renewing his invitation for June 1935. I put the letter in my wallet and carried it about without answering. I don't know – perhaps I was troubled by thoughts of home – but on the edge of my mind was a feeling that some decision I couldn't face, some calamity was lying in wait for me. I couldn't define the feeling. My dream persisted. Sometimes the dream went back to its original form (happy ending), sometimes it was ragged and broken (sad ending). I was getting used to it, like an old coat. Looking back, I can see that my symptoms, probably magnified in my mind by the approach of Christmas, would have presented a wonderful challenge to a Freudian psychoanalyst.

"I'm bloody homesick," I wrote in my diary, and that Christmas, my fourth in England, I escaped from Paddington to Oxford to stay with the Knoxes in Park Town. My home-sickness must have showed because Nesta Knox said, "What you need, son, is a trip home to see your mother." I remember standing by the window of a travel agent's in the High Street and thinking, All I need is fifty pounds. I could go. I walked about Oxford revisiting Parson's Pleasure and old haunts like the miracle well at Binsey, the one Alice fell down, and I tried to figure out how to get the money. I sang carols and ate turkey with the Knoxes, but the smell in my nostrils was a scent of pine needles below my Dunedin home as I ran through the trees above Anderson's Bay. I walked in mist by the Cherwell and saw instead a coastline of sharp hills splashed with yellow lupins and drenched with the sun of a blazing summer's day. Christmas at home, high summer, had always been for me a time of youth and abandon. Oxford, already, seemed peopled by ghosts.

In the new year, January 1935, I was back in Oxford again to see C.K. Allen at Rhodes House. I showed him a letter I had just received from home. It said that my mother had been admitted to an institution "following a severe mental disturbance".

137

I said straight out, "I shall have to go back, C.K."

"Just give me a moment, Jack." Dr Allen gave me a sherry and a cigarette, then smoked two himself, gazing into the study fire with an expression of concentration and perplexity that surprised me. But C.K. Allen, an Australian who had thrown up a professorship to become the second Warden of Rhodes House, was like that. When he decided to help, it was with everything he had.

I said, "I'm sorry to land this on you, C.K. I rushed straight up."

"You haven't told the Knoxes yet? Good. I know what Nesta would say, she'd say 'Go'. I don't think you should go, Jack."

"But — "

"I'm sure you're right to want to go. What more natural? But what will you achieve? Your mother is, it seems, under restraint. The position is serious but not irreversible. She is in capable hands. You have an older sister there and a brother."

"Yes, but I'm needed. I feel that I'm needed."

"Costly business, Jack. How will you pay for the trip?"

"I don't know."

"By the time you get there after five weeks at sea, the position will almost certainly have changed. You're not summoned, are you?"

"No. But — "

"My advice is to wait, at least until you get another letter. Your sister will write again. She says that."

We talked about it at length and in the end I agreed to wait.

C.K. said, "Now about this other problem of yours."

"What other problem?"

"Money, old son, money. Don't look aghast and don't ask how I know. It's my job to know these things. I understand a complication has arisen over your father's estate and your share in it. As a result you haven't the resources to complete your medical course at St Mary's. Correct?"

"I can manage all right until April."

"And then?"

"I honestly don't know. I thought I might possibly be able to raise a loan."

"On what? On your expectations? Better to go on the dole. I take it, Jack, you're still hankering after Berlin? Good. I

138

thought you might be starting to panic and getting cold feet. Well, you won't get to Berlin on the dole. Will you?

"Any other ideas?" he said.

"None, I'm afraid."

"In that case, just write down the details for me, will you?"

"I don't want special treatment, C.K."

"Perhaps not. You probably don't want a lawyer's gratitude either. Listen, young man. Four years ago when I walked into this job you were the first Rhodes Scholar I clapped eyes on. I had resigned a Chair of Jurisprudence to take up the Wardenship here and at the last moment I felt I was making a ghastly mistake. I felt – well, never mind my problems. There were difficulties. You waltzed in with that Cheshire Cat grin on your face and my difficulties evaporated. You've probably forgotten what you did for Dorothy and me in those early weeks in 1931. I haven't. You warmed this Chair for me. Don't say any more. I shall write to Lord Lothian. Just be a good chap and put down the details as I ask. Tell me what it is you need."

C.K. was as good as his word. Three weeks later in February I received a letter from the Board of Rhodes Trustees to say that the Board had approved a loan of two hundred pounds to finance the rest of my medical course at St Mary's. The letter was signed, "Lothian". A few days after this I heard from New Zealand that my mother's condition had improved. She was no longer under restraint. At this point, quite suddenly and unexpectedly, the dream stopped altogether.

School of Medicine
St Mary's Hospital
Paddington, W.2.
17 February 1935

Mr Asa Bushnell
Graduate Athletics Manager
Princeton University, N.J.

Dear Asa,
    Second Princeton Invitational, 15 June 1935
    Please forgive the delay in replying to your last letter, received in December. I am now in a position to accept your

kind invitation and look forward to competing in Princeton in June, and to renewing old friendships there. I read in a newspaper here that you are installing a stop-watch the size of Big Ben at the Palmer Stadium, especially for the event. Is this to amuse the spectators or merely to distract the runners?!

You ask about my trainer. I should like, if I may, to bring Bill Thomas with me. Will your hospitality, expenses and so on, extend to him also?

I look forward to hearing at your earliest convenience . . .

I made the decision to go as soon as I knew my mother was out of danger, and I began light training immediately. Then I had a thought. A London daily, the *Evening News*, had asked me to write an article on the preparations in Berlin for the coming 1936 Games. The Germans were said to be creating an extensive village on the edge of a pine forest to house a record number of competitors. Why not nip over? Do a recce? It occurred to me that if I could persuade the newspaper to send me, I could turn the visit to my advantage and steal a march over my opponents. As I thought this, I felt a red-hot pain grip my diaphragm. My cardiac rate shot up and I began to dance about the room. I did the oddest thing. I raided the hospital stores and that night I bult myself a patent elastic fire escape – I tested the efficiency of the elastic strap leaping out into space from my third-storey hospital window.

Well, I had to do something to contain my excitement.

But then came a shock. At the end of February I heard back from Asa Bushnell. I caught a night train up to Oxford to give Bill the news.

Bill read Asa's letter and gave it back to me. "Well, that's nice, sir. Very nice of them offering to pay my expenses and all, I'm sure."

"What's the matter? Aren't you *pleased*?"

"Do you mind, sir? I'll just finish this. It gets in the way of my molars."

Bill seemed embarrassed. I thought it was because I had disturbed him at home. I had interrupted him performing his ablutions. He was in shirtsleeves and braces; a ewer was beside him and a chipped enamel bowl. He was sitting in the kitchen

of his spartan little house off the Cowley Road trimming his
moustache with what appeared to be a pair of horse scissors.

"That's better." He fastened his cuffs, put away the scissors
and led me into the sitting room where there was a fire. He said:

"There are some people, sir, as think you are making a bad
mistake going back to Princeton."

"For pity's sake! Bill, last time we spoke, you were all for it.
Remember?"

"Yes, sir. Since then I have spoken to Joe Binks and Sam
Mussabini and one or two others. They are of the opinion that
the Americans are setting you up."

"That's nonsense."

"I think they have a point, sir. You'll be on your own."

"You mean you're not coming?"

"Have you spoken to Mr Abrahams, sir?"

"Yes, I have. Harold said — " Harold, I now remembered,
had also cautioned me. "If you go again, Jack, remember –
history doesn't always repeat itself." I could hear Harold's
voice now. Yet at the time, from the moment I had written and
accepted the invitation, it had felt right. I could *think* again,
I could concentrate – it was like the peace that descended at
home in New Zealand on rainy afternoons when my brother
switched off the wireless. It still felt right.

"And Mr Cornes, sir. Just before Mr Cornes went back to
Nigeria he said to me, 'Tell Jack not to go. They'll crucify him.'
His first words, sir – and his last."

"I don't understand. Why is everyone so anti-American?
They're our hosts!"

"Now don't be hasty, sir. Just think it through."

"Hasty? I've been thinking about it for six months. I've
thought of nothing else. Bill, I've told you what the plan is
– it was Bonthron in '33, the Empire Games '34, now it's
Cunningham in '35. One big effort. One all-out effort in a
season, you know that. I've *got* to meet Cunningham before
Berlin. I've simply got to. Besides, I'm not the only invader.
Beccali is invited."

"And Mr Beccali, sir, won't bite. Your little Luigi is as cagey
as a nun going shopping. You won't see hide nor hair of Luigi
Beccali, I'm picking, till you gets to Berlin."

"There's Ny. Erik Ny is invited."

"Ny has declined, sir. It was in the paper this morning. It will be just you against the Americans – Mr Cunningham, Mr Bonthron, Mr Venzke, Mr Mangan and Mr Glenn Dawson. One against five, and four of them have done a mile in 4:10 or less. Have you seen this?"

"No. What is it?"

"It is an article by Jesse Abrahamson from the New York *Herald Tribune*. Just listen to what he says, sir. 'Ever since they first saw Lovelock, Americans have been longing for one of their own countrymen to beat him.' There you have it, sir. That's telling you in a nutshell. It stands to reason — "

"That they'll gang up on me to spoil my chances? Bonthron wouldn't. Bonny's not like that."

"I do recall, sir, the look on the face of Mr Matty Geis, Bonthron's trainer, when you nipped his boy last time in the final straight. It was not a pretty sight. Seeing is believing, as the saying goes. I do believe also, sir, that Mr Cunningham and Mr Venzke are old mates."

"Buddies, yes. Of course they're mates, what of it? So are Cunningham and Glenn Dawson, they're both from the mid-West. They have the same coach, Hargiss."

"Exactly, sir. And Mr Cunningham, from what I hear, is a man without pity. And very jealous, sir, of preserving his world record, what he took from you."

"I'm not likely to forget it, am I? All right. All right. Just let me think a moment." I thought long and hard. "You honestly think, Bill, they're going to collaborate or connive in some way to wreck my chances? I don't believe it. I'll tell you why. How many of us are going to be left in the race at the last lap? I say, three runners – Cunningham, Bonthron, and yours truly. Three of us. Now if there is a plot, it suggests, doesn't it, that Cunningham – or Bonthron – is prepared beforehand to allow the other to win? Can you see those two collaborating? Can you see either of them admitting the other is superior? I can't. They don't quite hate each other but they don't sleep together either – which reminds me. Bonthron's coach and Cunningham's coach don't get on."

"I didn't know that, sir."

"They can't stand each other. I think you're all over-reacting."

"Very good, sir. Will you just excuse me, sir? The kettle."

He had gone into the kitchen. I followed him out, feeling edgy and uncertain, and watched him take a jug from the safe. He set it down, fetched some cups and stood, thumbs in braces, waiting for the kettle to boil.

"So we're quite confident, are we?" he said quietly.

Bill's crunchy voice was so quiet I thought he was mocking me. I lost patience.

"If you're going to be like that, I'll go alone."

"Now, sir — "

"I mean it. I'm beginning to feel like the man in the Bible who says 'I go and goeth not.' Well, I'm going!"

"I can see that, sir. I wish you would sit down. There isn't a lot of space as you can see. I'm not used to entertaining gentlemen in the kitchen. Would you like a biscuit, sir?"

"Thanks. Nothing." I collected my coat and umbrella. "I have to get back to London."

Bill had cleared a space and settled over his tea, his hams resting on the table. He dunked a biscuit.

"That's it then, Bill. I'll go alone."

"I was thinking, sir – it's a long way to go for one man, isn't it? This Mr Cunningham. I was thinking to myself, you will have to develop a longer sprint. He's a right stew, this Mr Cunningham. The human horse of runners, they call him. But pitiless. A pitiless runner, sir. I suppose you could go on your own. You seems confident."

"I'd feel a lot more confident if you were behind me."

"Did I say I wasn't?"

"You mean—?"

"I don't know as how I should hold my head up afterwards, sir, if you lost."

"You mean you'll come?"

Pieces of soggy biscuit had stuck to the ends of his moustache. Bill licked it. Somewhere in his belly he began to chuckle. "Just you try and stop me, sir."

"Bill, you fox. You bloody old fox. You gave me the fright of my life just now!"

We began to plan the race that night in Bill's kitchen.

I have a suspicion that it was only now that Bill began to

believe, truly to believe in the possibility of an Olympic Gold Medal. It was as if in his private, doggy way he had determined to sniff in the undergrowth and face for me some of the hazards that he knew lay ahead – either that, or his concern had to do with Cunningham. Before Cunningham, Bill had never shown emotion about any of my opponents, not even about Sydney Wooderson who would be waiting for me, as we both knew, when I returned from Princeton. Wooderson was still in the future. But Cunningham for some reason had got under Bill's skin and this started him coming down to London. We began a new routine.

I would get a note in Bill's handwriting – "Wednesday, 660 time trial", or just, "Wednesday – sprints". We would meet at Paddington Station, take a tube to Maida Vale, walk along Elgin Avenue and cross over beside the plane trees on to the rutted track of the Paddington Recreation Ground. Bill called it the coal-pit. It was an appalling oval, soul-destroying. I would change in the open pavilion. Bill would station himself on a bend below the cycle ramp and say, "Go!" I can see his bowler hat now as he held the stop-watch, the curl of the bowler framed between pollarded plane trees against a row of red Victorian mansions flanking Biddulph Road. He never wore a top coat. Sometimes in the rain only the hat would be visible. Afterwards if I had done something that pleased him there would be a glint in his eye and we would come back to the Fountains Abbey, the pub opposite the hospital, and talk. Sometimes he would return to Oxford without saying a word. Occasionally I would slip up to Iffley Road or off to Wimbledon Common for stamina training, but we always seemed to come back to the coal-pit at Paddington. It was here I learned to perfect my pace judgment until the watch was almost unnecessary. And I suppose Bill was unnecessary in a way too, yet he insisted on being there. It seemed to matter to him. He had become, in his quiet way, possessed.

And it had begun with my outburst in the kitchen – with Cunningham.

Glenn Cunningham was a machine-like runner. He seemed to irritate Bill in a way he could not define, and this irritated him all the more. Bill would chew over his many nicknames – the Kansas Cyclone, the Iron Man, the Iron Horse of Kansas,

Old Man River, the Camel – chew them over, spit them out, then a moment later he would contradict himself, saying "It's all hoo-ha, sir." Again and again he used the word "pitiless". Cunningham worried me too, but differently. I found his background intimidating. Cunningham's background was mid-West, God-fearing, Chapel-going, axe-swinging and, in my distorted imagination, violent. But Cunningham also fascinated me, in the way Peltzer had once fascinated me – as a freak, a kind of running miracle, a disabled backwoods boy who had fought his way up and become part of the all-American dream of invincibility. And on the edge of my mind was an itch for revenge, an urge to snatch back my 1933 world record that Cunningham had broken in '34 just when mine was about to be ratified.

One night in the pub I said to Bill, "What do you mean exactly – pitiless?"

"Like a dynamo, sir. On and on. That's not miling."

"But last week you said the opposite. You said Cunningham was unpredictable."

"Well, going on what you tell me, he always runs a second lap faster than the first. Now lately he is running very evenly. And yet, what gets me – he never seems to run the same race twice!"

"I still don't understand what it is about him that irritates you."

Finally it came out: "I don't like his manners, sir."

"Oh, Bill."

"I don't like any man who does what he does before a race."

Cunningham had won more races at the start, it was said, horsing around and unnerving rivals by keeping them waiting, than at the finish. He had a name for keeping his opponents waiting. But at San Francisco in 1932 I had observed him in a dressing-room, lying with his lower trunk swathed in blankets. I saw with what care the trainer Hargiss had the masseur work over him; saw the masseur bend right back the toes of one foot – the transverse arch seemed to have broken down; saw, when he rolled Cunningham over, how abnormal the muscles were under livid scar tissue on the backs of his legs. Throughout the ritual, Cunningham prickled and shivered. He lay shivering

145

under the blankets as if submerged in an ice bath. Yet the dressing-room was sweltering.

"You know what I think, Bill? I think he's got a psychological block about the cold. You know he was in a fire?"

"No, sir."

"Hargiss told me." Hargiss had told me the story after the 1932 relays in San Francisco and I had been fascinated. Cunningham, he said, had spent part of his childhood in a covered wagon drawn by mules. His family had trekked West. His people were originally Scottish farmers who had emigrated to Virginia in the South and then trekked north across five states. But Cunningham's father had brought Glenn and his brothers West to a place called Elkhart on the Oklahoma line, in the south-west corner of Kansas. The father raised broom corn and melons; the children attended a small one-teacher school. They arrived at school one morning in winter, Glenn, an older brother and a sister. Glenn was seven or eight at the time. The teacher had not arrived. The older brother picked up a tin labelled paraffin and saturated the stove with its contents. Usually the fire was out but on this morning the coals in the stove were live, and the tin contained not paraffin but petrol. Glenn had his back to the stove when it exploded and blew the windows out. His legs were practically incinerated from the back. Both boys caught fire. They ran outside. The sister, who was not harmed, tried to throw sand on them as they ran, and they kept running for two miles past the yards of astonished neighbours until they reached home. The older brother died in a few days. Doctors said that Glenn might never walk again, but the parents refused to send him to hospital and refused to let the doctors amputate. He remained in bed with his legs bandaged for two years. He returned to school on crutches with a limp. Yet within three years the legs straightened and he was running. According to Hargiss, Cunningham won his first race as a schoolboy aged twelve in 1921, the same year I competed at a boy scouts' camp in New Zealand. The distance was a mile in each case and we each won by five yards. Hargiss said Cunningham had learned to move spider-walking and then forced himself to run hoppity-hop like a bird because it was easier than limping. That was Hargiss' story. The rest I

146

knew from the papers. At fourteen when I was taking my first dancing lessons, Cunningham was shovelling wheat into railway box cars with grown men. He had developed a gorilla physique and a spirit of endurance which latterly, since 1933, had led him to a string of running successes on two continents that was almost unbroken. He trained every day and maintained fitness through the winter competing on indoor circuits. He had run in blizzards and in temperatures of Sahara heat that no Englishman can imagine – his reputation as the human horse of runners was not misplaced.

Yet he was, apparently, always cold.

I had never been in a fire. But I had seen deep burn cases similar to Cunningham's in London hospitals and I could imagine how a runner's pre-race ordeal might originate not, as with most of us, somewhere in the central nervous system but instead in the sensory nerves attached to the ends of muscles damaged by fourth-degree burns. Hence the elaborate ritual with blankets I had observed in the dressing-room.

I said to Bill, "You think I'm complicated? I think Cunningham's just as complicated. The reason he keeps his warms on making people wait is he can't bear to uncover his legs, he's frightened to peel off. I think it's something to do with peeling off the bandages as a kid when the doctors said he'd never walk again. It goes back to the fire. It's a sort of trauma he goes through before every race. That's my theory."

Bill's reaction was curious. He sipped his pint and heard me out without speaking. Then he said:

"Just like I've been saying all along, sir, the man is unpredictable. Like the weather."

We had three months to prepare for Cunningham. It wasn't enough. We were sailing on the *Normandie* – the new luxury liner was due to make her inaugural voyage from Southampton at the end of May – and at the end of May the English athletic season, still in 1935 emerging from the nineteenth century, had barely opened. I was reduced to racing in schoolboy events to get fit or not racing at all. There was very little advance publicity for Princeton, or so I thought.

Then on 24 May Harold Abrahams telephoned to ask if I

would broadcast from the Palmer Stadium on 15 June immediately the race ended? (Assuming, of course, I had won!) The BBC, he said, was rigging a special microphone in a booth inside the stadium. I agreed to do the broadcast and next day, 25 May, ran in a Kinnaird Cup contest at White City. I wrote in my diary afterwards, "Feeling v. fit in legs." On Monday 27 at Westminster Hospital I was vetted by Adolphe Abrahams who pronounced me "very fit". On Tuesday 28, three days before the *Normandie* was due to sail, I attempted to run a three-quarter-mile time trial for Bill. A hundred yards from home suddenly my left leg didn't come forward and I collapsed, barely able to complete the distance. We both put it down to nervous strain, but that night the knee came up and the heel was so inflamed I couldn't walk.

I telephoned Professor Abrahams at his home in Mayfair. He listened and said:

"Sure it isn't a stress fracture?"

"I think it's the Achilles tendon."

"You haven't torn a muscle?"

"I thought I had at first, but, no, I don't think so."

"Can you walk?"

"Not very well."

"Doesn't sound very promising. Why do you think it's the tendon?"

"I did something to it in Amsterdam last August."

"August last year? Have you been treating it without telling me?"

"Yes." I had tried everything – galvanism, short-wave treatment, a hot paste called anti-phlogiston, massage. I said, "I thought it had finally cleared up. It seems to have come back."

There was a silence on the line. Professor Abrahams said: "You might have to cancel the trip."

"I can't. I mean, I don't want to."

"Speak up. I can barely hear you, Jack."

"I said I don't want to call the trip off."

Another silence. He said, "Have you got a cold?"

"It's just my throat."

"It's – what?"

"It's just a throat infection I've picked up."

"You didn't mention a sore throat when I saw you yesterday. Jack, listen to me. Correct me if I am wrong. You've got an inflamed shin or heel, severe pains and stiffness in the leg around the knee and simultaneously an infected throat, correct? All within the last twenty-four hours?"

"No, not the throat."

"Don't follow."

"I mean the throat infection isn't new. I've had it before – it comes and goes."

"Right. It's worth a try. I want you to see Fleming in the morning. I can't swear to it but it might, just might be a form of blood poisoning – a remote infection in the heel from the throat."

"You think I'm toxic?"

"Just do as I say and see Fleming in the morning. You're sailing when? In three days? My aunt, you've cut it fine. I think what Fleming will say is that as a result of a persistent throat infection you have developed secondaries. Secondary sepsis. That will be his guess. Flem's got a theory about focal sepsis and I know he has been working on it. I don't know that he's right, mind you. It's just a chance. He might be able to help."

"You mean produce a vaccine? I don't see how he can in the time."

"He will make time if I ask him." Adolphe was Dean of the Medical School at Westminster. "See Fleming first thing. I'll ring him now. Goodbye."

I saw Alexander Fleming in the morning. Professor Fleming took a swab from my throat and I watched him smear the swab across the surface of a culture medium of agar jelly contained in a circular plate, cover the plate and then incubate it. In a matter of hours colonies of bacteria would appear on the plate; from these, he explained, he would select the offending organism, grow it as a culture and then kill it to produce a vaccine, but there was a problem because of the time factor. There wouldn't be time to make a pure culture or carry out the normal safety tests, so the result – little more than a suspension of dead bacteria – would be crude.

"Very crude," he said. He gave me a long stare. "It's taking a risk, Laddie." By crude I thought he meant painful to inject.

149

It never occurred to me to wonder what might happen if some of the bacteria were left alive in the vaccine; I didn't know at this stage that the organism would turn out to be the pervasive and dangerous *streptococcus haemolyticus*. I shrugged off any risk. He nodded and said, "We'll have something for you, Laddie, before you sail." And he had.

Fifty-six hours later with ten million organisms of the experimental vaccine in sealed phials in my luggage and a note of instructions from Professor Fleming, I met Bill Thomas on the boat train at Victoria Station. I had twenty minutes to spare. Later, after we had sailed from Southampton, Bill sat in the cabin and watched me prepare to inject 400,000 organisms into my thigh.

"That's a syringe, is it, sir?"

"Yes."

"And what's that stuff?"

"Well I call it 'Flem's Juice', after the maker. It's a new drug."

"Will it help?"

"I don't know yet."

Bill worked on the principle that if anything can go wrong at the last minute, it will. He picked up one of the phials from the bunk and sniffed it suspiciously.

"It might poison you, sir."

"It might."

"But it's been tried before?"

"No, Bill. It's brand new. I told you. It didn't exist till Wednesday."

"But you didn't buy it in a shop. Who makes the stuff?"

"A little Scotsman at the hospital. His name is Alexander Fleming."

Bill said, "Who's he?"

11

We sailed on 31 May and arrived on the 4 June in New York. Princeton the same night. Cunningham and the others weren't due in Princeton until the week following and the race was on 15 June. I arrived sun-baked and rested. There were ten days to recoup the form I had lost at sea and I kept saying to Bill, "It isn't enough." On the ship he had fussed and rubbed and soothed me as if I was a china doll. I was reduced to lying in a deckchair while Bill ran round the promenade area instead of me. The only reason he allowed me to swim, I think, was that I had finally convinced him that swimming at least took the weight off my legs. He winced when he saw me inject the new vaccine. Fleming's experimental "juice" was so crude, the injections were almost as painful as the inflamed tissues. Bill was convinced Alexander Fleming was poisoning me. "No, Bill," I said. "The poison is already in the system. The injections are getting it *out*."

I lay in the sun thinking, How fragile we are. And how complicated. We're not like other people. The fitter we are, the more prone to injury we become. A tiny microscopic area of fine tissue within the tendon sheath had been damaged months before. Then it had healed. Suddenly without warning it had flared again. Why? Because of a stupid throat infection, apparently – that was all. The poisons had spread through the bloodstream and as a result I had become a near-cripple. But chance – or the gods – had given me a hospital that contained a shy little Scotsman who played with microbes, a genius called Fleming. Fleming had saved me, I realised. Without him I would have stopped running altogether.

Already the knee had stopped aching; the inflammation was down. I was no longer hobbling. On the third day I was playing deck tennis. After we landed I followed Professor Fleming's instructions and gradually increased the strength of the injections; then, the night before the race, I took a risk and gave myself a double dose, injecting a million organisms in one shot into a muscle round the knee. At this stage there was, luckily, no reaction.

When we docked in New York a small army of press reporters came aboard. "Leave 'em to me, sir," Bill said.

Bill was lovely. He contradicted everything I said. Sample:

REPORTER: Mr Lovelock, is it true that in England the coach always calls you sir?

LOVELOCK: Not always.

BILL: Yes. *Sir*.

REPORTER: Are you in shape?

BILL: Look at him!

REPORTER: How do you plan to run the race?

LOVELOCK: No faster than I have to.

BILL: A bit faster than everyone else.

REPORTER: Bill Hargiss, Cunningham's coach, is claiming a time for the Princeton mile of 4:06. Matty Geis, Bonthron's coach, is predicting 4:04. What do you say?

LOVELOCK: (*Feigns a swoon and disappears behind trainer.*)

REPORTER: Do you think a four-minute mile is within the realm of possibility?

LOVELOCK: Well, possibly . . .

BILL: Impossible.

"His interviewers," Arthur Daley wrote in the *New York Times* next day, "were at a considerable loss in interpreting Lovelock's remarks." I was pleased about that. Bill was tickled pink.

It was Reunions Week when we arrived in Princeton. The race was timed to coincide with the climax of Reunions, and Princeton was going mad. We stayed in a small hotel at the end of an avenue of maples and elms, secluded from bear-leaders, processions, lion-hunters and the incessant grinding of the publicity machine. Bill developed a great longing to go into the country, he said, and see a horse. My reaction was to rush down to the Palmer Stadium and start sprinting. Oh peerless bowl!

152

Oh bowl of satin! Bill screamed at me to slow down, terrified I would pull a muscle.

He wanted two fast runs before the race, only two, he said; two time trials only. We found an out-of-the-way harbour at Choate School and I trotted around there on grass. Mostly we sat around watching, and waiting. "Bill, this is torture," I said. "Sheer torture."

But I was regaining form, quite quickly.

As the day of the race approached, Bill became not anxious exactly, but sniffy. He was distracted. He would go off to the stadium when I was resting. He would return. I would say something and get a non-committal answer. I would come back from a swim and find him playing Patience in the hotel lobby. He would put down the cards, pull out a fob watch from the folds of his stomach and go out. "Stretch the legs, I think, sir." But I knew he was off to the stadium. He scented something. He was sniffing for rats. Cunningham had arrived with Dawson – they were staying out at Trenton. I believe Venzke was staying at the same hotel. I knew Gene Venzke; he was from Penn State and known as the Bridesmaid. He was the first in a cluster of great American milers and seemingly unbeatable until Bonthron and Cunningham came along. He had become one of the eternal "seconds" – always when he would happen to beat either Cunningham or Bonthron, the other one was in front. Gene the Bridesmaid – an enormously popular runner, but unlucky. I knew little about the other two runners, Dawson and Mangan.

Cunningham arrived on Monday 11 June, fresh from a successful race on the Saturday, but Bill wouldn't let me near him. We met only once before 15 June. Cunningham was sitting on one of the tiered stone benches of the stadium and got up when I arrived. I said, "Hullo." Cunningham said, "Howdie," and looked around. I remembered this habit, the small quizzical eyes that looked around but not at you, mentally staring. I remembered it from Los Angeles and I was struck again by the contrasts in him – the bulging chest and the small tapering body; the big wrestler's arms and the small pointed head. His head was domed, rising on top to a cliff, then falling away at the back.

"I love this track," he said.

153

I said, "It's a beautiful track. But I think it's starting to lift in the heat."

He nodded and looked around. "I love it," he said again. "I love this track to death."

That was the extent of the conversation. It was a friendly encounter, yet it left me feeling tight and uncomfortable. Then a report got back to me from Seymour van Blake, the masseur Bill and I liked so much, that Cunningham and Dawson between them had the race "sewn up" and that Cunningham had called me a runt, a stuck-up little runt and a whippersnapper. It was probably a rumour. There were so many rumours buzzing about the stadium after Cunningham and the reporters arrived, you could believe anything. Cunningham brought reporters in his train like royalty. If a competitor ran anywhere in training, even if it was only to the dressing-room, you could be sure his recorded time would be published in a newspaper next day.

"I don't think Cunningham likes me very much," I said to Bill. It was the Tuesday before the race.

"There's something funny going on," Bill said. Bill had been at the track in the morning, come back to the hotel for lunch and gone out again. Now it was tea time. "You'd better come over, sir."

As soon as we came through the iron gate into the stadium I sensed that something unusual had happened. Cunningham, Dawson, their coach Hargiss and a few others were standing under the big electric clock bunched together. Further away near the finish line was a throng of murmuring supporters, officials and pressmen – apparently surrounding Bonthron and his coach Geis. Presently Bonthron appeared, shrugging off reporters, and vanished into the dressing-room. He was looking pleased with himself. Jesse Abrahamson of the *Herald Tribune* gave us the news.

Bonthron, he said, had just ambled through a 660-yard time trial in 1 min. 20 secs.

Bill stopped still as if he'd been kicked in the back.

That's it, I thought. That's the end. I had been planning when it got cooler towards evening to run my own time trial. Going all out, I reckoned with luck I might break 1:22. The best I had ever run was 1:23.

"I wouldn't credit it," Abrahamson was saying. "But there's the clock."

I looked up at the Great Western Union sports clock erected at the open end. The second hand showed twenty seconds exactly.

Hargiss, Cunningham's coach, was walking slowly across the turf towards Geis. After a short distance Hargiss stopped and tilted his hat. He seemed undecided what to do next. Arthur Daley was hurrying towards him. People had detached themselves from Geis and were moving about in twos and threes, talking animatedly. Everyone was having the same conversation.

And all the time, I thought, we've been concentrating on Cunningham! Not Bonthron. Bonny? A four-minute man? A time like that was as good as a four-minute mile. In fact, it was under.

I was so shaken I turned away. I picked up my bag and said, "I think I'll go back to the hotel, Bill."

Bill had disappeared.

I spotted him a moment later with Keane Fitzpatrick, one of the Princeton officials. I couldn't think what they were doing at first. Bill was kneeling with his jacket off on the far side of the track; Keane, walking away from him anti-clockwise. Now Bill had collected his jacket and they were walking towards Geis.

I saw them take Geis to one side.

I waited.

Bill came back, opened his mouth to speak, remembered Abrahamson was listening and coloured slightly.

"Nothing wrong, Mr Thomas, is there?" Abrahamson said.

"Wrong, sir?" Bill put his great St Bernard's head on one side and the crow's feet round his broody eyes expanded, almost hitting the brim of his bowler. "Wrong? Not as I am aware of."

"All right, tell me," I said to Bill as soon as we were alone.

"Geis, sir. He made the boy run short. A bleeding long way short."

"Are you sure?"

Bill nodded. "He made Bonthron run twenty-one yards short of the full distance."

It took me a moment to digest what Bill was saying. "You mean, deliberately?"

"If you ask me, sir – well, it would be better if you don't ask me. A trick like that, it makes me wild! I told you in Oxford these birds would get up your snout, didn't I? Mind you, I'm not saying it's deliberate. Mr Geis has apologised just now, he is most apologetic. Very apologetic. Well sir, when you're found out, what else can you be? Twenty-one bleeding yards short, sir. I measured it."

"Does Bonny know?"

"No. The boy does not know, sir. And don't you go telling him neither. His supper's spoiled, whichever way you like to look at it. And so is Mr Cunningham's. Just four people know now – you, me, Mr Fitzpatrick and Mr Geis. And that's all, I'm picking, till after the race on Saturday, that's all as will know."

Just then Venzke arrived. We waited to see if he or Cunningham or Dawson would come out and run, but they didn't. Later, when there were fewer people about, I ran my own time trial. Bill wouldn't let me start until he had spoken to someone and made sure that the hand of the Western Union clock, looming over the bowl, wouldn't start creeping round. I told Bill he had bats in the belfry. "Are you ready, sir?" he said. I ran flat stick over the full distance of 660 yards and returned a time of 1 min 21.5 secs. It was the fastest 660 of my life.

I sometimes wonder if horses are as mean to each other as humans before the start of a race. I'm very mean.

The race was timed to start at 6 p.m. and it did, more or less. There were six of us stripped and lined up before the referee and the starter and the hands of the awful electric clock. The hands of the clock showed midnight. I was third out from the pole-line. Bonthron, strung taut, was inside me, Cunningham on my other side, then Dawson. Rather, Cunningham should have been on my other side. At five past six he was still prancing around in his track suit.

Whenever he came within earshot the referee called out to him. Cunningham ignored him and went on jogging in a wide circle.

"Blow your whistle," Bill Bingham the referee told the starter. But you couldn't hear the whistle for the wind.

156

At noon conditions had been ideal. Now a small gale was coming down the back straight. It came round us in gusts, magnified by a stropping sound like sailcloth tearing – the spectators were equipped with little American flags that tore in the wind. The stadium was jammed to capacity.

"Blow it again," Bingham said.

I know the man has problems with his legs. I know he's only got half a foot. I wanted to murder Cunningham. I was standing straight up the way I always do, head slightly bent, my hands playing across the knees – "in the old-fashioned English mode", as the Americans say. Finally I lost concentration and spoke to Cunningham. He nodded and took his place beside Dawson. Then Bonthron's nerve snapped. He broke just before the gun sounded, taking the others with him. I stepped back with a grin. The crowd roared with laughter.

"There's no particular hurry just yet, my dear," I told Bonny as we lined up again. I said it with malice. It was a remark designed to hurt a man already too nervous to speak. As I say, I'm not a nice person at the start.

One reason I stand erect is so I can turn my head and notice what's going on. And I *did* notice, as we again faced the starter; I noticed that Cunningham and Dawson had abandoned their normal stance and were crouching. They were crouched down low, side by side. I felt the sweat trickle down the inside of my thighs as I registered the fact, too late. The starter had raised his pistol. We were racing.

Racing? We were shuffling along like old women. Dawson had stepped clear, clear of Bonthron, of Cunningham, of Venzke. Venzke gave me an elbow. I had determined to shadow Cunningham and slid on to his heels, almost knocking Venzke off the track. I cut in too sharply. And Dawson led at a crab's pace. Cunningham second, outside him, playing bridesmaid. Dawson looked left, looked right. Then, as if he couldn't believe his luck, he looked back in what I took to be amazement. At the time it never dawned on me that he was connecting with Cunningham, just as it had not dawned on Bill or me beforehand that in order to spoil my chances Cunningham might be prepared to deliberately wreck his own. It was the one possibility in planning the race we had overlooked.

So we crawled, with Cunningham at Dawson's elbow. It was so slow, that first lap, that when we should have been passing the post the first time we hadn't even entered the straight.

Suddenly Cunningham had slipped the field and was racing. He discarded Dawson and the rest of us like so much loose change. It seemed a suicidal thing to do. It was such an erratic thing for Cunningham to do. I couldn't understand it. If Dawson's opener was, as I heard later, the slowest first lap in the history of first-class miling, Cunningham's second was the fastest, despite the wind. Cunningham was attempting what Paavo Nurmi had done in Paris in 1924, to kill off the opposition. It was horrible trying to hold him, and equally horrible for Bonthron – his face was twisted as he went past me, sensing, as I did, that Cunningham was starting to wilt. The strain told. The wind blew. Cunningham, Bonthron, Lovelock. Entering the back straight for the third time, I managed to close on Bonthron. A gust tore at him and he seemed to hang there, vest and sash billowing. Then he sailed backwards with a faint rushing sound. The wind was eerie. It tore and sucked. It blew Cunningham back to meet me so unexpectedly that I suspected a trap to force me past him on the corner. He was leaning in. The cinders raining from his heels got up my pants. I moved out of the rain of cinders on to his right shoulder and I stayed there, sheltering. The man was so broad, he covered you like a shield. There was no sound apart from the wind. Nothing is more maddening or distracting than to have a lightly stepping shadow moored to your shoulder within sight and hearing, re-fusing to pass you. Yet he didn't flinch. I watched Cunningham's shoulders tighten, I felt his knees starting to go and I knew I was beginning to madden him, yet the man was so stocky and powerful and remorseless he was able to walk through the buffeting wind without swaying by as much as a millimetre. We stayed glued for almost a lap and a half. I overtook him on the final bend and went on to win by ten yards. By then I don't believe he cared. As I caught the finishing breeze and ran past him, Cunningham half-turned. His knees were crumpling, the eyes staring and glassy. He half-turned and for an instant we were joined by one of those visual threads which are in the nature of the only real conversations runners ever have. There was no anger in him, not even defeat, only a nod. In that nod I read satisfaction. "You're late," he seemed to say. "The party's over." And then a queer nod as of satisfaction.

Cunningham shook hands with me afterwards – at least he got as far as parting the spectators and extending an arm. Some woman got between us and began clawing and kissing me. I saw Cunningham reel away, his vest was torn. I had my fern badge ripped off. Bill had his bowler – never mind Bill's bowler. "Oh Lord," I heard Bill say, as I got to my feet. I was knocked to the ground. I couldn't stand up anyway. I got up to see Bill, minus his bowler, throwing people around. Ken Fairman, an official, was there, with the police. Women screaming. Spectators engulfed us. I think we were taken off under escort, who remembers? Who remembers what happens after a crowd turns into a mob? There was mass hysteria. Police punched a corridor so we could get through into the dressing-room and an hour later we were still sitting there, unable to get out. I didn't even get to look at the clock. Arthur Daley, the only journalist who got in before they put guards on the door and locked them, said the time of the race was 4 mins. 11.2, or nearly five seconds outside Cunningham's world record. I gathered that Bonthron had also passed Cunningham in the straight. A great race, Geis was saying. Bill was talking about a broadcast. I kept saying to Bill, "Why did he do it? Why did Cunningham kill himself off like that?" Bonthron announced he wasn't coming to Berlin. "Don't you believe it, fellas," Geis piped up. "The broadcast, sir," Bill said. He had to shout above the din outside. What broadcast? I said. "You are supposed to be broadcasting to London, sir." I had forgotten all about the broadcast. There was no chance of getting to the microphone room now.

Just then Cunningham came out of the shower. He sat down against a locker, rubbing himself, his face expressionless. I suddenly felt cold and called for a blanket. Somebody brought me a glass of water. I drank it and lay back. Bill was bending over me with a blanket. Arthur Daley was speaking, saying something about a moment.

"That was the moment, Jack."

"What?"

"The moment, the moment. The moment when you passed him, that was the moment." He went on saying it. I closed my eyes and thought, yes, the moment. I remembered the moment.

I remembered it very clearly. But more than the moment, I remembered Cunningham's queer nod.

I was still puzzling about it a week later when we sailed back to England.

I had come on deck with Bill, it was late at night. Sunday 23 June 1935. I had been dancing in first-class after dinner. Bill had gone down to the wireless room where he had made friends with the operator, then we had met for our customary turns together on deck before retiring. We were leaning against the stern rail yarning when an elderly gentleman in a bow-tie came up to me and introduced himself, an American. I had noticed him before in the dining-room. He spoke for some minutes. When he had gone Bill said, "What was all that about?"

"He wants to stop the Games. Can you beat it? He wants to stop the Games in Berlin next year. He's off to Germany to 'monitor the situation', he says."

"What situation, sir?"

"Exactly. He seemed to think I knew what he was talking about. Said he was a sports official of some kind, a judge, some bigwig. Judge Mahoney, I think he said. He asked me what was being done in England to boycott the Games? Precious little, I said. How should I know? He's formed a Committee for Fair Play in Sports, he said."

"Stop the Games, sir? He hasn't got a hope."

"I told him that. Apparently there's some movement in America to boycott the Games. I haven't heard about it."

"Sounds like a right crank, sir, if you ask me."

"Or an alarmist. Bit of a badger, I thought. Anyway it's got nothing to do with us. What were you saying just now, Bill, about Wooderson?"

"I was saying, sir, that Wooderson had his first race of the season at Guildford yesterday. The wireless operator told me. Bert Hill has the boy, as you know."

"Yes." Albert Hill was the London middle-distance coach, a former double Olympic champion.

"Wooderson won. He beat Reeve."

"I thought he would."

I was watching the ship's wake. From our perch over the stern the sea was black. The moon had grown and gone behind a cloudbank. Only the lower deck lights were visible in the sea, making reflections at the edges of the wake. I was enjoying the reflections, the way they made patterns streaming through the sea like a giant pony's tail. We fell to talking about Princeton.

"You were right about one thing, Bill."

"What's that, sir?"

"Beccali didn't come."

Bill chuckled. "And you were right, sir, about the Prof's vaccine."

I didn't say anything. After the last massive shot, on the eve of the race, the tendon trouble had cleared up completely. Now it was back again. I was beginning to think the injury might be permanent.

"I was thinking," Bill said. "About the race and Mr Cunningham and one or two other things. You saying it never felt right and being bothered with the wind. You will have to develop a longer sprint at the finish, sir."

"Why?" I waited for Bill to enlarge but he didn't. I was used to this.

"Just bear it in mind, sir. I liked your little stalking trick, I've told you that. You had your ears pricked. You had us on our toes. It's a pity though you had to do it now. You won't be able to do it again, in Berlin. Never mind, we'll think of something. We usually do, don't we? But if you look at the race in terms of profit and loss, you and Mr Cunningham, I'm not sure that his Nibs didn't have the profit and us end up with the loss, if you see what I mean."

"No, I don't."

"I've changed my mind about that gentleman. If you'll just bear with me, sir. Another thing you did. You did it again, you know. You got past him and then slowed up. You slowed right up. Another few yards, Bonthron was catching you."

"I always do it, Bill. I don't know why I do it."

"It's foolish, sir. And I think you *do* know why. You say you're bored. I don't understand that. You'll have to cure yourself, sir. It's dangerous. Now about this other thing that's been bothering you, that second lap."

"I can find reasons, Bill. I still can't find an explanation. You mean, you *know* why Cunningham killed himself off like that?"

"I think so, sir. I've been cogitating. You will recall what you

161

said to those reporters when we first landed? You said you hadn't come all this way just to run against a clock or beat records, only Cunningham. The clock didn't matter, you said – only winning mattered. They thought you was joking. They couldn't understand your attitude. Well, that's it, a question of attitude. The Americans don't think like we do, Mr Cunningham don't neither. So I put it to you, sir. Why does his Nibs go out with his mate Dawson and run a lap as swift as a pudding would creep? To save his world record, that's why. That first lap, sir, took more than 65 seconds. Slowest first lap in history. Then what? He's destroyed any possibility of a record. You can sprout wings, turn into a cannonball if you wants, you can't touch that record of his – it's safe. Next thing, he goes asbestos and runs a lap that is the fastest in history. Second lap, 60 seconds. I put it to you again, sir, why?"

"To win, of course."

"Ah. But put yourself in his shoes. What are you to him? A whippersnapper, a little black smudge away in the heat. 'I wants to know,' says he, 'what little Smiler is made of.' He's running one way and looking another. He wants your measure. When you come up to him and begins your stalking trick, he's got it, hasn't he? You're giving it to him on a plate. He's picking your brain, isn't he? One way and another, sir, you had the stalking of him, but he had the pickings of you. He took us both to the fair. Mind you, it's only a guess."

Guess or not, I thought, it was the only explanation that fitted the facts. "Then he's very clever," I said. "He's cleverer than we are."

We stayed on deck talking. The moon came out between clouds and remained sitting above the horizon like a flattened cheese. We talked about Berlin and I surprised Bill telling him I had already been there in May, for the *Evening News*. Told him what I had found behind the Olympic Village that the Germans were erecting beyond the Havel, beyond the western approaches to the city. Bill seemed both surprised and pleased.

"I was thinking," I said presently. "Is it possible do you think to run a perfect race?"

"What's that, sir?"

"A perfect mile. Bill, we don't really know anything about

162

the human body, do we? Not about its *potential*. I was thinking about it on the ship coming over and then now, just now, something reminded me. I was thinking about a pony I used to have in New Zealand called Gipsy. She was roan and her tail was flecked with white. Looking down at the sea reminded me – I mean, the wake. A ship's wake is perfect. Gipsy was like that."

"I didn't know you rode, sir."

"All the time when I was young. I used to ride Gipsy down a steep sandhill. In some parts of New Zealand the sand is very fine, almost powder, and it's the colour of poppyseed. You don't see it in Europe. I don't know if you can imagine it. Her fetlocks went right in. But it was very steep, the sandhill, almost perpendicular, and at first she couldn't do it. She stumbled. It was quite dangerous, for her – not me. We were high over the sea. But gradually she learned to adjust her stride to the slope and if she didn't hit a rock she used no effort coming down and very little effort lifting the hooves up – gravity was carrying her. In the end she could make a uniform smooth descent at great speed without a falter. She was actually flying. And it was perfect."

"Oh yes, a horse can do it. A horse doesn't know any better."

"But I trained her, Bill. Gipsy was half wild when I got her. She had complete control over her environment. Another thing. She had beauty and style. She knew it too. As if she was saying to all the other ponies, 'Look what I've discovered. Why haven't you thought of it?' "

"Are you – You're not thinking of Berlin, sir?"

"Yes, I was, actually."

Bill was silent.

"I don't see why it shouldn't happen in a race. I mean, what are the Olympics all about? What were the Greeks about if it wasn't that, perfect harmony, perfect movement? Why do I run, Bill? What's it all about?"

"What do you want exactly, sir?"

"I used to think it was a Gold Medal. Well, sure. Who doesn't? We've talked about it often enough. I don't know, Bill. Somehow winning doesn't seem to be enough any more. You're right in a way – as soon as I've won, I seem to lose interest. I'm bored. I've beaten the man, I have a little grin, a little chuckle to myself, and then I slow down. End of episode. Next week

163

another episode. But who remembers the last one? Now a story in a book, a story by Chesterton, for example, that can be perfect. I think a race should be built like a book, to be remembered.

"What I want, Bill, I think, is to win a great race in a fast time without a falter. Yes, without a falter. What do you think?"

"I think a lot of things, sir. I'm not saying it can't be done. On a sunny day at the Ponders End Fête you might bring it off, p'raps. At the Olympics? I'm just an old-fashioned masseur trainer getting old before my time, but I've seen a thing or two in my day and this isn't one of them. Perfection, eh? That's what the Almighty is for, I was taught, not mortal man. I don't know if they run races in heaven, sir, but I reckon the Archangel Gabriel would have his work cut out to do that, even if you gave him a start. Oh no, sir. You're whistling for the moon."

"You don't think that a race is a performance?"

"I'm a bit out of my depth here. Oh *yes*. Of course it's a performance, if you put it like that."

"And if it is a performance, should it be remembered?"

"Blimey. Well all great performances are remembered, aren't they? I dare say if I scratch the old head I might even think of one or two that was, you might say, immortal."

"That's what I'd like, Bill."

12

The idea germinated like an orchid sprouting in the brain. It was such a beautiful thought, such an original thought, that even before the ship docked at Tilbury I began to think that my idea of "a perfect mile" was as good as accomplished, forgetting it was only a brainstorm. Back in London, I returned to digs in Bayswater and walked to the hospital each day where I was due to join Mr Fitzwilliams' firm working as a surgical dresser. I went around in a trance. At night I would lie relaxed in my awake-but-resting state as I had done as a child listening to my father's rhythmic slapping in the bathroom – only now the sounds were translated into gasps of astonishment at my latest discovery. Then came dreams in vivid colours, my invention unfolding before an Elysian stadium with the brightness of a sunburst. This would continue walking to the hospital the morning after. I would sometimes find myself prolonging a dream sequence, standing with a blissful grin on my face at the end of a long bus queue, waiting for a vehicle going in the wrong direction. Everything about which I had thought or read was made to bear directly on the new idea. It would have been more intelligent to think instead about what Sydney Charles Wooderson was up to, Albert Hill's young protégé. Wooderson was now reaching peak fitness running round the streets of Camberwell every night in flannel trousers and a pullover after a day spent clerking in the city; on weekends, with his brother Stanley, Wooderson had for months been walking deep into the Surrey and Kent countrysides, sometimes covering thirty miles in a day. I was due to run against him in the British Championships at White City. But Wooderson at this time was hardly a serious consideration. Serious, in July 1935, were the communiqués reaching the newspaper offices in London from the German Olympic Committee headquarters in Berlin, unfolding the preparations for the coming XI Olympiad. Harold Abrahams and Bevil Rudd kept them aside for me. The first of these illustrated reports appeared at the beginning of 1934; now they were arriving from Berlin in a steady stream. I read them as I had once read the *Boys' Own Weekly* or a new adventure by Rider Haggard, devouring each instalment. Serious too at this time, if only I'd realised it, was a letter that came from Otto Peltzer, also postmarked Berlin. But the envelope when I opened it was empty. There was no letter. There was a number stamped on the envelope; beside it was stamped, "Opened for a check on Currency Regulations". There was no return address. I thought it a bit strange. I stuffed the envelope in a drawer and forgot about it.

Of course in a way, I told myself, Bill was absolutely right. I was whistling for the moon. Perfection might apply to something like gymnastics, say, or a score in marksmanship, or parachuting where you could hit a target dead on. It could apply to a short story. A story has a beginning, a middle and an end – that was perfect in itself. But how could you "perform a race" in a manner never to be improved upon? It was silly. Yet the germ, once implanted, continued to seethe in my brain like a new and irresistible strain of bacteria. Maybe simply because I was working in a hospital where other inventions and discoveries were "in the air", the idea took on an added potency, I don't know, but I did know it was no longer a question of just winning or losing. I was past that, I told myself. I was on a different plane altogether. "The great thing about victory, Jack," Harold Abrahams said when he congratulated me on my return from Princeton, "is that it takes away the fear of defeat."

What could go wrong? I had formulated an original idea. All I had to do was execute it.

My euphoria lasted two weeks. The first doubts came one afternoon after I had spoken with Professor Fleming. We had met in the pool. Alexander Fleming was a terrific swimmer – we often met in the pool in the basement of the Medical School in the lunch-hour and I would envy him his style, the large head and bent nose only visible when he came up to turn. On this day I swam my usual steady four lengths and later after we had spoken I came to his room in the Clarence Wing. The door was open. He was pottering about in an old lab coat, a cigarette hanging from his lips. Fleming's room was half laboratory, half art gallery. He loved visitors. His favourite laboratory game was to grow patterns and designs on agar plates sown with bacteria and from these he would produce as if by magic brightly coloured paintings. Around his bench, filled with capillaries, test tubes, syringes, swabs and Petri dishes, the walls were dotted with these paintings. I had already told him how the experimental vaccine he had made up had saved me for Cunningham and how as I stepped up the dosage I occasionally experienced a reaction, sometimes feverish symptoms, sometimes a rash, sometimes a temporary worsening of pain. Now he asked again about the reaction. I told him it wasn't serious.

"I'd rather have the reaction, sir, than not have the vaccine," I said. "It saved me, it really did."

166

He nodded and produced some phials, a fresh supply he had made up, from the refrigerator. "The question is, Laddie, will it get you to Berlin?"

"I hope so, sir." I couldn't resist adding, "I'm working on something."

"Oh?" he said. He gave me a disconcerting stare. Alexander Fleming had clear blue eyes and an acid stare that reached you from behind square lenses. One of the stories about him was that he had passed his Vivas as a student not by studying hard but by predicting with uncanny accuracy the questions his examiners were going to ask him, but I always felt he did it by staring them into submission. He was doing this to me now.

"Oh?" he said. "Something original?"

And I was tongue-tied. For I had come not just because of the vaccine, I was burning to ask him a question. In 1935 the medical profession was at loggerheads about how micro-organisms worked inside the body. But Fleming had already discovered lysozyme, the ancestor of penicillin, and his discovery of penicillin itself in the room where we were talking was seven years old. Outside St Mary's, however, nobody had heard of penicillin and even inside St Mary's nobody, not even Fleming, had an inkling of what he had accidentally done. Inside Mary's the initial excitement following his discovery had died and Fleming himself appeared to have lost interest in the substance. Nevertheless I had seen him using penicillin in the hospital as a local antiseptic – he used it sometimes to dab wounds; in class he had dinned into us the notion that normal body fluids possessed bacteriological activity; and his belief that the body's natural defences were more effective against germs than chemical antiseptics was something I had vaguely come to accept. There was an aura of the magician about this modest Scotsman with the bent nose and large head who played with microbes, and to me at any rate he was already a great man.

I remember him giving each of us once at the start of a lecture a test tube and asking us to drop into it a tiny nail paring. The tubes, which held a cloudy liquid, were full of bacteria. At the end of the lecture when we looked again the liquid was clear. In forty minutes a natural substance in the body found in the superficial layers of skin had killed off the germs – a perfect solution. He sometimes used the term "perfect solution" and when, the month before, he had drawn off mucus from my infected throat, explaining as he did so his theory about focal sepsis, I had gained an insight into the way an inventive mind works. This had started me thinking about my own needs. I was interested in my body's potential. I wanted to beat the world's best. I was also interested in harmony and I wanted to beat the world's best running in complete and perfect harmony. I wanted to find a way to conquer fatigue so I could win a Gold Medal without strain. Fleming's great search was to find an ideal antiseptic – a way to conquer disease without harming the body. To me this was a search for perfection, and I wanted to pick his brain. I suppose I was looking for a short-cut. But now, under that penetrating blue gaze of his, I couldn't get out what I wanted to say. My thoughts were so woolly and unformed, the question I had come to ask him suddenly seemed ridiculous. So I dithered and tried to draw him out another way – how was it, I said, in the case of penicillin, he had pounced on that particular strain of mould when there were hundreds of other moulds he might have chosen to investigate?

"Just chance, Laddie."

But I already knew from hospital gossip the story – later to become legendary – of how he had "kept the plates". The story was that in 1928 he had been routinely typing a microbe he had grown on a jelly and then, after examining the culture plates, instead of discarding them had kept them in case he wanted to look at them again. Ninety-nine out of a hundred bacteriologists would have destroyed the plates, but he hadn't. For some reason he had kept the plates. A bit later, wandering into his room and picking up one of the plates at random to show to someone, he had found it contaminated by a rare mould that had floated in from Praed Street and round the mould the bacteria had completely disappeared.

"I didn't do anything," he said to me. "Nature makes the penicillium mould. I just found it."

"But you kept the plates," I said.

He wouldn't be drawn out. He swivelled the cigarette between his lips and said, "What's on your mind?"

"All discoveries, sir – I've read it somewhere. Every discovery or invention is said to consist of a number of ideas apparently silly in themselves, but if some original idea is added to them — "

"Yes, yes, Laddie, I've heard that too. Toss in an original thought, rearrange the ingredients a wee bit and out comes a winner. But you mind what Pasteur said? 'Opportunity comes to the prepared mind.' There's a lot in what he says. In fact, there's everything in what Pasteur says. What's up? What are you looking for?"

"I think I'm trying to find a simple way of hitting several targets all at once. A sort of magic bullet."

He didn't say anything. He stared. I blurted out, "How long was your preparation?"

"Let me see." Alexander Fleming stubbed out his cigarette, wiped his lenses on a fold of his old coat and said, "I joined Mary's in 1902 and I became a junior laboratory assistant to Almoth Wright in 1906. I first became interested in the bacteriology of wound infection working with him during the First World War in France in 1914, that was four years. Until 1918. We had a laboratory on top of a casino, you know. Then came some work with the influenza epidemic. Then I got married and caught a cold. I took a blob of the nasal mucus and cultured it and after a bit of playing round found that it contained a natural antiseptic, we called it lysozyme. That was in 1922. That started me thinking. In 1928 I was made Professor of Bacteriology on my birthday and the following month I hit on penicillin. I don't know why you're so interested in the penicillin mould, but anyway. To answer your question: about fourteen years."

My heart sank. He had answered my question and I wished now I hadn't asked it. He had said fourteen years. I had exactly fourteen months.

I was down, as they say, but not out. I was far from discouraged. I hadn't forgotten Otto Peltzer's words to me in New Zealand, the magic "key" of which he had spoken. There was still time to uncover the body's secrets. Obviously no stray mould or thunderbolt was going to descend on me from the blue and blow the murk from my eyes as it had done with Alexander Fleming but, as Bill had said to me on the ship, "We'll think of something, sir." Sooner or later, I told myself, something would turn up. Three days later, at the British Championships on 13 July, it did. It was not at all what I expected.

It was almost a year since I had seen Sydney Wooderson. We had met three times in the previous 1934 season and on the two occasions that mattered I had won, comfortably. Wooderson sat now in the dressing-room at White City with one leg crossed, his straight hair parted at the centre and neatly brushed back above the round spectacles, his features composed. His bag was at his feet. The newspapers said that he lived at home with his parents and walked every day to the office. He might have been going to the office now. But when he stood up I was surprised how compact he was. Previously I had thought of him as puny. Jerry Cornes had once referred to him facetiously as the Running Article (Wooderson was articled to a firm of solicitors). On this day, the day of the final, I had no particular qualms. We exchanged a few words in the dressing-room.

"I wish it was wet," he lisped, almost gloomily. He seemed to have lost none of his diffidence or shyness.

I knew what he meant about the wet. After rain, the red of the cinders dulled and the cinders seemed to compact, binding together. Today, as I came out to defend my British title, the track was dry and cut up with potholes. But I liked this stadium – I liked the excitement of emerging from a tunnel in the middle of the track and I liked the tight turns inside the greyhound racing circuit. I had won my Blue here. I had outwitted a hare on this track. That was in 1932 when the track was relaid and the White City management celebrated the occasion by inviting an Oxford pair, Jim Mahoney and me, to demonstrate Guy Butler's infallible mechanical pace-maker. Jim and I ran it off the track. The "hare" got lost on the turns. There was a technique for the White City turns, just as there was a technique for the final bend of Fenner's at Cambridge – you hadn't to fight to get into them but drop down like a motor-cyclist, then, whoom, you were out.

As we emerged from the tunnel, I looked up and saw the stays in the stand and felt the excitement at once. In places the crowd had spilled forward almost to the edge of the greyhound track. Wooderson wore black. The last time we had met in the 1934 Empire Games I had worn the black of New Zealand and he, the white of England. Now it was reversed – he in the dark uniform of his club, Blackheath Harriers, I in the white of Achilles, and when during the race the crowd began calling his name and a black shape ran past me I thought I was seeing double. It was like chasing my own tail. I had an even stronger impression. Watching his leg muscles which had filled out and were curiously white against the flapping black pants, I had the impression I was following an elderly professor who wore knickerbockers. It was hard to believe Sydney Wooderson was only twenty years old.

Until the spectators surged forward and began calling out, "Come on, Syd!"

He's got a following, I thought.

It had been on my mind to experiment in this race with something Bill had been urging on me for months, namely a longer finish. An opportunity had never come before, and it didn't now. I decided to wait and unleash my usual short overpowering burst at the entrance to the front straight. He was playing into my hands for that.

The bell had sounded. We were entering the back straight. Wooderson ran past me with a sort of hectic flutter, going past Normand, a Frenchman, on one side while I followed on the other. Joe Binks wrote later in the *News of the World*, "Lovelock went with him easily and I thought he was playing to the gallery. He looked at Normand as he went past him and he smiled." Dead right. I was killing myself, thinking Wooderson had miscalculated again – he had a reputation for poor tactics – by moving too soon. I was even beginning to feel sorry for him. But then twenty yards before the front straight just as I was gathering myself to sprint, at my favourite spot, Wooderson fled. I accelerated. Nothing happened. He accelerated, and became a human piston. His elbows jerked, his knickerbockered muscles went up and down. He sailed away from me.

This Running Article.

This articled product of Mother England.

"Come on, Syd!"

"Amid indescribable excitement, Wooderson piled on pace and beat him in his own special style. What a cheer went up for young Wooderson . . ." Joe Binks again.

171

Pandemonium. New British champion.

Wooderson won by seven yards.

"What happened, sir?" Bill kept saying afterwards.

It was so ludicrous that twenty yards from the tape I had burst out laughing and let him go. Bill seemed put out. I said to him, "There was nothing I could do."

I wasn't going to bust myself for a kid.

I congratulated Wooderson. I had no excuses, no regrets. Wooderson pushed a hand through his hair, blinked, lisped a few words, wiped his lenses and managed to look stern, triumphant, modest, shy and wistful all at once. Chiefly he looked puzzled. He seemed just as puzzled afterwards as I felt.

In the tunnel going back to the dressing-room Aubrey Reeve looked up at me in disbelief. Aubrey, who was going out to run in the three-mile event, was bending over the basin being sick. He looked up as I passed, pale green. In the dressing-room one of Wooderson's supporters was waving a Blackheath rosette the size of a cushion and singing:

> *Randy pandy sugardy candy*
> *Buy me some almond rock.*

I showered and changed and waited a few minutes for Harold Abrahams to put his head in, as he usually did. When Harold didn't appear I joined Bill in the stand to watch the rest of the meeting. "That was pathetic, Bill," I said.

Aubrey Reeve won the three-mile event.

"Bit stale today, Bill," I said. "That's all." Bill didn't say anything. He was unusually thoughtful. Later as we were walking to the tube together it crossed my mind that nobody apart from Tommy Hampson had come near me after the race. Normally there would be a string of visitors to the dressing-room or a note would come down from Harold or someone else in the press box inviting me up. "Bad luck, Jack," Tommy Hampson had said. Tommy had come into the dressing-room looking for Wooderson and gone out again. That was all.

On the tube I said to Bill, "Everybody seems to be taking this very seriously."

"Local boy, sir."

"I mean it's not as if it's a sensation or anything like that. It's not a matter of life and death."

"Local boy, sir," Bill said again. "One of us. I've seen it before. I've seen it all before." Bill lapsed into a moody silence.

We changed at Notting Hill Gate and I got off at Bayswater. Bill went on to Paddington. I came out into Queensway and noticed a poster outside the station. "SENSATION – LOVE-LOCK MEETS HIS MATCH". The evening papers were on the street. I bought a newspaper and some lozenges – my lips were dry – and turned down towards my digs, then changed my mind and went into the park instead. The sun was still warm. I stretched out on the grass with my face in the sun and thought how I had underestimated him. Four races. Two to Wooder-son, two to me. Two all. He appeared to have developed a rousing finish, almost a replica of my own. How odd. And how odd to be licked by a boy. I was feeling not sad, just disoriented. Disembodied almost. I still couldn't bring myself to take Wooderson seriously – he was such a busy little runner. His arms were working all the time, almost hitting his nose. I was surprised that Bill didn't see the humour in the situation. And what did he mean by "I've seen it all before"? Anyone would think I was written off, I thought. Then I spread open the newspaper and read the headline, "DOMINATION OF LOVELOCK AT AN END". Even then I didn't understand what was happening.

"They've gone over. That's all, Jack."

"It makes me sick, Arthur."

"It isn't surprising."

"I thought they were my friends!"

"Weathercocks. Fair-weather friends, Jack. You mustn't expect too much from the sports writers."

"I must be naïve."

"A bit sensitive, Jack. You always were a bit sensitive."

"Sensitive?"

"It's the New Zealander in you. Yes, I think you are naïve. You mistake admirers for friends."

"One week they're cheering you, the next they're spitting in your face. Makes me sick."

"People change sides."

"But not overnight. After one race?"

"I've seen it before."

"That's what Bill said. They've written me off, Arthur. Do I look written off?"

"You look to me like a man who's been bottling up fury all weekend. Care for a sherry?"

It was the Monday after the race. I was sitting with Dr Porritt in his Regent's Park flat, smarting from the yelps in the papers – "Britain has found a man to beat J. E. Lovelock" – "outwitted and outpaced" – "Beaten at his own game" – "Where is the famous Lovelock kill?" – "unable to cope with the challenge of a boy" – It wasn't what the critics had written that hurt me, it was the cold-shouldering way they had rallied to the new champion, almost to a man. Even Tommy Hampson had deserted me.

Arthur handed me a sherry and lit his pipe. Ten years older than me, dapper, unflustered, a successful athlete, a successful surgeon, Arthur Porritt epitomised the expatriate New Zealand Rhodes Scholar who had made the adjustment to English society. We had been friends for a long time.

"In a way, Jack, they've paid you a high compliment. You've been making their English athletes appear third-rate for so long, they were beginning to think it might be permanent. Now they've found one of their own and reminded you that you're a New Zealander. Which, thank God, you are. Mustn't blame them for being patriotic." Arthur's baby-blue eyes twinkled. "Look at it this way. Your stature is increasing with every failure."

"What do you mean, *every* failure? I shan't underrate young Wooderson a second time."

"When's your next race?"

"Against Wooderson? In two weeks' time, at Glasgow." I drank my sherry and said, "Well, that settles it. From now on I shall stop reading the newspapers. I shall go my own way."

"You always have, Jack. You always have." Arthur was amused. He said, "I've a spot of news. You know I've been named manager of the New Zealand team for Berlin? Well. You're captain."

"Oh come off it. The team isn't picked yet. You've named me yourself."

"Why not? Manager's privilege. You always said you wanted to carry the flag in Berlin."

"I do, I do. Yes, that's marvellous. How big is our team?"

"It isn't fixed yet. But I should guess – hold your breath. Six."

"Six! Good God. We sent three times that many to Los Angeles."

"Makes you realise where you come from, doesn't it?"

"Six!"

"Including you. You'll probably get tenpence a day expenses and be expected to buy your own embrocation."

"They'll probably send the chaps over steerage."

"Mustn't grumble, Jack. Mustn't grumble. I was talking to Jozsef Sir, the Hungarian athlete – he was here last year with a team from Budapest, travelling third-class rail. 'Why third?' I said to him. 'Dr Porritt,' he said. 'The only reason they sent us third-class, is that there wasn't a fourth-class.'"

We both laughed. Arthur said, "You've been away too long, Jack. You've forgotten what New Zealand is like." New Zealand was so small and out of touch with the rest of the world that we always ended up grumbling about it. Somehow it helped.

"Are we at least sending a newspaper correspondent?"

"For a team of six? We haven't got a national anthem yet. You realise, Jack, don't you, that New Zealand has never won a Gold?"

"I thought we had, Arthur. One. Yes, in 1928 for boxing. Ted Morgan won a Gold Medal in Amsterdam for boxing."

"Boxing doesn't count, I'm talking about athletics. *Athletics*, Jack. I looked up the literature. I was amazed. We've won a bronze medal, that's all – the one I collected in Paris. Nothing else. Zero, Jack. No New Zealand athlete in the history of the Olympic Games has ever won a Gold Medal."

"Well I'm darned."

"You didn't know that?"

"No. It never occurred to me."

"Well, there you are. Amazing, isn't it?"

Arthur poured another sherry and said, "You know, they're expecting five thousand athletes and half a million visitors in Berlin. Extraordinary, what they're doing. They've already got a full-sized Olympic Stadium in Berlin, built by the Kaiser for the 1916 Games which were cancelled. Nothing wrong with it, big Stadium. This chap Hitler comes along and says, Scrap it. He gets an architect to design a Stadium seating 100,000 on top of the old one. When he sees the plans for the new one Hitler says it isn't impressive enough, so they start again. He's a weirdo, this Hitler. They're building now like billy-o, I hear. Pity you can't nip across to Berlin, Jack, and see it. Do a recce."

I didn't say anything. I was keeping what I had found in Berlin a secret, even from Arthur.

Arthur had recently attended a meeting of the International Olympic Committee in Athens. At thirty-five, he was the newest and youngest member of that august body.

"I told you about the last IOC meeting, Jack? What I hadn't realised, until that meeting, was how near the Olympic Movement came a few years ago to collapse, after the 1924 Games in Paris. The incidents! The booing that went on! I was incensed. It was chiefly directed against the Americans – terrible sportsmanship on the part of the French. After that, several countries voted to pull out altogether. It very nearly happened. That would have been tragic, an end to the Games. It's all right now, of course.

"What I didn't tell you is what old Lewald said. Forget now how it came up. I think one of the Americans was spouting about Los Angeles, yes. He called Los Angeles the 'Olympiad of Records'. Up jumps Lewald, the chairman of the German Olympic Committee, and says in that case the 1936 Games will be remembered as the 'Olympiad of Miracles'. I thought Lewald was boasting, but when he outlined some of their preparations – Do you know the Germans are laying on a 3000-kilometre relay across Europe? With torches? All the way from the sacred grove at Olympia? Think of it. A chap called Carl Diem thought it up. Diem's the chief organiser. I met Diem in Los Angeles, little man with a paunch, very like a beaver. He was going round with a notepad noting down everything the Yanks were doing so the Germans could go one better. You can't blame them. Lewald told us they're importing 150 chefs to do the catering. The army is running the show. Some film actress woman called Riefenstahl has got an open cheque from Hitler to film the entire shooting box, every contest. She's invented a camera to shoot the swimming events under the water! But this torch run – David Burghley said to Lewald, 'What if it rains? Won't the flame go out?' "

"Well it will, won't it?"

"No, apparently they've found a way to keep it alight night and day. Three thousand runners lighting one torch from the other all the way to Berlin – pretty terrific, I thought. Things like this, Jack. I was impressed by what Lewald had to say. We all were."

"Sounds terribly exciting," I said. "I take it the Americans *are* coming? I met someone on the boat coming back from Princeton who said it was doubtful. Something about a boycott movement in the States."

"Oh that. That's blown over. It was some unpleasantness about the Jews in Germany – there were rumours that German Jews weren't being allowed or invited to participate. The IOC's looked into it. There won't be any discrimination. As a matter of fact, the American Committee sent a chap specially to Germany to look into it. He saw Hitler, I believe. We heard about it at the meeting. Hitler has given his solemn promise that there will be no discrimination on the field of sport and the IOC is satisfied. The Yanks are quite satisfied too. There's too much national pride at stake for the Germans to try and pull a fast one like that. The IOC's got Hitler under its thumb – *that's* what I wanted to tell you. Count Baillet-Latour, the chairman of the IOC, gave Hitler an ultimatum. He told Hitler that unless the Jewish chairman, Lewald, was allowed to stay, there would be no Games in Berlin. Hitler said all right. He gave in like a lamb. The Germans were going to sack Lewald from their Committee. Exzellenz Dr Lewald. Awfully nice chap. But a Jew.

"Oh, the Americans are coming all right, Jack. In force. Aha, tick-tock. The penny's just dropped. You were rather hoping that Cunningham might miss the bus. Weren't you just?"

I grinned.

"You've got Cunningham on the brain. If I were you, I'd worry about young Wooderson, not Cunningham. Let me say something. Apart from Wooderson, I have a sneaking suspicion that this country – I mean England – hasn't got an earthly of winning a Gold Medal."

"You think Wooderson is that good?"

"All respect to you, Jack. Yes, I do."

"He's an automaton, Arthur."

"He's cool, he's fast, he's collected. What more do you want from a runner?"

Experience, I thought. But I didn't say it.

"So you meet Wooderson again in a couple of weeks?"

I nodded. I was due to run in Stockholm on 26 July and the following Saturday, 3 August, against Wooderson in Glasgow. "It's an invitation event, Arthur."

"Bit soon, Jack, isn't it? To meet him again?"

"I shall regard it as a training run."

"That's what you *say*. I wonder if you realise how much that American trip has taken out of you? You're stale, Jack. Why not give Glasgow a miss, take a rest? Come up fresh for Berlin next season?"

"Arthur. He's only a kid."

"All the same. I'm thinking of Berlin. I'm thinking of what it might do to your self-confidence if you lose again."

I didn't say anything.

"So you won't give it a miss?"

"I can't. I've said I'll go. It's a special handicap event."

"Handicaps? That makes it worse. Who's setting the marks?"

"I am." Arthur looked at me as if I was shooting a line. "They've asked me to suggest the handicaps for the other runners. I'm arranging the handicaps myself."

"Are you? Oh well. In that case it might be all right."

13

I put Wooderson and myself on scratch, naturally. Oh yes, I arranged it all. I worked out the ideal combination for my revenge – ideal for me, ideal for Wooderson. I gave Aubrey Reeve the three-mile champion a start of twenty-five yards,

Tommy Riddell the Scottish champion thirty-five yards, and Reggie Thomas the former English record holder seventy yards. An end to boredom, I thought. A good flick of the whip is what you need, Jack-o. Stimulate the antibodies. I was planning to thrash Wooderson. Massacre him. I arranged the weather too. A mild summer's afternoon, a light breeze – ideal conditions in Glasgow. I arranged everything. I even forecast the result. After the race, I ignored what the newspapers said about it; didn't look at them. There was no need. In the London *Evening News* of 2 August 1935, the eve of the race, I had already described what would happen (I was writing a regular column for the *News*). Before I telephoned my article to London from Glasgow, I walked on the golf course and pondered what I should write. Should I say that Wooderson was a world-beater? That his victory over me a couple of weeks earlier was only a beginning? That to underestimate him for Glasgow – or Berlin – was lunacy? That was exactly what I told my readers. It was a bit cheeky what I wrote. At least it was accurate.

At Glasgow, as at White City, Wooderson ran rings round me. As he surged past me, the sunlight caught his glasses, transforming them into two white shields, and 50,000 people went wild. One of the handicap men tried to help me, I remember – he moved out on the last bend to let me through, anticipating my famous kill. He needn't have bothered. I cracked in the straight. *Again.* It was an exact replica of the British Championships at White City, except that this time I didn't laugh and Wooderson won not by seven yards but by fifteen yards.

It might have been twenty yards.

After this defeat Bill Thomas, Arthur Porritt, common sense and some of the few admirers I had left told me to retire for the season, as Wooderson, very wisely, did. I didn't. I was in no mood to listen. I went on running. I had the usual sickness, I think. Why do I say "I think"? I *know*. It's called depression. Somebody said once that a crown shouldn't be so weak on your head it falls off. Mine was lying in the gutter. I don't know how other people cope in this situation but I had a fit of the mads. I'm not apologising. When I feel mad, I claim the right to feel mad and to hell with common sense. I'm a loner. Sometimes I think it's the New Zealand condition.

I travelled about Europe and went on running. Ran at Zagreb, ran at Budapest. I was supposed to meet the Hungarian champion Szabo in Budapest. Szabo didn't come. I was supposed to meet Beccali at the Student Games in Zagreb. Beccali didn't come either – and I had known this in advance. At twenty-five I was technically still a student and eligible to compete, but at twenty-eight Beccali wasn't. I knew this before leaving London. Yet I still went. I was rash, you think? Behaving like a nut? Well. The Medical School was in recess and nobody in England had invited me home for the summer. What else should I have done?

It wasn't all bad. Travelling, I find, is one of the secret pleasures of life. I'm secretive by nature. I love waking in strange bedrooms in strange lands. I enjoy the feeling of being temporarily disoriented. Things happen to you when you're alone. And I never had the feeling I had as a child when I used to go off to the hills and mope for hours, I never felt I was running away from anything. I took three books with me, *Lost Horizon* by James Hilton, a shocker by Ellery Queen and for some reason instead of Chesterton, my usual travelling companion, I had thrown in a copy of *Alice in Wonderland*. I hadn't read *Alice* since I was a child. Perhaps that explains something about me.

In Budapest, strolling by the Danube under all those cupids outside the Parliament, I met a charming Hungarian, a brunette with shingled hair. Her name was Maya. She was an English student. We spent the day together at St Margaret's Island and I read her passages from the Mad Hatter's Tea Party. At Bellevue we danced half the night. Maya asked me what I would do if I could disappear and pop up in another world like Alice. I said, "Go on running, darling." It was the truth. Next morning I awoke in an unfamiliar bedroom and said to her, "What am I doing here?" At Zagreb three days later I found out. On the day the Student Games opened in Zagreb I lay by the Sava River and fell asleep in the sun. I dreamed I was back in the Fellows' Garden of Exeter College, Oxford, talking to Walter, the college tortoise.

"Hullo, Walter," I said. "You're looking old."

"But I am old. What are you doing back here?"

"I'm looking for my finish."

"Have you mislaid it?"

"No, Walter. You don't mislay a finish, it's not an umbrella. I've lost it."

"Well you won't find it here, Jack."

"I'm supposed to have the fastest finish in the world. It's famous."

"Have you looked in Binsey? I'd come with you but my arthritis is giving me gyp."

"I've been looking for it everywhere, Walter."

"I'd try Binsey if I were you. It's probably fallen down the Treacle Well."

I woke up then. I didn't find my finish in Zagreb either.

In Zagreb I circled a floodlit stadium whose name I didn't know against competitors who didn't matter, looking for something that wasn't there and, strange to say, my depression began to lift. I had gained no experience for Berlin. The opposition was mediocre. But the Slavs applauded – at least, I thought, I'm popular here. The applause fed my vanity and perhaps that helped. I ran in black with the silver fernleaf, my New Zealand colours. Perhaps that helped also. Who knows? Who knows what goes on in the mind of a man who goes on running in circles like a monkey on a string? Somewhere deep inside me there is a joker. When things go wrong either he insists on engineering a breakdown or he plays the fool. Just now he seemed to be playing the fool.

Back in London in September, with winter looming and the left leg far from stable (despite the vaccine, the knee was up and I was limping again), I continued to feel something of value was being hatched inside me. I summoned all the mental detachment I could muster and contemplated the facts. The facts were these.

At Princeton in June I had pushed myself to the limit, my state being such that on the eve of the race against Cunningham Bill had stayed up all night, terrified I would not sleep. Since then, I had met a youthful opponent with no international experience, Wooderson, who made me look like a novice. Wooderson was no flash-in-the-pan. In a sense he demonstrated what I had been telling Bill all along – how seldom I could give of my best in one season. The fact remained, Wooderson appeared to have the stronger finish. Even at my best, people were saying, he could give me ten yards over the last hundred and win. Even Bill, I think, thought this. Common sense dictated that I accept Wooderson's superiority, scrap the 1500 metres event at Berlin and train instead for one of the longer distances. There was still time to do this. It was either that or shut up shop altogether.

Even then I believe I had the ability to suck the full flavour out of an experience. Maybe I was lucky in having finally become aware that the winner of the last race is already forgotten as soon as the next one starts. At all events, returning to London from Zagreb, I continued to walk to the hospital each day and train through the winter as if nothing had happened.

According to my diary, it was an uneventful winter. I swam. I walked. Twice a week I pumped Professor Fleming's vaccine into my body to prop up my wonky knee. I sat my Pathology examinations towards my final B.M. and took a course of instruction in fevers. Elsewhere, as I now know, there was ferment. In America somebody invented the Richter Scale, somebody else "nylon". Sulfa drugs came in. A Scotsman pioneered radar. In Germany the first tape recorder with plastic tape was produced and laws were enacted depriving Jews of German citizenship. The first baby farm to produce an Aryan "super race" was started. Herr Hitler invented ways to expand the German navy, create a Luftwaffe and prepared to send in troops to reoccupy the Rhineland. I knew nothing of this, of what was going on. If anyone had told me in the winter of 1935–6 that Hitler was planning to use the coming Olympic Games as a showpiece, an elaborate stage setting to buy time and mask his intentions for war, I would have laughed in his face. For I too was preoccupied. But in my dreams, you understand.

That winter my dreams returned and I made my discovery.

In fact I did know something, I remember. In November when I went to Oxford to watch the Relays against Cambridge, Godfrey Brown spoke to me. Godfrey Brown was a young Cambridge Blue and an admirer of mine – it was he who coined the phrase "continuous contact running" to describe my particular style of stealing along the ground. "Bespectacled

Brown" we called him. Godfrey was another short-sighted athlete.

I always think of him as the unlucky man' of the 1936 Games. In Berlin in the 400 metres Godfrey drew the outside lane successively in the heat, quarter-finals, semi-finals and final, four times in a row, and as a result his internal clock was broken. In the final he lost to the American Archie Williams by inches. That's by the way. In August 1935 when I was in Zagreb, Godfrey was in Munich running for Britain in a match against Germany. He told me about it in Oxford. "Nice crowd, there, Jack. We were well received. But there had been an incident. We were taken on a sightseeing tour of Munich and we ran into a demonstration. All the traffic had to stop. Up the middle of the street came lorryloads of brownshirts shouting abusive remarks about Jews, ghastly cartoons on the backs of the lorries. Slogans plastered all over them. It was one of these revolting Jew-baiting parades. The people came and stood on the edge of the pavement and gave the Nazi salute. Our guides in the bus turned bright red. We'd been a jolly lot until then, talking and laughing. After that nobody said a word." And Godfrey looked at me as if to say, "What d'you make of that?" I didn't make anything of it. I think I said, "Well it's nothing to do with us."

That winter my dreams were so peculiar and so engrossing that I almost lost the knack of conversing with people. About dreams: I have probably given the impression that my nights were agony. They weren't. At Oxford for example I discovered I could rest just as well lying awake and dreaming in the dark as by sleeping. Nobody could prove to me that my muscles and recuperative machinery didn't go on functioning just as well resting as sleeping. From a neurological and physiological point of view, there was no proof whatsoever. My nights in Oxford were never monotonous and it was the same now in London, that winter before Berlin. I had stopped cursing the darkness. I felt I was one of the select – I was alive when everyone else had died. Night was a magical and mysterious time and I thank God now that the psychiatrist I saw in 1934 didn't try to cure my insomnia. He was a wise bird, that Dr James. I thank Sydney Charles Wooderson too. He was the one who got into my dream in the garden and interrupted it. I can't thank him enough. Syd woke me up.

Sometimes I think that my whole mission in sleeping (or not sleeping) has been to dream. I'm coming to the dream in a minute.

All discoveries are simple once you have made them. But you have to get there. After Zagreb I was in a blind alley. I had to make a leap into the unknown, and I was scared. That was what Wooderson did – he pushed me from the known into the unknown. I could never have got there without him.

I have just remembered what Alexander Fleming said – about his apprenticeship before he hit on penicillin taking fourteen years. I began to dream in 1922 when I was twelve. I made my discovery in a dream at the end of the winter just after my twenty-sixth birthday, in February 1936. That's fourteen years. Amazing.

Almost as amazing as the dream itself.

I am walking through a garden deep under the ground. It is very still and the air smells of pine needles and fresh sand. I can hear wood pigeons. The paths are swept and planted and dotted with neat bungalows. Flags are flying, displaying the five-circled Olympic rings and the red and black swastika. Beyond in a woodland clearing I can see a small lake wreathed in mist and surrounded by larches and silver birch trees; and beyond the lake, a dense forest of pines.

Jutting over the lake is a log cabin built like a bath-house. Male athletes are disporting themselves and diving from the cabin into the misty cold waters. The scene is both strange and strangely familiar.

A voice says, "You're late." It is Walter, the tortoise.

Walter is beside one of the bungalows, examining a rose bush. He says to me:

"What kept you? The other athletes have been here for weeks."

"Is Cunningham here?"

"I expect so."

"It's very cold, Walter. Much colder than in Oxford."

"I should say so! Just be careful where you put your feet – it's damp underfoot. It's because of the sand. Berlin is built on sand. Jack, do you know anything about earwigs? The earwigs are eating the roses."

184

"What you do, Walter, is put crushed balls of paper in the rose bushes at night. In the morning you go round and shake out the earwigs which have crawled inside the paper into a pail of boiling water."

"However did you think of that?"

"I thought it up in New Zealand. My mother was always having trouble with the earwigs. I'm a very inventive fellow."

"I suppose," Walter said, lifting his carapace and scratching an ear, "you want me to show you round?"

"Yes please. This *is* the Olympic Village?"

"Well it isn't Covent Garden. They call it the Village of Peace. That's Hindenburg Haus where they give concerts and film shows. Over there is the dining-room. Goering says it's the best restaurant in town."

"Is Goering here?"

"He was here yesterday. He was showing the American aviator Colonel Lindbergh round. Air-Marshal Goering has been displaying his Luftwaffe, doing stunts – that's one of his planes up there looping the loop. What kept you, Jack?"

"I took your advice and came down the Treacle Well. It's all overgrown."

"Oh yes, I remember. Weren't you looking for something?"

"I still am, Walter."

"Oh look. See? Over towards Spandau. There was a balloon up there yesterday."

"I can't see anything."

"Of course you can't, it's gone. Yesterday there was a balloon up there. It's one of Leni's – Leni Riefenstahl. She's got balloons everywhere fixed to the ground with cameras tied to them. She wants to film the marathon event from the air. That one must have floated off. You know, Jack, there are a lot of funny things going on here."

"It seems very peaceful to me."

"Oh it is, idyllic. I told you, it's the Village of Peace. It was built by the army. When you chaps have gone, the army moves in again."

"You seem to know everything."

"I read about it in a booklet. This place is called 'The Cradle of the German Army' – it's in the booklet. You'll get one if you ask. They're giving them out free. There's probably one in your room waiting for you."

"I wonder if you can help me, Walter."

"I'll try."

"It's about my finish. You know I've lost it. The thing is, can I do without it?"

"It's a bit unusual, Jack. What would you use instead?"

"That's the problem."

"How about something heroic? Something big like Wagner? They're very fond of Wagner round here."

"I wish you'd be serious for a minute. What I need, I think, is a magic bullet, something that goes round biffing things but isn't harmed itself."

"It would have to be something new, wouldn't it?"

"The thing is, I'm on the threshold. I can feel it. I feel I'm right on the threshold."

"I'll think about it. Oh hullo, Max . . . That was Max Schmeling the boxer. Max is always out here, he's very popular. Max has just knocked out Joe Louis at Madison Square Garden in New York. Herr Hitler is absolutely thrilled. Do you want to see the track?"

"Please. Wait a minute. Is that a stork? How did that get here?"

"Well storks are traditional, you know. The English asked for them. No German village, said the English, is complete without a stork. So the Germans have provided storks. They've thought of everything. That's the French team over there."

"What are they doing?"

"Practising the Nazi salute for the opening ceremony. It's the new salutation. Everyone has to do it. I can't manage it, I'm afraid. And over there – you see the log cabin? That's the sauna. Those are the Finnish baths, specially made for the Finns. The American athletes went down and gate-crashed them. Now they've all got colds."

"Has Cunningham got a cold?"

"No such luck. Here we are, this is the practice track. It is an exact copy of the track at the Reichssportfeld. There's Cunningham."

"But – who are all the others?"

"Well, you know Wooderson. And Harold. Harold Abrahams

186

is talking to Alec Burns, I think. That's Jesse Owens giving autographs. They call him the Tan Streak, he's said to be America's sharpest weapon. Wooderson told me something funny. Wooderson was invited to see one of the Nazi 'baby farms', but he didn't go. Alec Burns went instead. Alec was shown all over. They're purely for breeding purposes. Alec said they'd invited him to participate.''

"Is Peltzer here?"

"Who?"

"Otto Peltzer. He wrote to me but the envelope was empty when I opened it."

"Never heard of him. By the way, I should steer clear, Jack, of that chap in uniform."

"The little chap in the shiny boots with the eyebrows?"

"Yes. His name is Tschammer."

"He looks like a riding instructor. Is he important?"

"Important! Tschammer came up to me yesterday when I was watching Earle Meadows practising. He said to me, 'The American athletes are unsportsmanlike. They are behaving in a very un-German manner.' 'How is that?' I said. 'Well look,' he said. 'There's one of them using a pole to get over the high jump.' "

"But, Walter. Earle Meadows is a pole vaulter!"

"That's the point. Tschammer doesn't know the difference. His full name is Reichssportführer Hans von Tschammer und Osten – he's Hitler's Sport Leader. He's the Minister in Charge of Sport. Herr Hitler appointed him. Apparently Tschammer's brother was meant to get the job, but Herr Hitler made a mistake."

"Is it true, Walter, that the Germans have installed television in the Village?"

"Quite right! Television! You'll be able to see your race on the screen the same night. Talking of films, I don't see Leni anywhere. Nurmi is here somewhere. That's the British ambassador being shown round, over by the long-jump pit. Mr Phipps. Sir Robert Vansittart of the Foreign Office is with him. And the one showing them round is Herr Ribbentrop. Herr Ribbentrop made his money out of champagne. He's the new German ambassador to London."

"They seem very pally."

"I'll tell you something about Herr Ribbentrop. He's throwing a big party at his villa in Dahlem. If you win, you might get an invitation. Ah. There she is."

"Who?"

"Leni. Leni Riefenstahl."

"Which one is Leni Riefenstahl?"

"You see the old gentleman in national costume being photographed? He's holding an olive branch. Leni is wearing a jockey cap and sweater. She's the young woman in the background directing the cameraman."

"Wow."

"She used to be an actress. You should see what she's done to the Stadium. Her speciality is low-angled camera shots – she's dug trenches for the cameramen all over the Reichssportfeld. Of course they're concealed. The place is bristling with trenches. She wants to film your race."

"Wow!"

"Now you watch it, son. Leni is bespoke. You know what they call her? The Imperial Crevasse. She is said to be very close to Herr Hitler. Incidentally, the old gentleman with the olive branch is Spiridon Loues. He's Greek."

"It can't be, Walter. Surely he's dead? Spiridon Loues won the marathon in Athens back in 1896!"

"That's the one. He's nearly as old as I am. Mr Loues is the guest of the German Olympic Committee and the olive greenery is from the sacred grove in Olympia. It's very appropriate. Tomorrow he will present the olive branch to Herr Hitler at the opening ceremony."

"I think I'll sit down for a moment. My head is spinning."

"But you haven't seen anything yet. Buck up. Half the crowned heads of Europe are here."

"It's too much to take in, Walter. It's like a dream. I must sit down and rest before my race."

Now I am running through a forest of pines. It is early morning and the Village of Athletes is asleep. There is an aroma of pine needles and rotting bark. The forest floor is broken and carpeted with needles over wet sand, the boles of the Kiefern trees grow straight out of the sandy soil and the forest envelops me like a cloak. I am running between the boles of the Kiefern watching my shadow and inhaling the pine-scented air. I pass a woodcutter's cottage, the smoke curling upward from the chimney. A deer starts up. Further on beside a snow-break firewood is roped together and stacked in bundles. I find a hollow where the snow has melted and curl up in the hollow to rest. It is very still and peaceful and all the time I am resting in the hollow I have the feeling I am protected, as if someone is watching over me.

The scene changes and I am in a tunnel. I emerge from the tunnel into a granite Stadium. I sense the excitement of the Stadium. Somewhere a choir is singing. The air is suddenly full of the beating of pigeons' wings and for a moment the sky is blotted out. Now I can see flags on the ramparts. Below on the vast floor of the Stadium are more flags carried by marching men, all the men and all the flags of all the nations in the world. Spiridon Loues holds up the Greek flag. Walter is carrying the Union Jack. I say to Walter, "I can't see the New Zealand flag anywhere." Walter says, "That's because you're carrying it." Now a runner appears, all in white. He is blond and Aryan and carries a torch. The Stadium rises in a tumult. "It is Fritz Schilgen," Walter says, "the torchbearer." As the torchbearer runs past the Tribune where Hitler is seated and begins to circle the Stadium, I drop my flag and give chase. "Faster," Walter shouts. I am running as fast as my legs will carry me, but it's no good. Every time I try to pass the runner in white I fall back exhausted. At the fourth attempt he turns and I see that he is wearing glasses. He pauses and says:

"I wish you'd stop following me." It isn't the torchbearer. It is Sydney Wooderson.

"I'm sorry, Syd. It's a habit I've developed."

"Well, give over. Try following Cunningham instead. How big are you, Jack?"

"I'm five foot seven and I weigh 133 lb."

"Well I'm five foot six and I weigh less than that. If it comes to a fight between you, me and Cunningham, he'll eat us both."

"Syd. Why are we standing here in the middle of the Stadium?"

"It isn't Thursday, you know."

"Isn't it? I thought the final was on Thursday."

"Today's Wednesday. I'm waiting for the heats to start. The final isn't till tomorrow."

Now I am racing again. I have overtaken Beccali and am trying to get past Cunningham, but there is a runner in white in the way. From the back it looks like Wooderson, but it isn't Wooderson. It's someone else. Where is Wooderson? Why isn't he running? People are calling my name. "Come on, Jack!" Harold Abrahams is calling. Godfrey Brown is calling. Sydney Wooderson is calling. "Jack! Jack, come onnnn!" I don't understand it. I don't understand it at all. Why is Sydney Wooderson calling my name?

Silence.

From the granite bowl of the Stadium rises a single gasp.

I woke up crying.

"What was that?"

"It's me."

"What did you scream for?"

"Sorry, Chook. I was dreaming again."

"What are you doing?"

I was sitting on the end of my bed in Westbourne Grove trying to stifle the tears. Tears were spilling down my cheeks. I had woken one of my flat-mates, Chook Henley, an old New Zealand friend. Chook said, "What the hell are you doing?"

"I can't stop crying. I'm so happy, Chook. Chook, I've seen clean through it. *Clean* through."

"What? What?"

"I've made the most – it's stupendous, stupendous. I've made the most stupendous discovery. I've just sprinted the whole of the last lap in Berlin."

"Eh? Oh for God's sakes. Go back to bed, it's three o'clock in the morning."

14

I stood at the window. I didn't go back to bed after my dream. I stood at the window looking over the area on to the street and I thought, That's it. That's the answer. I was breathing rapidly, my breath coating the inside of the pane. I was shivering. I couldn't see out properly. I had forgotten to take down the milk bottles. I must tell Bill, I thought. Presently I thought, Forget it, he'll think I'm crazy. Anyway it can't be done. I pulled on a jersey and went down two flights of stairs into the bathroom. I lit the gas jets and ran a bath. I lay in the bath until the house woke up to go to work. Then I thought, Why not?

If it could be done in a dream, why not in reality? Nobody had ever sprinted a final lap in Olympic competition before – at least, I didn't think so. That evening, when I returned from the hospital, I took out my notes and records and began to pore over them.

I found that not only had it not been done before, nobody appeared to have attempted anything remotely like it. The most spectacular finish in the annals of the 1500 metres, I saw, was Arnold Strode-Jackson's at Stockholm in 1912, but a staccato burst of 40 yards only. Larva's final sprint over Ladoumègue at Amsterdam in 1928 was shorter still. Sheppard's sprint seemed to be the longest – in 1908 Mel Sheppard of America had launched a winning spurt 100 yards from the tape. Was that the ultimate? What about Nurmi? I saw that in Paris in 1924 Paavo Nurmi had covered the last lap unopposed; he was so far ahead he just had to dawdle round. Nurmi didn't need to sprint.

I had forgotten Beccali. At Los Angeles in 1932 Beccali had accelerated and shot the field from perhaps 120 yards. OK, 120 yards then. That appeared to be the absolute limit.

Outside it was raining. I turned up the gas fire and went back to the collapsible card table where I was working. My eye fell on a report I had copied out, dated 1925. In an address at Southampton given in 1925, the physiologist Professor A. V. Hill had said, "The most efficient way in which to run a race is that of uniform speed throughout." This theory, the so-called even-pace theory, had been adopted as an iron rule by Wooderson's trainer Albert Hill. It was one of Bill Thomas' hobby horses too. It was also, I knew from experience, a totally sound theory. But did it negate variations, massive variations, or the sort of variation I was contemplating?

At what speed, it occurred to me to wonder, will my opponents in Berlin be travelling over the last lap?

I picked up a folder and saw that half a century earlier an Englishman, W.G. George, had run a final lap in 65 secs. That was in August 1886 when Walter George, a Victorian phenomenon with a drooping moustache, ran a mile as a professional in under 4 mins. 13 secs., a time that was hardly scratched until Nurmi's performance in 1923. And even Nurmi didn't break 4:10. I had spread my notes and journals beside me on the bed. As I worked through them, I realised by how little Walter George's ancient time of 4 mins. 12.75 secs. had been reduced in the intervening fifty years. Beginning with Nurmi in the twenties, then Ladoumègue, then me a few years later, the mile had been whittled down and whittled down. But only gradually. Only very gradually. And exactly the same appeared to be true of the shorter Olympic distance, the 1500 metres. Strode-Jackson's time at Stockholm in 1912 was 3 mins. 56.8. Twenty years later in 1932 Beccali had not broken 3 mins. 50. Beccali's winning time at Los Angeles was 3 mins. 51.2. That was equivalent to an annual improvement of only a quarter of a second – or two yards. The Olympic times were almost static.

It's like nibbling an orange, I thought. Nobody's taken a proper bite.

I picked up another folder containing sectional times and began to analyse final laps. Final lap? Walter George, 65 secs. Paavo Nurmi, no better. Jules Ladoumègue, 61 secs. Who had broken the one-minute barrier? I had. I had done it twice – at Iffley in 1932, at Princeton in 1933. Who else? In first-class competition, hardly anyone. The fastest last lap in history seemed to belong to John Paul Jones of Harvard, a time of 58.2

secs. That had been recorded in 1913. I checked the figures again and blinked. That *can't* be the limit? I thought.

In August 1935 I had written in my journal, "I am unable to see where, as our knowledge of physiology and psychology increases, there can be any limit to the human capacity for speed."

Now I turned to a new page and wrote, "It seems absurd that today in February 1936 after twenty-three years John Paul Jones' time of 58 seconds for a final lap should still be the ultimate. Yet, apparently, it is.

"A time of 58 seconds represents a speed of less than 16 miles per hour which sounds slow and, on the same basis, what I am now contemplating in miles per hour is very little faster. But in fact, in performance, the dream-lap I am contemplating represents a gain of some twenty to twenty-five yards. According to forty years of Olympic history, this is an impossibility.

"Common sense dictates it is crazy to attempt to burn oneself out in a final sprint of this nature. But it is crazy only up to the point where one knows one cannot carry on."

So who – I did some calculations – who did that leave in the race? Assuming it could be done. Who did it cancel out? On paper it appeared to cancel out everyone except five runners – Cunningham, Wooderson, Beccali, Bonthron and Ny. They were the only men, it seemed to me, capable of breaking 58 seconds.

I did a further calculation. I looked at the performances of these five men and allowed for a maximum improvement under ideal conditions. I translated their projected speeds into feet per second, set these figures against what I was contemplating and transferred the result to the physical layout of the Berlin Reichssportfeld. I drew a scale plan of the track, which I had measured when I was in Berlin, and marked the start of the race. The start was on a bend. At this moment I had a fright, realising that in Berlin the actual last lap and the *psychological* last lap were not the same. I saw that the difference could be important. I made some coffee, wrapped a rug round my knees and began on a fresh set of calculations. I worked late, filling sheet after sheet of notepaper. It was after midnight when I got up. I got up from the table feeling I had survived a horrible examination. But I felt I had passed. At that moment almost twenty-four hours after my emergency waking dream I was absolutely certain of it.

It was 27 February 1936. I had five months.

As it turned out, I had less than two months. I realised it the next day. Reason told me that if I was going to stake everything on a mad gamble, I had better "do the experiment". That meant a race and preferably one in which Wooderson was not competing. I looked at the athletic calendar and saw that the first likely date wasn't until 13 June, a Kinnaird Trophy meeting at White City. On that day there was a three-mile event. I would have to settle for that. The Games were due to open in Berlin on 1 August, six weeks later.

I hesitated to face Bill with what I was planning. On the one hand I was bursting to tell him. I needed the seal of Bill's approval. On the other, I feared a rebuff. Bill's doubts were sometimes better than my certainties. So I waited, undecided.

In March Bill came to London. I said nothing. Early in April he came again. Still I waited. Then everything went haywire. I had hoped to begin hard training in April, May at the latest, but at the beginning of April my hospital duties were switched. On 6 April I began an intensive maternity course at Queen Charlotte's Hospital that lasted three weeks. Back at Mary's in Paddington, I began a two months' stint "on District", going out with black bag, gloves, umbilical string, a supply of tow and female catheter to deliver my first babies. Absorbed as I was with the labour of my own dream-child, I had forgotten, if I had ever known, what the business of real birth was like. I remember that in this period, 26 June, the New Zealanders landed in London – I had been on duty continuously for fifty hours with three hours' sleep. Cecil Matthews, a member of the New Zealand team, told me later I had arrived on St Pancras Station platform to meet them wearing an Achilles blazer, a tie and a pyjama jacket. I seemed to be perpetually tired. There was no on-call system at Mary's, so you could be woken at any hour day or night. As soon as the night porter touched my door I was awake. But very often I would get outside the hospital and ask myself, Now am I coming back from a case or am I *going*? Paddington at this time had a population of 500,000

194

served by one hospital – ours – and in the crowded back streets families were living in tenements often six and eight to a room. Sometimes the father was drunk. I recall one delivery in a poor street off the Edgware Road. The electricity failed and the district nurse was held up. The eldest child held a lantern. One of the windows was boarded over with cardboard; there was no hot water and I delivered the baby on to a sheet of newspaper which was the cleanest item in the room. Usually we cleared the father and the children out and put them on the landing while the delivery was made; then, my job done, I would subside on a chair and fall fast asleep, to be woken again by the arrival of the midwife or the jubilant yelps of the children as they swarmed back into the room. As medical training the experience was superb; as Olympic preparation, heart-breaking. I thought of Wooderson coming home from the office each night at five and training monotonously, running through suburban streets, such a drab life, such a dull unbroken routine. Such bliss! How I envied him that routine. I managed to compete twice in May. After one race, a charity mile at Imber Court in Surrey, Harold Abrahams said to me jokingly:

"One of these days, Jack, you're going to do the impossible."

"How do you mean?"

"You're going to fall asleep during a race."

"Pardon me, Harold. I have just done so."

I had succeeded in finishing third. Halfway through the race my lids felt heavy and I had closed my eyes for an instant. When I opened them again I was careering off the track at an angle, running full tilt towards the spectators. I had actually dozed off.

Afterwards I had a long talk with Harold about Berlin. I was so demoralised after the race I told him I was thinking of chucking the 1500 metres and concentrating on a longer distance.

April became May and May, June. Bill came and went. Still I waited. Bill was worried about my knee. It was still unstable, despite the vaccine, and never quite free of pain. The toxins had remained in my system. All I could do now was pump in more and more dead organisms, never less now than a million organisms at a time, and hope for the best. I wasn't panicking, but I was beginning to drive myself, using what spare time I

195

had to extend my interval running from three-quarters of a mile to two, three and sometimes five miles at a stretch.

On 26 May I attended the annual dinner of the British Olympic Association at the Dorchester Hotel. It was a glittering and formal occasion and I was half-expecting to drop off during the speeches. But then the chief guest, Exzellenz Dr Lewald, the chairman of the German Olympic Association, came on. When he spoke the atmosphere changed. I found myself banging my fork against my plate and crying "Bravo" with all the rest. Dr Lewald spoke of the coming "Festival of Peace" in Berlin, he spoke of Hitler's enthusiasm for the Olympic ideal, and at that the room burst into spontaneous and prolonged applause.

Yet I have a memory of Harold Abrahams who was sitting nearby with Douglas Lowe – of Harold clapping politely but without his usual enthusiasm – and thinking how strange this was, for Harold was a fervent supporter of the Olympic movement and had told me before the dinner that the BBC had commissioned him as chief commentator to report the events live from Berlin. At the dinner Harold seemed subdued. I put it down to approaching middle age – the former Olympic hero who could no longer recapture the spark of electricity and anticipation that I was experiencing.

One other speaker received an ovation that evening. This was Lord Portal, chairman of the British Olympic Association. Lord Portal replied to criticism in the *Manchester Guardian*:

"Now one leading newspaper says it is opposed to British participation in these Games. The *Manchester Guardian* is demanding sanctions against Germany.

"Surely," Lord Portal said, "we should not consider such things as sanctions in sport? Here we have a wonderful country offering hospitality and guaranteeing everybody fair treatment. We shall go to Germany with the esprit de corps and the confidence of all right-minded Englishmen behind us. In these times of anxiety and trouble, might we not all welcome the Games as a happy augury of peace for Europe?"

Two hours later I was back on duty at the hospital. But the excitement and feeling of well-being generated by the dinner was still with me three days later. I was walking up Regent Street to meet Bill. I noticed a sign in the German Tourist

Office saying that all Lufthansa flights to Berlin for July and August were sold out. I could contain myself no longer and that night, after training, brought Bill back to the Fountains pub in Praed Street and told him what it was I was contemplating.

"A whole lap, sir?"

I nodded.

"You wants to sprint a whole last lap?"

"It's a new concept, Bill. A completely new concept."

To my surprise Bill accepted it. There was no argument, no row as I had feared. Bill wiped his lips, swallowed his beer and said:

"You'll have to test it first."

"You think I can do it?"

"I look at it this way, sir. The cardinal rule is never begin your final dash until you know you're within sprinting distance of the tape. Now. Your normal sprint is 60 to 80 yards, that's how you've won all your races. I've been at you to make it longer, haven't I? – maybe 100 yards. Maybe 150 yards. But you've gone asbestos, you have. You wants to do the blooming lot. It's drastic."

"Can I do it?"

"Drastic, sir. It's very drastic."

"But can I do it, Bill?"

"If you – " Bill pondered. He put down his glass. His broody eyes got bigger. "If you can produce the form at Berlin you know you're capable of, sir, yes – I believe you can."

"My God," he added. "I like it."

A moment later Bill said, "But how will you test it?"

"I thought on Saturday week."

"The Kinnaird meeting?"

"Yes. I'll try it in the three-mile event."

"Why not the mile?"

"Because Wooderson will almost certainly choose to run in the mile. The trouble with Wooderson, Bill, he seems to produce a crisis every time he starts. I'm not ready for Wooderson yet." I showed him a schedule of races I had planned, starting with a three-mile event and ending with a two-mile race on 25 July, the day before we expected to leave for Berlin.

Bill nodded. He seemed puzzled.

"It's confusing, sir. There's hardly a mile event in it. You're

197

avoiding Wooderson, are you? I suppose it's deliberate, you wants to hide your intentions? I can see that. But this race on Saturday week at White City, three miles, and you try and bust yourself on a last lap, don't think they won't tumble to it. They'll tumble all right."

"But they won't know what I'm thinking."

"They'll time you every inch of the way. Mind you, if you stick to this schedule you've worked out, they'll think you're a variety turn. So who's to know? Who's to know what's on your mind?"

"The only other chance to try it, Bill, is at Birmingham on 25 July. That's too late."

"I can see that. Seems you've got no option, sir." Bill swallowed his beer and expelled a satisfied burp. "Saturday week it is."

The track at White City was wet that day after heavy rain. June 13. Jack Powell won the half-mile. Wooderson as anticipated ran in the mile and won easily. I ran in the three-mile. Three hundred yards from the tape at White City there is a pole-vault pit, corresponding to the 1200-metre mark in Berlin. At this point after eleven laps I left the bunch and began a long sprint which I managed to hold almost to the end. It wasn't a total sprint but it felt that way. Bill timed my last full lap at under 60 secs.

"Let me check that, sir." A little later Bill came back saying, "The press box is buzzing, sir. They're all talking about that lap."

A pity, I thought. It couldn't be helped.

Bill showed me his notebook. He had jotted down Wooderson's last quarter, and Powell's. "Wooderson, sir, 60 seconds. Powell, last quarter, 59.2. As against you, sir, 59.4."

So Wooderson and Powell running over much shorter distances had done no better?

It looked promising.

That week I swapped my roster on District and took a break. I went up to Oxford and lay about like a tourist. I walked, jogged a bit, swam, sun-bathed at Parson's Pleasure, danced at night. I talked with Bill every day. Once at Iffley Road I broke into a sustained finish in simulation of what I was planning for

Berlin. I felt groggy afterwards and told Bill I wouldn't attempt it again until the race itself. On the day.

"But you must, sir."

"I know what I'm doing, Bill. And don't," I said – with six weeks to go I was starting to become paranoid – "don't breathe a word of it to anyone."

"What about Doc Porritt?"

"No. Not even to Arthur."

After one session at Iffley Road, Bill said to me:

"You wouldn't consider changing that schedule?"

"Why?"

"You'll get on the train for Berlin exhausted."

"I know."

"You've got a race every Saturday until the day we leave, sir, and on some Saturdays, two races. And solid training every afternoon, you reckon, every blooming day. Where's the sense in that? You'll get on that train at Victoria Station like a Lyons bun, dead stale. *Dead* stale, sir."

"Yes."

"You've thought about that?"

"Yes, Bill. It's what I want."

We trust what feels and smells right. A couple of years earlier at Princeton, I had trusted to the reassuring smell of bodies in the dressing-room. That day everything had smelled right. Now I had gone past that. A pattern, as of discarded jigsaw pieces acquiring new shapes in the mind, was beginning to formulate itself from what I had already discovered. I couldn't put it into words. It had to do with understanding the way my body worked, with staleness.

"You say that, sir. But you don't give me any reasons. It's a feeling you've got, is it?"

"Just a theory, Bill. I can't explain it."

The following Saturday, after the Southern Counties events at Chelmsford, Bill brought up the subject again. On that day, 20 June 1936, I chose a short half-mile distance, still avoiding Wooderson. Wooderson stuck to the mile. After my race I sat in the stand and watched – I was rooting for Jerry Cornes against Wooderson. Reggie Thomas, the former triple champion, was also in the race. After two laps Wooderson went ahead of them both. Soon he was twenty yards clear. A lap from home by the

1200-metre mark I watched Wooderson's busy figure become busier than ever and my throat went dry. At the finish he was forty-five yards in front. When the time was announced, Wooderson was cheered to the echo. At one stroke he had knocked my 1932 Iffley record for a six, run the fastest-ever mile in British history and become, so Harold Abrahams wrote the next day in the *Sunday Times*, the most talked-of miler in the world.

"Only twice in the whole history of athletics has Wooderson's time been beaten in Europe," Harold wrote.

A week before this *The Times* had speculated, "One wonders if Lovelock, like Nurmi, might not now adopt a policy of lengthening the race to suit his years." Watching young Wooderson, I was starting to wonder too.

It was Wooderson's last lap that did it.

Afterwards Jerry joined me in the stand. He said, "The press boys are going berserk, Jack. Even Harold. Harold's predicting a world record for Wooderson at Berlin."

"It won't happen," I said. "Not in the Olympics. Not in the Olympic mile. Olympic record, maybe; world record, no. It's never happened yet."

"Try convincing Harold, old fellow."

Until then Harold, almost alone of the critics, had remained my supporter. I had never questioned his allegiance. I didn't now. We were sitting in the old wooden stand, to one side, with Bill, Arthur Porritt and a few old faithfuls like Sandy Duncan the long-jumper. Sandy, a New College man and double Blue, was one of the few wholehearted admirers I had left.

Jerry said, "Where does he get it from, Jack? I mean his power. What is the secret of Wooderson's power?"

"Oh come on, you two," Sandy said. "He's smaller than either of you. He's just a rather funny little man going along wearing spectacles."

"Good point," Jerry said, and we all laughed.

"Isn't it strange," I said, "the way camps form? Here we are, and there they are." Wooderson had entered the stand with his trainer, Albert Hill. They had immediately become the focus of an excited swarming crowd. I said to Jerry, "I feel quite out of it."

"What about me?" Jerry hooted. "You realise, Jack.

They've brought me back from Africa just to run for England in Berlin? Must prop up the Motherland, mustn't we? I arrived a week ago and already I'm redundant. That rather funny little man, as you call him, Sandy, has just made me utterly, absolutely and powerfully redundant. Re-dun-dant."

And on grass, I thought. Wooderson's record run – he had broken 4 mins. 11 secs. – had been recorded on an English grass track.

"Cheer up," Sandy said. "I'll tell you a story that will tickle you, Jack. Remember Sam? Our mutual friend Sam Ferris? Sam was out East the other day, Baghdad I think he said, poking about in the markets. Sam wanted to buy a carpet. Gets into conversation with an Arab carpet-dealer, wizened-up old fellow smoking a water pipe. Age about two hundred. Sam tells him he's an athlete. Then, bang. 'Sir. Please. Can you tell me, when is the next Wooderson-Lovelock duel to be?' Just like that. Not bad, eh."

"Not bad!" Jerry hooted with laughter. Jerry said to me, "As a matter of interest, when are you going to meet him?"

"In three weeks, Jerry." On that day, 11 July, Wooderson would be defending his British title at White City. The British Olympic selections would be announced the same weekend.

A hand touched my arm. Bill was standing there. "Might I have a word, sir?"

As soon as we were out of earshot Bill said, "I thought we had agreed you wouldn't meet Wooderson that day, sir."

"Well, I need one hard race before Berlin. I can't go on avoiding him for ever."

"You don't have to run in the same event."

"But I want to, Bill. I want to meet Wooderson. I'm not changing the schedule, if that's what you mean."

"I thought you were, sir. Then what's this Doc Porritt has been telling me? That you've gone and entered for the three-mile race at Berlin – the 5000 metres?"

"I told you, Bill."

"You told me as a joke, sir."

"Don't you like the idea?"

"I'd be a lot happier if I knew what you was up to. No, sir. I do not like the idea. And Dr Porritt doesn't neither."

"It's been in the papers."

"Speculation. There's always speculation in the papers. You're not serious about the longer race, sir?"

"Perfectly serious. I wrote to the New Zealand selectors and asked if they would enter me in both events at Berlin, and they have done so."

"But sir. You're a specialist *miler*!"

"Nevertheless. That's what I have done."

"You're swinging."

"Swinging?" I grinned. "I've got a swinging chemistry, Bill."

It wasn't like me to be sarcastic, and it was even less like Bill. "I suppose," he said, "that's another of your pet theories you won't tell me about. Like staleness." He walked off.

"Secrets?" Jerry said when I rejoined him.

"Oh, it's just Bill. You know what Bill's like."

Jerry and I sat on talking about old times. I saw Bill reappear between the deckchairs set out below and walk slowly round the track and then stop in a dismal loitering sort of way. He had his hat pulled down hard. He hadn't moved when the meeting ended and Jerry stood up to go. Bill had stationed himself on the far side just off the curve, by the 1200-metre mark; he seemed to have taken up residence there, whether by design or accident I couldn't tell.

"Run?" Jerry said. "Little run-run? Come for a trot for old times' sake."

"I'd love to, Jerry. But I'm waiting for Harold. He's invited me down to Rickmansworth for the night."

"Oh?" Jerry made a face and started to say something, then changed his mind and went.

In other circumstances Harold and I would have enjoyed each other's company enormously. I had been looking forward to the visit, but on the train going down to Rickmansworth where Harold lived we barely spoke. I was feeling sorry for myself, brooding on Wooderson and my own performance that day. In the half-mile event I had been beaten by Jack Powell. Wooderson's coup in the mile had left a scared rabbity feeling in my stomach. Harold too seemed preoccupied by something.

"Adolphe is coming down," Harold said, "if he can manage it."

"Oh good. Splendid."

When we arrived Harold disappeared into the study, I presumed to telephone his weekly article to the *Sunday Times*. Adolphe and another of Harold's brothers were there. After dinner Adolphe and I sat together and discussed a number of medical things. Adolphe spoke to me of a 1921 discovery by Otto Loewi, the man who, after a dream, had carried out a crucial experiment on the nerves of the autonomic system. I told Adolphe something of the theory I was evolving on "staleness". Adolphe listened and said:

"The Chinese, Jack, say you should think of the body as a hollow vessel through which the air passes endlessly. You seem to think of it as a vessel capable of storing up fatigue, is that it?"

"Subconsciously, yes. In the sympathetic system. And then releasing it."

"Releasing what?"

"The nervous energy. I mean the energy needed for a peak performance."

"Interesting. You're imagining a kind of general 'sleep' within the autonomic system, the nervous anticipation stifled or smothered? Locked away? Then, at a given moment, the subconscious is unlocked and the adrenalin is released in a great splurge. Like turning on a tap?"

"In my case, yes." I grinned. "Something like that."

We were still discussing the question after the others had gone to bed. Afterwards, in my room, I wrote in my diary:

Upset Bill today at Chelmsford. I wish I wasn't so secretive. Yet I can't discuss these things with him. I'm still groping – towards perfection, towards something. Adolphe *very* amused when we talked tonight. It's the first time I've discussed my "sleep" concept with anyone. Adolphe very knowledgeable, an authority on the body as a Human Machine. He listened to my theory then very quietly, very patiently pointed out all the factors I had overlooked. But I feel that I'm right.

I also think I'm right to continue with Professor Fleming's strep. vaccine, even though it doesn't seem to be doing the knee any good. I can't seem to rid myself of the pain. Sometimes the inflammation goes altogether. Then, for no reason, it's back. It's maddening. It's like a chronic toothache. I think I've torn a tendon. It isn't serious enough for an operation, but irritating enough to wear me down. Adolphe thinks that it is a low-grade, persistent and deep-seated infection, possibly from the throat, but that to continue after twelve months injecting more of the same bacteria into myself is useless and even dangerous. I said, "I've put my faith in Fleming." Adolphe said that I'm "clutching at straws".

Six weeks to go. Twenty-two laps to Berlin. The scared rabbity feeling is growing, but that's good I think. It forces the concentration. The human capacity for sustained concentration isn't infinite, and I know how easily I can be thrown or upset. If *only* I can stick to the schedule and not let myself be panicked by outside events, e.g. Wooderson.

Wooderson ran the greatest race of his career today. That shook me, but not as much as it shook Jerry and one or two others. Powell beat me in the half-mile. I'm not really a half-miler. They are all running too fast too early, I suspect.

In the morning before breakfast I jogged on the golf course. Harold's house was built beside the Moor Park golf course. After breakfast we sat round the table talking. Sybil, Harold's actress-wife, brought the Sunday papers, and I saw from one of them that the day before, in Italy, Luigi Beccali had run a flashing 1500 metres. Harold was reading the *Sunday Times*. Presently the discussion brought up Wooderson.

"For heaven's sake, Harold," Sybil said, "why don't you show us what you've written? Show Jack, anyway."

"Jack's a guest."

"Don't be so embarrassed, Harold. Show him the paper."

"I think I can guess," I said, glancing at Harold. "You're tipping Wooderson."

"No, I'm not." Harold got up to pour more coffee.

"Let me see." Adolphe took the paper and read out what Harold had written. "Yes, you are. 'The world record,' you say, 'may get a rude shock in Berlin.' Of course you are, Harold, you're backing Wooderson. Wooderson, according to you, is unbeatable."

"Harold, you rotter. Think how Jack must feel."

"Sybil, you know nothing about athletics. You weren't there yesterday. Nor were you, Adolphe. And I do *not* say Wooderson is unbeatable at Berlin."

"Well you certainly imply it. Of course you're tipping Wooderson. What do you say, Jack?"

I didn't say anything. I had taken my coffee and crossed the room to the French doors giving on to the golf links. Two men and a young woman were approaching the green, playing out a hole. The young woman had red hair. As she walked her wrist flashed in the sun. She dropped her bag at the edge of the green and measured with her eye the distance from the ball to the hole. I watched. Behind me, I heard Harold say, "Oh fiddlesticks. Jack's been to the house before. He knows he's among friends here. I just think, Adolphe, that on Jack's recent form, he should forget the 1500 metres at Berlin and run in the 5000 metres instead."

I might run in both, I thought.

The red-headed woman had squared up and was about to putt. Her companions were watching intently, as I was. The French doors were open, the green directly in front of me about twenty yards away. It was a short but not an easy putt. On the point of making her stroke, the woman appeared to hesitate, as if changing her mind. It was a momentary hesitation and her companions relaxed. I felt rather than saw this happen. By then she had followed through with the stroke and the ball was down. I gave an involuntary gasp.

"That's extraordinary," I said, out loud.

"What is? What's extraordinary, Jack?" Harold had come up behind me. I pointed through the French doors. Harold peered on to the green. "Aha. Cherchez la femme." He chuckled and squeezed my arm. "Care for a walk? Let's go out."

"The reason I asked you down this weekend has nothing to do with Wooderson," Harold said after we had left the house. We were crossing the golf course. "I have to write what I think and I'm sorry about that. But there you are."

"Of course. I don't mind."

"Of course you mind. In your place I'd mind very much. Before we leave the subject let me just say this. I admire Sydney Wooderson and it's got nothing to do with his being the underdog and being on top at the moment. I admire his guts. I detest the way some writers are bragging about 'our Syd'.

'Our Syd' versus 'Lovely-Locks Lovelock'. You've seen the cartoons? Things like, 'Our Syd will run Lovelock and Cunningham ragged at Berlin.' It's the English class thing, you realise. In Germany all we seem to hear about is politics in sport. Now in England it's class. And you, my dear Jack, are on the receiving end. Does it bother you?"

"A bit. Yes."

"Well don't let it. You get to Berlin, you'll breathe new air. I'm not a fatalist, you know, but sometimes I almost think the gods do smile on us. I imagine them having a little talk over morning coffee. One says to the other 'You know, I like the look of this chap. Think I'll pop down and say hullo before he starts.' A funny thing happened to me at the Paris Olympics. It was something Sam Mussabini said before the final, some little thing, something terribly obvious, and I forgot about it, but just before the gun went I remembered it. My mind must have been receptive to what he said. I'd been feeling rotten until then, like a condemned man going to the scaffold. Then I remembered. It made all the difference."

"It's the little things, you mean?"

"You'll know when it happens. If it happens." Harold had taken my arm, steering me towards a copse at the end of a fairway, his face tinged with concern. He continued, speaking rapidly, "I've been writing about you for some years. Oh, I know what people are saying: 'Poor old Jack, he's past his prime' . . . 'His finish is gone'. I imagine you're having a tussle with yourself – you've entered for two events and can't make up your mind which to plump for. And this hospital work, night-shift, doesn't help, does it? That's knocked you. You don't say much. I suspect because of this Wooderson business you've entered two events so as to keep your options open – very wisely. Anyway that's none of my business. But I do know what Berlin means to you. Now let me throw you a crumb of comfort. If you do start in the 1500 metres you won't start the favourite."

"The hardest thing, I find, Harold, is to simplify."

"My dear fellow, it gets more complicated. It's torment. All I can tell you – " Harold had been walking me along almost as quickly as he was talking. He stopped and threw up his hands. "All I can tell you is until the last moment, until the very last moment when the gun releases you, nothing will appear simple.

But *then*, if the gods do decide to add a cubit to your stature, the scales will fall from your eyes and everything will suddenly be clear as a bell. Jack, it's the most wonderful feeling in the world."

I felt closer to Harold at that moment than I had ever been. I felt the warmth of his affection, the emotion behind his words. I said lightly to hide my own feelings:

"Anchovies on toast? If I win? Celebration in the Village afterwards?"

His face clouded. "That's what I wanted to speak to you about. It's by no means certain that I'll be there."

"But – the BBC? I don't understand."

"You forget. I'm a Jew. Oh I want to go and the BBC wants me to go too – there is no problem with the BBC. 'Go. Go and show them in Germany, Harold, there is no anti-Semitism in England. Show them the BBC employs Jews.' The Head of Outside Broadcasts is pressing me. There's no problem with the family either. We had a conference about it. The problem is with me and the Orthodox Jewish community in London. If I go to Berlin and report the Games for the BBC, they see it as a silent acceptance of everything the swastika stands for. They see it differently. They're up in arms. You know Helene Mayer, don't you? The Jewish fencer?"

"Well, slightly. We met in Los Angeles. But I haven't kept in touch."

"Oh. Somebody told me you had. I thought you might have had some first-hand information."

"As a matter of fact, I didn't even know she was Jewish. I thought she was American."

"Jewish-American. Her people still live in Germany. She's one of the few German Jews the Nazis have selected for their Olympic team."

"I haven't even kept in touch with Peltzer."

"Who?"

"Otto Peltzer."

"Oh yes, I know about him. Douglas Lowe was talking about Peltzer at the dinner. Got me to sign something to do with Peltzer, if I remember rightly. Peltzer's another one."

"I didn't know Peltzer was Jewish."

"He's not. I didn't mean that. I'm undecided, Jack. There

207

are so many rumours going round about what's happening to sportsmen in Germany, it's hard to know what to believe. So what do I do?"

"*Do*? Go, of course. Don't be an ass, Harold. You're the best commentator in the business."

"That's what Adolphe says. Sybil too." Harold was walking again. We came round the copse and started uphill, Harold leading with long ungainly strides. Ahead and walking parallel to us, the red-headed woman and her companions came into view.

"I suppose it will be all right. I'll probably go. I might have a word with Sir John Simon at the Foreign Office. Lady Simon's a patient of Adolphe's. It will probably be all right. I know Vansittart is going from the Foreign Office – of course, 'only in a private capacity'. He wants to see the Games. It's ticklish, Jack. My view is, the Games must go on. It simply won't do to treat the Germans as mad dogs. It's nonsense to talk of the Games as being held 'under the Nazi swastika'. They're not, the Games will take place under the Olympic flag. You heard about Hitler's reaction? What he said to the Count? Graf Baillet-Latour of the IOC went to see Hitler. 'Herr Hitler,' the Count said, 'I would ask you to remember that when the Olympic flag flies over Berlin, you are no longer master in your house but a guest; you are the host to these Games, not the initiator, and at the opening ceremony your function is to speak only one sentence.' 'What is the sentence?' Hitler said. Baillet-Latour told him. It's a very short sentence. Hitler gave a hollow laugh. He said, 'I shall have no difficulty in learning it by heart.' So there you are ... Are you listening? My God, he's glued to that red-head again."

"Sorry, Harold. I was trying to remember something."

I had paused beside the fairway to watch the young woman again – she was chipping out on to a green. I was remembering the scene I had witnessed earlier from the breakfast room and trying to connect it with something that had happened to me in Norway. Two years before at Tönsberg I had been showing off in a race and had done something unexpected that made the crowd gasp. The crowd had gasped involuntarily, just as I had done watching the red-headed woman half an hour earlier. In my mind the incidents were connected. What was the connection?

Something clicked. I had it.

"Jack, I don't think you've been listening to a word I've said. Now what's got into you?"

I had leaped in the air and was sitting down on the grass hugging my knees, squirming with excitement. It was a very little thing, something terribly obvious, but I knew that when I got to Berlin I would remember it. I got up in a minute. "Sorry, Harold. I get these fits. It really is extraordinary. I've remembered something that happened to me in Norway in 1934. It's been puzzling me for two years."

As we walked on, I turned and looked back on to the green where the three players were finishing the hole. I watched to see if the red-headed woman would do her putting trick again. But she didn't.

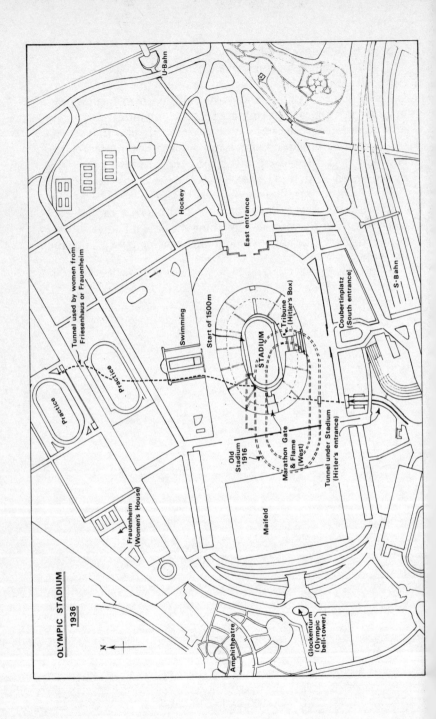

OLYMPIC STADIUM
1936

N

Frauenheim (Women's House)

Practice

Practice

Tunnel used by women from Friesenhaus or Frauenheim

Swimming

Hockey

U-Bahn

East entrance

Start of 1500m

STADIUM

Tribune (Hitler's Box)

Coubertinplatz (South entrance)

S-Bahn

Old Stadium 1916

Marathon Gate & Flame (West)

Tunnel under Stadium (Hitler's entrance)

Maifield

Amphitheatre

Glockenturm (Olympic bell-tower)

Part Three

August 1936

"It was a great moment not only in the history of the Games but of our entire era that on 1 August 1936 young people of all nations united in a holy quest marched behind their national flags into the Berlin stadium."

BARON PIERRE DE COUBERTIN,
founder of the modern Olympic Games

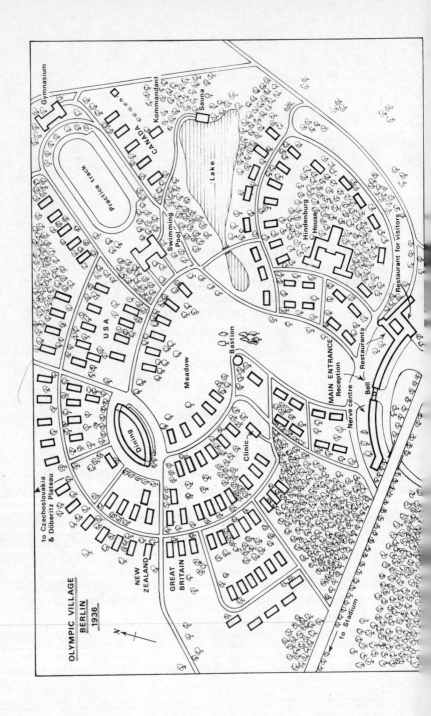

15

Six weeks later Harold came to Berlin for the BBC, as I had assumed all along that he would. Because of Harold's broadcasting duties, I didn't expect to see him in the Village which was eight miles out of town; nor did I want to. We had had one more talk in London – inconclusive – and after that when Sydney Wooderson's star soared even higher, eclipsing me altogether, I didn't want to talk to anyone much. Anyway Harold seemed to have vanished and I assumed he'd gone right off me. In Berlin Harold stayed at the Hotel Kaiserhof near the Potsdamerplatz. He walked into my room at the Village late one evening out of the rain – it was the day the track events began – and went again without explaining himself. I said to Bill, "Is he telling us something?" Bill didn't know, and I didn't know, and to this day I still don't know what exactly was in Harold's mind, not that it matters a great deal. I only remember the incident because of Harold's condition. He arrived in a state of bemused shock.

Shock, euphoria, a feeling that anything could happen to upset the most carefully laid plans was a common experience, I believe, at the 1936 Berlin Games. And rain. It was pneumonia weather when we arrived, cold and grey. It rained. It blew. It cleared and was sunny and then rained again. On the day of my heat the wind almost blew out the Olympic flame and Hitler and Mussolini's two sons who were in the box that day left the Stadium in disgust.

Yet Berlin smiled.

Coming from England, we felt Berlin's "vast substantial smile" already crossing the Dutch frontier. The normally plain station at Bentheim was decked out like a carnival tree. All the way to Bahnhof Friedrichstrasse in central Berlin the smile grew and when we stepped down on to the platform we found that not only the girders and stays and oval glass roof of the station were festooned with garlands and roses, but so was our train too. Two bands were playing. Everyone made a speech. We drove to the town hall past a curtain of swastika banners forty feet high (more speeches), and from the town hall past cheering crowds along a five-mile Olympic Way, down the Linden and the Charlottenburger Chaussee, under the clipped hedges and waving flags of the Tiergarten, up the wide Heerstrasse, every wall, every tree, every lamp standard looped and smothered with scarlet and black flags – I had the feeling of driving into a crimson sunset. The smile was endless. The silly thing was, we were only seven people. Seven on a train. Seven on a grey army bus with curtained windows. Seven New Zealanders in flannels and straw boaters driving into the greatest pageant the world has ever seen (well, since Agincourt) – and it was all for us. I remember Cec Matthews gawking out of the bus window and saying, "Christ they've laid it on, Jack, just for us!"

It was dark when we reached the Olympic Village looking out towards Spandau. A band played us to our quarters. The Kommandant came too, a tall elegant man in an elegant army uniform, and ahead of him marched a procession of guides in Olympic white holding torch flares. It was like a scene out of grand opera. Golly, I thought. I was exhausted and slept. I was awoken in the morning by bells in the Village playing the Olympic Hymn – I guessed it was the Olympic Hymn because there was a booklet at the bedside telling us about the Village and the belltower at the gate and also about the hymn, which was composed by Richard Strauss. The first thing I noticed when I went outside and stretched my legs was a stork walking beside a lake. It's not real, I thought. It was so incongruous that I walked down to the lake and stood looking at the stork, expecting it to vanish. The stork was real. I was smiling to myself. Already Berlin and its pageantry of the night before seemed far behind, a forgotten memory. Yet the illusion remained – that vast substantial smile remained, and I basked in it.

"I can do anything here," I said to Bill when he showed up later in the day. "Anything at all."

Our bungalow was between the British and the Japanese quarters. It was red-tiled, neat and orderly; it had a gravel path edged with flowers, a wooden bench and sun chairs outside and

214

there was an agapanthus growing on the terrace. It was like a chalet in a Butlin's camp except, I noticed, the windows and doors were very thick. After breakfast I pinned on the obligatory identification badge, collected the post and returned to the bungalow and laid out my kit: black running singlet and shorts, black spikes, black blazer, black track suit, white sweater and flannels – grey flannels for walking-out, cream for the parade. I checked the phials of vaccine, hypodermic syringe and needles I had brought, also my sleeping draught. It was my usual mud-coloured sleeping draught, chloral, bromide and tincture of opium mixed in equal quantities. For emergency I had brought trional, a longer-lasting hypnotic. I hadn't taken trional before, but then I hadn't been in a situation like this before. I knew it was addictive.

I kept going to the window to look out. We seemed to be on the very edge of the Village, remote from the nerve centre – actually there were two nerve centres: 1. the gate complex where the telephones were, and, 2. the three-storey egg-shaped dining-room which had its own meadow sloping down to the lake, and we seemed to be tucked away from both. I kept returning to the window and peering out through the gauze frame. I couldn't believe my luck. There, beyond a screen of birch trees, was the pine forest. It began less than a hundred metres away.

I unpacked very slowly, my thoughts fidgeting. I couldn't sit down. I was overweight. I had to lose two pounds. For some reason that worried me. I kept putting things in drawers and taking them out again. There was a squirrel outside my window. I could hear wood pigeons warbling. Bill hadn't come yet. Bill was somewhere else, looking for digs. Today was Wednesday. The Games were due to open on Saturday and my first race, the 1500-metre heats, was less than a week away. The Americans had brought ten track coaches for their team, 357-strong – so Godfrey had told me at breakfast. I had breakfasted with Godfrey Brown and Jerry and Godfrey was already spitting about their late arrival. The Brits had come only 24 hours ahead of us, flouting all the accepted theories of acclimatisation. The chief American track coach Lawson Robertson, Godfrey said, was "astounded". The British team was the third last to arrive, New Zealand second to last and after us there were only the Maltese. Godfrey was saying that the training track, after weeks of sun, was hard and the British sprinters after only one day had sore calves. Now it was raining. "Wooderson's upset," Jerry said. "Oh, why?" I said. "Bloody British Olympic officials. They won't let his trainer Albert Hill stay in the Village." I nodded. "They won't let Bill stay here either." It didn't matter that Albert Hill was a double Olympic champion or that Bill Thomas was the elder states-man among trainers in England – men like them were considered a "cut below" athletes and officials. Bill was hunting for digs somewhere along the Heerstrasse. I hoped he would be all right.

There was a knock. A young officer stood at the door, Oberleutnant Joachim van Wick – our official attaché. He looked junior. New Zealand rated only a very junior attaché. He saluted – "Heil Hitler" – and addressed me as "Captain". He was young and friendly and insisted on explaining to me the literature alongside the bed – a map showing the route to the Stadium, a programme of entertainments provided in the Village. He picked up a leaflet depicting an oak cluster superimposed on a picture of the Village and said, "Dorf des Friedens."

"Yes, the Village of Peace," I said. "Yes, I know."

"Welcome to the Olympic Village!" he suddenly boomed. He had removed his cap, placed it under one arm and assumed a striking pose, holding the leaflet at arm's length. I realised he wanted to practise his English and intended reading out the lot. I sat on the bed and he read out:

This is your home for the immediate future . . .

The Olympic flags, including the flag of your country, wave over this Village. The bells each morning ring out the Olympic Hymn.

May the Olympic spirit and Olympic peace rule here from the first day to the last.

Help us to preserve and honour this peace.

The Village has been built by the German Army for the Olympic Games. For the Army, inspired with love of sport and loyal to the Olympic ideal, this has been a joyous task . . .

When he had finished I thanked him and saw that the address of welcome was signed

The President of the Organising Committee
for the XIth Olympic Games, Berlin, 1936
Dr Th. Lewald
Reichs Minister of War
von Blomberg
Field Marshal.

The Oberleutnant clicked heels and I waited for him to go. But no, he wished to escort me to the practice track. Nein? The gymnasium perhaps? The swimming pool? I smiled, showing all my teeth. Ah, the *dentist*? Beside the Oberleutnant had appeared a youth, alert and spotless in white duck uniform. He too offered his services. Hairdresser? Sauna? Solarium? I declined, saw them out and continued with my unpacking. Then Godfrey's spectacles appeared at the window, his tousled chipmunk face pressed up against the wet pane looking in. "God, you're neat," he said. Then: "Coming?" Godfrey was on his way to the track. Automatically I reached into a drawer for my spikes. Then I remembered and put them away again. I waved him on. There is only one thing worse than having a race inside you that can't get out because it's raining, and that is a race that wants to get out too soon. I'd made that mistake once before, at Los Angeles. I wasn't going to make it again.

I took my brolly and went out, walking due west until I reached the perimeter giving as I thought on to the forest. There was a containing fence patrolled by soldiers in grey-green uniform. I had expected a gate, an exit of some kind. There was no gate. I walked round the perimeter to the north, then scouted back in the other direction. Clearly the fence was designed to keep out the public, especially women (no women were allowed inside) and effectively it did this. It also locked me in. The fence was about eight feet high, built of double steel mesh and topped with coils of barbed wire. It was more like a fortification. Bloody hell, I thought.

I went back to the bungalow, got a plan of the Village and explored some more. The plan was picturesque but not drawn to scale and the more I explored the more confused I became. After half an hour I walked down the meadow below the dining-room and up steps on to the raised terrace of an open-air

217

kiosk like a rotunda, called the Bastion. From here the Village seemed to disappear into a moat. According to the plan, I was at the centre of the Village. The rain had stopped. I stood on the terrace and tried to figure it out. To my right was Hindenburg Haus and further round, some distance away, the belltower and main gate. From here once the Games began buses would leave for the Stadium every ten minutes. The dining-room was behind me. Ahead, beyond a ring of birches, the ground fell towards a serpentine lake behind which were the Finnish sauna and the quarters of the German team. Ahead and left were the swimming pool, gymnasia, massage rooms and, on a high plateau, the practice areas, but I could see none of this – only a maze of paths criss-crossing and disappearing into trees. At the time of my visit a year earlier, it had all been rolling fenland open to the forest and the hinterland beyond, just a few houses and marsh, the marsh still being drained by youth workers. Now there were trees everywhere. In the transformation, tens of thousands of trees had been brought in, fully grown, and planted in the earth. The trees blotted out everything.

I got a glass of lemonade at the bar and returned to the terrace, completely flummoxed. There had to be a way out other than by the main gate. We were six thousand bodies, athletes, officials, masseurs, trainers, distributed over an area as extensive as Regent's Park. I didn't believe we were locked in. There had to be an entrance for service vehicles, there had to be a break in the wire.

My thoughts were interrupted by a babel of tongues as athletes, returning from the gym and practice areas, appeared through the trees and split off in various directions around the meadow, calling to one another or climbing up on to the terrace around me, dragging stools across the flagstones and invading the bar inside clamouring for drinks. Godfrey Brown was among them. He saw me and came up, a bit stooped, a bit round-shouldered, walking slowly, his tousled hair flopping across his glasses. He glanced round with one of those ferocious frowns common to people of short sight and slumped into a chair beside me.

"I hate this place, Jack."

Godfrey was the best quarter-miler England had produced

in years, though barely twenty-one. He wasn't long down from Cambridge. These were his first Olympics.

"Drink, Godfrey?"

"Yes, a gallon. Beer."

"Better not." I brought him apple juice. There was no beer anyway, no alcohol was allowed.

"No beer. No alcohol. No women. I can't even see my sister. I hate this place."

"Track still hard?"

"It isn't that – it's a madhouse up there. Can't run, can't think. Either someone's pushing a camera in your face or you're blundering into spectators. I can't see the lanes properly anyway. Bloody great weight suddenly lands at my feet, a 16-pound shot. Here's me trying to wind up to sprint. Here's Beccali screaming his lungs out to clear a passage, and this American Jack Torrance heaves the shot. The Louisiana Giant, they call him. He chucked the shot to clear the spectators. Missed me by inches, almost brained Beccali. I can't wind up, Jack. I just can't."

I was laughing to myself. We were both frustrated. Godfrey couldn't wind up and I couldn't wind down.

"It's worse than Hyde Park Corner up there, Jack. Phil Edwards sends you his regards."

"Oh good. How's Phil?"

"Said to tell you he's qualified, he's now a doctor, so you'd better be polite. Oh Phil's all right. The Canadians have got the best pitch, he says – they're living in clover, right by the sauna. Lucky them. Where we are, God it's gloomy."

"Gloomy?"

"Yes, all those pines we look out on. Glooming great black pines on the other side, like looking into Hades."

"How's Wooderson?" I said. "I heard he'd done something to an ankle?"

"Not that you'd notice. Oh Syd's all right, the little man is thriving. Actually Sydney is in danger of becoming as popular as Cunningham and Jesse Owens. Cunningham got voted the most popular man on the American ship coming over, I'm told. Strapping beast, isn't he? I was watching Jesse Owens run and thinking of you, Jack. The difference is extraordinary. When Owens runs he doesn't seem to touch the ground. You never leave it. Oh, you know what he did? Just now? The photographers asked Jesse Owens to do a long jump for them, just a little one, so he did 25 feet 9 inches. Olympic record. The man is amazing. You know, the Yanks have been here for weeks. *Weeks*, Jack."

"Sadly," Godfrey said, when he'd been to the bar and returned with more drinks, "sadly I have to report that our mutual rivals are looking 100 per cent. Wooderson's fine, Cunningham and Beccali are looking fine and so, alas, are Lu Valle and Archie Williams." Jimmie Lu Valle and Archie Williams were Godfrey's American rivals for the 400-metre title, both blacks and both 46-second men. Godfrey had only once broken 48 seconds.

"Compared to them," he said, "I've had almost no hard competitive experience. It's pitiful."

"Don't underrate yourself," I told him. I had a soft spot for Godfrey. Four days before, in Birmingham, he had broken training and spent a morning sweeping the inside lane of a churned-up track for me, a gesture that had enabled me to complete my preparation for Berlin later in the day with a two-mile race victory and a British record. That race, the culmination of my "circus schedule", as Bill called it, had been just right. I still ached from the race, but it was the sort of physical animal ache this side of exhaustion I had been planning for.

"Take it easy," I told Godfrey. "Don't try and flash too soon."

"I don't know how you do it, Jack – you look so damned composed. You haven't even changed yet."

"It's just a pose," I said. The sun had come out, glinting on a van going by. It was a funny little red van, going along like a sewing machine, buzzing in and out of the trees. I sat back and watched it, twirling the straw boater on the point of my brolly. I said, "Where do you suppose, Godfrey, the service vehicles get in here?"

"Through the main gate. Don't they?"

"Don't think so. It's too official." The main gate was at the wrong end of the Village, remote from the forest of pines. "You've got a week yet," I said to Godfrey, my mind still on the van. "They say there are two sorts of athlete – those who

220

are scared and show it and those who are scared and don't show it."

"That's us then, you and me." Godfrey had the look of a furious muscular owl.

"That's us. Then there's the other sort."

"Who are they?"

"The sort that don't make champions. You'll be all right," I said.

"It would be all right, I think, if Ralph was here." I nodded. Ralph was Godfrey's brother, a hurdler. He'd missed the team. Godfrey had a sister, Audrey, also an athlete – a sprinter. She was in the women's team. "Ralph was sick as mud about missing the team. I'd give anything to see him. Or Mary. Mary's the girlfriend. Mary's staying with a Nazi family somewhere in the town, Charlottenburg. She came out to see me yesterday but they wouldn't let her in – we had to talk in the restaurant outside the gate. It's pathetic. I can't even see Audrey. She's stuck in the Women's Haus over by the Stadium. I can't visit her and she can't visit me, you're so cut off here, Jack. Alone, somehow. I feel like a Christian being thrown to the lions."

"Well at least, Godfrey, you know which race you're going to start in."

"Yes, well. That reminds me – Bevil was asking about that. Bevil Rudd wants to know which event you're starting in. Everyone's asking about it."

"I haven't decided," I said.

There was the red van again. It had vanished in the direction of the swimming pool and now reappeared chugging up the incline behind us, apparently heading for the dining-room. I watched it follow the curve of the almond-shaped meadow. Suddenly it swung right and disappeared. It seemed to be heading north. I grabbed my plan, left Godfrey and followed it at a fast walk.

The van kept stopping. The driver left the engine running as he went among the bungalows. He wore a natty blue uniform and a peaked hat; he seemed to be delivering telegrams. He made a couple of stops by the Mexican quarters, doubled back, went past China and then breezed north for half a mile flat stick to pull up in the middle of a densely planted thicket where the

221

house plaques said "Tschechoslowakei". I had to run to keep him in view. I saw from the plan that I wasn't too far from the New Zealand house but further round on the edge, a sort of hidden bulge like a piece of geography stuck on that I hadn't suspected. The sun was high and growing warm. The van had left the houses, threading back, and was now puttering away over gravel down a lane of beech trees leaving a trail of yellow exhaust fumes. It was gone from sight. Looking back, I saw that the Village was disappearing. I ran on. The route grew narrow, the trees on either side less tended; sand appeared, river sand speckled with broom and couch grass. I emerged as from a bottle-neck on to a clearing, half-ploughed, under an immense sky. A few trees lay where they had fallen. Ahead was the perimeter fence. I saw the fence, the gate in the fence, the red van passing through the gate on to a highway and the tall remembered pines beyond the fence all at once. The pines crowded to the edge of the highway.

There was a soldier on duty beside a sentry box. He wore a small burnished eagle on one lapel, the five-looped Olympic rings on the other. He stopped me.

I said my name. He said, "Zur Verfügung," and saluted. He closed the gate.

"Nummer?"

He peered at my identification badge and wrote the number into a book. My number was 1066. I moved forward, expecting him to open the gate. He restrained me. Now what?

"I, willkomme," he said.

"I, Lovelock."

"You, Lovelock. Nummer eins null doppelsechs. Ten doppel six." He bared his teeth in a grin. "You, Englishman?"

"New Zealand. Neuseeland."

"Ah so! New Zealand ten doppel six."

"Sixty-six," I corrected. "Ten sixty-six."

"Ah so! Ten sixty-six."

"And all that," I said. He opened the gate. I passed through, crossed the road and entered the forest.

The Olympic Village of Döberitz was situated on the edge of a vast three-sided plateau in East Havel-land in the Mark Brandenburg; a genuine hinterland, much of it untouched by human hand. Tall stands of Kiefern – Prussian pines – such as the one I now entered, alternated with fields and moorland and marshes lying beside old river valleys. I had discovered the forest the previous autumn and walked through it on to the plateau, marvelling at the light and the clouds dissolving under wide horizons; returning in the late afternoon, I had lost my bearings; dusk had fallen rapidly and I was taken home for the night by a farmer I had met in a white straw hat ploughing alone with two horses. In the morning he had shown me his tiny village – houses crumbling, pigeons nesting in the red brick and yellow straw roofs, a romantic church and, beside the church, a monument of some kind, an obelisk, which he saluted with immense dignity. He thought I was English. He showed me some barracks where he had trained to be a soldier in the First World War and, as we drove about in his dog cart, pointed out to me ancient cannon shells dating from I don't know when which littered the fens. Then he took me on to a height above the embryo Olympic Village and showed me a cemetery dating from 1914 where English, French and Russian prisoners-of-war were buried. Later when I returned to London I looked up the Mark Brandenburg in an encyclopaedia and discovered that Döberitz was famous in Prussian military history. It was called "the Cradle of the German Army". The Heerstrasse, the main Olympic highway leading from Berlin past the Stadium and on in a straight line to the Village, was also mentioned: a famous military road. I didn't read the details which seemed to be mostly a recital of Prussian armies, battles, and manoeuvres, but my eye was caught by a striking phrase, "the white hot sands of Döberitz":

> *Thunder, hail, storm, lightning!*
> *God created the white hot sands of Döberitz.*

And that explained something to me. I was puzzled by an area into which I had strayed which was so alien to me and yet at the same time had seemed totally familiar. It appeared to be a kind of "sandbox"; and sand, hot white sand mingled with the tang of pine needles, had been in my blood since childhood.

Nothing brings back the past like a stench or a perfume. That day, after I left Godfrey and plunged into the forest, long rays of light were streaming down through the boles of the Kiefern. The Kiefern grew straight up, tall and spindly, growing straight out of warm sand, the needles warm and comfortable under my feet. And everywhere the smell of mulch and pine cones and the peculiar aroma of rotting bark, steaming after rain, invaded my nostrils. I walked and walked. My brain emptied and I began to relax. I found a sand dune, kicked off my shoes and lay with my face buried in the sand, the remembered itch of hot sand between my toes, and dreamed of all the things I hadn't thought of since I was twelve. I had been born beside sand dunes and river sands blowing in from the sea; I had spent the best parts of my childhood swinging through rain forest and hanging upside down from the boughs of macrocarpa pines. I had been happiest then. Now I was less than an hour from Berlin and nothing was the same as New Zealand, yet it felt exactly the same.

The Olympic Village was not, as Godfrey complained, a "madhouse". But it was a place where you never set foot outside without recognising somebody or being recognised in turn by somebody. I knew before I came that I would have to escape from it, and why, and in the days that followed leading up to my race I returned to the forest whenever I could. Once I found an abandoned hay cart, climbed in and slept for two hours. Best of all was to come in the early morning when the light was an apricot haze and the Village was still sleeping. Only a tall melancholy Indian would be about at that hour, a strange bearded figure with a knot of blue ribbon tied on top of his head. I would meet him sometimes trotting past the Czech quarters on my way to the wire and he would greet me, pressing his hands together with a little nod, and trot on. I would cross the perimeter wire to run between the boles of the Kiefern, choosing a path at random, sometimes to put up a deer, sometimes to emerge unexpectedly at the margin of the forest looking out on vistas of cereal and corn ripening in distant river valleys. The vistas were endless. I was running over broken ground, yet it was easy. Directionless. Unimpeded. Uninvolved. And sometimes to find a hollow in the sand formed by melted snow and curl up there for ten minutes under the Kiefern where no one else had been. I felt like a dawn mouse scenting its way. It was perhaps the best part of me.

"This is getting too easy," I said to Bill on the evening of the fourth day. We were in the dining-room with Arthur Porritt. Arthur had come out to the Village from an IOC meeting in Berlin to discuss the parade the next day and I hadn't long come in from the forest.

"That's a nice song to hear, sir," Bill said. "A change from the tune I've been getting up on the practice track all day – I was just telling Doc Porritt. 'Ooh-ess-ah, Ooh-ess-ah!'"

"'Ooh-ess-ah', what's that?"

"The latest yell, sir, from the spectators. 'Ooh-ess-ah' – USA. Yell, yell, yell. I'm referring to the American Negroes, sir, that's causing all the yells and consternation – Mr Jesse Owens, Mr Cornelius Johnson, Mr Dave Albritton, Mr John Woodruff, and so forth. There are ten of them Negroes on the American track team, superb athletes. They are superb, sir. The Doc tells me that the German press has referred to them as America's 'Black Auxiliaries' and his Nibs, Mr Führer, has deemed them to be an inferior race. Isn't that so, Doc?"

Arthur nodded. "This chap Hitler has a nerve. He is reported to have said the Negroes are not Aryans and it is 'unfair to allow such flat-footed specimens to compete against the noble products of the German race.' Well! Mind you, Jack, just wait till you see the Stadium. They took us there today. You have to give him credit for that. Majestic – I can find no other word. Baillet-Latour claims it is nobler than the Coliseum. Take a look at this."

Arthur, who was in semi-formal attire with cravat and tie-pin, took out from a box a bronze chain, elaborately gilded and looped with rings of coloured enamel. The rings ended with an Olympic emblem fixed to a medallion showing the head of Zeus. "Handmade," Arthur said. "Specially cast. They've had sixty of them made, one for each member of the International Committee." Arthur would wear the chain at the parade.

We admired the chain and Bill tried it on over his blue suit. He looked like the Lord Mayor of London. I said to him:

225

"Know what I think, Bill? I think the Negro has a longer Achilles tendon than we do. So he gets extra acceleration."

"Ha!" Bill snorted. "That isn't what the British press is going to print, I'll warrant, thanks to Frank Wright. Frank is looking after the British aches and pains as you know, sir, and he is putting it out that Jesse Owens and the rest have undergone thigh operations so as to increase their speed. Frank Wright is telling all the English reporters that."

Arthur said, "Sounds like sour grapes, Bill. They're as bad as Hitler."

"Yes, Doc. So I said to Frank Wright, I said 'If that's all you can find to tell the readers back in England, I hope the Negroes win every event on the track.' They will too, Doc."

"Except the 1500 metres. Eh, Jack? I wonder – " Arthur surveyed the dining-room and said, "Could we move to the bungalow, Jack? It's a bit less public. Bill has something to show you."

Outside the dining-room Bill was buttonholed for a moment by Harold Whitlock, the long-distance walker, and Arthur and I paused, looking down across the meadow on to a scene which probably sounds ordinary, and was certainly not new, for I had imagined it before many times and I'm sure Arthur had seen it in his mind's eye previously, and yet we both responded to it in the same way, just standing there and looking. Maybe it was the night air which was soft and warm, or the sound of mouth-organ music drifting upward through the trees, maybe it was simply the date – it was Friday 31 July, the eve of the opening of the Games. The scene is engraved on my mind still. Everywhere athletes were sitting out in the warm air, lounging on the grass, their voices murmuring and blending, with here and there a face caught in the shafts of light spilling down the slope from the dining-room. A Frenchman was rolling oranges down the slope, Jesse Owens was sitting on the steps talking to a blond-haired German, a group of Aussies was carolling about with a kangaroo, the team's mascot, showing it off to an audience of Japanese.

"The youth of the world, Jack," Arthur said quietly.

He spoke with feeling and I thought, yes, it's true. It's really so. I had heard the phrase before. I knew it by heart, Jugend der Welt – it was in the bedside literature. I had seen it in the

226

communiqués in London engraved on the mighty Olympic Bell that overlooked the Stadium from the adjoining Maifeld. It was engraved again on a miniature bell at the entrance to the Village, Ich rufe die Jugend der Welt! I had read it in newspaper headlines in Berlin that would be blazoned across Europe:

DIE JUGEND DER WELT DARF SICH NIE WIEDER KÄMPFEND GEGENÜBERSTEHEN

– "The Youth of the World must never again confront one another on the Battlefield" – I knew it so well I'd come to take it for granted like an advertisement for toothpaste. But at that moment as I looked down the meadow with Arthur from the steps of the dining-room, it actually came true. It's true at last, I thought. It didn't sound like an empty phrase.

"All set for the march-past tomorrow?" Arthur said, as Bill rejoined us and we moved on.

"Yes, Arthur. We had a dress rehearsal this morning."

"Go well, Jack?"

I thought of the seven of us slouching along that morning in boaters and bathrobes, me in front with the flag, trying to get the turns right, and I tried to sound convincing. "Well enough, Arthur."

"General effect, not good?"

"I don't think New Zealand will win any medals for marching."

"For what it's worth, Doc," Bill put in, "the Americans have had three dress rehearsals and are still up the creek about it."

"About what, Bill?"

"About what salute to give to Mr Hitler. I gather they don't know what to do with their boaters. They can't decide."

"Neither can we," I said.

"Jack." Arthur spoke sternly. "I shall be with the official party tomorrow, as you know. You know the drill, surely?"

"Oh yes."

"You don't sound very confident. Jack, we're talking about a solemn occasion, the most solemn and ritual Olympic Games opening there's ever been. Half the crowned heads of Europe will be there. You have to get it right. I'll have a word to the chaps now."

227

"They're not there, Arthur. They've gone to the flicks."

"Oh. But didn't you tell them I was coming?"

"Yes. But the Schmeling film is on." Max Schmeling the boxer had knocked out Joe Louis in New York. A copy of the film, which was apparently being rushed to cinemas all over Germany, had arrived in the Village that morning. Half of our team were boxers. I said, "You can't blame the chaps for going, Arthur."

"So what about the march-past then? Olympic salute?"

"Hell no, it's too much like the Nazi greeting. The chaps won't wear that. No, we'll give Hitler the eyes right, same as the Brits."

"Surely we can do better than the Brits?"

"We might doff our straw hats as well."

Arthur sighed. "Just get it right, Jack, that's all. Just so long as you get it right."

16

I took Arthur and Bill into the day room of the bungalow we shared with the Belgians. The room was carpeted and simply furnished with a glass-topped coffee table against one wall and a long wooden table with chairs against another. The walls were decorated with murals showing the Black Forest and a Rhineland scene depicting the Lorelei rock. I sat under the Black Forest, Bill on my right under the Lorelei. In a corner was the New Zealand flag which I'd parked there after the morning's rehearsal.

Arthur closed the door and sat with his back to the French doors giving on to the terrace and trees. "Before we go any further, Jack, I want a straight answer. I can't get it from Bill and every English newspaper I pick up tells me something different. Which event are you running in?"

"I haven't decided."

"You haven't decided or you can't decide?"

"I can't decide anything, Arthur, until the heats are announced."

The programme was:

Saturday 1 August	Official opening
Sunday	Games and track events begin
Tuesday	5000 metres, heats
Wednesday	1500 metres, heats
Thursday	1500 metres, final
Friday	5000 metres, final

I said, "Let's see what I get for Tuesday. If I get an easy heat in the 5000, I may run in that as well."

Arthur eased his collar stud and did something to his cravat. "You mean you want to run in *both*? This is new."

"Nurmi did it."

"Four races in four days?"

"Nurmi did it in Paris."

"Jack, in Paris Nurmi was facing a weak field in the 1500 metres. This year's field is exceptional."

"I know."

"Then I shouldn't have to tell you. It is so exceptional that even Hitler has heard of it, and I'm told Hitler knows nothing about sport. He can't even ride a bicycle. You've *got* to concentrate on the 1500."

"At one time, Arthur, you were quite keen on me running the 5000. Anyway what's Hitler got to do with it?"

"It's because of Schaumburg, the German champion. Hitler's interested because he's been told that the 1500 is the only event, apart from field events, where Germany stands a chance. It happens to be the classic event on the programme."

"Schaumburg's a policeman," I said. "I met him in Munich. He's good, but he's not that good."

"Hitler doesn't know that. I can't think what's got into you, Jack. In London three weeks ago it was either-or. But not both."

"I feel so well, Arthur. I've got air on the brain. I feel I can do anything. Incidentally, three weeks ago Wooderson had just clouted me in the British Championships and that, if you remember, was three times in a row he'd beaten me over a mile.

229

You know how I was feeling that day. I don't remember what I said. My finish wasn't there."

"You're being inconsistent. In London you told me you'd win the 1500 in Berlin if it killed you. You'd gone cold on the 5000, you said. A week later after a turnout at Ponders End you told Harold Abrahams that if you ran the 1500 in Berlin it would be a disaster."

"I may have said that to Harold, but not then. It was much earlier. I don't remember."

"You're dithering."

"I'm not ready to decide, Arthur, that's all. I'm not frightened of Wooderson, if that's what you're thinking."

"I wish I knew what you were thinking."

"I shall probably run the 1500, Arthur."

"But *will* you? I am your team manager, dammit. Jack, you cannot – repeat cannot – afford to enter an Olympic contest in a divided state of mind." Arthur found his pipe and lit it. He said, "I've got meetings, parties, official receptions from now on non-stop. I shan't see you again until Tuesday. Tell me straight: are you in a bind?"

"Actually I'm feeling a bit sleepy – no, not sleepy, detached, quite detached from it all. It's a very pleasant state to be in. I've stopped thinking about technical details. The truth is, Arthur, I had a long talk with Harold in London and he made me realise that my best chance of a Gold might be in the 5000."

"Against the Finns?"

"It's within my range."

"This is madness. Why listen to Harold? He's rooting for Wooderson. Harold is not a New Zealander!"

"The 5000's an interesting prospect, Arthur. I'm considering it."

"But it is *not* your race."

"Harold thinks it is. Anyway since Harold talks to everyone and everyone seems to listen to Harold, I find it amusing to keep my options open."

"If I might speak, Doc?" Bill ran his finger round the gutter of his bowler and coughed deferentially. "I think Mr Abrahams would like a Gold for England in the 1500 metres 'cause he knows it's the only one they are likely to get."

"It is also the only one New Zealand is likely to get."

"Yes, Doc. If I might continue. I'm in the dark, same as you. I don't know if Jack has worked out a strategy for the 5000 or not, he hasn't told me; but as for the 1500 – if he wants Mr Abrahams to think the medal will end up on Mr Wooderson's chest, there's no harm done, is there? Myself, I don't think it will. Who are the favourites? Cunningham and Wooderson. Those are the names being spoken. But Mr Abrahams is a bad guesser if he's picking Wooderson – he forgets that young Wooderson has never run the Olympic distance in his life. There's a lot of guessing games going on. Jack hasn't spoken to reporters since he came and he has instructed me to say nothing, and I haven't, so the guessing has grown a treat. That's the way Jack likes it. We did it at Princeton last year. You've known Jack longer than me, Dr Porritt, but the way I see it – he's got a large secret garden in his top storey that he doesn't distribute to his friends or his trainer. So who am I to argue?"

Arthur sucked on his pipe and said nothing.

I said to Arthur, "You wanted to show me something."

"Yes, Jack. Bill's got a list that you may find interesting. All the managers and coaches have been meeting today, comparing time trials. Bill did a walkround before you came and we've got a complete rundown on the 1500 runners except for the Germans. Bill didn't get the Germans or the Frenchman, Goix. Have a look."

I scanned the list of names that Bill gave me. Cunningham and Beccali had recorded three-quarter-mile times, I saw, as had a new young American star, San Romani; Jerry Cornes and Venzke had run 800 metres; Phil Edwards, Erik Ny and the Hungarian Szabo, 600 metres. Archie San Romani's time made me whistle. He was a handsome olive-skinned youth from the mid-West, like Cunningham, and had flashed to within a yard or so of Cunningham in the American Olympic trials ahead of Venzke and Bonthron. It was San Romani who had edged out Bill Bonthron. Bonthron hadn't made the team. I said, "Apart from San Romani's time, Arthur, there's nothing spectacular here."

"Look again."

I did. I said, "Wooderson's not here."

Arthur nodded.

231

I said to Bill, "Was Wooderson out there today?"

"Yes, sir. Running very well too, and timed. There were two clocks on him. I couldn't get the time."

"Why not?"

"Not available."

"Wooderson's foot was bandaged," Arthur said. "The ankle, Jack."

I sat up then. There had been rumours about Wooderson's ankle since his 11 July victory over me in the British Championships. On that day he had finished strongly to beat me by two yards, but someone said he had been limping after the race.

"Was Wooderson wearing a sock, Bill?"

"No, sir. A plain bandage around the ankle on the open foot. He wasn't hiding the bandage. That's why I think it's nothing serious. But the Doc, he thinks it's significant."

"Yes, Jack, I do. I think it's very interesting, don't you?"

I thought about it. "Could mean anything, Arthur. They're obviously keeping his time a secret." To be honest, I didn't know what to think.

"Captain Lovelock, Captain Lovelock, please to wake up! Where is the flag?"

I heard the attaché's voice as from a long way off and sat up slowly on the bed. Outside it was drizzling. What was he saying about a flag?

"Captain Lovelock, where is the flag?"

Have you ever been a herald? An official standard-bearer to a march of nations? On a most solemn day? In 1936 a ceremonial Olympic flag measured seven feet across and almost four feet the other way. An Olympic flag is quite light when dry, but carried in a procession at the end of a long pole in the wind on a rainy day, it can be an alarming piece of equipment. It is a heavy responsibility, especially if you happen to have mislaid it and have your mind on something else. After Arthur and Bill had left the night before, I slept badly. I had woken at five, jogged in the forest and then, returning to the bungalow, flopped in my track suit still turning over in my mind what Arthur had said the night before. I must have dropped off. Now it was 10 a.m. and Oberleutnant van Wick was in a fine tizz.

"I left the flag in the day room," I said. "Isn't it there?"

We went into the day room. Amazing, it wasn't there. We went from room to room looking. Eventually we found it. It was outside lying under the trees, soaking wet. The attaché recovered the flag, thrust it into my arms and helped me on with the leather belt and harness. "Practice," he said, as we moved off into the drizzle. "Practice." I nodded. I remembered now. There was a final flag drill scheduled on the meadow below the dining-room.

The Village seemed half empty. In the distance I could hear phantom sounds like guns reverberating, boom boom. A giant shape like a dirigible was hovering over Berlin. Then a gangling man with the Union Jack painted on his track-suit top appeared striding towards us through the trees, his limbs streaked with moisture. I recognised the "Guardsman-gate" of the race-walker Harold Whitlock. He stopped for a moment, wiping a hand across his moustache and panting:

"They're out in the rain, the whole town's out in the rain, Jack. The streets are jammed." Whitlock had taken an early morning bus into Berlin, he said, and walked back for practice. "They're releasing pigeons," he said.

"Already?"

"Thousands and thousands of pigeons. You can't get near the centre. There's bands and parades, it's gas and gaiters everywhere. They're chucking garlands on me from the windows. Perishing cold. Lovely fun, Jack. Boom-boom, hear the guns?" He panted on.

"Herr Lovelock. Kommen Sie!" I followed the anxious attaché down to the meadow and joined the other team captains and flagbearers who were spread in a U-formation rehearsing the oath-taking manoeuvre that would mark the climax of the parade after Hitler had declared the Games officially open. The rain was easing. The Village band struck up the tempo of Handel's *Hallelujah* chorus and the Village Kommandant, Oberstleutnant Freiherr von und zu Gilsa, made a speech that seemed almost as long as the rehearsal. Three hours later, dismissed, lunched, called out, embussed and driven to the Stadium – on the Maifeld now between the Belltower and the Stadium – we reassembled in teams. Cream-flannelled, black-jacketed, boatered, with white Olympic guide – we seven. Placed behind Mexico and Monaco, seven

233

out of 4269 athletes and officials, New Zealand came somewhere in the middle of the procession; and then like iron filings
we were drawn through an arch and were marching on to a
shrieking field. No, not a field. A bunker stupendously beflagged,
with a bright emerald circle of grass at the centre. Not even
that. An arena, a colossus, a sunken stone architecture that had
become a monument made of people. You knew. You knew
from the seething within, from an internal roar, when the right
arms were raised in tumult. You knew the power of so many
people together. We were not even inside yet – we were outside
the Marathon Gate on the open space of the Maifeld still
waiting to march in. But we had known for hours. They had
locked the gates to the Stadium at one o'clock. We had felt the
frenzy of the waiting throng as we drove in from the Village.
Along the Heerstrasse the inhabitants of Berlin were standing
forty deep. The Horst Wessel song was playing. Every thousand
feet we passed big metal loudspeakers announcing the impending arrival of the Führer. I saw a child held up by his father, a
child of two or three at most, who was clasping a huge beer stein
and raising the right arm in salute. Seen now from the Maifeld,
the Stadium was circular, surmounted by columns. The floor
forty feet below where we were standing.

Hitler drove on to the Maifeld at the head of a fleet of
silver-grey cars bearing the fifty or sixty members of the
International Olympic Committee. They wore their gilded
chains of office; they wore gloves, top hats and frock coats, their
coat-tails billowing in the wind. Hitler wore a simple brown
uniform. He was tiny. I was struck by his modest appearance
and by the slow dignified manner with which he mounted the
steps to the Marathon Gate between two top-hatted civilians.
The programme said he would arrive at 3.50 p.m. It was
3.50 p.m. precisely. The Stadium had grown strangely quiet.
Harold Abrahams, who was watching through binoculars from
a broadcasting box perched in the sky, later described to me the
scene when Hitler appeared between the towers at the top of the
Marathon Gate and descended to the floor of the Stadium. But
we had no need of description. We heard the trumpets sound
and the roar that followed. We felt the power as we marched in
behind. We were sucked in. Nothing could have prevented it –
we were sucked in by a magnetic power.

The march-past has since become history. Who can describe it? Years later I met a former Luftwaffe lieutenant, Hans Fritsch. Fritsch carried the flag for the German team on that day. He told me that the German team had been trained to march to the air "Frederikus Rex unser König und Herr"; but, as they entered the Stadium, the last of the 49 nations, the crowd of 100,000 spectators burst spontaneously into the German anthem, "Deutschland über Alles", throwing Fritsch completely. He missed the beat and the whole team lost step. Afterwards, he said, his fellow Luftwaffe officers cut him dead. They never forgave him for shaming Germany.

Believe me, it was a serious occasion.

I had a moment's panic as we marched in behind Monaco and swung right, approaching Hitler's stand. Everything happened quickly once we had come through the Marathon Gate. I had to make a snap decision, dipping the flag. I thought New Zealand performed rather well. Incidentally we copied the Americans and took off our boaters in salute, which is more than the Brits did. The British kept their hats on and gave a perfunctory eyes right; they got a cold reception from the crowd. You heard about the French? They brought the house down. At one stage, we had heard, it was in doubt if the French would send a team to Berlin at all. But they came. They gave Hitler the Nazi salute to a man. "Suddenly," Evelyn Montague wrote in the *Manchester Guardian*, "a forest of arms shot out in return and the German spectators broke into deafening applause which continued unabated as long as the French team was on the track. The symbolism of the German and French arms bridging the gap was so sudden and vivid as to be intensely moving . . ."

I had tears in my eyes when we sang the *Hallelujah* chorus at the end. Everyone was moved by something different. For Harold Abrahams, broadcasting live to England, it was Richard Strauss conducting his own Olympic hymn – Harold described the choir, massed in white, forming a gigantic iceberg against the dark tiers of the Stadium. But for Arthur Porritt, standing with the official party below the Tribune, it was the sound of Baron de Coubertin's voice relayed over the loud-speakers:

235

"The important thing about the Olympic Games is not the winning but the taking part, not the victory but the struggle."

I remember looking up after these words were spoken. A moment before, the sky had been filled with the sound of cannon and the beating of pigeons' wings. Momentarily it cleared and there, directly above our heads, was the legendary Zeppelin Hindenburg, so close I could see the smiling faces of the crew peering from the gondolas. It hovered there, engines roaring. The hymn was reaching a climax. The air was full of pigeons again. Then a runner in white appeared holding aloft a torch and I wanted to drop my flag and run after him as he circled the Stadium – I remembered the runner from my dream. But the dream was blotted out in noise. As the runner plunged his torch and the brazier on the skyline came to life, the noise that went up from the multitude was like a torrent of fire. Everything else passed in a blur. My arms ached from holding the flag.

The only other thing I recall is a German athlete taking the oath, his name was Ismayr. We were grouped in a ceremonial U before the Tribune where Hitler sat in a cantilevered box; in front of us was a raised box draped like an altar; the athlete stood inside the box, right hand raised; as he spoke the words of the oath into a microphone he reached out, as if to steady himself, to grasp the Olympic flag in his left hand, but clutched instead the Nazi banner. He held the red and black crooked cross fluttering at his side.

That evening after we returned to the Village I went into the forest and jogged quietly until the circulation returned to normal. The whole of my upper body seemed paralysed. It was about eight o'clock when I entered the dining-room. Going through the concourse and up the stairs, I heard snatches of conversation:

"All the little countries did."

"The Danes didn't."

"Well the Bulgarians did, the Austrians did. And the Czechs certainly did."

Everyone seemed to be discussing the march-past. On the stairs I passed our attaché, van Wick, who didn't greet me, and ran into Phil Edwards. Phil told me to have a look in the French restaurant. Upstairs around the French tables there was uproar – it was either an argument or a celebration. Knives and plates were being banged, voices raised, wine was flowing (only the French were allowed wine in the Village). Bottles of red wine were being snatched up and shared out among a mêlée of athletes who had battened on the Frenchmen with hilarity.

On my way to the New Zealand end, I stopped a moment by one of the English tables. Bespectacled Brown was saying to Jerry:

"The French are disgusting. But it wasn't just the French, Jerry. The Bulgars were goose-stepping! Everyone was poking their arms out for Hitler except for us. Oh hullo, Jack. You're not very popular round here either."

"Eh?" I said.

"Congratulations."

"What for?"

"Take a look round you."

I said, "The French seem to have stolen the show, don't they?"

"What about *you*?" Jerry's high-pitched guffaw reached me across the table. "Godfrey and I were just wondering who could have put you up to it? Nice work."

"All the same, some of your New Zealand chaps seem to think you've landed them in queer street," Godfrey said. "They're not taking it very well."

"Taking what very well? What on earth are you talking about?"

Jerry said to me, "Perhaps you should pay them a visit?"

There was a kind of muttering gloom surrounding the table in the New Zealand room. The five men who were hunched over their steaks and salad barely looked up as I joined them, though Clarrie Gordon the boxer, our youngest member, grinned and kicked me under the table.

"Something wrong, Cec?" I sat down alongside Cecil Matthews, our 5000 metres man. "What's on the menu?"

"Whatever it is, you won't get it. They kept us waiting half an hour."

Normally we were waited on by willing stewards. As I looked round, two stewards who were chatting nearby turned their backs and moved away. "Are we in some sort of bad odour, Cec?"

237

"You can say that again. We're the worst smell in the Village."

"I don't see why."

"You mean you don't know? The march-past, Jack!"

"Well?"

"We buggered it up."

"I thought we did rather well."

"So did I till we got back here. Have you seen Fritz, our liaison chap? Van Wick? Feel a bit sorry for him, actually."

"I passed him coming in. I thought it was a bit queer. He looked straight through me."

"He was frothing at the mouth a few minutes ago. He blames you, says you did it on purpose. Says you've made him an object of derision and dishonour before his fellow officers." Cecil suddenly chortled and dug me in the ribs. "*Was* it deliberate? Christ, you really don't know what I'm talking about, do you?"

"No, I don't."

"And I thought *I* was being thick. Jack, you remember marching us in through the Gate? You looked right and said, 'Which one is Hitler?' I took a dekko and saw there were two uniformed blokes with zipper moustaches standing up on platforms on the edge of the track – they were spaced out ahead of us."

"That's right."

"You turned round and said, 'Which one's him, Cec?' And I said, 'Hold your water. Not yet.'

"I didn't hear you. There was a lot of noise going on."

"So you dipped the flag and we all looked right. Took off our hats and clapped them over our chests. We did that bit all right."

"I took a stab, Cec. They both had little moustaches, it had to be one of the two."

"Damn right he had a zipper moustache. Did you see his dial? He nearly fell off the pedestal with fright. It was just a trooper, Jack, some little counter-jumper in a brown tunic. Jack, we still had fifty yards to go! I was screaming at you, 'Hold on.' You didn't listen. Next thing, you'd hauled in the flag and that was it, we'd shot our bolt."

"Oh God. You mean – ?"

"I'm telling you, we ignored the bugger. By the time we'd got abreast of Hitler's box we had our hats on again and were staring straight in front. You saluted the wrong man."

17

From my diary:

Sunday 2 August, 1936: Woke to wind and drizzle and went outside, the Village still asleep. Only the strange bearded Indian with his topknot of blue ribbon about when I reach the practice track on the plateau, the silent and melancholy Mr Singh. He is always first up in the morning. Jogged six laps followed by the trotting Mr Singh. We ran silently in a thin string rain. Afterwards he bowed, hands pressed under the chin – first he bowed to the east towards Berlin, then to me, quickly and silently, a gesture that I understood. As if to say that we alone know the beauty of the wind and the rain and the gods will favour us. I took it as an omen.

After grass and forest paths, the cinders felt easy – wet and soggy but easy. So easy.

As I came off the plateau, Cunningham and Lawson Robertson emerged from under the verandah of one of the houses. They had evidently been watching me. Cunningham in a flapjack raincoat and leather pumps, Robertson, the most famous of American track coaches, holding up a brolly for them both. Cunningham greeted me with a Howdie and joked about me "cocking a snook" at Hitler yesterday. My stock seems to have risen in his eyes. He was sucking a lozenge and offered me one. (He's worried about throat infection. So am I.) Lawson Robertson volunteered that he had banned visits by the American team to the Finnish sauna bath – half his boys apparently have colds – and as good as warned me off the sauna too. Cunningham said, "The Lord looks after fools and little children." He's a shrewdie is Cunningham, but for the first time I actually like the guy. He added, "See you Thursday" (the final of the 1500 metres is on Thursday), and I thought to myself, He wants me there. He really wants me there.

Cunningham has made me realise something about the Olympics – how utterly alone we are. He is already a hero, the most famous American miler of all time, with more records, awards, trophies than most of us put together; he's tough-minded, unsentimental, popular; yet his burning desire to win an Olympic prize sets him apart. He's alone. Worldly affairs don't touch him, as they don't touch me. All we've got is ourselves, and a slender chain of hope or pride linking us to some people back home that we care about. Deep down we think only about ourselves: but we feel for one another. I even begin to understand and feel for Wooderson's hopes and fears. Somebody said Wooderson has unlucky feet. I don't *want* these rumours about his foot to be true. I really want Wooderson to be there on Thursday.

The Times, I see, is doing Sydney proud – "Wooderson . . . a diminutive marvel of pace, stamina and pluck", and "the most popular of all the British competitors". Yet in an odd way I feel closer to Cunningham.

Afternoon: Beccali is going "great guns", Bill says. Bill came at 9.30 and sniffed about for me up on the track. Beccali, fighting fit, and screaming at spectators to get out of the way in sheer exuberance. Erik Ny, the German Schaumburg and Phil Edwards of Canada also, according to Bill, "impressive".

Wooderson, Bill says, didn't show.

Today are the first track events. At one o'clock the Village empties, and the buses leave for the Stadium at ten-minute intervals. Spend the morning swimming and hiding from reporters, all asking the same question: "Will you run the 5000?" I walk and walk, but can't decide. Nurmi's presence only increases my indecision – I keep bumping into him and thinking about his 1924 feat in Paris. Nurmi, now almost forty, seems to have an attaché all to himself. He's here with the Finnish team as guest of the German Government. Nurmi wears a crumpled overcoat and fedora, awkward when he sits, energetic and impressive when he moves. This morning we were photographed together. He said to reporters, looking at me with his blank farmer's eyes, that no new records would be set in Berlin – "only in the 5000 and 10,000 metres". That sort of thing makes me itch to run in the 5000, it's as if he is goading me. I can win the 5000 metres easily, Jerry thinks. It is certainly the easier prospect.

Now it is five o'clock. Through the rain from the window of one of the recreation rooms I look out towards Spandau, towards the Stadium, and read and re-read the letter to my mother I have been carrying about since yesterday.

"Village of Peace", Berlin
Sunday 2 August, 1936

Mrs Ivy Lovelock
c/o Miss Olive Lovelock
Opoho, Dunedin
New Zealand

Dearest Mother,

Your letter is such a welcome surprise, after a long silence. To have it *here* at this time makes all the difference. Some sixth sense told me you would write.

Everyone else is at the Stadium (today it begins). I read and re-read your letter and laughed, because you thought I would be "lonely" here. Remember when I first went away to boarding school? You had the same fears and apprehensions. But at school I had a key made that opened every door and on weekends when I was alone in the school I used to go into all the rooms, even the Rector's study, to find out things. I was never lonely. It's the same here. I have found a forest, a secret garden which is just like home – the tree-stems drip, the needles reek of home, it's like finding a cul-de-sac where I can slip in and out opening any door without a soul hearing, because only I have a key. It relaxes me. Who's lonely? Everyone else is under tremendous pressure, especially the Germans who are marched everywhere by their trainers, one-two, one-two. Fritz Schaumburg, a nice man whom I've met before, tells me some of the Germans are beaten before they start, "because our Führer wants only winners".

241

Schaumburg is their miler, unbeaten in this country since 1931, a great talent and a mature runner, but even he seems to be wilting under the pressure. I am free of all this.

I wrote to you once years ago about Lovelocks not being able to rise to an Occasion. But now I remember some lines that Father used to say from Longfellow – "He moved, he stirred, he seemed to feel, The rush of life along his keel." Well. It's true. The sap is rising. I can feel it. I am here to do great things and this time I won't let you down.

I don't like writing to you at an institution, so I am sending this c/o Olive. But you do sound calm and cheerful and that is a comfort to me. You've been praying, you say – it almost seems a miracle that thoughts and prayers written across 12,000 miles of ocean manage to arrive intact. I have already had an unexpected prayer delivered to me this morning (by an Indian). Yours is the second to reach me. It means so much.

Arthur is worried because I can't decide which event(s) to run in, but you will know long before this letter comes. Whatever happens, dear, a Lovelock is going to be remembered in Berlin. Yesterday was the parade and something terrible happened – I'll write of that another time. Now I have the Village to myself, apart from chefs, Japanese ducks, storks, rabbits, a kangaroo and a springbok belonging to the South Africans. There is no kiwi but me, and you always said I was a solitary bird!

You know, it has taken me eight years to get to Berlin and I don't know why it has to be Berlin, at least I didn't until yesterday. There is a sense of danger here. I don't mean personal danger. I felt it yesterday, at the Stadium – there are in fact nine stadiums, but *the* Stadium dwarfs us, like an empire in stone. The stone statues at the gate are so powerful and the walls of people so frightening, like gods of thunder, that you feel to succeed here requires something that is almost superhuman. You remember the tonic I used to ask Father for when I was a child? When I was sick? You brought me cocoa once and he put rum in it. Father called it cocoa with meaning, and I always wanted that when I was sick. So that is what these Olympics are to me, "cocoa with meaning".

The first buses are arriving back from the Stadium. Eureka! I have just realised something. I know now what I am going to do. I shall stop now and write again later . . .

Your loving son,

Jack

Dining-room, evening: The dining-room is littered with paper raincoats. Everyone has returned drenched. I am sitting at one of the tables with Godfrey Brown and Sandy Duncan and a few others, waiting for Bill who has gone off with Jerry to borrow some dry socks. Bespectacled Brown is telling me about Hitler's treatment of the two Negroes, Cornelius Johnson and Dave Albritton, who finished one and two in the high jump today. But before that, BB says, the pair lay about just below Hitler's box shooting craps in the rain and not bothering to take off their warms until the German competitors and all but a couple of others had been eliminated. By then the height had become "interesting". Earlier Hitler was wild with delight, according to BB, because a German, Hans Woellke, won the shot-put. "Mine host congratulated Woellke afterwards and also the Finns. Snubbed the blacks."

"How's that?" I say.

"He shot through. Just as Johnson and Albritton were called up to the dais, Hitler got up and left the Stadium."

Apparently Woellke, who is a police constable and the first German athlete ever to win an Olympic title, left the box, after receiving Hitler's congratulations, three ranks higher than he went in.

"Joke," Sandy suddenly says, passing round a drinks coaster on which he is collecting signatures. "What should the perfect example of Aryan manhood be? Blond like Hitler, slim like Goering, tall like Goebbels."

Everyone laughs, but not so convincingly, for there is tension now after the first day. Godfrey's tousled monkey face shows it; he can't stop blinking. Everyone is talking louder, faster, more furiously – or, like Sydney Wooderson, saying nothing. Wooderson is sitting at another table peeling an apple. The Finns, who finished one, two and three in the 10,000 metres, have gone to bed; the French and Italians are subdued; this pneumonia weather is getting to everyone and the English are

243

the glummest of the lot, having today lost all three of their sprinters, Pennington, Sweeney and Holmes at one go, with pulled thigh muscles.

"Holmes didn't start, Sweeney crocked and Alan Pennington stepped in a hole warming up, would you believe it?" Godfrey says. He adds, "I suppose I'll be next."

"Don't be silly, Godfrey."

All the same, Bill's prediction about the English appears to be coming true. British chances now remain in only two events, the 400 metres (Godfrey's event) and the 1500 metres (Wooderson's). Odd to think that after one day the hopes of Great Britain rest upon two men who are so short-sighted they wouldn't pass medicals for the Boy Scouts.

Presently Bill returned, bringing with him cups of Horlicks malted milk on a tray. He passed them around but didn't drink himself. He remained standing, looking preoccupied. I knew that look.

"You all right, Bill?"

"Headache, I think. Do you have some aspirins, sir?"

"Lots, in the room. Come on."

"You don't normally get headaches," I said to Bill when we reached the bungalow. "Two aspirin enough? Water?"

I gave him two and a glass of water and watched Bill take the bottle and tip several more aspirins into his hand. He folded the aspirins into a handkerchief and put the handkerchief away. He sat on the spare bed and sighed. "Aren't you going to take them now, Bill?"

"No, sir. Thank you, sir. I'll go now." He got up.

"Bill, you were going to get me the heats for the 5000 metres," I said. "Didn't you get them?"

Reluctantly, with another sigh, Bill reached into a pocket of his woollen suit, produced his notebook, extracted a piece of paper from it and read out some names. I lay back with my elbows behind my head and listened.

"Easy meat, Bill."

He held out the piece of paper. "Don't you want to see the heats?"

"Not much."

Bill sat down again. The bed sagged under his weight.

"Are you playing games with me, sir?"

"Bill, tell me something. Do I look ill?"

"No, sir."

"Worried? Depressed? Do you see anything wrong with me at all?"

"You're two pounds overweight, that's all."

"But that *is* all. I couldn't stand up on the train, remember? I was dropping from exhaustion. I should still be a cot case! Instead I'm dying of health – no knee trouble, no sleeping problems. I can't even catch a cold. You look terrible by the way. What's got into me?"

"You're in the pink, sir."

"I'm confident."

"Maybe. I don't like to hear you talk like that, sir."

"To tell you the truth neither do I, and that's what worries me. I'm worried because I'm not worried. Incidentally I can win the 5000 metres. Easily. How did the Finns go today in the 10,000?"

"It was a great race, sir, but slow, very slow. The Finns ran as a team. The winner was nine seconds behind Nurmi's record."

"There you are, Bill. Slow in the 10,000 metres, they'll be slow in the 5000 metres. The 5000 metres is a cinch." I grinned. "It's easy."

"Don't provoke me, sir."

"Bill, when did I ever do that? Now the 1500 metres, that's different. That's difficult. I can't possibly win that."

"You give me the creeps, sir."

"At least," I taunted, "not easily."

"You give me the creeps when you talk like that. Do you mind, sir? I'll go now."

"Oh Bill, don't go. The question is – Hullo? Come in."

There was a knock and Harold Abrahams walked in.

"Evening all. Hullo, Bill. I'm looking for a man called Jack Lovelock. There he is, he's grinning, just like Jesse Owens. Is it Owens? It can't be Jesse Owens, he's got small ears. You've got ears like mudguards. You must be Lovelock. Now you . . ." Harold shook out his umbrella and waved it at me. "You think I'm being facetious, don't you? I'm not. Every time I go into the press box someone says to me, 'Where's Lovelock? What's he up to?' So I decided to find out. Where have you *been*? Don't

245

answer. I can't stop. The weather forecast by the way is awful. Jack, dear boy, the Americans have got the wind up about you.''

"Oh? Really?"

"Yes. But I shan't go into that. I've told them you are having a second childhood playing hide and seek. Is it true you're training in a private park? Jack, it's coming to something when your own manager Arthur Porritt is (a) in the dark (b) won't speak to me and (c) is circulating a rumour that *I* don't want you to start in the 1500. Did I say that?"

"Yes, in London. Several times."

"Dear me. 'The greatest field of milers ever to be gathered together in one race' . . . A race 'bristling with world-beaters' – I am quoting the *Times*, you understand. 'And what of Lovelock?' our mutual friend Evelyn Montague is asking. 'What of a temperamental genius called Lovelock, the only one in the race with *brains*?' That's what Evelyn is writing in the *Manchester Guardian*. And I – *I* don't want you to start? Well if I did say that, I've changed my mind."

Harold glanced from me to Bill and back to me again, his eyes bright, amused. But he seemed shocked. He was in evening attire.

Suddenly he peered down at the carpet where his brolly, on which he had been leaning, had punched a neat hole. He straightened up and said, "Well, I must be going. Nice room you have here, Jack. Good night all."

"Now what do you suppose that was about?" I said to Bill when Harold had gone.

"He's telling you something, sir."

"Yes, but what? Do you think he knows something that we don't?"

"He's telling you not to run the 5000."

"I suppose he is. What a strange man Harold is." I sat up and said, "It's all right, Bill. I have no intention of starting in the 5000."

"Are you – are you on the level, sir?"

"I had to be sure, you see. I've always known, I think, what I was going to do – I knew what, but not why. Now I know why. I was writing a letter this afternoon and it suddenly hit me. Actually . . ." I laughed. "It's worth it to scrap the 5000 just to see the look on your face, Bill. In a minute you're going to smile."

"I am smiling, sir. Keep talking."

"I got a fright last year over Wooderson. I admit it. Ever since, I've been looking for a way out. I haven't been stringing you along."

"You said just now, sir, that your best chance is in the 5000 metres. Maybe it is."

"And that's why, Bill. It's too easy. Look, I've got little to gain and everything to lose by running the 1500. It's *dangerous*. I've never won a race in my life where I've had to worry about more than one man at a time, two at most. Six of the finalists from Los Angeles are going to be in the final on Thursday in all probability. Six! Plus Wooderson. Plus Schaumburg. Plus San Romani. How the hell do I stay out of trouble in a field of that class? It's just starting to get to me. The 5000 metres is a breeze by comparison. But Arthur is right – I can't walk away from the 1500. I know these people. I can't funk it, Bill. I daren't."

Bill didn't say anything. He sat there with his hands clasped across his paunch. His eyes were moist. "Keep talking, sir."

"Nothing more to say, Bill."

Bill dabbed his eyes with a corner of his handkerchief. As he did this, aspirins spilled out on to the carpet. He collected them one by one and put them back in the bottle, screwing down the cap.

I said, "I thought you wanted them for a headache?"

"Not now, sir. I just said that about a headache. I've had a spot of bother sleeping these last nights."

"Because of me? Oh Bill, surely not?"

"I thought the aspirins might help me to sleep."

"Oh Bill!" I got up and put my hand on his shoulder, then withdrew it. He was embarrassed.

"I've been worried that you'd make the wrong decision, sir. Worried stiff. I'll have to put another handle on my name, won't I? 'William G. Thomas, masseur, trainer, insommiak', I don't know how you say the word, I'm sure. But it will be all right now, sir. I'll go to sleep now like an angel in a pink nightie, even if it is a German bed."

*

247

Two days later on the Tuesday afternoon we got the draw for the 1500 heats. That was the day Bill got lost. We had expected the draw on the Monday but on Monday evening Jerry returned from the Stadium shaking his head. Jerry flopped on the spare cot in my room, said he was "worn out" with watching and confessed to being anxious about the race. Subconsciously, we both realised that this would be our last chance in the Olympics – Jerry was 26, and so was I.

On the Monday I had again stayed behind in the Village. I started out after lunch to go to the Stadium, but had no sooner got into the bus with Bill than my heart began to pound erratically, so we got down again. It was only after walking and swimming and sitting very still, willing it not to burst, that the thumping ceased and my heart-beat returned to normal. I noticed that Wooderson had also stayed behind, also Schaumburg. I met Wooderson in the afternoon by the perimeter fence. He pushed a hand through his hair and said, "Heats out yet?" "Not yet," I said. He nodded and ran on. He wore long baggy trousers. I couldn't tell if his foot was bandaged or not. Cunningham appeared on the practice track on Monday and again on the Tuesday morning, unsmiling, unflagging. Bill watched him and said there was nothing to report. Bill had a new word for Cunningham now, not pitiless any more, but "relentless". "He's fit, sir," was all Bill said. Bill refused to go to the Stadium unless I went too. He was brooding, a mood I remembered from Princeton. "I'll wait," he seemed to be saying. "We'll suffer together." Bill confided to me later that those two days of waiting, Monday and Tuesday, were the longest of his life.

On the Tuesday I sat in the competitors' stand with Jerry; Godfrey was with us, Bespectacled Brown, and Sandy Duncan. It was cold and windy; hats and programmes were flying about; there was a constant blare of loudspeakers; we seemed to be continually standing up for victory ceremonies or hidden rituals over to the right where Hitler's personal standard flew and visitors to his box came and went, ushered up from the bowels of the Stadium. Sandy had brought along binoculars and picked out Goebbels and Crown Prince Umberto of Italy in the box, also the film-maker Leni Riefenstahl looking like a magazine model in sweater and jockey cap: the ground was pocketed with deep trenches where her camera crews were dug in.

"Those bloody loudspeakers," Bespectacled Brown said. "They get my goat. Let's go back to the Village." But Sandy said, "Let's wait for the long jump." Jerry was cold and fidgety. I said, "We've lost Bill. We can't go yet." Bill had gone off in search of the draw for the 1500. We were not to see him again until the end of the afternoon. By then American athletes had won four more Gold Medals and we had been caught up in a drama that would become a legend.

"Look at that," Sandy said. "The flag's up."

We were watching the long jump, the qualifying rounds. Jesse Owens had strolled up and, still in his pullovers, raced to the pit and ran right through. The red flag was up, signifying a foul.

"They've ruled no-jump," Sandy said.

"I wasn't watching. What happened?"

"Jack, he was just running through, warming up! Jesse always does that." Sandy, a long-jumper himself, had his shirt on Owens. Jesse Owens had already collected two sprint wins that day in a heat and a quarter-final. The previous day he had won the 100 metres final. Owens seemed unperturbed by the officials' mistake. He shrugged, gave a gap-toothed grin and trotted back. "He'll be all right next time," Sandy said. As he spoke a young German ran, hung in the air and qualified for the final: Lutz Long, Germany's champion. I had met Long once and liked him – he was a medical student from Cologne.

Owens ran again. This time he hit the take-off board, cleanly I thought, and exceeded the qualifying distance. Sandy chuckled. "He's all right now." Then his expression changed.

The red flag was up again.

"I don't believe it, Jack. That's his second no-jump. If he fouls a third time, he's out."

It didn't seem possible – Owens was the world's record holder. The long jump was his best event.

Owens was peering down at the chalked board. He blew out his cheeks and walked back very slowly. Lutz Long came up to him. Owens pulled a blanket round his shoulders and huddled under it on the grass. Long sprawled on the grass beside him. They were head-to-head, talking. Nice, I thought; nice contrast. The flaxen-haired Aryan and the black sharecropper's

249

son, side by side. They were sprawled directly beneath Hitler's box, but I don't think anyone noticed at first.

A Japanese jumped, then an Italian.

"Ar-tu-ro!" sang the Italians in the stand.

"Taj-ee-ma! Taj-ee-ma!" chanted the Japanese.

"Oh shut up," Sandy said, glaring round him. "Shut up the lot of you," he bellowed. Surprisingly our section of the Stadium became still.

"What's going on, Sandy?" Bespectacled Brown said, in what had become a long and unexplained pause. The wind blew. Big white nimbus clouds were tearing above our heads. The officials waited. Sandy swivelled the glasses and said:

"Hitler's standing up. So is Goebbels. They're walking down together."

"Who are?"

"Lutz Long and Owens. They're coming down to the pit. Hang on, there's a photographer in the way. Long is telling him something. Take a look."

We were sitting to one side above the Marathon Gate; the long-jump pit was on our right at an angle. I could see Owens under the blanket walking down beside the run-up lane, the German walking beside him and pointing at the ground. Near the take-off board a camera lens had appeared, sliding out of the ground. The pair had stopped. The German was pointing again.

Sandy snatched back the glasses and said, "Lutz Long is telling Jesse to change his run-up. He is, he is. He's telling him to take off before he gets to the board. My sainted aunt. He's *coaching* him!"

Apparently he was. And, at the third and final try, Owens did what the German said – instead of pumping wildly with his legs he ran carefully, took off a good twelve inches before the board, hitched, ran through the air, sprawled and rolled out of the pit to qualify. Around us American loudhailers and Bronx cheers came to life and a murmuring tide of approval crept round the Stadium – although it was by no means full, there were only about 90,000 spectators at this stage. Jesse Owens had run back to Lutz Long and the pair were dancing round like puppies, grin-happy. I grabbed Sandy's binoculars and focused them. Hitler, I noticed, was no longer visible.

"How extraordinary," Jerry said.

250

More was to come. When the final began at 4.30 p.m. the Stadium was overflowing. The qualifying distance had been 23 feet 5 inches. Excitement began to mount when Owens, with his first jump, broke the Olympic record, leaping 25 feet 4¾ inches. The Stadium roared. Then Long also broke the old record, matching Owens exactly – 25 feet 4¾ inches. The Stadium roared again. "This German crowd . . ." Jerry was yelling. "Fair. They're very fair!" We kept nodding to each other and smiling with the excitement. But it was true. I could detect no partisanship or meanness in the German spectators, no bad intentions beneath the excitement. It's true, I thought. All through I was thinking, It's really true. All these stories we've been hearing about the Nazis, they're lies.

"Oh boy," Sandy said, after a huge ovation. The loudspeaker announced the distance in metres – "Sieben, vierundachzig!" Long, in the third of six rounds, had cleared 25 feet 8¾ inches.

But Owens was still an inch ahead – he had meantime increased his first jump to 25 feet 9¾ inches.

Long concentrated. Light, feathery. Leaned gently forward. Ran. Threw up his arms and hung in the air, suspended, like an insect. The loudspeaker blared, *"Sieben, siebenundachzig!"* – 25 feet 9¾ inches.

Owens rushed up to Long and congratulated him.

Sensation. A wait.

Owens told a German reporter later that he would have broken under the tension if Long hadn't taken him aside once more and talked to him, advising him yet again to check his run-up to the board. I didn't see this. There were other competitors still jumping. Sandy was making gobbling noises like a hen and Jerry was holding my arm in a vice. All I know is that Long in his final jump missed the board and Owens in his last two jumps hit it exactly, walked through the air, broke the record twice more and became the first Olympic man in history to exceed 26 feet. The Stadium seethed like a cauldron. The clamour never stopped – I suppose at some point it did stop, for Jerry was saying, "Does the heart good." He kept repeating it. "Does the heart good, Jack. Terrific spirit."

It's more than that, I thought. I was remembering the scene of three nights before, standing on the meadow outside the dining-room in the Village with Arthur. All these people who have been making war on each other, I thought. They've come to Berlin. The whole world is here. I was bubbling and chiming inside with youth and happiness – I half-expected a bell to ring out and sound the Pax Olympia. Presently it did. It was the Olympic bell mounted on top of the Glockenturm over the Maifeld. "The Youth of the World", I thought.

We watched Lutz Long congratulate Jesse Owens on his triumph. It was almost the end of the afternoon. Bill still hadn't returned. Just before we discovered where he was, after someone spotted him through the glasses, we watched the final of the 800 metres in which my old friend Phil Edwards was attempting for the fifth time to win a Gold Medal for Canada – but he didn't, the Gold went to the American Negro Woodruff. Phil came third, falling back after launching a long witless sprint from the 300-metre mark. As he dropped back, I automatically turned round to say something to Bill, forgetting Bill wasn't there.

"There's Bill," Sandy said. Far below us was a sunken path where the competitors stood while they waited to be called up on to the track. Bill was down there. Sandy could see his bowler hat projecting over the rim of the trench. We went down. As we made our way down, one of the heats for the 5000 metres was lining up and I saw that the melancholy Mr Singh was a competitor. I recognised him by the topknot tied with blue ribbon. Mr Singh seemed content to trot along philosophically far behind the field, tall, thin, bearded and quite detached. He was somehow perfect.

"Bill, where on earth have you *been*?"

"Sorry, sir. I tried to get back but they wouldn't let me through. I lost my pass. I've been wandering in and out of tunnels, hoping . . ." Jerry interrupted.

"Never mind that. Have you got the heats?"

"Here you are, Mr Cornes." Bill fished out his notebook from his mac. "J. F. Cornes, Grossbritannien – Heat 2. Ten starters." Bill passed Jerry the notebook and added, "You won't like it, Mr Cornes." He turned to me and winked.

"Jack, this is marvellous," Jerry said. "What d'you mean, Bill, you old devil? Jack, we're in the same heat!"

"True? Who else?"

"Boot, Nakamura, Velcopoulos, never heard of them. Oh yes, Venzke. Venzke's there. We'll have to watch Gene Venzke.

252

Nobody else that seems to matter. Jack, you know what? We'll do a fixer. We'll *fix* the race. Oh, pack up your troubles – !" Jerry began to sing. He had grabbed my brolly and leaped out of the trench and was pirouetting on the track above our heads in the rain. "What's the USE of worrying?" Jerry sang. It was starting to rain. I turned to Bill and said, "I reckon we can fix it, you know, Bill – just like at Iffley Road. We'll do an Iffley." "Do more than that, sir" – Bill nudged me. "I reckon with that heat you can do a bleeding Charleston."

"OH! Pack up your troubles in your old kit bag . . ." Jerry sang. It was one of the ditties Jerry had regaled us with at Oxford during my first winter in 1931 when Jim Mahoney and Tony Leach and I had chased him in a mud-bespattered dance round the track at Iffley Road. Jerry had a terrible voice. Just then there was a downpour. Rain pelted down and we scuttled for cover under the Stadium.

That night in the Village when Jerry and I were sitting together in his room planning what we would do in the heat, Pat Boot came looking for me. Pat was a New Zealander, another miler, he came from South Island as I did and the same South Island school and by a further coincidence he had drawn the same heat in the 1500 metres. Jerry gave Pat some advice. "Nice lad," he said when Pat had gone. "Silent type. Doesn't say a lot, does he?"

"Like me, Jerry."

"Bit of a worrier, I'd say."

"Like me. Pat's all right. I was the same at Los Angeles."

"You were worse." Jerry's hooting laugh exploded in the room. "At Los Angeles you were insufferable."

The heats were run next day.

18

"Blast, I wish they would hurry up," Jerry said.

"It's the pole vault," I said.

"No, it's not."

"They're waiting for the pole vault."

"It must be something else."

"Der Nächste," the loudspeaker said every few minutes. Nächste – Next one. "Nächste . . . Nächste . . . Nächste."

"Can you see?" I said. Jerry hoisted himself and peered over the rim of the trench. "It's blowing. I can't see a thing, only umbrellas. I hate this."

"Think of England," I said. "What's the matter with Wooderson?"

Jerry didn't answer. Wooderson was huddled in an ill-fitting World War One greatcoat. He looked so thin and tortured and the wind up there was so strong, I felt he needed ballast in his pants, some lead nails or fishing sinkers to hold him to the earth. Even the sinewy Beccali, poking faces at a lowering sky, was looking unhappy. I was wearing two jerseys under a track top. We were all cold, waiting to be called out from the trench, forty of us – the four heats. "That bloody pole vault," someone said. Little did we think that the pole vault which had begun an hour before in streaming rain would continue another five hours into the darkness to end at 10 p.m. under floodlights. We had been waiting since 4.15. It was ten to five.

Jerry said, "I forgot to tell you. Saw a friend of yours yesterday as we came in."

"Tell me later, Jerry. I can't think."

"Sorry! Thought you'd been asking about him. Otto Peltzer."

"I don't know why we bothered to warm up, Jerry. Who? Peltzer's not in Berlin. I asked Schaumburg."

"He had a goatee. It may not have been Peltzer."

"Then it's not him. According to Schaumburg, Peltzer has disappeared. Anyway he's not in Berlin."

"Hullo. Here we go."

We were marched up a flight of steps on to the track. We had been marched from the dressing-rooms through a cavernous tunnel into the trench; now we were marched across a red circle to the other side of the track. It was blowing hard. The start was beside a tall camera platform. The first heat was away immediately, bang on five o'clock. God, they're efficient, I thought, as Jerry and I drew lanes and lined up for the second heat. We had decided that at lap three we would take control and slow the field right down, to conserve ourselves for the final. But we hadn't planned on wind. It was the same wind Cunningham and Dawson had used to slow me down at Princeton in 1935, except that here it was inhuman. We seemed to be running in a crater. The sides of the Stadium joined the sky – there was no physical separation – and the wind plunged down. If it's like this tomorrow, I thought, I'm finished. Pat Boot led for a lap and a half, disregarding Jerry's advice. Pat came last. The cinders felt sticky. I had made a mental note the day before of the position of the camera platform, at the 1200-metre mark, and now, passing it, where the back straight opened up, I looked up through the stays of the platform to a gap on the skyline where the twin pillars of the Marathon Gate broke the sky. In the gap flickered the Olympic flame. Each time in the heat I passed the platform, 300 metres out from home, I looked up to the flame and said a prayer: God give me the strength to go tomorrow. *Here.*

"That was close," I said to Jerry when the heat had ended and we were walking back to collect our jerseys. Coming down to the finish we were preparing mentally to join hands and cross the line in a dead-heat as we'd done four years earlier at White City when I had won my Blue. Jerry had waited for me on that occasion. Now, again, he had waited. We were well in front, as we blithely thought. Then two men hurtled up, Scholtz and Venzke. Ten yards from the tape Venzke went past my right shoulder "Help!" Jerry shouted, and we scrambled in second and third to qualify, heading off, but only just heading off, the South African Scholtz.

Our heat was the slowest of the four.

The third heat had already started. We stood by the camera platform and watched Beccali control it, running beautifully, well within himself. But it was black Phil, lazy old Phil Edwards who amazed me. Edwards, the Hungarian, Szabo, and Britain's Robert Graham were all there. "Go, Phil," I yelled as the bell rang for the last lap. Phil was lying third, behind Graham and Szabo and ahead of the Olympic champion, Beccali, Phil just loping along. Then, passing the point where we were standing, almost lazily Phil accelerated, beginning a long sprint. "He's mad," Jerry said. "He can't sprint from here." "It's not impossible," I said, but my voice was coming from outside my body. I was seeing forwards and backwards at the same time. I had already had moments of dream experience since coming to Berlin, but this was different, uncanny. Annoying too. It was as if Phil were rehearsing my dream for me, trying to gatecrash it. It amazed me that he should so casually attempt to anticipate what I had been so carefully and secretly planning all this time. He had tried to pull off a last lap like this at Los Angeles in 1932 and failed. Yesterday in the 800 metres he had tried it again. Failed. Now he was trying a third time.

"There, what did I tell you?" Jerry said. "He's cracking." Phil was cracking in the straight. "He's cracked. Beccali, one, Szabo, two – Edwards, three."

"Graham, four," I said. But Phil, third, had qualified for the final. Robert Graham, the Scotsman, was out.

"Another British hope down the drain, Jack. Damn."

That left Sydney Wooderson. There was one more heat. Wooderson's heat was the last and toughest heat. We were walking over to wish him luck but we'd left it too late – the heats were being rushed through to clear the track for the end of the 50-kilometre walk which had been under way outside the Stadium since one o'clock. The wind blew. Rain was slanting down, holding up the pole vault in the centre of the field and sponging out the ten runners who had already taken their marks. A loudspeaker crackled, announcing the impending arrival of the long-distance walkers. I heard the names "Schwab . . . Whitlock". The starter was waiting for the announcement to end. I saw Albert Hill dart across and pin down Wooderson's number which was flapping loose – I don't know how Hill the trainer got on to the field. Hill stepped aside and gave Wooderson a thumbs-up sign. Wooderson was standing outside Schaumburg. He put up a hand to wipe his glasses, and the hand flopped to his side. I turned to Jerry – and I don't know how I knew. I said, "He isn't going to qualify."

Wooderson lay in fourth place for two laps. He ran erratically, as if the eyes were fogged and he couldn't see the lanes. Going past us the last time, he made a tremendous spurt along the back straight that took him within striking distance of Schaumburg and the Frenchman Goix, the two leaders. Then he stopped. "Come on, Syd!" I wanted to yell, as in my dream, but the dream was reversed somehow, it was all back to front.

256

The words died on my lips. Wooderson had stopped. He limped across the line in seventh place.

Only later back in England did we learn that he had been hiding – with what care, with what consummate secrecy! – an injury that turned out to be a fractured ankle bone. Out walking, months before, he had stepped in a rabbit hole.

"That's it," I said to Jerry.

"Come on!" And we ran across to see if there was something we could do. But Albert Hill was already there at the finish line, leading Wooderson hobbling from the field. "Another British disaster," Jerry was saying. "Damn, damn, damn. An absolute unmitigated thundering disaster." Thunder, there now was. A clap sounded. I looked up and couldn't see the Olympic flame. Flame's gone out, I thought. Peals of thunder crashed about us. White rain began to fall in torrents and, with this, a man with a little moustache and a Union Jack on his vest, body heaving, his number spattered with mud or vomit, appeared under the arch of the Marathon gateway and advanced on to the track. "Whitlock!" Jerry said, and rushed across to cheer on an Englishman winning the long walk. Harold Whitlock, a mechanic from Deptford, walked – or rather, waded – a final lap in triumph. But I was thinking of Wooderson, hobbling away in pain and in tears. I thought of Peltzer leaving the field in tears at Los Angeles four years earlier. The rain lashed down. The air had grown black – the air was black with umbrellas. I stood there looking up to where the flame had gone out. For a moment the Stadium seemed turned to night.

Arthur Porritt was waiting when I got down to the dressing-room. I changed and drove with him into town for a bath and a talk. Arthur as an IOC member had a car and driver at his disposal. We dropped Bill in the Heerstrasse, arranging to meet in the morning, and went on to the Adlon on the Linden where Arthur was staying. In the car Arthur said, "All set for tomorrow?"

"I think so, Arthur."

"I thought you ran the heat very nicely, you and Jerry. Like a couple of wise old sheepdogs." I nodded. "But you will have to watch young San Romani. He's a dark horse, that one." Running in the last heat the unknown San Romani had, according to Arthur, come from ninth to second place, passing six runners in the last eighty yards. "He was invisible till the last hundred yards. Did you not see it, Jack?"

I shook my head. I had been too intent on watching Wooderson. All I knew was that in the final next day there would be three Americans, Cunningham, Venzke and San Romani. They had all qualified.

We talked about Wooderson and I mentioned to Arthur the dream I had had in February. "I don't understand it. You know, I dreamed Wooderson wouldn't make it. Now it's happened, but it hasn't happened as I imagined it would. It's just the reaction, I suppose."

"What is, Jack? You *are* feeling all right?"

"Bit flat, that's all."

"You'll be all right tomorrow. Bath and a rub-down at the hotel. Good sleep tonight. The car will take you back when you're ready."

Harold was in the Village that night. After supper Burghley arrived – Lord Burghley was Commandant of the British team – and champagne was brought out to celebrate Whitlock's win. "About time they remembered him," a reporter said to me. The reporter said he had come upon Whitlock after his victory in the walk in one of the underground tunnels of the Stadium, limping in bare feet, quite lost, unable to find the dressing-room. At that stage none of the British delegation had bothered to come near him. Harold Whitlock was a motor mechanic, Britain's first – and, as it turned out, only – individual athletic victor of the Games.

I looked in on the celebration for a few minutes, but somehow the atmosphere wasn't right. Wooderson's failure seemed to have thrown a pall over the English camp. I avoided the public rooms and walked down to the lake, enjoying the aroma of pine needles coming from the sauna hut and listening to the rhythmical sounds of the Finnish athletes beating themselves with pine branches. I paused on the wooden bridge spanning the lake and tried to think of all the things I had to think of for the race next day, but my thoughts were outside my body and I worried instead about the weather. The storm seemed to be over. The night sky was sombre – there was no way of knowing what it would do next. The slapping sounds coming from the hut had stopped. "Hoch. Hoch. Hoch," I heard, followed by a splash, and I jumped. One of the Finns had plunged from the sauna raft into the lake. "Helling-GOA," he cried, breaking the surface. "Helling-GOA! Helling-GOA!" And all I could think of was Cunningham. For the chants that had accompanied Cunningham's win in the first heat that afternoon had sounded just like that – "Cunning-HAM! Cunning-HAM! Cunning-HAM!"

I went back to the room, wrote in my diary and took a sleeping draught. I swallowed half the bottle and lay down. About ten thirty I awoke with a raging thirst. I could taste the chloral in my mouth. I noticed a message impaled on one of my spikes which were lying on a chair. It was written on green and red Village stationery and it said, "England expects". No signature. I walked through the Village to the gate, found the restaurant there still open, went in and ordered a drink. I lit a cigarette and sat there smoking it. Harold walked in.

"Do you think that will do any good?" he said, wagging a finger.

"Don't know, Harold." I smiled. "Tommy Hampson smoked one at Los Angeles the night before his final. 'If I can't have a smoke when I want one,' Tommy used to say, 'I can't run.' It helps my mood."

"And why not? What's that you're drinking?"

"Horlicks."

"Oh. You poor thing. I've been drinking champers with Burghley." Harold was wearing a dark overcoat and a long silk scarf. He pulled up a chair, signalled to a waiter and waved him away again. "Now then," he said. "Tell me the worst."

"It's strange. I'm sitting here thinking, Tomorrow is the final. Tomorrow is the final. I can't grasp it, Harold. You know, I'm half-convinced that if I don't turn up tomorrow, there won't *be* a final."

He laughed. "You should be in bed."

"I'm wide awake."

"In that case we'll talk. I suppose," he said, glancing round conspiratorially, "this is where the fraternising takes place?" There were about twenty people in the restaurant, mostly couples, among them a Hungarian woman athlete I vaguely knew. The restaurant, although part of the complex at the entrance to the Village, was beyond the gate on the main road, its glass-fronted panels facing the road where we could see soldiers patrolling and a free biscuit van was parked. Behind the van, opposite where we were sitting, a small car was stationed. "Nice arrangement," Harold was saying. "No Exos here, I see." Exo (for Exotic) was a term the Berliners had coined for the American Negroes.

"You know what they do with the Exos, Jack? The poor beggars are so starved for alcohol and sex, the Germans have taken pity and begun running transports for them into town to the brothels. So the story goes. Not your style, I suppose?"

"Not my style, Harold." But at that moment there was nothing more I wanted than a woman. "I just hope," I said, "I don't draw the second to outside lane tomorrow."

"Why? Was that what you got at Los Angeles?"

"How did you know?" I laughed. "Yes, Lane 11. I've drawn the second to outside three times in my life and each time I've lost."

"Omens like that don't mean a thing. Mustn't brood, Jack. Whatever you do, you mustn't brood. Would you like the Abrahams weather forecast?"

"Please."

Harold moistened a finger and held it up, his eyes playful, mischievous. "It won't rain. No, seriously. Hitler has been to the Stadium three times without an umbrella and each time he's got soaked. Tomorrow he's bringing the King of Bulgaria *and* an umbrella. It won't rain."

"Harold, you're drunk."

"I told you, I've been drinking with Burghley. David has all the gossip on the Royals. Lots of intrigue going on, secret police guarding them. Half the visiting Royalty are at the Adlon and half at the Kaiserhof, staying incognito. They travel to and from the Games separately for safety. As for tomorrow, Hitler is entertaining to lunch Boris of Bulgaria, the Princess Maria of Savoy and the Crown Prince of Greece. The cars are ordered for the Reichskanzlei at 3.50 which will get them to the Stadium just in time for your race. Command performance."

"They'll have to gobble their dessert then. The race starts at 4.15. Harold, who do you suppose is in that car?"

"Which car?"

"That one, behind the biscuit van. It was here when I came. There are two men in it. They keep looking."

"Well they can't be interested in us. Now listen. Did you get my message?"

"What message? Oh, yes. Somebody pinned 'England expects' on one of my spikes. Was that you? I thought it was a joke."

"It is no joke, my dear fellow, that England's sprinters have crocked and it is no joke that Sydney Wooderson has now crocked. Who does that leave? Work it out for yourself. *'Sail on, sail on, thou ship of state!'* Don't look so mystified. I thought you liked poetry. How does it go?

> " *'Humanity with all its fears*
> *With all its hopes of future years*
> *Is hanging breathless on your fate!'* "

"Oh shut up," I said.

"I won't shut up. God, I wish I was a performer and not a commentator here – I'm sick of this Hitler and his daily ration of Heils. I'd like someone, just someone to show these Nazis what England and the Empire is made of. You can do it. You've got to do it. Don't laugh. Half an hour ago the pole vault ended. Who won? Another American. They went for six hours and ended under floodlights, Earle Meadows won – I've just heard. Another Olympic record, another American. Jack, there have been ten, twelve competitions so far. The black Americans are sweeping the track events and the Germans are winning everything else. The Germans think they're the only Aryans in sight."

"I'm not sure I like being called an Aryan, Harold."

"Nordic, then. You've got blue eyes, blond hair and you're white. Don't be so dense. You know that Jesse Owens has already collected three Gold Medals. The press boys are now calling him American's sharpest weapon – they're right, he is. And you're ours. You may not think you will be carrying England's hopes with you tomorrow, but by God in most people's minds you are. You're the only challenge to Hitler we've got."

"So who's for tennis?"

261

"I wish you'd stop grinning and be serious for a moment."

I didn't say anything. I ordered another drink and sat there getting the taste of chloral out of my mouth and thinking confused thoughts. "I just want you to win, Jack," Harold said. "Thanks for the Horlicks," he said, when he finally left. He pressed my hand. "I must try it some time."

Harold's weather forecast was accurate. Next day it was dry, flat calm. Before breakfast I walked in the forest, jogged gently. I did nothing silly. I returned to the Village, swam quietly in the pool, dried and weighed myself. A hundred and thirty-three pounds, just right. Back in the room, I changed, cleaned my spikes and was just leaving the bungalow to go to breakfast when I felt the knee go. For a moment I stood rock still. Very gently I flexed the leg. I went back to the bungalow and sat down on the bed.

Cecil Matthews my room-mate came in from the bathroom. "What is it?"

"Nothing. I'll see you at breakfast, Cec." I went into the day room and waited until Cecil had gone, then returned to the room and lay down. I waited a few minutes and tested the leg again. The knee was stiff. Bill arrived shortly after 9.30. By then I had got out the equipment and was calculating how much of the vaccine I dared inject.

Bill took one look and said, "Oh God. Oh my God, sir."

"It's the tendon, Bill."

"When?"

"Just now – a few moments ago. Would you mind closing the door? I must have done something without realising it."

"How bad, sir?"

"I don't know yet. Would you pass me that phial? No, the other one, the one with coloured glass. I want to get the stuff in before Arthur comes."

I pushed a needle on to the syringe, unscrewed the cap of the phial and perforated the rubber bung. I was drawing up the contents of the phial into the syringe when Arthur walked in.

He took in the situation very quickly. "The knee?"

I nodded. "It was bound to happen, Arthur." I forced a grin. "Serves me right, I suppose. That's what comes of saying it's getting too easy."

Arthur asked a couple more questions. He said, "Would you put down that needle, Jack," and took Bill outside. I could hear them speaking in the corridor. Arthur came back and said, "No vaccine, Jack." He added, "Mickie Mays will fix it."

"I don't want Mickie Mays, Arthur. The vaccine works. It worked at Princeton."

"I've sent Bill to get Mickie Mays. If it's the tendon again, you want massage, heat, anything but that stuff of Fleming's." Vaccine therapy was a sore point with Arthur. Like many surgeons he was sceptical about the value of absorbing dead toxins into the system. He said, "I thought you'd stopped taking the drug."

"No."

"As a matter of interest, how many organisms in that dose? A million?"

"A million and a half." Arthur swallowed. I added quickly, "There won't be a reaction."

"You've had a reaction before. Jack, if you get one now, a sudden implosion, you're out of the race."

"Arthur, if I don't take the vaccine, I may not be *in* the race." I drew the rest of the contents of the phial into the syringe.

"Please wait. Have you got anti-phlogiston?"

"No. I didn't bring any anti-phlo with me."

"Lie back." He examined the knee. I winced, even though the pain was slight. "Stand up please. Now walk. Flex the knee. Well, you can move it."

I said, "It may be nothing at all."

"All the more reason not to inject."

"Arthur, it's a *recurring* injury. I've had it for two years. I've been injecting the stuff for so long, my body is used to it."

"It's too risky, Jack. No, no. God, I wish you'd allowed me to operate on the tendon in London."

At one stage I had consulted Arthur about the possibility of an operation, but had decided against it in favour of continuing the vaccine.

Bill came back and said he couldn't find Mickie Mays.

"Arthur, at Princeton last year the knee was far worse – I'm telling you. And it worked."

"On the day of the race?" Arthur turned to Bill. "He injected himself that day? The same day?"

263

"Yes, Doc." Bill's face didn't twitch. He lied beautifully.
"And there was no reaction?"
"Not as I am aware of, Doc. He won."
"Here." I gave Arthur the needle. "Would you like to do it?"
Arthur hesitated.
He looked at the needle. "It's blunt."
"I've sterilised it."
Arthur was meticulous. He removed his jacket, rolled up his sleeves, washed his hands, sharpened the needle and resterilised it, using a small stone and an ampoule of methylated spirits from my kit. Deftly, he injected the opposing arm. Bill looked on approvingly.

"Beautiful, Doc. But I don't know why you puts it in the arm. Jack usually bungs it in the knee."

"In the *knee*? No wonder you've been getting a reaction. Jack, what is he saying?"

I didn't answer because at that moment I felt an excruciating pain, as if the knee had been wrenched in its socket. The pain was rioting from ankle to thigh. I had doubled up on the bed against the wall. One minute I was cramped in a stiffened agony against the wall, the next I had rolled back with tight-shut eyes and the pain was flowing out of me. "It's all right," I said a moment later, sitting up. "It's going. Look – " I was sweating. Something like cool cream or melted snow was coursing down the back of my neck and across the ribcage. My toes tingled.

"What is it?" Arthur said.

Very gently I leaned forward and touched my toes. I lay back and worked the knee. "Look. It's coming loose." I waggled it. Lay back and bicycled in the air. Kicked. Then I got up and ran a few steps on the spot. "It's going to be all right, Arthur. I can feel it." Arthur was shaking his head in bewilderment. By mid-morning when he left, still shaking his head, the stiffness had gone completely.

Looking back now, I am inclined to think that though inwardly calm I was more strung up than I had realised and that the incident was purely psychological. Something similar, I learned later, had happened the previous year to Jesse Owens: on the eve of a famous meeting at Ann Arbor in Michigan, Owens had been overcome by a searing pain in the joints, knocked sideways; then the pain had passed and he had gone out to establish four world records in seventy-five minutes. In my case, Arthur was I think right to be sceptical. But my faith in "Flem's juice" that morning was absolute. Arthur was right and I was right. We were both right. I don't understand it.

After Arthur went, I took Bill for a late breakfast. I ate fruit, a slice of cheese, a poached egg. Bill ate all my toast. At noon when we returned to the room I was keyed up. I said to Bill, "Arthur says everything is going to depend on the way the first lap is run. What do you think?"

"Depends." He had taken out a pack of playing cards and was laying out patience on the bed. "Depends how you look at it, sir. When a man is as fit as you are, it don't do him much good to think. He knows. It's like this game of patience. I've been playing this particular patience, sir, for twenty-one years and it hasn't come out yet, but on the day when it does I reckon I'll know. Won't I? I'll know before I start. So will you." Bill fastened me with his mournful eyes and I thought he was about to make a profound statement. He said, "I've got another pack of cards here, sir. Would you like a game?"

There were still two hours to wait. I said, "Yes, Bill. I think I would."

19

"Plenty of time, sir," Bill said.

"They'll start without me."

"No, they won't."

"Bill, I have to go. They'll disqualify me."

It was 4.05 p.m. We were alone in the dressing-room in the bowels of the Stadium. We had left the Village with Jerry at two o'clock and Jerry and I had warmed up on an outside track near the Friesenhaus where the women were quartered; we had walked back through a sealed tunnel that ran beneath the arena and emerged deep down in the catacombs of the Stadium where Hitler drove in each day. Jerry and I then separated on the stairs to go to our allotted rooms. Ten minutes later I was called out, taken down and ushered through a wire fence and up through a door with a guard on it into a sort of diffused whiteness full of staring faces. "Achtung!" Voices barked outside the door. More runners were brought in, the door closed. I found myself in a cavernous chamber, bare, ill lit, with wooden seats around the walls. I sat down beside someone smelling of hair oil. "Ciao," he said, flashing his teeth, and moved across. Beccali. Across the room I made out by another gash of white teeth the ebony frame of Phil Edwards and, beside Phil, holding his spikes in one hand and a roll of tape in the other, the Swede Erik Ny. I couldn't see Jerry. Cunningham appeared from somewhere, shook hands and said, "What's your number?" I told him.

"What's yours?" I said. But he had turned away.

That annoyed me. Bill had been refused entry by the guard on the door and that had also annoyed me. I was starting to feel mutinous. A low hum issued from one of the ventilators above our heads. I don't know how long we waited. At one stage the door opened and there was a scurry and scraping as everyone stood up to go, but it was only the German finalists, Schaumburg and Böttcher, coming in. They arrived with an escort of Nazi officials, then the officials left except for an umpire of some sort in mufti with a pointed chin. He had taken Fritz Schaumburg aside and appeared to be lecturing him. I heard the words "Führer . . . unser Führer" repeated. Schaumburg said nothing. His mouth was white, probably from glucose. He licked the top lip, his thin body trembled and I had the impression he would have liked to throttle the umpire but felt powerless to talk back. When the officials eventually returned and marched everyone out for the start of the race, I stayed put. I sat down and refused to go.

"That's the stuff, sir," I heard Bill say, beside me. Bill had nipped in when the others went out. A man in white uniform was plucking at my arm, saying "Endlauf. Komm!" Bill got between us and said in his best Cockney, "If he don't want to go, Fritzie, he don't want to go!" The official shrugged and retired. Bill sat down with me and said, "Let the buggers stew."

I said to Bill, "How long to go?"

"Plenty of time, sir."

They had left at five to four and been gone several minutes. The race began at 4.15. They would be on the track, drawing their lanes. I couldn't stand it any longer.

"If I don't go, Bill, they'll disqualify me."

Bill took out his fob watch, consulted it and put it away again. He folded his hands across his paunch. "Let 'em stew," he said.

The room was made of concrete, like an underground garage, walled high; pipes and tubes ran up the walls, meshing at the top, and continued across the ceiling. At this moment somewhere up there, Godfrey Brown was running a 400-metres, his quarter-final. I could feel the weight of granite tiers pressing down on me. The silence pressed down. Without warning the hum of the tubes changed to a high-pitched whine and a clamour of sound entered the chamber. Godfrey's race, I thought. It must be over.

"All right, sir?" Bill stood up.

We went down together.

As I came up on to the track, I glanced quickly across to the starting line on the far side – the runners were there waiting. Seconds before, having a last word with Bill, he had put a hand on my shoulder, and it had felt so heavy. Now, released on to a gigantic stage, the heaviness slid away. It seemed to me that I had imagined this moment all my life, every detail, yet I had imagined it somehow wrong. White-suited officials accompanied me, advancing like penguins. They waddled. I tiptoed. Do you know what it means to cross a field on tiptoe? A field of Aschenbahn baked rust-red, the red painted on a green ground? The air was dry and warm. I walked silently, yet I knew that every step, every footfall, every breath I took and every pulse that beat in my body was being carried to the uppermost tiers of that arena.

I remember thinking, I hope Bill remembers to watch. And: Mother wouldn't have liked this. She hates crowds.

I had forgotten to find out if the lap times were being called.

Cunningham was already on the cinder path, knee-stepping. I went up to him and waited until he'd taken off his track top. I didn't say anything. I just wanted to see his number. An umpire held out to me a small canvas bag. From the bottom of the bag I drew out a numbered stick, Number 11. Just my luck, I thought. I had the second lane from the outside.

The starter, Franz Miller, stood back, one arm crooked, the right hand holding a pistol from which snaked a coil of black wire to some remote timing device. Miller was an experienced starter, the best. I remembered him from Los Angeles. I remembered the ankle-length white surgeon's coat. Miller nodded to me and tapped his watch, telling me to hurry up. I sat down on the grass and very slowly began to lace on my spikes. I had to delay everything now. Ny's feet, I noticed, were striped with tape; that, and his blue pants and flaxen hair, made the Swede the clearest runner on the field. Ny appeared to have one of the inside lanes, with Beccali. Beccali's chest and lips were moving. He had his head down. He didn't have a number on his vest at all. I had a feeling that Ny or one of the Germans would try to lead. The two Germans, in white, were in the middle lanes with Jerry and Cunningham, also in white, but side on I couldn't see the numbers and the white vests were blurred; almost indistinguishable one from the other. Jerry's hair, which was black, showed. Cunningham's number was 746.

"Seven four six, seven four six" – I was memorising the number aloud to myself when Phil Edwards came over and said in his sing-song voice, "Doin' fine, boy. You're doin' just fine." I nodded and smiled. I had already told Phil I intended to keep Cunningham waiting. Miller's whistle had gone and as Phil trotted back I stood up and waited for Cunningham to turn round, knowing that he would turn round, knowing exactly how he felt, knowing that every second's delay after the starter's call would be agony to him. Cunningham was already in line but a little back from the line and gazing ahead, his eyes taking in the back straight and scouting the top corner where it unwound anti-clockwise and emerged by the Marathon tunnel marking the beginning of the front straight. He stepped to the line. His eyes went down and he waited, fists lightly clenched. On the grass, I waited for him to turn. He didn't turn, he half-turned. The head swivelled and I caught the whites of the eyes – oh, there was anguish there. Deliberately, keeping an eye on the starter, I prolonged his agony by bending down and doing something to the lace of one shoe. I got my comeuppance then – on cue.

One minute I was keeping Cunningham and 110,000 spectators waiting while I tinkered with a shoe, the next the starter, Miller, who short and dumpy, appeared to have grown ten feet tall. Franz Miller had come bolt upright. All the runners changed personality. On the inside lane I saw Beccali's right arm shoot skyward and in the middle where the Germans were two arms more and then all around hitting the air a rain of arms uplifted as the Reichssportfeld came to its feet in tumult – "Sieg Heil! Sieg Heil! Sieg Heil!" It went on and on, the most terrible noise. Quite wonderful. It was for Hitler, entering his box with the King of Bulgaria, right on cue.

Upstaged again, Jack-o, I thought.

The demonstration lasted several minutes. According to the official German Olympic Committee's Report, Hitler's arrival delayed the start of the final of the 1500 metres by a full six minutes. But the rush of electricity that I had dreamed and plotted and prayed for, when I finally stepped off the grass and on to the cinders, lasted longer than that.

Nobody broke. Phil and I had to run an extra few yards at the start because of the outside positions – six lanes only, for twelve runners. I didn't see the jockeying at the front. Phil tore off with a loud "Yaaah!" I glanced in and saw that one of the runners, San Romani, had been caught off balance. I lay back deliberately and after 50 metres found I was running last. I looked for Cunningham but couldn't see him, swore, blinked, wiped a grit from one eye, focused and was startled to read the number "746" immediately in front of me. I was on his back! So Cunningham had also opted to stay out of trouble. From the yells as we came round the Marathon Gate corner into the front straight, I guessed that Beccali and one of the Germans were in front. In fact Jerry was in front. Already at this stage, as some Frenchman has written, I was drowsing on the alert and beginning to command the race – "Hare-watching," he wrote, "ears pricked. Hypnotising the field from the back . . ." That's a pretty phrase. But Cunningham in the wake only a pace ahead of me was doing exactly the same thing. We were both starting to wonder, Why are we going so slowly? I know this because at the same instant we were both dominated by an identical impulse to overtake the field. We moved as one man, propelled by an unseen force. Cunningham went through blocks and pockets of runners as if they weren't there. I followed. We rolled up the field. I was pocketed once, by black Phil. "Look out, Phil. I'm coming through," I shouted and he moved over. That's what you can do with another runner if he's friendly. Just touch him, he moves over. After 600 metres passing the Marathon tunnel a second time, Cunningham led and I was stepping in his holes. The track was so cushioned, so clean and swept, you could do it. Where was the effort? I swear the pair of us hadn't moved at all. Relatively our positions hadn't changed, except that now we were at the front of the field instead of at the back.

"Attaboy, Cunning–HAM!"

Loud and clear the chant came from loudhailers. I knew where the American supporters were now – they were right over the Marathon tunnel. But the chant seemed blown by bellows from the mouth of the tunnel and the universe of spectators was receding. In that enclosed yet limitless space only the danger was not receding – the danger of bunching, of being bumped on to the grass. There was a lane of grass inside us. Schaumburg was outside me on Cunningham's shoulder; Jerry and Beccali immediately behind on my heels. Cunningham up to now had gone fast. Now he went faster. Approaching the bend into the third lap, I heard slapping sounds behind me like the beating of wings. Someone was coming faster yet. This is getting interesting, I thought. I didn't look round. Into the bend, the bottom bend leading to the camera platform where we had started, everything began to happen very quickly – for the spectator. For a runner it isn't like that. It happens slowly. Outwardly I could see a photographer climbing down from the platform on to the grass verge; inwardly I sensed that Cunningham was bothered. He was in a dilemma – to let the oncoming runner overtake? Or fight him off on the bend? I know what I'd have done. Cunningham didn't do that. It sounds elementary, but it is moments like this that decide races. There is no second chance and Cunningham, it turned out, was given no chance because of a fool of a photographer. And because of Ny. I'm not saying the incident decided the race, though you may think so. The slapping sounds behind me had changed to grunts. I could hear Beccali's name faintly shouted and I thought it was Beccali coming. Or Schaumburg. The cry "Schaum-burg!" was revolving like a continuous wall. But Schaumburg had fallen back. It wasn't Schaumburg and it wasn't Beccali, it was Sweden's Ny – such a beautiful runner. And so brainless. Erik Ny came with a flash of blue and yellow and he grazed Cunningham's shoulder as he drew level right on the curve. Cunningham fought, using his elbows. He fought Ny round the curve. Ny had his fists clenched. I sat up and watched this – sat up on the tips snuggled in behind, letting them take the wind. Twice Ny tried to cut in. The third time – maybe the photographer was to blame. On the grass lane at eye level here is a photographer lunging with a camera at the pair of them. Ny lost his nerve and cut in, grazing Cunningham a second time. Cunningham spun on to the grass, off balance, and oh boy I thought, blue manna from a Swedish heaven – Cunningham's out of the race. But you know what that man Cunningham can do? He can swerve, topple, recover, and get back in a race without anyone noticing. That's what he did. Cunningham ran four paces on the grass and got back on the cinders without wobbling or losing momentum, as if he had been practising the move all week. I spoke to him about it later and he didn't remember a thing. That's how good he was. I had to brake very slightly at this point to keep Cunningham ahead of me, that's all. Cunningham was so little disconcerted that in a few more strides he had overtaken Ny on the back straight, going inside him – why let a man *inside* you? – and had recaptured the lead. It was then I realised how Cunningham was feeling, on fire. Me?

I was running on slippered feet. I had a charmed position.

I don't know why Cunningham didn't let Ny go and destroy himself at this stage. Maybe his emotions were too strong. Maybe he had contempt for the Swede, as I did. Even without the times being called, I knew that third lap was the fastest ever run. Now the pair were neck-and-neck and still duelling. They had been neck-and-neck at the start of their duel on the bottom bend with half the race to run, neck-and-neck down the back straight and around the Marathon curve, and coming down the front straight past Hitler's box to the bell for the start of the final round they were still fixed together, Ny breathing at Cunningham's shoulder, hands flapping now. Ny being kept on the outside, running wide all the way, Cunningham's upper body stationary, arms rhythmically stirring, and both men moving quickly and easily within themselves. Schaumburg had reappeared and was at my right shoulder. He needed to cut in. I moved on to Cunningham's heels and shut him out which meant whoever was in fifth place behind me – I guessed Beccali – would have to go wider still. I imagined by now the other runners were strung out. Had no idea the rest of the field was still bunched closely behind. I had forgotten Jerry, he was in fact shadowing me but locked in by Beccali. I was half-expecting black Phil to burst from cover and lead us all a dance, it would have been in character. But he didn't. Nor did I hear "the low rumble of excitement" that the *New York Times* man described as the pace suddenly quickened passing Hitler's box and Ny, clenching his fists again, blond hair streaming back from his forehead, surged past Cunningham for the second time and the bell rang for the last lap.

I didn't hear the rumble, only a half-familiar echo like a key or a lock sliding into place in my brain. Something coalesced and fused. As Ny left Cunningham's shoulder, I moved out on to it. I hung there. We were brushing arms. Beccali was moving too – but from behind. I glimpsed the danger. I sensed Beccali's chest closing like a prow. Beccali ran with his chest. Now he closed with his chest. It was as if his chest was boring into the cavity of the small of my back, and at that instant my wits nearly left me and I almost made a mistake. I started to go. I felt I had to go. Cunningham on the inside was frictionless, his upper body rigid, erect, as if cast in bronze. Why didn't I go? Ny had gone. The bend was unfolding. But at the moment of leaving Cunningham's shoulder, I didn't leave it, instead I hung and went with him half-wide round the bend, knowing that Beccali couldn't get in and that Cunningham, squeezed up to the grass, couldn't get out to overtake Ny, at least not until we straightened by the camera platform at the 1200-metre mark. By then all my echo-states were vibrating in a single clear image (oh Bill!) and I had started my sprint.

I thought of Bill. Why not? The race was decided at this moment. It was as if there were no longer any secrets between

272

us. I was coming clean for Bill at last. It was a prophetic moment. With my inner eye I saw Bill standing at this exact point 300 metres from home where he had occupied it one day back in England at Chelmsford after that row when I had humiliated him. I saw the loitering figure, sorrowing with his hat on his head, as clearly as I see the words I am writing now, and I don't care what people tell you about running for King and Country, who you run for or why: at that moment rushing past the stays of the camera platform I began to sprint and it was all for Bill.

Ny was two yards ahead of Cunningham as the bend straightened. I passed Cunningham leaning in slightly and caught Ny at the entrance to the back straight bang on the 1200-metre mark. Cunningham had anticipated this. He was by my ear. I was accelerating and Cunningham was accelerating. If you look at the Riefenstahl film, it is there, precisely. If you've already seen the film and can remember the scene with Harold Abrahams and the redhead on the Moor Park Golf Course, you know what happened next. I hesitated. I passed Cunningham, moved to the line of Ny's shoulder and I hesitated, while behind me Cunningham on hare-alert also hesitated, thinking that I'd changed my mind. He relaxed. Subconsciously he relaxed. You think I don't know? But I heard the gasp that went up from the throat of the Stadium. And in that gasp, which was the split-second of Cunningham's relaxation, something ignited and I accelerated a second time and was clean away. Behind me where Cunningham should have been there was a space – how big? Some say four yards, some say ten. It doesn't matter. I had jumped the field. I was accelerating so fast down the back straight that as I rounded the top bend and looked into the square of black framed by the Marathon gateway, I began to hear voices. "Come on, Jack!" – Harold's voice, Sydney Wooderson's voice and Walter's voice and all the voices of my dream were distinctly calling. In fact I heard nothing. I seemed to be gliding, totally weightless, and everything turned from black to orange. I had to check only once, rounding the corner, to correct my balance. Then I spurted again. There was no wind. I couldn't understand why my opponents weren't catching me. The air had grown quiet. I was conscious of a feeling of great loneliness and silence and

273

since the tape seemed to be receding and I could neither see nor hear my pursuers, I thought that something had gone wrong and I looked back over the right shoulder. I mention the look because it is what people seem to remember, I don't know why. It wasn't like the look on Alice's face that Lewis Carroll describes when she begins to grow and it wasn't like Nurmi's when he consulted his stop-watch one more time before throwing it on to the grass after shaking off the field in Paris in 1924. My look was involuntary and unplanned, the briefest of backward glances, yet for some reason that is what people remember. *Of course* I glanced back fifty yards from home, I needed to see how far ahead I was. When I saw how far in front I was, I stopped.

I mean I slowed down.

Bill was disgusted with me afterwards for slowing down like that. Of course he was pleased too – I had carried out the plan we had conceived to the letter and I had won – but he was disgusted all the same. There is nothing so sad as a happy trainer. Many years later Bill's disgust still showed. We were sitting together in London listening to a replay of Harold Abrahams' running commentary on the race, the BBC commentary that had caused so much talk, and Bill said, "If *only* you hadn't slowed up, sir, you'd have broken the four-minute mile." Bill was getting old by then, he had retired from athletics and he was apt to get things muddled. Bill had forgotten that the race on 6 August 1936 ended at 1500 metres, 120 yards short of a mile, so not even Achilles could have gone a four-minute mile on that day. And I couldn't have done it either, glance or no glance, I was flat stick at the end. Yet, the odd thing is that, even though I slowed down and coasted the last twenty or thirty yards on to the tape, I still broke the world's record. So did Cunningham five metres behind me. Cunningham came second. Beccali was third – Beccali three, San Romani four, Phil Edwards five, and they all broke the old Olympic record. Five records in one race. That's another odd thing.

Even odder. I didn't realise at first that I'd won. Somehow on the track it didn't register properly. Across the line I went on sprinting, glanced back a second time, again a third time, stumbled, almost spiked myself, and finally pulled up round the curve where we had started. Somebody threw me a blanket. Everything continued quiet and loud at the same time and white rain seemed to be falling. Officials in white coats were falling about me like white rain. I had the impression they were surgeons mopping up after an operation. "Sir," Cunningham said to me at some point, "you must be the greatest runner in the world" – and that registered. No runner had ever called me sir before. I remember looking down at the grass and thinking, How bright it is. And thanking Phil – "Thanks, Phil," I said, "for letting me through." Phil just goggled. He had no recollection. He was just as stunned afterwards as I was. So many things became clear only later, just as the architecture of the race itself about which so much has been written began to dawn on me only with a passage of time. A man called Harris who wrote a book about my races said that I radiated happiness. Basked, was the word he used. He says I stood on the victory dais basking in the applause and grinning like a Cheshire cat, who knows? Who knows how the legend of a race is fixed in the popular imagination? You can't measure happiness. Everyone was standing up for the Victory ceremony. Blonde maidens had appeared on a carpet of leaves at our feet and were holding out to us green garlands. I was blinking up at Hitler's box which was on my right, wondering who was flashing mirrors at me. (It was in fact Goering in the box. Goering's medals were glinting.) At this moment Hitler is said to have entered my legend, reportedly turning to the French ambassador, M. André François-Poncet, and saying, "If *only* he had been a German." (Meaning me.) But that is pure fiction, since the French ambassador wasn't at the Stadium that day. I can understand the Führer's feelings all the same: the race was a climax of sorts and the two blond Germans, Böttcher and Schaumburg, had finished last. An anthem was playing. Beccali's hair had turned green. I was standing on the dais between Beccali and Cunningham holding a tree in a pot with both hands, one of the "Hitler oaks" from the Black Forest that were presented to winners. Winners at Berlin got oak trees and at the same time medallists had to bow down to blonde maidens to be crowned with circlets of fresh green oak clusters. I suppose, to Beccali and Cunningham, my

275

hair looked green too. I couldn't see Arthur. I'm on the peak of the world, I thought, but where's Arthur? I'm huge, and that's my flag up there – for the first time in history a New Zealand flag was flying from the ramparts alongside an Olympic banner. Where is he? I looked from the flag to the official party below the box and I searched for Arthur all round, knowing how proud he must be feeling at this moment, and I couldn't find him. It turned out Arthur was beside my elbow. He was standing beside me wearing a polka-dot tie and choking the tears back during the ceremony – he told me later. I didn't notice him. What registered instead as the Stadium got to its feet with a sound like a tempest blast was a youth at the front of the crowd holding up an elevated sandwich board on which a message was chalked below the words "zum Fernsprecher (Téléphone)". Beccali was giving the Fascist salute, Germans were saluting in German. A band was playing "God Save the King". It was all mixed up. I swear they forgot to give me the medal.

It was only when I got down to the dressing-room and put a hand in my pocket and felt something hard and solid – actually I took it out and showed it to Bill. "You'd better hold on to it," I said. "I'll only lose it." Bill wasn't a bit excited. He sat there talking to reporters in his seamy old suit, as calm and unperturbed as an October conker. Anyway it wasn't until I reached into a pocket and felt the medal and actually gripped it with my fingers that I realised I had won.

20

Even today, writing as I am years later and looking back, a feeling of disembodiment and trance still lingers. The trance-like states that I experienced before and during the race did not leave me afterwards in Berlin. It is like the fleeting apparition of the boy with the sandwich board, "zum Fernsprecher", glimpsed from the dais afterwards. It is like Arthur coming to the Village afterwards saying he had known I would win, because when the gun went he looked up at the sky and a pigeon dropped a message on his head. It is like Harold saying to me afterwards that he feared he was going to lose his job with the BBC and it would be all my fault. Afterwards and afterwards and again afterwards.

All was trance.

It was too late to send telegrams to friends when I got back to the Village. I was feeling a bit weary after the race and I didn't send cables to my mother or to friends until the next morning, Friday. Friday was the day of Bespectacled Brown's 400-metre final. In the evening, that is the Thursday evening, so many people came to my room to offer congratulations we had to evacuate it and hide in the day room to talk. Arthur came. Bill came. Harold came a little later. We talked and talked – that was the best part. I made Bill show Harold the Gold Medal. Harold looked at it, felt it. He said, "It's fatter than mine." He said, "It's more organised than mine." He said, "That's because the Germans are more organised than the French. When I won my Gold Medal in Paris, they didn't have one ready in time. I didn't get it for six days. They posted it on to me." Then he said in a perplexed tone, "I had a phone call just now when I got back to the hotel. De Lotbinière rang." De Lotbinière was Harold's boss at the BBC. Harold said, "I think they're going to fire me. De Lotbinière's up in arms." "I'm not surprised," I said. "What do you mean?" I said, "Well you did your bun, Harold. Lost your head. When I began to sprint you started shouting out, 'Come on, Jack!' Then you said, 'Hooray.' And 'My God, he's done it' – things like that. 'Hooray, hooray.' You silly chump. You forgot you were on the air." Harold looked at me. "But that's exactly what de Lotbinière says that I said. I don't remember a thing. Jack, how do you know what I said if I don't remember myself?" "I dreamed it, Harold," I said. Of course he didn't believe me.

In fact Harold wasn't fired by the BBC, he was promoted. On the strength of his bizarre commentary on my race on 6 August 1936, Harold's broadcasting career took a new turn and

277

in May 1937 he was chosen by the BBC to cover the coronation of King George VI. Such is the power of athletic games. But in those early days of radio the BBC had a regard for form; and de Lotbinière, who developed the art of "running commentary" and was the BBC's Head of Outside Broadcasting, was a stickler for the correct tone. Incidentally, and also for the record, my final lap which I had calculated needed to be run in 57 seconds or under was timed at 56.8 seconds and the time of the whole race was 3 mins. 47.8 secs. or about three seconds faster than Beccali's 1932 winning time at Los Angeles and a full second under Bonthron's world record of 3 mins. 48.8 secs. I told reporters that the only reason I had got away with it was that my plans for the last lap weren't leaked and the only reason I had gone so fast was that if I hadn't, I wouldn't have won.

Somebody asked me in the day room that night, I don't recall who, "What are you going to do now?"

I said, "Stop running and become a doctor."

A most disturbing thing. That night I didn't sleep. I got up and without thinking went for a run. The next day, the same thing: another run. It was automatic. I continued train-ing. The following day, Saturday, I jogged four miles. I ran every day that remained to us in Berlin and the first thing I did when I got back to England was go to Cambridge and run at Fenner's. Such is also the power of athletic games. But the significance of what was happening to me didn't dawn for a long time.

Friday came and with it, Godfrey Brown's "closing address". It was the day after my event, the last day of the individual track events at the Stadium and Godfrey's final was the last event of the last day. It was also the day I met the boy with the sandwich board again. Funnier things can happen.

The boy wore short blue Manchester trousers. He passed quite close to where I was sitting in D Block with Sandy and some others. I read the message on his face without somehow noticing the message on the board that he carried. He wore a tie, a blazer, his hair was cut short, he was skinny. He reminded me of myself at his age when I was a member of the Boys' Brigade in New Zealand, although now that I think of it he was probably a member of the Hitlerjugend. The Hitler Youth boys occupied a block near the Tribune and sang

> *Deutschland, Deutschland, Heil Heil Heil*
> *Deutschland Eagle, fly to Victory!*

and:

> *One for the Führer, two for the Führer!*

in tones that outdid the American and Japanese cheerleaders with their armoury of loudhailers. The boy was about thirteen. Going up the aisle of D Block, he held the pole with the message on it erect, his eyes level, roving the ranks of tiered spectators, his back to the arena, and as he passed beside me he looked at me with a sad mute appeal and I thought, Poor kid. He's missing the fun. Then Sandy Duncan and Jerry let out a groan between them and my attention was turned to the track where the final of the 400 metres was about to begin.

Bespectacled Brown was down there and five other finalists. The entire British athletic contingent of 240 souls seemed to be squashed into the seating area around us, scenting the prospect of a track victory for England at last. "Oh hell," Sandy groaned, with his glasses on the line-up. "Godfrey's done it again."

And Jerry. "He hasn't done it again?"

And me. "He hasn't done it *again*?"

"He's done it again, Jack. Godfrey's drawn the outside."

Poor bugger, I thought.

In four races BB had drawn either the outside lane or the one next to it, in a heat, quarter-final, semi-final and now, for the fourth time in succession, in the final. I couldn't see Godfrey's expression but I could read his attitude: his whole body had slumped. I watched him take up his staggered lane outside two Canadians, another Englishman Bill Roberts and the two black Americans Lu Valle and Archie Williams.

"Oh come on, Godfrey," Sandy said. "Don't give up now."

We knew Godfrey's plan. He would run the first part faster than normal, hoping to encourage the Americans to overdo it. Godfrey's strength was at the end and, like me, he had decided there was only one man in the race to beat – in his case the Negro Archie Williams, the world's record holder.

279

I said to Jerry, "He's half-blind as it is. He won't be able to see Archie Williams until they hit the straight, even if he looks."

Godfrey seemed to take hold of himself once he'd dug his holes. He went very fast from the beginning and approaching the final bend he was about three yards up on Williams. Then he seemed to hesitate. Williams shot through inside him and as the bend straightened Archie Williams was several yards clear. Godfrey crumpled. Lu Valle came through, then Godfrey's team-mate Bill Roberts. "He's had it," Jerry said. Godfrey had weakened to fourth, falling back with every stride. Then a girl spoke. Amid the roar of the crowd an English girl's voice was heard. "Come on, Bill!" – meaning Bill Roberts. It was uncanny, because sixty tiers below on the track it was as if Godfrey heard her too. As if until she spoke and reminded him, he had omitted to notice there was another Englishman in the race. And that, for some reason, seemed to infuriate him. I jumped up. I could feel the pants sticking to the backs of my legs. I was clutching at Jerry, just as I'd done at Los Angeles four years earlier for Tommy Hampson's finish. Only now it was Bespectacled Brown. His head came up, his mouth gaped sideways and with forty yards to go he began to drive forward close to the ground, almost skidding along. But with great ferocity. Godfrey overtook first Bill Roberts, then Lu Valle and finally right on the tape an exhausted Archie Williams. A stride past the tape, Godfrey was in front. Four men crossed the line almost together, Godfrey and Archie Williams not separated, it seemed, not even by the thickness of a cigarette paper. "He's there," Jerry said. "He's there!" Sandy and I cried. But he wasn't.

"I need a drink," someone said when it was over and the results were posted.

"Of all the luck," I said to Jerry as we went down and pushed through the promenade under the stand in search of a drink. According to the results boards, Godfrey had missed the Gold by a fifth of a second. But it was closer than that. The electric timer showed later he had missed by only the fiftieth of a second.

Jerry nodded disconsolately. "Drinks this way," he said and led off towards an exit. Sandy and I followed. Then Sandy stopped and stood on tiptoe, peering ahead and pointing. "Herr Doktor!" he said to me. "You're wanted."

"What?" Halfway round the concourse above a shifting mass of heads where Sandy pointed, there floated the elevated sandwich board – "zum Fernsprecher (Téléphone)". Underneath that, chalked on the black rectangle, I read

Herr Doktor LOVELOCK
Neuseeland.

I caught up with the message boy and he took me back round the encircling promenade, past granite columns and down stairs into an office where white guides were congregated and two men in homburgs sat with ledgers behind a rank of telephones. One of them consulted a slip of paper, rang a number and motioned me into a booth.

"Dr Lovelock?" a voice said at the end of the line.

"Yes, Jack Lovelock. Who is that?"

"My name is Martin Brustmann. We met at the Hochschule here in Berlin last year."

"Who?"

"Brustmann. Dr Brustmann."

"Oh yes. I think I remember."

"Many congratulations to you for your great victory yesterday. I would like to see you again, with a friend of mine. You are free tomorrow morning?"

I hesitated. "I don't know. I could be free."

"Excellent. Please come to the Hotel Kaiserhof near the Potsdamerplatz. Ask for Dr Brustmann. I am expecting you."

"Just a minute. Who — ?"

"Shall we say eleven o'clock?"

I started to say something but he had said goodbye and rung off.

I didn't remember him at all, but I knew the name. Dr Brustmann was a prominent sports doctor in Germany. It's probably an offer, I thought, just another request to run. I won't go. Already in the space of twenty-four hours I had been swamped with cablegrams, messages, offers of all kinds including three proposals of marriage. Requests to make public appearances in Scandinavia, invitations to lecture and run again in the States. That night, back in the Village, strangers kept walking into my room and next morning, Saturday, when

I went to one of the recreation rooms to write a letter autograph-hunters and calls to the telephone pursued me. It was becoming impossible to be alone in the Village. I looked at the programme for the day, saw there was little of interest at the Stadium before Sunday and realised I had seen little or nothing of Berlin. I would go. It would be good to get away for an hour or two.

I took a bus to the Stadium, then the U-bahn to the Potsdamerplatz. I was ten minutes early. I bought some postcards and a street map. The flower ladies were out and one of them, when I stopped to give an autograph, thrust a heap of carnations in my arms and grabbed my umbrella in exchange. She gave it back with good grace and kissed me on both cheeks. I was surprised how polite and jolly people were. Swastikas and Olympic flags were flying from the roofs of Government buildings and black-topped fiacres and cyclists were tacking down the wide Leipzigerstrasse in a busy stream. I turned into the Kaiserhofstrasse and entered the hotel just after eleven o'clock. In the lobby a commissionaire bowed, then took me to a glassed-in café terrace where a tall man in an overcoat and dark glasses was sitting with his back to the street. He rose and came towards me.

"My friend," he said, clasping my hand.

"Dr Peltzer!"

"My very good friend. You have come."

"This is a surprise."

He had grown a goatee, as I had heard. I had forgotten how thin and handsome he was, only now he seemed much older and even more pencil-thin and the bony angularity of his face made him look almost emaciated. There were shadows under the eyes and in the hollows of grey flesh where he hadn't shaved properly. He motioned me to his table then impulsively squeezed my hand a second time, smiling and holding it in a lingering grasp.

"I didn't think you would come," he said. "I knew you from the umbrella. I thought, Why does he carry an umbrella? I saw the umbrella from the window when you came in the Kaiserhofstrasse and I spoke to myself, Yes, it's he! Only Jack Lovelock carries the umbrella like that, perfection. Just like his race. Your race on Thursday was an artistic creation. I have

282

remembered the umbrella, you see, from Los Angeles. Now. Bitte."

We sat down by the window. "You will take coffee?"

"Tea. Thank you. It's good to see you, Dr Peltzer."

"Tea, of course. Please call me Otto. Kellner, ein Kännchen Tee. Kaffee für mich . . . Something to eat? Und etwas zu essen, belegte Brötchen . . . Oh my dear friend, there is so much to thank you for! You received my letters? No? But you have received the last one? Of course. Otherwise I would not be here. There. The waiter demands your autograph . . . I said to you once you will be a prince of runners, now in Germany they call you King. 'Der König der Meilenläufer', the King of Milers. Oh the lap, the last lap! We say in German, reibungslos, without friction, without effort. That is what Berlin is saying about you, reibungslos." Of all the lovely things, I thought. He said, "Never before has it been done. Such perfection." He said, "Your father will praise you," and his words made me start. I still glowed from the race but for the first time he made me think I might have done something that went beyond the reach of ordinary description. For an instant he almost made me believe I had reached my father beyond the grave – "What happened, son? You didn't make a mistake." "No, I didn't, Dad. Did I?"

I was nodding and smiling at him. Peltzer's words were like a confirmation.

"Your photograph is in all the papers," he was saying. "You were possessed. You ran in a rapture."

I laughed.

"It will never be forgotten, that lap. Never, never.

"And you know," he added, "you were running on my head? Yes, yes, on top of my head. Underneath you, below Hitler's Stadium, is the old Grunewald stadium built by the Kaiser where in 1926 I became the conqueror of Nurmi. Yes, yes, you were on my head."

His English had improved. There was something else that was different about him. The throaty, slightly grating voice was the same. He was speaking with his hands but not gesturing, pressing down with slender fingertips on the table surface, and I saw that the nails were broken and there were small weals on the backs of the hands. He had ordered fresh rolls with cheese

283

and cold cuts but when the waiter brought them he didn't eat himself until I had finished, then he bent over his plate and ate ravenously. He was strangely excited and I had the impression more than once that his eyes, hidden by the dark glasses, were taking in things over my shoulder that I couldn't see.

"Reibungslos," he was saying. "I turned to my friend, Martin Brustmann — "

"Oh yes. He said he would be here. Dr Brustmann telephoned me."

"Yes, yes, Brustmann. He could not come. We saw your race together. We came to the Olympische Dorf at Döberitz to see you. No, he could not come this morning. He offers apologies." Abruptly he said, "You are staying some more days?"

"Yes. Until Thursday or Friday."

"You wish to see something of Berlin at night?"

"It would be a pleasure," I said.

He nodded and went on eating. Most of the window tables were occupied. A man in a leather jacket with patch pockets stood up, tightened his belt and came across. He smiled hesitantly and asked in German if I would autograph his Olympic programme. He was suntanned and smelled of face lotion. I signed the programme and he went out. Peltzer didn't look up.

I said, "You came to the Village at Döberitz to see me?"

"Yes, to Döberitz."

"When was that?"

"Two nights since. I stayed outside. It was not permitted to enter the Village."

"But surely you have a pass? Why didn't you leave a message for me?"

"I saw you. It was enough." He smiled.

"Two nights ago? The night before the race? I was in the restaurant by the gate with Harold – Harold Abrahams. There was a car across the road. Was that you?"

"Yes. I came with Martin Brustmann."

"Why didn't you come in?"

"I did not wish to upset your concentration before the race." He added, "You are surprised?"

"Well. Not really. Only that you sat out there and didn't

come in." He was still eating. "Actually," I said, "I am surprised by your English."

"It is good, you think?"

"Very good, almost perfect. *Reibungslos*," I joked.

"Thank you. I have been studying your language."

"Here in Berlin?"

He took off the dark glasses and looked at me sidelong with shrewd grey eyes. The look was both warm and disturbing. "In prison," he said, "there is always time for studying. But you know about that," he said, and put on the glasses again.

"I don't understand, Dr Peltzer."

"Oh but you do. Very much you do understand. What you did on Saturday is a proof. A proof and a demonstration."

"On Saturday?"

"On Saturday at the marching before the Führer. The parade of nations. You have – snooted him. How do you say it?"

"Oh I see? You mean, cocked a snook."

"You cocked the snook at Hitler, the gangster man. The people of Berlin thanks you for it."

"But my dear Otto. That — "

"Nobody else at the marching was brave enough to do it. You know," he said, lowering his voice, "that this man is arming Germany for war?"

"What are you talking about?" I stared at him.

"So why do you think the doors and windows of your houses at Döberitz are so thick? Or have you not seen? And who builds these houses like forts in the 'Village of Peace'? Who will occupy them when you leave? It will not be the heavenly choir but the Reichswehr, my friend, the army of Nazi Germany. There will be manoeuvres for war in the forests of Döberitz. Of course not everyone can see it."

"Now wait a minute. This parade on Saturday – that was just a joke. I made a mistake."

"Ah so, now he makes it into a joke! That is typical modesty, typical Oxford. My friend, it is not a joke, it is an act of courage on your part. And then comes your race. You know what Hitler says his German youth shall be? 'As fast as whippets, as tough as leather, as hard as Krupp steel.' And where are the noble German youth in your race? Last. Who is first? A little smiling man who comes to Berlin with an umbrella. Once again you snap the fingers at this gangster man and his ideas, our Führer." He smiled sarcastically. "Our noble and glorious Führer. The people of Berlin are not so simple, my friend. They make of you a symbol of the goodness and strength of the free world and so they are laughing with you against this madman who thinks he can destroy the world. They see your picture in the newspapers, they see you on the 'Wochenschau', on the screen in the picture houses. Oh yes. They take you into their hearts with Jesse Owens. I will take you into the bars and cabarets and you will hear the jokes."

"Jokes? What sort of jokes?"

"There is time for that. Come, eat up, drink up. In a moment when it stops to rain we will walk outside. I think," he said, "that you understand many things. Why did you not answer my last letter?"

"No, I – " I started to apologise. He said, "That was correct. I wrote to you from the prison and it is correct that you do not answer. It tells me you understand what is happening here in Berlin behind the scenes – Hinter den Kulissen. Oh yes. You understood and then you acted."

"Acted? This is nonsense," I said.

"I owe you much thanks. But you do not want thanks, I can see that. Let us go outside. The sun is coming."

He had called the waiter. He put down some money and I followed him into the street, my head swimming. "Dr Peltzer," I began. "I think there is a big misunderstanding."

He had taken my arm. "Let us get away from these people . . . No, no. No misunderstanding. Here I am, Otto Peltzer, on the streets a free man. I am no longer in the prison thanks to you. Ask your friend Harold Abrahams. He knows. Unless," he said – "unless you do not wish to be seen with me?"

"Heavens. What an idea!"

Outside the hotel we had turned left and then left again into a busy thoroughfare; now we crossed an intersection and followed another busy street of pedestrians and yellow tramcars beside a line of trees. There had been a shower and the pavements were wet. Ahead rose the familiar landmark of the goddess and chariot atop the Brandenburger Tor. Passing a tram stop,

Peltzer turned off on to a path that dived under trees and after a few paces became a leafy park.

"This must be part of the Tiergarten?" I said.

"Yes. The Pariserplatz is over there. This is the start of the Tiergarten and tomorrow in the marathon race the runners will come by this way. Now I am taking you to a place the foreigners do not see. A place of beauty," he added. But he had paused beside a low column surmounted by heads in stone. "Noble Germans," he seemed to say, nodding at the heads in a confidential sort of way. He walked on. I read the names Beethoven, Mozart, Haydn cut in the base of the monument. The path meandered through chestnuts and birch trees closely wooded; then without warning emerged upon a hidden clearing where a lagoon or miniature lake was mirrored, the grassy verges dotted with wild flowers and lounging figures in sun-hats. It was very like a river scene in Oxford except that instead of boathouses and punts there were swans and water lilies and a policeman giving directions with an upside-down coal scuttle on his head. The lake, elongated like a lozenge, was spread about with luxuriant old trees.

"You see?" he said.

Families with small children sat about on rugs or picnicked on wooden seats; lovers sauntered by the bank or paused to gaze into the clear water.

"It is very lovely."

"You see the Berlin of my childhood – my mother brought me here to see the goldfishes. The pond is famous for the goldfishes."

We stood side by side looking down at our reflections in the water. Below the surface small fish darted as if painted on glass.

I said, "Dr Peltzer. You were arrested?"

"More than once. The last time for eighteen months."

"But why? For what reason?"

"You don't know?"

"I know nothing."

"Aber? You signed the letter? You signed the letter with Douglas Lowe and Harold Abrahams that obtained my – my — "

"You mean your release?"

"Yes, release, my freedom. Last week. I am released to

freedom by the good Minister Präsident Generaloberst Goering. The good Field Marshal Goering and the good Mr Hitler, they like to make a good impression for the Olympic visitors to Berlin. I too, my friend, was once a national hero."

"You were released from prison only last week? On the eve of the Games?"

"Actually two days before the Games started." He knelt down and plunged his hands into the water, bathing his lips and cheeks and his eyes under the glasses with the tips of his fingers. He stood up and gave a sardonic laugh.

"But how could such a thing be possible in Berlin today? You are quite right to ask the reason of my arrest. Shall I tell you what my mother said? I was just a little boy and she had brought me to Berlin to see the doctors – it was when my legs were paralysed."

"When you had poliomyelitis?"

He nodded. "I was in a wheeling chair. Afterwards I asked my mother to show me the pond of the goldfishes because, like every child who comes to Berlin, I had been told the story. I had been told that in the winter when the freezing comes all the goldfishes come to the top of the pond and freeze with a look upon their faces, then in the melting time of the spring, hop hop hop, off they go and swim away again. 'But why?' I said to my mother. 'Why do they do that? What is the reason?' 'You must ask the goldfishes, Otto,' my mother said. So, my dear friend. If you want to know the reason why so many people are arrested in Germany today, you must ask the goldfishes. Shall we sit down? I am a little tired."

We sat together on a seat with our faces towards the sun and I remembered something. "Los Angeles," I said. "Your last Olympics."

"Yes?"

I had remembered the incident when he left the field in tears, after the German starter Miller had ordered him to retire from the race. I reminded him of it. "There seemed to be an argument," I said. "You seemed to be in disgrace with Miller."

"Why do you ask?"

"I didn't understand it. I just wondered if that had anything to do with it – I mean with your arrest?"

"What do you mean? Miller? What has Franz Miller to do

with Otto Peltzer being locked up in the Moabit Jail?" He had
become agitated. He jumped up and strode sharply away from
me to the water's edge. He remained there without speaking
with his back to me. He was breathing rapidly. Then, as
abruptly as he had left me, he returned, turned up the collar of
his overcoat and spread wide his arms along the back of the
seat. He tilted his face to the sun and fell asleep.

I looked at my watch. Ten past twelve. It crossed my mind
that the man was ill, not normal. He had been angry with me,
yet in an obscure way he seemed to need me. He had lost his
pride, then been ashamed; now he slept like a child. I
remembered his habit of cat-napping in the middle of a
conversation from our meeting in New Zealand. I took out one
of the postcards I had bought, addressed it to my mother, wrote
a few words, then stopped, aware that someone was observing
me from the opposite side of the pond.

The man had one hand crooked in his belt. He stood just
back from the pond up against the treeline and was making no
effort to conceal himself. It was the suntanned man in the leather
coat from the Kaiserhof café. Peltzer awoke, rubbed his eyes
under the glasses, looked up and saw him at the same time. The
man stood there a moment longer, then moved off into the trees.

Peltzer said nothing. After a minute he got up, squeezed my
shoulder and walked away. When he had gone about twenty
yards he turned and looked back at me with a curious sidelong
stare, as if to reassure himself about something. Then he was
gone.

21

I went straight back to the Kaiserhof where Harold, I
remembered, was staying and by good luck caught him as he
was coming out of the restaurant from lunch. He was on his way
to the Stadium.

"I'm in a rush, Jack. I've got to do a round-up with Bevil Rudd – we're on the air in half an hour."

"This won't take a minute. Harold, did you know that Otto Peltzer had been in prison?"

"Peltzer? Yes, of course I knew. He got put away on some trumped-up charge last year. I think he's out. Why? Somebody told me that he's out again."

"I've just seen him. Harold, did you have anything to do with his release? Did I?"

"Well I don't know. We both signed the letter that Douglas Lowe drafted, don't know who it went to. I think Douglas was sending it to Goering. I told him it wouldn't do a scrap of good, but – you mean it helped? I'm delighted."

"But what letter? I didn't sign anything."

"Yes, you did."

"No, I didn't."

"I'm sure you did."

"Hold on. When was this, Harold?"

"Last May, at the Olympic Association dinner at the Dorchester. You remember? Douglas brought along a petition. That's right, it was addressed to Goering as Minister in Charge of Police. Douglas had kept in touch with Peltzer after Peltzer beat him at Stamford Bridge in 1926, then he got wind Peltzer had been put in a camp. Was it a camp? Anyway at the dinner Douglas showed me an appeal he'd drafted calling for Peltzer's release and afterwards he got everyone to sign he could lay hands on. You must have signed it, everyone did. Of course you did. I saw your signature."

"Well I'm blowed."

"You were probably tight. Jack, sorry. I must run."

I waved Harold into his waiting car and thought, So that explains it. Probably I was tipsy that night at the Dorchester, more likely in a stupor from continuous night work and emergency calls at the hospital. I dimly remembered being buttonholed by someone after the dinner before going back on duty. I must have signed the thing automatically without noticing. Yet I was still mystified by Peltzer. I couldn't make the man out with his abrupt changes of mood, his dark hints of persecutions and preparations for war, while all around me the Berliners – it wasn't just the visitors – were amusing themselves and giving the lie to everything Peltzer had said. I crossed the hotel foyer and bought a paper at the desk, noticing a headline ("LOVELOCK'S WIN ... *Scene in Berlin* ... *Crowd's Frenzied Scream*") and my photograph on the front page of the London *Telegraph*. But I couldn't concentrate to read, my eye kept skipping to billboards and posters, "THEATER – KONZERTE – VERGNÜGUNGEN", round which people were gathered exclaiming and jostling. The foyer was crowded. Some of the revue turns made my mouth water.

BERLIN BIETET
BERLIN VOUS OFFRE
BERLIN OFFERS YOU

The Don Cossacks, I noticed, were in town. Peltzer's mad, I thought, staring at a film poster of Jean Harlow, the It girl. Shuts his eyes to things, doesn't know how to enjoy himself. Well, the Berliners obviously did know how to enjoy themselves. Jean Harlow was starring with Clark Gable at a movie palace on the Kurfürstendamm. Marlene Dietrich was on in *Shanghai Express*. I was thinking, I haven't had a night out since when? – when a familiar voice said in my ear, "Are you coming or going?"

"Oh hullo, Toby. Kicking my heels actually."

It was "Toby" Horsfall, an Australian athlete – we had once run together in Norway for the Achilles Club. Toby was a Trinity man from Cambridge who had been seconded as "Commissariat" to the New Zealand team at the last moment. But he had been so busy carrying messages and running errands into town I had seen almost nothing of him. "Where are you off to?" I said.

"Just off to the West End to collect some film for one of the chaps. Have to find the Agfa shop. Come along?"

We took a tram to the West End, found the camera shop Toby wanted and after a quick lunch near the Friedrichstrasse Toby jumped up saying, "Come on, let's strut. I've got a couple of hours. Let's do a Bummel." So we wandered through an arcaded passage swinging our brollies and down the Friedrichstrasse, that funny old street with its hanging globes and top-heavy wrought-iron balconies, and on across town. There

291

seemed to be a fever on the streets. Already the night-club barkers were out, chatting to each other, hands in pockets or calling across the streams of black-topped cabs. Girls were on the pavements. They pulled us into shops or under awnings or stepped from slowly cruising cars to demand autographs or practise their English. Yet it was easy to be anonymous. I was amazed at the garishness and pulse of the Friedrichstrasse, intoxicated by the holiday atmosphere. The department stores were crawling with people. Further down on the tree-lined avenues crowds of soldiers in brown and grey uniforms and businessmen in homburgs were congregated in groups in the open air, their expressions rapt, their faces turned upwards listening to the progress of the Games issuing from loudspeakers concealed in the branches overhead. It was as if the whole town had become an annexe to the Stadium. On the Savignyplatz I had a sudden urge to go with a woman in bobbed curls who plucked my arm, unbuttoning her short black raincoat. But Toby shook his head and said there wasn't time for that. Toby wanted to get into the Delphi where Teddy Staufer the saxophone king was playing – "Le Jazz Hot", the poster said. "Dancing until dawn." But the Delphi, where people were already queuing for tickets in droves, wasn't open yet. Undecided, we bought English and American newspapers in the Hardenbergerstrasse and settled in the end for a Thé Dansant where ancient waiters served us English tea and Torten from brown trolleys and all the girls looked over fifty. This is really living it up, I thought. The waiters wore black jackets and white aprons to the ankle; above the swastika on their lapels they wore little flags, denoting the number of extra languages they spoke. Girls with mahogany-table legs which bulged in the centre sat about on dark red Biedermeier furniture – or what Toby told me was Biedermeier furniture – and a three-piece band played "Until the Real Thing Comes Along". Toby danced. I read the accounts of my race in the papers.

On the train returning to the Village Toby said, "What are you going to do when we get back to England?"

"Don't know," I said. "I've said I'll retire, but now I've been invited to run again in America."

"Princeton?"

I nodded. "I honestly don't know what I'm going to do."

"Difficult. I've still got examinations when I get back."

"Same with me. I don't want to think about it, Toby. Actually, I feel like a night on the tiles. Met a German friend today who wants to show me the night life."

"Lucky you."

"Trouble is, I've got a calendar full of official receptions until we leave."

"Swap you, Jack. Any time. The town's at your feet. Me, I'm just a rouseabout. I get a top second in the Economics Tripos at Cambridge and all I'm good for in Berlin is making cups of tea and running errands."

"Anyway," I said, "it probably won't happen. I've lost him."

"Who? The German friend?"

"Yes, don't know where to reach him. Funny cove."

"Funny, in what way?"

"I was thinking about something he said. 'Why do you suppose the doors and windows are so thick?' he said. In the Village, he meant."

"What did he say that for?"

"Well, you know. Godfrey goes on about it sometimes, saying the Village will be taken over by the German army after we move out. Turned into an arsenal, he says."

"Why shouldn't it? The army built the place. It's their country."

"Good point. No, it just stuck in my mind, what he said. Come to think of it, our bungalow is built like a fortress."

"Oh, I've heard yarns like that – 'Protection from gas attacks' and what have you. Chaps saying, 'The Germans are rearming for war' and 'War will follow.' I've even heard it said that the Stadium will be taken over by the SS for initiation ceremonies after we've gone. Sinister stuff, eh."

"Do you believe it?" I said.

"*Do you*? Oh come on, Jack. Be your age."

"Of course I don't believe it."

"Thick windows, eh. Ever heard of double glazing?"

"Double glazing? Of course. The whole of northern Europe's built like that, isn't it? Amazing, isn't it, how easily one can be taken in by rumours."

"I'll tell you something. People talk about conscription in Nazi Germany and press censorship. Hitler's supposed to have

293

'muzzled' the press, total censorship. Stamped out 'the free expression of ideas'. I heard that at Cambridge. Utter balls. There's every damn newspaper in the world on sale here. I bet your German friend didn't tell you that. What else did he say?"

"Oh nothing directly. He sort of makes you feel there's a spy in every bar and every second official you meet in white Olympic uniform is a member of the Gestapo. I don't see it."

"We had a chap at Cambridge last year. He'd been to a Nazi youth camp. He had a good line. His line was, the Germans are using sport and gymnastics as a cover for rearming. A German army on the march in two years – I remember his words. 'They're re-educating the German youth of today for the army of the future.' Just look around you, Jack! Oh yes – 'Guns instead of butter' – that was another line he was shooting. 'The Germans have given up eating butter to buy guns,' he said."

I laughed out loud. "I've never seen so much butter, Toby, since I left New Zealand. What did you say to the chap at Cambridge?"

"Howled him down."

"Quite right."

"Absolutely right, Jack. You know, I got to Berlin before you did. I've been to Berlin every day. See anything, do anything, talk to anyone. I don't think I've been in a cleaner, sweeter, more orderly, more friendly place in my life. Berlin must be the most law-abiding city in Europe."

"It's wide open, Toby."

"That's it. I mean, that *is* it. Nothing hidden. These Games are the proof of what we've been saying. *The* proof. OK, Versailles, the Treaty of Versailles. I know about the Treaty of Versailles. And maybe the Nazis have got a problem with a few dissidents, homosexuals and Communists and a few Jews. What have you. Heavens, it's a new system. Who hasn't got problems? It will all settle down. But can you imagine a man like Hitler – *any* statesman – throwing a party like this and inviting the whole world to come and poke around in his back yard if he's planning a war? Can you? Can you?"

"Ludicrous," I said.

I don't now remember exactly where I met up again with Otto Peltzer, but I know it was right at the end of our stay and we were in a lovely old Berlin garden. It was night. Music was playing. Lanterns hanging from poles between ornamental trees spilled a honey-coloured light which seemed to soften even the heel-clicks of the aides who flitted across a lawn bearing salvers of carp and canapés. Was it Charlottenburg? It was one of the innumerable German cocktail receptions to which in the second week journalists and athletes, gold medallists in particular, were invited. In the second week the swimming, equestrian and other events were held; all the stadiums of the Reichssportfeld came into use; the weather was continuously hot and there were performances of Greek opera in the open air and mass gymnastic displays under a night sky transformed into a weird forest of searchlights. When it became obvious that Germany was ahead on points and that the host nation's tally of medals would far exceed that of any other country,* German official hospitality which was already lavish became overwhelming. Our party, the one at which Peltzer appeared, was quite small, about two hundred guests. The biggest parties were thrown after we left. Herr von Ribbentrop, the new German ambassador to the Court of St James, had an ox roasted on a spit in his private park at Dahlem, but then Dr Goebbels, the Minister of Propaganda and Popular Enlighten-ment, went one better with an "Italian evening" on an island in the Havel River. According to Harold, Goebbels had an army of engineers throw a pontoon bridge across to the island, the Pfaueninsel, and the 1500 guests, arriving down an avenue of fairy lights, were led to their places by troupes of girls dressed as Renaissance pages. At midnight Goebbels initiated a bombardment of fireworks. By comparison our party was tame.

Marquees were set out in the garden and a string quartet played under the trees. Nobody danced. There were several generals present. The most exciting thing was the American swimmer Eleanor Holm Jarrett in a see-through rose dress. Eleanor had been suspended from the American team on the voyage across for getting plastered on champagne, but had now

* Germany dominated the gymnastic events, and was the overall winner in nineteen competitions ahead of its nearest rival, the USA, when the Games ended. German contestants won a total of 89 Gold, Silver and Bronze medals, compared with the USA's 56 medals.

been hired by an international press agency as a reporter. Neither Toby nor I could get near her for heel-clicking attachés. I had wangled an invitation for Toby, and Freddie Wolff, the English quarter-miler, also came. Toby had heard that somebody big was coming and when the chamber music suddenly died and a band which nobody had noticed struck up "The Great Elector's Cavalry March", we all rushed out of the marquee expecting to see the dazzling sky-blue uniform of Field-Marshal Goering, or at the least Himmler or Leni Riefenstahl, but it was only a little man with eyebrows who looked like a riding instructor. He was smaller even than Sydney Wooderson, primped up in a uniform with a lot of rings on his left hand and his face was bronzed as if he had stepped from under a sunlamp. He was announced as the Reichsminister in Charge of Sport, Hans von Tschammer-and-Something, and we stood about with our glasses of Pommery champagne waiting to be introduced. Everybody was polite and jolly, except the British who huddled in undertones and were getting quietly tight. Then the Reichsminister in Charge of Sport, holding his baton across a chestful of ribbons, came up to Freddie, clicked, bowed and said in well-rehearsed English, "Ah, Lovelocks. Die Gazelle aus Neuseeland. You have a very fine moment."

"He means you, Jack," Freddie said.

"Ah, Mr Lovelocks." The Herr Reichsminister turned to me and offered his left hand. I shook it. "You have a very fine moment."

"Movement, Herr Reichsminister," an interpreter prompted.

"Ja, movement."

"Thank you," I said.

"The Führer has asked me to convey his very big wishes. Our Führer saw your race. He said you 'came'. Nein, not came. What is the word?"

"Came on," the interpreter prompted.

"On, ja. On, on, on. 'Came on'. Came on, Lovelocks. You came on, genau. Very good. The Führer said you were grim and watchful."

"Slim and watchful, Herr Reichsminister."

"Ja, slim."

"Thank you," I said to the Minister.

"And we shall see you in Tokyo, Mr Lovelocks? The next Olympic Games will be held in Tokyo in Neunzehnhundertvierzig."

"Tokyo in 1940? Yes indeed," I said. "Unfortunately I — "

"And," he added, pausing, smiling, showing a handsome profile, he really was a handsome man, gazing around the Olympic-blazered gathering as if he had rehearsed a punchline and was undecided in which language to utter it. "*And*," he said, "the entire German team will travel there in airships!" Then he clicked, whacked his leg with the baton and made a beeline for Eleanor Holm Jarrett.

"This is terrible," I said to Freddie Wolff. "Let's get out." Freddie hiccuped. Ever since the previous Sunday when he had helped win Britain's only Gold Medal on the track in the 400-metre relay, Freddie had been on a high, but he wasn't accustomed to Pommery champagne.

"It isn't," Freddie yelled at the top of his wispy voice, "it isn't the sort of party where you're encouraged to do 'Knees up Movvah Brown', is it?" So saying, Freddie swayed and gently collapsed against a pole looped with garlands which was holding up one of the marquees. As Freddie subsided on to the lawn, a hand reached out of the darkness and helped him to his feet. I looked, and there was Otto Peltzer.

He was grinning. The grey eyes shone. Gone were the dark glasses, the overcoat, the huddled look of four or five days earlier. He wore a suit. The thick toothbrush moustache was trimmed and he had shaved off the goatee beard. He stood there smiling expansively like a contented elder statesman.

"Dr Peltzer! Otto, I mean – what are you doing here?"

"I came with my friend." Beside him was a white-suited young German, very blond, very Nordic, with blue eyes.

"Fritz Schilgen," I said, recognising him at once. I shook hands with the blond athlete and made the introductions all round. "You carried the torch into the Stadium. You were in white."

"Fritz is a former pupil of mine," Peltzer said, and spoke to Schilgen in German. "But how do you know him? He says he has never met you."

"Oh we've met," I laughed. In a dream last February, I almost added. But that would have sounded silly. Instead

297

I said, "Otto, we're bored to tears. Can you get us out of this?"

"Certainly." He turned to Toby and Freddie. "You are in pain, gentlemen?"

"Nicely put."

"Bored stiff, actually."

"Come. We go. I show to you Berlin by night." Peltzer gathered the three of us up and twenty minutes later we were strolling down the brightly lit avenue of the Kurfürstendamm with the strains of jazz and honky-tonk spilling on to the sidewalk around us. Schilgen for some reason had vanished.

It was after nine o'clock, nearly ten. The tree-lined boulevard was thronged. The glass-enclosed verandahs of the coffee houses were full, also the bars and dance parlours, and wherever one looked Olympic rings and lights floated. "Odd," Toby said to me. "Hardly any Nazi flags in the street." He said to Peltzer, "Why are there so few swastikas?" Peltzer shrugged and strode on without answering. He took us into a bar where a dog, dressed in SS uniform, was being encouraged to walk a tightrope and an American Negro athlete was jiving with a dark voluptuous woman in a black dress. They stamped their feet and sang "Goody Goody". A zither was playing. Peltzer seemed determined we should enjoy ourselves. On the Lehninerplatz patrons, coming off the pavement, were storming the entrance to a cabaret. Peltzer strode imperiously across the foyer, sweeping people aside, and got us as far as the door. Looking in, I glimpsed a man in round spectacles spotlighted on an otherwise darkened stage. He seemed shy. He stammered as he spoke. His audience, crammed into the auditorium at small tables, was convulsed with laughter and rolling in the aisles. But we couldn't get in. We took a cab and alighted at another establishment in the Nürnbergerstrasse. "What were they laughing at back there?" Freddie said to Peltzer when we were seated at a table.

"Ah, Werner Finck. I tell you. Moment – Ein Kirschwasser bitte," he said to the waiter, ordering a shot of clear colourless Schnapps. He ordered Sekt for Freddie and me. A pianist was playing. We appeared to be in an OK sort of night club. Couples and unattached girls sat about at numbered tables and on every table was a white telephone. There was a smell of wine, rouge and powder.

Toby drank mineral water and kept his eye on an unattached bosomy girl with coral fingernails seated nearby.

"The man at the cabaret is Werner Finck," Peltzer said. "He makes jokes."

"What sort of jokes?"

"I tell you. He makes jokes about Jesse Owens and Leni Riefenstahl. Hitler does not like the American Negroes to take part in the Games and Leni Riefenstahl, she makes the film of this Olympic Games with many shootings of Jesse Owens winning his medals. So Werner Finck tells the audience, 'Und plötzlich sieht sie's negativ, wie positiv der Neger lief' – but it is not funny in English."

"Sort of political jokes, you mean? Against the Nazis?"

Peltzer smiled. "Then Werner Finck tells a joke about Himmler. Himmler is in charge of the police in Berlin. 'The police in Berlin,' Finck tells, 'have three different uniforms, vite, blue and green. If blue, it means you are a police official. If vite, you have the power of the police behind you. If green, it means you must be obeyed absolutely."

"And that is the joke?"

"That is the joke, my friend."

"Do you get it?" Freddie said to Toby.

"I wasn't really listening, Freddie."

The bosomy girl with the red nails was smiling at Toby. Peltzer leaned across the table and said to Toby, "You like this woman?"

"Toby thinks she's a wow," I said.

"You wish me to telephone to her?"

"Let me," I said. I exchanged a wink with Peltzer and dialled the illuminated number on the girl's table. She joined us at once. Presently she and Toby got up and danced. The club was on two levels with freshly painted walls and was decorated with international flags. Behind the pianist a door, discreetly curtained, led to another part of the establishment. I recognised Peter Wilson, a British journalist, among the clientèle at the bar. Peltzer's smile took in the scene with the expression of an amused parent chaperoning a birthday party. "Your friend is tired," he said, nodding at Freddie. Freddie had fallen asleep.

Some time later Freddie woke up and left. Toby lost his girl

299

to an Italian weight-lifter in a black beret. Then he too left.
"Now we are alone," Peltzer said to me. I nodded.

"You are enjoying yourself, Jack?"

"Yes, Otto. Very much."

"May I call you Jack?"

"Of course," I said.

"You wish to go with one of these women?" he said,
indicating the white telephone.

"Not particularly." I was feeling not tight from the champagne and Sekt but a bit goofy. Pleasantly disembodied. I
pushed the telephone away.

He smiled. He touched me lightly under the table on the
knee. "If you wish we can go to another place. Would you like
that?"

"Would you?"

"My dear Jack, I am at your disposition."

Why not? I thought. One last fling. Aloud I said, "Why not?
It's my last night in Berlin."

22

We didn't go very far. I think it was somewhere off the
Rankestrasse. There was a bakery on one corner. A tattered
limp swastika hung from a balcony of stone cupids and
armorial designs and below, opposite the bakery, steps led
down. The steps descended to a half-basement giving on to a
corridor and then, after crossing a courtyard with a sudden
view of clear sky and descending to a lower level again, we were
in a room faintly misty filled with a lurid pink light. The first
thing I saw was a man who might have been a bank manager
except he was clothed entirely in pink – pink rouge, pink hair
dye, pink silk shirt and necktie, pink silk handkerchief –
reclining on a plush sofa. He had a sailor on his knee. They were
embracing. The room was divided into alcoves; perfume drifted

about; lights fastened to chains hung from a low ceiling; there was a bar and a space for dancing. Beside an old-fashioned iron stove sat a man in a monocle playing chess. Rouged couples with Eton-cropped hair were dancing very close together. They appeared phosphorescent, like rotting fish. I drew back.

"Komm." Otto had taken my elbow. Then he too paused, irresolute. The man in the monocle was looking up. The proprietress or Madam, a woman in black, oozing flesh, her fingers bulging with rings, came forward – she had a little drawstring bag of silver mesh dangling from her wrist. She wobbled towards us in her flesh and kissed Peltzer on both cheeks. Even so it wasn't until a youth appeared and greeted Peltzer with a quick smile that he seemed to relax: he allowed the youth to guide us to a table. Peltzer seemed drawn, despite himself.

"Gut," he said, glancing round as we sat down. On the walls were photographs of boxers and male torsoes with outrageous muscles and biceps, but it struck me that each of the patrons in the room was more outrageous still. The man in the monocle wore a creased evening suit with an overblown lilac rose in his lapel; he was smoking a Turkish cigarette which seemed to grow from a long polished fingernail.

"What is this place, Otto?" Little gasps directed at my Olympic blazer had greeted our arrival; phantom boat-shaped eyes were nodding in our direction. I sat down feeling permeated by something slimy. Yet I was strangely exhilarated. The air was tinged with excitement.

"Ja, gut. It will be all right, Jack." Petlzer had put on his dark glasses. He motioned me to remove my blazer.

"What is this place?" The blazer was sticking to me.

"I thought it was closed. Yesterday it is still closed." He was drumming his fingers on the table top. Notes from a pianoforte which I couldn't see gushed out. Abruptly in time to the music he intoned, "Yesterday we are closed, today we are open. If we are open today, we shall be closed again tomorrow." He said, "It seems the Nazis allow it for the season."

"What season?"

"The Olympic season, of course." His lip curled. He was suddenly contemptuous. Then as the youth returned with drinks he smiled and said, "We call it the Olympic Pause, my

301

dear. The Nazis like to show that all things are possible in the new Germany. Ja, ja. Berlin knows how to 'faszinieren' her guests. Take off your jacket. They like to create an impression for the foreigners. You see?" But he was watching the youth.

"You mean this isn't normal?"

"What is normal, my dear? Drink! Prosit. They know me here."

"Prosit, Otto," I said, raising my glass and sniffing Schnapps. But Otto, his angular face creased into a grin, had eyes only for the youth. He had set down a stone bottle and poured three drinks; he shot a glance in my direction. Peltzer held the glass by the twisted stem, grinning widely, and he allowed the youth to ruffle his hair, grinning and appraising him, their eyes interlocking, neither of them speaking until the boy reaching in the waistband of his tights produced a ring and held it up: Peltzer chuckled and murmured the word "Hans". Hans smiled. He wore black tights and a shirt open to the navel; he had a hot open face. He bent forward, slipped the ring over Peltzer's finger and kissed him gently on the mouth. Then he sat down beside him and they broke into a flood of intimacies in German.

I sat there disapproving, aware of a network of signals I didn't understand. Some current running deep underground held me. Presently above the notes of the piano I became conscious of a thrumming sound at my back, together with a hint of perfume. A low attractive voice was crooning in my ear. Peltzer was leaning across the table spreading his long fingers, displaying a signet ring initialled "O.P."

"Hans saved it for me while I was in the prison. Hans is a good boy." He added, "Hans says, why don't you dance with Anna?"

"Anna?"

I turned, and there was a girl in a slim black eye-mask strumming a balalaika. Her lips parted in a smile.

"My name is Anna," she said in German, speaking in the same bewitching voice which a moment before had been singing. She wore a maroon velvet suit – starched shirt, bow tie – and had coal-black eyes that flickered behind the mask. She put down the balalaika, bowed, and we danced. Despite my feather feet I am, so people tell me, a clumsy dancer, full of inhibitions. But with Anna I became daring. Anna crooned as we danced, her dark hair flopping over one cheek. The space was tiny. The tunes were unfamiliar and melancholy, matched to Anna's crooning voice, and the pianist copied our steps. Her hands brushed my shoulder. We moved sinuously, barely touching yet in supreme intimacy. Anna undid my Olympic tie and looped it at her throat, I removed my blazer, made little jokes, rolled my eyes and imagined I was being seduced in a closed black cab (only it was better than that). This is the real Berlin, I told myself, letting the atmosphere seep into me and winking at Otto who sat, tie loosened, chin cupped on one hand, his eyes feasting on Hans. Hans was alternately flaunting his body and talking excitedly, smoking small cigarettes and passing them round when he poured the drinks.

"*Ich hab*'," Anna sang, "*ich bin, ich bin verliebt in Dich.*" Whenever we sat down Anna picked up the balalaika and crooned. A sense of delicious languor overcame me. I felt I had penetrated to the core of a mysterious new world and was sliding through layers of milk-green moss.

> *Ich hab', ich bin, ich möcht' mit dir sofort*
> *Ich würde wenn Du gerne auch*
> *Es fehlt nur noch ein Wort . . .*

Surely, she seemed to be saying, you understand what I'm trying to tell you?

She sang song after song. At one stage the man with the monocle got up and spoke to the proprietress, putting something in her drawstring bag; then he returned to his chess game. The sailor on the sofa left. It grew late. The man in the monocle sat on, smoking Turkish cigarettes through an ebony holder. Later, after the sailor left, or it might have been earlier, I became aware that something was passing surreptitiously from table to table. At first I thought it was a magazine, then realised it must be a programme. I saw the word "Olympische" on the cover. It seemed to have a curious riveting effect, almost a paralysing effect on people, as it circulated among the alcoves. Then it reached our table and Peltzer became agitated.

I had been dancing a Charleston – the pianist had broken into a snatch of honky-tonk. Yielding to a sudden temptation to show off, I had left Anna's side and was whirling and stamping like a dervish, letting go with a solo number I had learned in America. Hans jumped up and kissed my hand. Otto said:

"Hans says, will you teach him? And what is the name? Say it for him in German please."

"I can't, Otto. It's called, 'Would You Rather Be a Colonel with an Eagle on Your Shoulder, or a Private with a Chicken on your Knee?' I learned it in Princeton during Reunions Week."

"Wunderbar! But say it in German for Hans."

"I can't." I grinned. "What is Anna singing now?"

"*Gestern*," Anna crooned, "*waren wir geschlossen. Heute sind wir offen . . .*" Otto translated, " 'Yesterday we are closed, today we are open. If we are open today, we shall be closed again tomorrow'. I said it to you before. Aber, it is not a song. It is a joke from Werner Finck at the cabaret where we have been earlier tonight."

"What does it mean?"

"It means what it says." He up-ended the stone bottle to pour a drink. It was empty. "It is better you don't understand."

"But why?" I said. "Don't be so mysterious."

"It is a pity to spoil such a nice evening. Go, dance with Anna."

"I'm not a child."

"No, a sportsman. Only a sportsman, my dear." He patted my arm. "I keep forgetting that you are only a sportsman. In Germany it is no longer possible to be only a sportsman."

"Otto, are you angry with me?"

"Go, dance. Anna is waiting."

"She's not waiting, she's singing. What does it mean?"

He shrugged, turning the ring on his finger under the lamp as if absorbed. I thought he was about to doze off. "Very well! This evening you have been with me on the Ku-Damm and your friend says to me, why are there no swastikas? There are no swastikas on the Ku-Damm because it is a Jewish street. Ah so! You remain puzzled? Berlin is a stage and for the visitors, we have the stage dressing. Instead of swastikas on the Kurfür-stendamm we have American jazz music and cabaret and Werner Finck who makes jokes about the Nazis. You think this is normal? Tomorrow there will be no more jazz. Werner Finck will vanish."

"Vanish?"

"Normally, my friend, in normal times, even to think such things as Werner Finck is saying is a form of treason. You are an innocent, I see that."

"You *are* angry with me. Don't be potty, Otto. The place is wide open."

"Potty? I do not understand the word. This bar where I bring you is verboten."

"Forbidden? Then why bring me?" I laughed. "Why are you here if it comes to that?"

"You are an innocent, Jack."

"Well don't snap at me." I laughed, getting up to dance. "You're so theatrical, Otto."

Anna tugged me up. They were playing a tango. As I got up, Hans fetched the Olympic programme which had been circulating and brought it to the table. I saw Peltzer pale and push it down. One minute he was looking at the programme over Hans' shoulder, the next he had pushed it under the table saying "Nein" to Hans. "Nein, nein, nein," he said in a kind of stifled scream. Hans had a stupid grin on his face. "If that's a German programme," I said to Otto, "will you sign it for me?" Hans was pulling at it under the table.

"For a souvenir, Otto? I mean, I haven't got one in German."

I didn't see what happened to the programme. Anna tugged me back on to the floor. Even then I didn't take in what he had been saying. My alarm signals had long vanished. It never occurred to me to wonder why he was agitated about the programme, or what it was, just as it never occurred to me to wonder that Anna might be a boy or that we were indeed in one of the boy bars forbidden and closed down by the Nazis since Hitler's rise to power. We danced the "Tango Marina". Anna had snuggled into my shirt. I closed my eyes. Not even when she stiffened in my arms and I heard the word "Achtung!" spoken by one of the dancers on the floor did I open them. The pianist continued playing for a few moments and then stopped. It was only when the music stopped and I opened my eyes and saw Peltzer, white-faced, half-risen against the slatted back of the chair, slewed round in the chair as if frozen, that I realised something was happening.

Everyone in the room was standing and saluting in the Nazi manner.

A man in black SS uniform had come in. He was young. He carried gloves which he flicked as he walked. He had a round fleshy face, thin lips and a small chin. He had paused near the stove where the man in the monocle, smirking slightly, was holding out to him the programme like a trophy. The SS officer took the programme as if it was something obscene and moved quickly round the alcoves peering at faces; he seemed to know without looking what was in it. He came to Peltzer. Peltzer had slumped down. He was the only one not standing. Hans was rigid. Beside me Anna was breathing rapidly, clutching my wrist. I tried to go up to the table but my legs wouldn't come forward. Anna's fingernails were digging into my wrist as if in spasm. She had removed the mask, revealing a face in terror. It was then I realised I had been dancing with a boy. By the stove the man in the monocle had stepped aside. In his place an official in a grey Party uniform had materialised. The official beckoned across the room and the proprietress, who was balancing a tray with one hand and trying to salute with the other, the little drawstring bag dangling absurdly from her outstretched arm, wobbled towards him. At the same time two guards positioned inside the door whom I hadn't seen enter advanced upon her from behind. Beside our table, a few steps in front of me, the SS officer in black was slapping the pages of the programme across Peltzer's face, forcing him to look at them. Peltzer was shaking his head. He seemed to have lost the power of speech. "Papiere," I heard spoken. Peltzer was fumbling in his pockets. Nobody spoke. I heard a thud and saw the proprietress lying on the floor. Loose change had spilled from her mesh bag and was rolling under the tables. She was dragged out by the guards, leaving, where her body had lain, a damp stain. Nobody moved. Peltzer's hands shook as he emptied his pockets and produced his papers. The SS man glanced at the papers. He inclined his body and continued to slap Peltzer's face with the programme. Then he spat in it.

"Aufstehen," he said. Peltzer didn't get up, didn't move. He was looking down with an expression of peculiar horror.

"Aufstehen!"

306

Two guards rushed up and stood at Peltzer's elbows. More guards had appeared in the room, expanding and contracting before my eyes like a brown twilight. They wore brown shirts, flared trousers and high polished boots. All this had happened in the space of perhaps two minutes. By then I had left Anna's side and managed to cross the intervening space to the table.

Peltzer, still seated, was saying something in German. The officer's back was towards me.

"What does he want?" I said to Peltzer.

"He wants – " Peltzer took off his glasses and managed a sickly smile. "He wants that I stand to greet him. Please tell him, Lovelock" – and he repeated the name. "Tell him, my dear Lovelock, that as someone already convicted of a crime like treason, Hitler has said I must not use the German greeting and I never must put my dirty hands on the German flag."

At the word Lovelock the man in black uniform had spun round. Face to face his pink eyes seemed to bulge and yet didn't. The eyes went blank.

"Lovelock?"

This is ludicrous, I wanted to say – the whole thing's ludicrous. What I said was, "Good evening." I tried to sound plummy and relaxed but all that came out was a squeak. The saliva stuck in my throat.

"Lovelock?" he said. "Ausländer?"

"Ausländer," Peltzer said. "Engländer," he added. He picked up my Olympic blazer and gave it to me. I put it on.

"You are English?" The man in the black uniform had stepped back, snapping upright. His manner had changed. He pocketed the programme and spoke rapidly in German. The guards went out and the man in Party uniform followed them.

"I am so sorry, Mr Lovelock. A most unfortunate occurrence. The bar, you see, has no permit. It is necessary to have a permit. It is most unpleasant for you. Come – " He bowed slightly and someone moved a table, making a passage to the door. "Please come.

"Please come," he repeated.

Anna was trying to say something. She hadn't moved from the dance floor. I still thought of her as a girl. Her hands went to her throat, to my tie. She held the tie to her side, slightly out from the body, in a helpless imploring gesture. I turned away.

Hans kept his eyes averted. Peltzer's chin had slumped forward on to his hand. There was spittle on his face, slime-tracked by perspiration running down his cheeks. The perspiration dripped on to the table. He made a sign to me and I went out.

I went up the steps and through the courtyard on to the street. There was a small garden in the courtyard and chairs beyond where two people sat talking under a pale pink sky. On the street day was breaking and the light was again pink. Groups of young people were waiting outside the entrance to a U-bahn station. They carried packets of food and rucksacks and tenting equipment. Traffic was still flowing. I remember the details. There was a girl sitting on the pavement under the sign "Bäckerei" nervously clutching a handbag between her fingers. I remember everything. Then a car pulled into the kerb beside me. Perhaps the car was already waiting at the kerb when we arrived? The officer in black who accompanied me spoke through the window to a man sitting in shadow behind the driver, passing something through the window to him, then opened the door for me to get in. I remember the feel of the upholstery as I sat down and the car moved forward. I even remember the aroma of face lotion as the man beside me leaned across after we had gone a few yards and switched on the panel light illuminating his face in the back seat. He introduced himself. It was the man in the leather coat from the Kaiserhof café. So why didn't I scream?

I just walked out.

It seems to me there are two possible explanations for my conduct. One is fear. For the first time in my life I had smelled terror and was afraid. Yet I was not so afraid, walking out of the bar, that I didn't remember where to put my feet. Walking out, crossing the room with thirty pairs of eyes watching me, I carefully avoided putting down my feet where the money had spilled on to the floor. And what of the others? I could say that they pitied me. True, one or two of those watching gave me pitying looks. But the fear that I felt was as nothing compared to the anguish and numbness I read in their eyes. I just walked out. I abandoned them. A man however traumatised he may be, however petrified, can always scream. Why didn't I scream?

I went gladly, willingly.

The other explanation is disbelief. Even today, writing this down from memory, I seem to be describing an incident that happened to someone else. People who have witnessed a bullfight tell me the same thing – afterwards they cannot grasp that what happened to the bull or to the matador really happened. Reality was suspended, they say. There are voices whispering to me about that night. But are they telling me my own thoughts? What in fact did happen? Perhaps nothing happened. A woman had fallen down. Did somebody hit her? I didn't see it. She might simply have fainted. I saw nobody harmed. Did I dream the whole thing?

I shall never know the answer to these questions, just as I shall never completely unravel the mystery of the Olympic programme that produced such a violent reaction in Peltzer.

Ten years later in 1946 I was visited in London by a German woman, Frau von Richard Falkenberg, who brought me news of Otto Peltzer. She talked of many things, one of which was the anti-Nazi underground which survived in Germany, she said, until 1938 and was active in Berlin in 1936 during the Games, activities of which I, like so many other athletes who took part, were totally unaware. She mentioned that one of the illegal documents distributed by the underground was a fake Olympic programme got up to look like the original, *Der Olympische Reiseführer* – "A Travel Guide which no visitor to the Olympic Games in Berlin should be without". Inside, illustrated by maps and photographs, were listed more than 200 concentration camps and prisons in Nazi Germany, together with the names of sportsmen who couldn't take part in the Games because they had already been arrested or executed by the Gestapo. I can only assume it was one of these "programmes" which was circulating that night and which caused Peltzer to react as he did – presumably so I wouldn't be involved. After all, as he said, I was "only a sportsman".

Did something die in me that night? I have no comment. I can't even swear that I was especially miserable or depressed the next day when I left Berlin, although a certain niggling doubt remains. Sydney Wooderson and others of the British team will tell you that when I arrived on the platform of Bahnhof Friedrichstrasse at two o'clock in the afternoon, I had a hunted look. Wooderson wondered if I was on drugs. Most of the British team went back that day. According to Wooderson, I sat down on my bags on the platform apart from the other athletes and refused to talk to anyone. When Lord Aberdare came up and asked if I was feeling all right, I ignored him; then David Burghley whom I had known for years approached me – Wooderson says I got up and walked away. That is one piece of evidence.

But against this: Cecil Matthews who travelled with me in the same compartment back to London has a different story. Cec claims that on the journey I chatted with him about running and in all respects behaved quite normally. You can make of this what you will. Cec remembers me talking about the oak seedling I had been given on the dais after the race: how I asked him if he would look after it and take it back to New Zealand for me and present it to my old school: how I nursed the seedling in its pot and how concerned I was about its long sea voyage. Cec said to me, "It mightn't survive the trip, Jack." "Oh but it must, Cec," I said. "It must." That is another piece of evidence.

I know that at times of great stress or excitement your eyes can play tricks with your surroundings and many competitors at Berlin have subsequently gone on record saying they can't quite believe that certain things at those Games which they witnessed actually took place. Ask them. It isn't just me. There are lots of survivors from Berlin 1936 still around, although of course many of the German athletes – Lutz Long, Rudolf Harbig, Werner Böttcher – were killed or crippled in the war. Maybe some will even tell you about experiences similar to mine – I know of two other cases. But I'm not going into their stories here. You will have to take my word for the events of that night. There is no reason why you should. On the other hand there is no particular reason why you shouldn't. I'll tell you why. I went back.

When the car had travelled a short distance from the bar, it stopped. It crawled forward and stopped again. I said to the man seated beside me, "Where are we going?"

"We are returning to Döberitz. To the Olympische Dorf."

"Why have we stopped?"

310

"A small delay. It is nothing."

He spoke to the driver, then sat back with one leg crossed looking out of the window. He seemed indifferent to my presence. His movements were quick and catlike but he was not menacing, unless indifference and silence can be menacing. There was a silence in the air when he spoke. His tanned face merged with the leather of his coat and the padded upholstery, and if he had not left the light on in the back I would hardly have known he was there.

"And have you enjoyed your stay in Berlin, Herr Lovelock?" There was a glimmer of gold in his mouth. He spoke in fluent educated English.

"Who are you?" I said.

"I shall explain. It is my pleasant duty to look after our more important guests and see that they come to no harm."

I said nothing. He had explained nothing. I sat as far away as possible on the edge of the seat and pressed down on one leg which was jumping. I tasted bile in my mouth. I was going to vomit. I pressed down, forcing my foot to the floor, and didn't vomit.

"You have another question, Herr Lovelock?"

I didn't answer.

"About this, for example?" He flattened something on his lap and tilted the cover towards me under the light. "Dr Peltzer wished you to see it, I believe? Come now, Herr Lovelock. There is no cause for alarm. You have signed dozens of Olympic programmes like this one since you came to Berlin. You signed one for me, you remember? In the Hotel Kaiserhof."

I said, thinking somehow to save the situation, "It's mine." My brain was working. "It's not his, he had nothing to do with it," I said, "it's mine."

"Ah."

"Somebody gave it to me."

"Ah. You mean showed it to you?"

"No – I mean. Yes, a souvenir. For a souvenir," I repeated stupidly. "Somebody – I wanted a souvenir. I don't know who gave it to me, he wouldn't sign it."

"Yes?"

"Dr Peltzer had nothing to do with it. He – " I stopped. He

311

was smiling broadly. I had made some dreadful error. "Please go on," he said. The car moved forward and stopped again.

"Herr Lovelock, do you speak German?"

"No."

"In that case there is no harm done. Is there?"

I said, "I'm going to be sick," and opened the door and got out.

"Are you feeling better?"

I was standing by the door at the kerbside leaning against the chassis breathing in air. The driver had half-turned; the other man had slid across and was holding the door handle from the inside, waiting for me to get back in. The sickness was passing. When the sickness had passed I looked around and saw we had come no more than forty or fifty yards. There was the "Bäckerei" sign on the corner. It was then I left the car and ran back.

I don't know what was in my mind. Even as I ran and turned in by what appeared to be the same swastika hanging limply over the pavement opposite the bakery and reeled down the steps into the courtyard, I knew it was hopeless and stupid. An act of senseless bravado. But I had to do something. I was out of control. The rush of air as I ran had made me drunk, sleep-drunk. The courtyard was deserted. I crossed the courtyard. I seemed to hurtle down the steps from the courtyard and collide with the door at the entrance to the bar and bounce back from the closed door, recoiling in shock, and lunge forward and turn the handle and fall inside the room all in one movement. It was a moment before I caught my breath and realised my mistake. The room, enveloped in darkness, was empty. It wasn't the bar at all. I had come to the wrong place.

I started to laugh. I could hear an inane laugh echoing from the bare walls as from a vault, some cellar or deserted workshop I had stumbled into by mistake. I was groping about, laughing hysterically: the encircling walls contracted and expanded at the sound of my laughter like shadows waving at nightfall: and as the echo of my voice died away a door closed and reverberated at the back of the premises. I heard footfalls. Then nothing. I was turning away to go out of the door. A light came on. A pallid light was shining from a bulb hanging in a corridor beyond, throwing shadows into the room and up one wall. Perhaps the light had been there all the time? I stepped on a nail or a screw, scuffed an empty cigarette packet. A cigarette packet was scraping under my foot, adhering to the shoe – I bent down to free it and felt a tug of elastic in my hand and something else, not a cigarette packet but a piece of crumpled cardboard to which the elastic was attached. I felt the card give in my fingers and in the same moment caught a whiff of perfume, no, not perfume, nor even fumes of stale alcohol which must have been clinging to the air, but an acrid tang like the aroma of a Turkish cigarette, and then I knew, even though my eyes told me otherwise, that I had returned to the right place.

Everything had vanished. The bar counter had gone. The photographs from the walls, the tables, the chairs, the lamps, the chains holding the lamps, the pot-plants, the sofa in the alcove, even the low wrought-iron balustrades dividing the room into alcoves had vanished, the old-fashioned iron stove, the piano, all was gone, swept away. Where the pianist had sat on a tiny stage was only a space and a pile of boards stacked along the wall. A film of grey dust was settling. The bar had ceased to exist.

I stood just inside the doorway and felt my skin blanch and grow cold. I couldn't scream. I wanted to scream and I couldn't. The piece of card I had picked up fell from my hand. It was Anna's mask. I stood there feeling cold in my clothes and then I went out, closing the door, and retraced my steps on to the street. The car was waiting, pulled up at the kerb. The chauffeur held the door for me.

I got in and was driven back to the Village. The clock under the belltower at the gate said 4.50. a.m. It was 11 August 1936. We left on the afternoon train.

Part Four

1949

"The horror of that moment," the King went on, "I shall never, *never* forget." "You will, though," the Queen said, "if you don't make a memorandum of it."

LEWIS CARROLL
Through the Looking-Glass

23

And then? And afterwards?

Afterwards I ran one more major race in America. Then I stopped. Finish. End of career.

And what was the lesson of Berlin?

There used to be a saying in the thirties: "It is later than you think." But who cared? Who listened? I, for one, didn't listen and one of these days quite soon when my daughters are a little older – I have two daughters now – one of them is going to say to me, "And what did you do in the war, Daddy?" I am going to find it very hard to look her in the eye and give a straight answer. I was "only a sportsman" – and how right Otto Peltzer was to tell me so. I have never seen him again. In Germany he was known as "Otto the Strange", but Peltzer, for all his strangeness and tortured air, was a noble man. When I returned to London from Berlin in 1936 I wrote an article for the journal of the British Olympic Association in which I said, "Success is glorious only when nobly achieved." Was my own achievement noble? That is what I am still asking myself today. Was it?

I am not going to make any judgment upon it. I am retired now, living in New York. I am trying to embark on a new career here in the US. Athletics are over, the war is over – all that is behind me and I am in the fortunate position of not being qualified or able to pronounce on these things with any certainty. Yet I keep feeling the need to go over it all in my mind.

At one stage, after the phoney war ended and the real war began in 1940, I became noisy and full of myself – what is commonly called a bore. I'm told that among other things I was uncivil to a general in the presence of senior officers. I may even have tried to bite him. I threw a tantrum. But the army has a way of looking after its own. I was given a lieutenant's uniform, quite a baggy one, and put into a small medical rehabilitation unit at Aldershot. It was a safe place for me to be. I didn't mind. I was at Aldershot for the duration. I wasn't exactly idle during the war but I wasn't particularly active either.

This was after my accident, of course. I went through a period of depression. Some of my friends as a matter of course relate the depression to the accident, rather than the accident to the depression. But here again, I can't pronounce. You will have to decide for yourself. The accident happened in 1940.

I was demobbed in 1946. Otto Peltzer, incidentally, survived the war, although his family didn't. His entire family perished. Otto was the sole survivor. At one stage he was paraded in handcuffs through the streets of his old town, Stettin, where once he had been received like royalty as the conqueror of Nurmi; his property was confiscated by the Nazis and he was sent to a concentration camp. I don't know the full story. After the war he wrote a book, *Sport, a Way to Freedom and Culture*. I have a copy, here in my study. Peltzer is now in India, I understand, studying yoga.

As I sit here in my study in New York, leafing through old scrapbooks and journals, Peltzer's name and photograph – such a thin, lean, passionate man – is the first thing I see. He's still someone I look up to.

It is thirteen years on. I'm trying to set my life in order, trying to simplify these thirteen years and make some sense of them. A great deal has happened to me since Berlin – and obviously I shall have to go back and pick up the threads. But there is a difficulty. When I began this account I was in Oxford convalescing from a cartilage operation on my knee. My memory was A1. Now I am no longer in England and my memory is faulty. In other ways too I am not the perfect engine I once was. My eyesight is bad. I suffer from vertigo – occasional giddy spells – and headaches and at times am so restless I don't know what to do with myself. When the headaches began, after my crash – I'm coming to that – I was given a prescription containing morphine. I was never addicted to it but when the pain behind the eyes is especially bad I still take morphine occasionally, although my wife Cynthia doesn't know this. I sit up here in my study in Brooklyn reading papers and textbooks – I'm trying to complete my State Boards. And

Cynthia is always telling me to cut it out. Don't overdo it, she says. Don't load up.

"It's past midnight. Stop straining, darling, and come to bed," she says.

But I have to keep going. I have to pass these medical examinations if I'm to complete my life's plan and become a successful doctor in New York. And that's another difficulty. I'm nearly forty, and still cramming to pass examinations. I'm still a student.

There's a great mystery somewhere.

A small mystery. It concerns my last race which was run at Princeton in the autumn of 1936 just a few weeks after my victory in Berlin. I was honouring my signature, so to speak. I lost. "It is very strange the way in which my condition has altered in the last month," I wrote then. "Before, I felt in perfect mental and physical condition – now I feel worse than for a long time – sleepless, restless and very easily tired." I wrote that on Wednesday 30 September 1936, three days before the race at Princeton and the same day that I injected two million organisms of "Flem's juice" into a muscle, the biggest dose I had ever taken. After Berlin the knee had flared up again worse than ever. "Still," I wrote in my diary, "with a couple of good nights' sleep I may yet avert a fiasco on Saturday." Conditions at the Princeton bowl that day were perfect, I was twenty-six, at the height of my powers, I even had Bill there with me, and I lost. I have a photograph here in my scrapbook showing San Romani beating me by half a street – San Romani who was fourth in Berlin and still only eighteen years of age. Archie San Romani was a mine boy from Kansas, turned cornettist and music student. I did my damnedest to beat him but – well. What does one say?

Evelyn Montague wrote in the *Manchester Guardian*, "It should have ended in the sunshine of Berlin . . ." Well. In a way it did, didn't it?

The date of this race was 3 October 1936 and in the same month I sailed from San Francisco for New Zealand, the first – and only – time I have been home. I was the guest of the Government, but what should have been a conqueror's return and perhaps (who knows?) actually was a visit to remember,

319

has remained in my mind only as a pattern of jumbled images without highlights. But there is a reason for this. I have nothing in my diary to fasten on to and excite the memory. For some reason after my last race at Princeton, the diary stops. It just stops.

When I saw my sister Olive again in New Zealand she said that I seemed in many ways a stranger, and I don't think she meant just my plummy Oxford accent. We talked about Mother – she had been cared for by an aunt in Auckland but was now in a home – and Olive and I agreed that it was the shock of Father dying when I was thirteen that had begun her troubles, I mean her real troubles. I knew Mother had been ill before that. Indeed, looking back now, ill health seems to have been considered quite normal in our family. My mother had found Father dead in his bed one morning and according to Olive, there were times even now when she could not forgive him for having done that to her. Her great loneliness had begun then. I asked Olive when it was we started calling Mother Janet, or sometimes Jane, but neither of us could remember.

Olive wasn't sure if the Olympic success had registered properly with her, although news of my victory had been brought to the home by special Government messenger. However when I saw my mother, she surprised me. I hadn't seen her since 1931 when I left for Oxford. She spoke more slowly and in a deeper voice than I remembered and as I came into the garden where she was sitting, when I was still some distance off, she said without turning her head:

"Was it a good race, son?"

She wore a veil. She was very thin and birdlike, sitting up straight on a chair outside in the garden of the home. The veil lifting in a spring breeze, the head turned towards the harbour as if she was speaking to me out there on the deck of the liner *Monterey* which had brought me in. Her legs were braced, there was a great activity going on in her thoughts and for a moment I thought she was about to spring. The nurse had warned me about that. But then she made a movement and seemed to adjust to my presence. Afterwards the nurse said it had been one of her good days.

"Yes, Janet," I said. "A lovely race."

She made me come very close and peered at me in a way I

320

remembered and looking down where the breeze was shaking the tassels of the rug below her knees I saw that she was holding my letters in her lap. They were in bundles done up with rubber bands. She was wearing the engagement stone my father had given her. I stroked her head and sat beside her.

"A lovely race," I said. "Cocoa with meaning," I added, and watched the ghost of a smile flicker behind the veil.

"I hope they're making a fuss of you at home," she said.

I wasn't sure if she meant New Zealand or England. "It's no joke being famous," I said. "Sometimes I have to read in the papers to see what I'm doing the next day. I don't like all the fuss."

"Your father would have been pleased, son."

"Yes."

"He always wanted you to win."

"Yes, he did."

"To do a thing, no matter what. That's what he said. *No matter what.* You were at school when he died."

"I never knew what caused it," I said, although I did know. It was a coronary attack.

"The temperament was too active for the body, that's what caused it, and you're the same, Jack. He got up to do a thing and it was wintertime. You were away at boarding school. He got up to do a thing and he wasn't well, I begged him not to go outside. But he had to do it, he said. He drove himself. And the next day he was gone."

"You don't have to worry," I said, because I knew it would please her more than anything. "I'm giving up this silly running. I shall become a doctor now, no matter what." Once again she surprised me, saying:

"They brought me the papers to show me your photograph, it was in all the papers. Then the nurses couldn't find my glasses. I said to them, 'What do I want glasses for? I know what he looks like.'" She said to me, "But I could tell it was a lovely race, son. Your eyes were so bright."

Jean Batten, the aviator, was in New Zealand at the time. Jean had just landed in a single-engined plane having flown solo from England, the first woman to do so, and like me she was engaged in a marathon round of speaking engagements as guest of the New Zealand Government. Jean was my contemporary –

321

we had met at a ceremony in London the previous month. And now, travelling those long empty New Zealand roads that seem to separate rather than join the towns, we met again in the middle of nowhere. We were in two Government cars. The cars stopped. We got out, shook hands and drove on again in opposite directions. I have often wondered if Jean, returning home from the northern hemisphere after an absence, had a similar reaction to mine. It was like coming out of a polar night. I had forgotten the intense ultramarine blue of the sea: the houses coloured like boiled sweets: the lushness of the grasses. The combination of lushness and hard brittle light was quite foreign to me. But then I visited the house in Dunedin where we had once lived – I opened the pantry door and automatically, as I closed it, flipped the lever with my thumb so it would stay shut. It was as if I had never been away.

I see from a cutting in my scrapbook that I visited my old school – "a tumultuous occasion". I remember that visit. Simply gorgeous. But otherwise – I don't think I said anything that people wanted to hear. Early on, when I was introduced at a civic reception as "the world's champion cyclist", and there followed a ghastly silence with everyone too polite to laugh, I realised I wasn't going to bring it off: I mean the speaking part. I played down the business of being a champion. It was a mistake. I've never been asked back. People expect you to have some special wisdom or secret knowledge to impart, and I didn't have any. Not down there.

Being a champion – the winning note – that was the one thing people wanted to hear about. It's like the guy who played the violin – he always played one note. Time after time, just the one note. His neighbour finally went in to him and said, "Other people when they play the violin, they go up and down. They make different notes." "No, no," the guy said. "They're looking for the right place. I've *found* it." Well I'd found it too. I had found my note in Berlin. But I couldn't talk about it in New Zealand. Anyway, my motto then, as now, was: Don't burden your friends with a gloomy face. So I talked to my old friends in private and in public gave exhibition runs and smiled and said that the Olympics were a good thing but they were not just about producing champions. I think some people may have thought I was slanging the Games. I felt a bit lost down there actually.

322

When you have had a private experience, it's like being dropped on your head. The world looks different. In the end I cut the tour short, pleaded ill health and left quietly. I didn't belong any more.

I didn't talk about Berlin in New Zealand. But in North America on the way back to England I gave an interview to a Canadian woman journalist in which I said that the spirit of the Olympics was being corrupted. She didn't approve of me slanging the Games either.

"Having taken part in two of them," I said, "I am definitely against." Against what? she said. "Against the idea of glorifying individual victors. Against the idea that the Games should be used by nations to further their national ideals and interests." I talked about the principle, the whole principle of the Olympics being the taking part and not the winning, "and the only difference," I said, "the only difference between winning and coming second is that the winner's name lasts longer. The system of values is all wrong. The emphasis placed on the winner as against the second or third placegetter is wrong, it's all wrong. And somebody — "

"You're going too fast," she said.

"And somebody has to put a check on this – this racial attempt by the host nation to outdo all previous hosts," I said. She missed that point, I think. I was getting steamed up. She sucked her pencil.

"So you think there is too much emphasis placed on individual champions, Mr Lovelock?"

"Dead right," I said.

She was persistent, this Canadian interviewer. Smart girl. Her name was Hazel. She sat up half the night with Bill and me in the hotel bedroom (Bill Thomas was there, I remember, so it must have been going out to New Zealand, not coming back). She had freckles and she sucked her pencil. She annoyed me. She wouldn't stop asking questions. I don't know why I bothered to talk to her. It's the only time in my life I've ever said anything to a reporter. She wrote a whole page in the *Toronto Star* afterwards in which she said among other things that I was a woman-hater. (*Me?* A woman-hater?) Finally she asked what would have happened if I had come second in Berlin instead of first, and I was stuck for an answer. I'm still stuck for an answer.

I'm not disillusioned any longer. I'm not defunct either. My running days may be over but I have fathered two children, two beautiful girls, and there is a great activity going on somewhere inside me, if only I can reach out and grab hold of what it all means. I'm trying.

Today is 5 January 1949 and it is my birthday. Some people count their lives in threes, and some in sevens, but we Lovelocks seem to come in thirteens, or in multiples of thirteen, and that is another mystery.

I was thirteen when my father died, a turning point in a way, and I was twenty-six when I won my race in Berlin. Another turning point. My father was thirteen when he contracted pleurisy, which is why he left England and came to New Zealand. He was thirty-nine when he married my mother and my mother was thirty-nine when he died. Today is my thirty-ninth birthday. I can't help thinking that this year, 1949, is going to be a momentous one. I dreamed about it last night. I woke up suddenly with tears in my eyes, just as it was years ago in London with my dream about Berlin – I saw clean through it, the whole year.

It's a wonderful feeling to start the year with snow on the ground and know that something unexpected is in store.

I am writing this at No. 203 Marlborough Road, Brooklyn, New York. It is evening and below the study window, all along the avenue, the tree trunks are frosty white. As I look down Marlborough Road the boughs and trunks of the trees, maple and birch and dogwood, are aglow in the frosty air, phosphorescent.

In a minute Addie will appear. I can see Addie's blue track top turning into Marlborough Road now from the direction of Church Avenue. Addie is in training for the Olympics. When he passes the house, he will look up and wave. He's a runner. Addie is someone I have to tell you about.

I wish I could remember what was in my dream last night. I don't think it had anything to do with my State Boards. Since arriving from England, I have had to sit my medicals all over again to get my New York licence and it is something on my mind. Last year when I sat, my thoughts were fuzzy – I couldn't remember things properly in sequence. But I have a funny feeling that this year it's going to be all right. It has been a goal of mine ever since Berlin to succeed in practice as a doctor: I'd like to have my own practice or at least run a hospital department. I didn't bring it off in England. Maybe in New York I'll be lucky.

I am waiting for Cynthia to come in. Probably when she does she will ask about my medicine: something I take to relax the eye muscles when I go out. I am ready and dressed in a suit and tie – we're going out for a birthday dinner with Cynthia's family. Cynthia will come in wearing a white silk dress and ask me to fix the pearl necklace that looks so good on her. "How long have you been ready?" she will say. "A couple of hours," I'll say. "A couple of *hours*?" And I might add, "I don't like to keep you waiting, darling."

She won't say anything. But going out, after I have fixed the necklace, she will pause and float her brown eyes at me and I will get a look. "Oh brother. I could bean you," is what the look is saying, a very special neat look that only I can recognise. She's a very neat lady is my Cynthia. I only have to mention it, make just the slightest crack about keeping her waiting, and out comes the look. It is because of our wedding.

Cynthia and I were married in London in March 1945 two months before the end of the war. I was in a major's uniform and Cynthia looked stunning in a white costume with big buttons and a spray of orchids, and as we came out from the church in Vere Street I turned to her and said something. Cynthia gave me a look. It's the same one I shall get tonight if I make a crack about keeping her waiting. I admit that I was late for the wedding, I was late by several years. Eight and a half years, to be precise. That's late by any standard. I can't explain it. How do you explain something you don't understand?

We met at Cambridge. September 1936. Cynthia claims it was later than that, after I returned from New Zealand; but I say it was before, in September, right after Berlin when I was preparing to go to Princeton and they were running heart tests on me at King's College Hospital in London and Adolphe Abrahams had let it be known what a phenomenally low pulse rate I had. Of course today when athletes are recording times which would make even Nurmi blink, a cardiac rate of 39 is not startling. In 1936 I was considered such an oddity, "the man with the 100 per cent heart", that plans were under way to amplify the heart-beats and broadcast them to the Empire. I was all set to make the broadcast when I met Cynthia. My heart rate shot up and wouldn't come down again and the BBC had to cancel the broadcast. We did the broadcast the following year, in 1937. Cynthia ruined everything.

You know how it is? You're on the lion train. Being invited out – presentations, country weekends, house parties, dinner parties. And what do they want you to talk about? You've guessed. It is the guy with the violin and the one note all over again – I don't have to spell it out. Mind you, part of me was loving the adulation. Who doesn't enjoy being lionised? Like Byron. And Oscar Wilde. But Oscar Wilde could sing for his supper with witty sayings. I can't do it very well. Anyway here is this girl at Cambridge in 1936 at a cocktail party. A roomful of athletes and hangers-on, all hearty, all talking athletics and wanting to hear about nothing except athletics. And this fresh-faced young girl with nut-brown hair and a bubbling smile and bedroom eyes. "Hullo," she said. "I'm Cynthia James." "My name is Jack Smith," I said, with polished arrogance. "Oh thank God," she said. "With a name like that you can't possibly be an athlete. I hate sport." That's how it began. I was totally unprepared.

Why is it always the eyes? Some eyes just send signals. Cynthia's sent Brooklyn thunderbolts. Imagine, if you can, if you live in a city full of smog, a city that you hate, waking up one morning on an island where there are no cars. How would you feel? You'd be delirious. That is how it was with me and Cynthia. She was twenty-one, American, fresh out of Smith College, Northampton, Mass., reading history for a Master's at Newnham. She was the youngest child and only daughter of a wholesale drug manufacturer in Brooklyn, she had three brothers, dressed not at all according to the fashion and had a face – according to an English admirer – not in the least favoured by God. But it bubbled. It bubbled over in laughter. And those eyes. And she had money. And I had fame.

It was love at first sight. My cardiac rate, I'm telling you, went haywire.

And then? I proposed? Not exactly. But we saw a lot of each other when I returned from New Zealand and one night that summer, the summer of 1937, when we were out together in London Cynthia said, "Darling, what are we waiting for?" It was after a show. I was back at St Mary's where I had been studying to take my finals. I had sat finals in June, gained my B. M., qualified, and we were celebrating. It was a double celebration because in the same month I qualified as a doctor I had published a little book, *Athletics for Health*, to rave reviews by the critics and had been assured by friends that it would be a runaway success. This was important to me: I was broke; I desperately needed funds. Housemen in hospitals were paid nothing in those days, not even a laundry allowance. I had published the book myself, borrowing money to do so. In my ignorance, knowing nothing of publishing, I assumed the proceeds from book sales would make me rich, or rich enough to become independent and set up in practice.

After the show we went to the Ivy for supper. We were both a little tipsy. We drank champagne. We looked at each other, and – "Let's get married," Cynthia said. "Yes, let's," I said. Cynthia was ready, I was willing and we both were able (*Ready, Willing and Able* was the name of the show we'd been to that night). We talked dates. Cynthia was anxious about her father, Warner James – she wanted to have everything settled and present him with a fait accompli. Warner James, the drug wholesaler, was Brooklyn aristocracy. I gathered that even though he had allowed his only daughter to come to England and study, and was footing all the bills, it was only a temporary kind of lend-lease arrangement. There was no provision in his mind for a penniless athlete like me. He seemed to have some deep hold over Cynthia.

"Yes, let's," I said brightly. "We'll get married in Oxford in the spring." In spring the bluebells would be out. "No, that's too far off, darling. How about October?"

"October this year?"

"In the autumn."

"Autumn would be neat," she said.

We talked of an autumn wedding.

But the following day I got cold feet and next time we met I asked Cynthia if she would mind waiting for a year.

327

"I've been thinking," I said. "I have to take my MRCP first."

"Your what?"

"Royal College of Physicians, darling. Membership of. It's an examination."

"How long will that take?"

"Not long. About a year. Besides," I said, "that means you will be able to finish your Master's degree."

"But I don't need to finish my Master's if I'm marrying you. What's the point? What's bugging you, darling? It isn't money, is it?"

"No," I lied. "I just need my MRCP."

"What for?"

Cynthia was very direct. It was one of the refreshing things about her. I tried to explain that in the hospital scene in England if an Englishman and a colonial were up for the same job, and equal on merit, the Englishman would always get it.

"But you're not going to stay in hospitals all your life?" she said. "Shucks. Why do you have to stay in hospitals all your life?"

"Anyway," I said, "I need the extra qualification."

"And what makes you think even if you get the qualification, the Englishman won't still get the job? Gee, the English really bug you, don't they? Oh come on, darling. Famous runner, famous author – you don't have to be a famous doctor as well. Let's not wait, let's do it now."

I hesitated. We were madly in love. Cynthia was right – I didn't need the qualification. But I had the fixed idea that I had to shine in everything I did. "Second-best won't do" – even now, although he has been dead twenty-six years, I can hear my father saying that. I think I was probably paranoid about security. In a way, I still am. "Save the string." That was another thing my father used to say. And Mother: "Think carefully. Don't be a spendthrift." I sometimes wonder if in those days we were really that poor in New Zealand. I know that in New Zealand I used to repair my brother Jim's shoes. Every holidays when I got home I would set to and resole little Jimmy's scuffed-out shoes and still to this day, although it makes Cynthia mad, I like to repair my own shoes although in New York money isn't a problem any more. I don't know why

328

I've always worried about money. It's a meanness in me. Fear of poverty, imaginary fear, is a terrible thing. Still, there has to be a better reason than money for putting off the woman you love. I am stressing this because if I'd had any guts – or what the English call gumption – I would have married Cynthia lickety-split, preferably the same night, and my future would have looked quite different. So would Cynthia's. As it was, that night in the Ivy, I hesitated and turned on what a friend of Cynthia's, Dossie, calls my famous charm. I talked Cynthia out of it and persuaded her to wait.

Dossie, the friend, comes into the story. Dossie always said I could charm a monkey out of a tree.

Janie Van den Bosch, I remember, was in London at the time. I have a fleeting memory of her turning up in the early summer of 1937. It was during Coronation week (George VI). I hadn't seen Janie since Oxford days. She had come over from New York to cover the Coronation for the *New York Daily Mirror* and afterwards while the festivities were still going on we walked about the streets trying to get back to Queen's Gate where Janie was staying, but she couldn't get back. All the streets were blocked off. I brought her back to my digs. We sat by the fire and I told Janie I was going to marry Cynthia. I think I also outlined to her my medical goals. Janie listened and said, "Sounds like a life plan, Jackie." I said, "What's wrong with that?" "Still the same old Jackie," she said. "What do you mean?" Janie said, "Well. Where does Cynthia come in?"

I remember, Bill Hawksworth was there. We were exhausted and went to bed. We offered Janie the sofa but she jibbed at that. "Don't be so stuffy," I said, "we're going to bed." In the end she asked for a pillow. I gave her a pillow and a cover and she slept in the bath.

So it wasn't as if Janie had anything to do with my putting off Cynthia that time. Something else was happening to me with my metabolism. Not me, you understand, but my metabolism. And while Cynthia and marriage had nothing to do with it, yet in a way they did, for throughout 1937 instead of drawing closer to Cynthia I seemed to be moving away, as if I was deliberately insulating myself from her. Maybe I was scared of the relationship. I've never been able to make up my mind about fundamental problems like relationships anyway. What had

329

happened was (surprise, surprise), I had started running again. For a time I even began training again in secret. What for? Did I imagine I could make a comeback? But I was restless and fidgety – I seemed all the time to be going through a series of revolving doors leading nowhere. Running was the only thing that helped.

"What's the matter?" Cynthia said to me at one point. "Isn't the book selling?" That was another thing. The book, after all the praise heaped on it by reviewers, wasn't selling at all. Actually it was a flop.* I wasn't drinking. I was partying a lot. I deluded myself into thinking I was getting to know everyone from Horder and Dawson down, that I was finally breaking into the "old boy network" and getting somewhere in England. Of course I wasn't. I wasn't getting anywhere, and I knew it. I was extremely busy. I was working full-time at the Brompton as a house physician. I was writing newspaper articles and broadcasting. I must have been mad to think I could become an ace broadcaster like Harold. Through Harold's influence I was commissioned by the BBC as a sports commentator. I covered several meetings for them – I thought I did the commentaries rather well. But apparently my mind wasn't on it or I waffled too much. The BBC gently dropped me. I was thoroughly mixed up. As I say, running – I used to take myself off to the country or sometimes to Barnet and run on a school track – was the only thing that satisfied me. I talked about it with Harold once down at Rickmansworth.

"My dear, there's always a reaction when you stop," he said. "You can't just stop dead, it's too silly."

"Well, you did, Harold. You stopped. But that isn't what I mean. You huff and you puff and blow yourself up to achieve these things and suddenly phut, it's like a piece of elastic that's gone phut. You're dead inside. You're nothing, total letdown. What's it mean? What's it all about, Harold? All these years running round and round a track, what's it all for?"

Harold laughed. "Have I told you about Uncle Solly? Uncle Solly was once long-jump champion of England – think he jumped 23 feet. Different generation, Jack. Solly's generation,

* *Athletics for Health*, designed, written, printed, published and distributed by J. E. Lovelock, cost a shilling. The New Zealand Government eventually took unsold copies off my hands and distributed them to schools.

that is my father's and my grandfather's generation, they were practically illiterate when they came to England. The old people spoke with heavy accents. Now Solly got engaged to be married. One of the old uncles said, 'Well, who is this Solly?' 'Oh didn't you know? The English long-jump champion. He jumped 23 feet.' The old boy put his head on one side and said, 'Für was? For why?' So there you are. We're a source of wonder not only to ourselves but to everyone else."

Me and Uncle Solly, I thought.

I said to Harold, "But how did you stop? You did, didn't you?"

"No and yes. I was lucky. I broke my leg long-jumping, so I didn't have to go on striving. Then I was called to the Bar and eventually took up broadcasting. In a way the decision to stop was made for me. I've often wondered, you know, if my accident wasn't intended as a piece of good bad luck."

"Good, I'd say, Harold. So maybe I should go and fall on my head."

"Don't be an idiot, Jack. Don't say these things. You're not depressed, are you?"

"No." I had never talked about my depressions with Harold. Maybe he had guessed. "Come on," I said. "Let's go for a run on the golf course."

So it went on, partying, journalism, hospital round, running, clandestine training. I was doing all these things and none of them well. I wasn't preparing for the MRCP at all, though I told Cynthia I was. And Cynthia was waiting. We still talked about marriage. I was beginning to see that athletic training was futile – I would never return to the track.

"It's no good," I said to her finally. "I can't possibly contemplate marriage before 1940." I had come clean at last and told her the MRCP was a more difficult examination than I had led her to believe. It would take me another two years at least. "Fine," she said – she seemed relieved. Cynthia's plans had changed too. She was going back to the States at her father's bidding to take a job. "Fine, darling. Just perfect – 1940 it is. I'll be back."

That was in 1938. Then the war came and she couldn't get back.

24

Warner James, Cynthia's father, must have been a wise parent besides a doting one. When Cynthia returned to the States in 1938 he gave her as reward for finishing her schooling an open Packard roadster with white sideboard tyres. But he also insisted, Cynthia claims, that she go to work for a year and learn to be independent. "You mean," she said to him, "in case I'm left a widow at thirty-five?" Cynthia was joking of course but that, it turned out, was exactly what he did mean. And she did what her father said. Cynthia returned to New York with a Master's degree from Cambridge and she took a job as a secretary. Cynthia adored her father. Frankly I think the reason she went home was simply to put things right with Warner James before coming back to straighten me out. She had a terrific feel for the idea of a relationship which is something, growing up in sheltered monastic places like Oxford, I have never had. She had total loyalty, total dedication. She also had tenacity of purpose. So that when in the spring of 1940 I surprised myself by getting my letters, MRCP, and sent her an ecstatic cable ending, "Topsy, come back", and then a little later sent a short note cancelling the cable and saying don't come, and at this point stopped writing altogether, she became more than ever determined. She tried to get back to England in 1940, failed. She tried repeatedly through 1941, failed. By now she was gung-ho about the war in Europe as well as about me, despite my silence, and at the beginning of 1942, by a smart trick through an Intelligence connection of her father's, she got herself posted to Oxford as a volunteer in a hospital helping war wounded. I was lying low. According to Dorothy Stevens, her American friend Dossie, Cynthia was leaving messages for me all over England and I wasn't responding. This was a period when the army didn't know what to do with me and had begun sending me from depot to depot, to Hendon, to Loughborough, to "the Convalescent Depot, Richmond Park", to "the Convalescent Depot, Ballymena, County Antrim". Because of my condition and lack of battle-worthiness, and a tendency I had developed to fly into rages, I had become an embarrassment to the army. I was finally brought to rest at Aldershot in the Army School of Physical Training. I was given an office. I was made Medical Officer in Charge of Physical Medicine – I ran fitness courses and helped disabled soldiers to rejoin their units. Later when the war machine got going I did some useful work with commandos, but when Cynthia arrived there wasn't much happening. I wrote a little poem at Aldershot:

> They don't need a doctor
> And certainly not me.
> I shall do experiments
> Upon the human knee.

I had decided, after a good look at my own knee, that the construction was faulty. The rotation and jointing was wrong. My own knee still plagued me, but it wasn't just me – almost all the recruits I saw had knee problems. I concluded it was a basic fault in design. I would improve upon it. To this end I rigged a block and tackle in my office; I had weights and pulleys running from the ceiling; I designed trusses, requisitioned a stack of paper and laid down that anyone going on sick parade should be told off to report to me for manipulation and knee jerks. I ran tests every afternoon. I had begun to fill dozens of loose-leaf folios with the results of these experiments. It was known as Lovelock's Punishment and it explains why so many men in the Army School of Physical Training at Aldershot were reluctant to report sick during the war. It also explains my reluctance to meet Cynthia again. There was no kudos attached to my job – it was a sinecure. I felt unworthy, and unworthy of her.

At Aldershot I got a message from Cynthia early in 1942 asking me to meet her in Oxford. The day before we met I had flown into a rage because a bunch of recruits had refused to dive into the outdoor pool when I ordered them. Admittedly it was winter. "Milk sops!" I yelled, throwing down my cane. "Cream puffs! Call yourselves soldiers? You don't know what fitness is."

I got rid of my cane, stripped, took off my glasses and dived in. Even with my glasses on, I hadn't seen that the water in the pool was iced over. I had to be fished out, half drowned. I wasn't in very good shape when I met Cynthia next day. We met at the hospital in Oxford where she was working.

"Hullo, Topsy," I said. "What's that you're wearing?"

She seemed to be in something shapeless and grey.

"It's called a uniform. See?" She showed me her shoulder flash and said, "'American Hospital in Britain'. I'm a volunteer."

"Terrific. I can't see a thing."

"You look swell," she said. In fact she must have been crying inside. In a letter she wrote home at a later date she described ". . . a man in uniform who walked as if about to stumble. He carried a stick. He had glasses and one eye shaded. The other glass similar to the crinkly glass in a toilet with a very small circle of clear vision. He was groping."

She said after a pause, "What happened?"

"Fell off my horse, darling."

"No, tell me. Tell me properly. You don't ride, do you? Tell me what happened."

"I've told you. I went zooming off."

It's funny. Seven years later – to digress for a moment – Cynthia has begun to use the same expression: zooming off. She's picked it up from me. I am reminded of this now, hearing her on the telephone downstairs. Cynthia is on the telephone talking to someone from Princeton who wants to come and see me here in Brooklyn – she's giving him directions for the train. She is saying, "Take the train to Brighton Beach and change at Church Avenue for Beverley Road. That's it, Brighton Beach. Be *sure* to take the one marked Brighton Beach, otherwise you'll go zooming off."

"I've told you," I said to her that day in Oxford. "I went zooming off. Let's go somewhere for a drink. I don't want to talk about it."

"Oh Jack. Darling." She caught her breath. I felt rather than saw her step back. I couldn't see her very well in that awful grey volunteer's thing she was wearing, but I knew she was making a mental comparison between what she had last seen in 1938 and what she was seeing now in March 1942 and trying desperately

334

to reach a decision. Most women in her situation would have
told themselves, forget it. The marriage is off. It wasn't as if she
was short of admirers.

Cynthia burst into tears.

Afterwards we went to the Mitre for a drink and talked. I told
Cynthia I couldn't marry her, not her or anyone. Not then. Not
ever. It was a cruel thing to say but it was all I could say in the
circumstances.

She said, "Tell me what happened."

I wasn't a keen huntsman. I was a keen horseman – I had had
ponies as a boy in New Zealand and had ridden on farms and I
think "Hoddie", who was with me when it happened the first
time, had been taught to ride by his father. Hoddie – John
Hodson – was a rugby scholar at St Mary's and in 1940 we had
been posted together to a sector hospital at Harefield in
Middlesex. Hoddie wasn't a keen huntsman either, but his old
father was mad keen. Hoddie's father would ring him up at all
hours and invite him down to the country and after a day's
hunting Hoddie would return to the hospital nicely boozed and
ready for the week's work. I was jealous. Hoddie was chunky,
shy, a lovely mimic. We shared a room at Harefield. The war
had started. All the London hospitals had been evacuated to
emergency sectors like ours – ours was a converted sanatorium
– and by March 1940 we had a ward full of trauma and were
getting civilian casualties from the south coast. It was an
emotional, highly charged time and although Hoddie still
blames himself for introducing me to hunting, it wasn't like that
at all.

"Do you think your father would mind if I joined you?" I
asked Hoddie one day.

"Mind? The old boffin would be delighted, Jack." And so I
hired a natty black suit with breeches and boots. It was nearly
twenty years since I had ridden, but the excitement was there –
it came back at once – and I had Hoddie's old man to guide me,
the boffin. He was a genuine boffin, incarcerated at that time
at Bletchley busy cracking the German code. He had been
hunting since boyhood, he knew the countryside and was
always one of the first to get away when the hounds were on a
scent. I loved the cry of the chase. I loved being in at the kill.

335

But more than that what I loved was hacking home afterwards with Hoddie and his old father at the end of the day. No more foxes, that's over. You're twelve miles from home. You're blue from the cold, liver-coloured – I was bloody-bottomed as well. The horse is tired. You've settled to a quiet unhurried non-competitive jog. You're in a group but apart from the group – there is this magic apartness, like in running, a feeling of extraordinary isolation. And you can't hear. If you want to hear, you have to turn your head sideways. In the fading light with the rooks coming home to roost. The trees are disappearing, not defined any more, going from well-defined silhouettes to a shapeless blur, but uniform, and stable. With the damp. The dew is beginning to fall. Hacking home at a hound's jog, one-two-three-hup, one-two-three-hup, with the horse's rhythm, but it's really a collection of rhythms, a dovetailing of rhythms that I can't describe, except – here again, like running, you're in control, in mastery over your environment. It wasn't quite like running but very nearly. A compensation of sorts.

Afterwards Hoddie and I would be round the hospital wards shouting at each other ("A nailing good gallop, what!" "'Ware wire!" . . . "Yoick! Yoick! Yoick!"), guying the County folk.

"Better get yourself a bowler, Jack," Hoddie's father said to me on one occasion. "For protection." I had lost a stirrup taking one of those stiff thorn fences known as bullfinches. For the first couple of meets I stuck very close to the old man, learning the etiquette, copying everything he did. I was sitting my MRCP at the time, cramming nights and worrying about my pathology viva. It was my second try.

We were in a wood, moving out of one cover to another. Hoddie was behind me. We had had two false scents and the Master was peevish, nothing much was happening. It was a sunny spring day but there had been a heavy frost followed by a thaw and when that happens you get "bone" in the ground. The ground is frozen hard under a superficial layer of soft earth or mud – the horse sometimes knows it. We had been warned about crossing bridges and indeed as we emerged from the path above a stream someone called out "'Ware bridge!", and everyone slowed on the path to a walk before descending on to the bridge. The bridge was below in a dip with a sharp rise up the other side. Just a short stout wooden bridge made of railway sleepers. An elderly woman in a cockaded hat crossed in front of me. Then two youngsters crossed together. My horse walked on to the bridge, dribbled forward and stopped – it wouldn't go. Or it wanted to go, I don't remember which because at this moment the two youths, reaching the opposite bank, plunged up it wildly spurring their mounts and I lost my head. I was fuming at the horse for stopping. I didn't know the form. Hoddie's father wasn't there. There was a line of horsemen banked up behind me waiting to cross. Something went tick-tock inside my brain – I lost my temper and kicked it hard. Next thing I knew, I was lying on my head hanging from a stirrup and being dragged across the bridge by a slithering horse.

"Bloody thing slipped, Topsy," I explained to Cynthia. "Damn horse slipped. All my fault of course."

"You must have been in a filthy mood, darling."

"I'd been up half the night before, cramming. I didn't pass the viva either. I knew I wouldn't. Oh it was all right," I said. "Hoddie grabbed the horse. He got me up and sat me under a tree – I was all right. I was back in the wards next day."

"Just a minute. You weren't concussed?"

"No. Oh probably, my bowler came off. For a few minutes."

"But – ?" Cynthia's relief came out in a bubbling sigh. "But that's wonderful, there's really nothing to worry about, if that's all. And that's all?"

"Oh no." I smiled. "That was just a beginning."

"You mean," she said. "It happened *again*?"

It was a few months later at a place north of Oxford near Grendon Underwood, a place that came to be known later as the Bombing Ground. It was in the late summer or early autumn – cub-hunting time. Cubs and bombs? But it was 1940, the Battle of Britain was on. Dunkirk was in June, but already by the late summer, when there was a big aerial shoot-up and the Spitfires took charge, we were getting a lift, and there was a feeling that the war might not last long. That summer and autumn produced cloudless skies. There was cricket at Lord's. The events of these months are joggled in my mind by so many images: overcrowded wards reeking of carbolic: Hoddie's beavering "'Ware wire!" shouted at me down a hospital corridor: the Stukas coming over equipped with screaming wind-whistles to scare the populace: Gracie Fields at the London Palladium: the daily quota of bomb casualties coming in: plumes of smoke: the luminous melancholy of a fine September mist at Grendon Underwood on the day it happened: a newspaper article I wrote entitled, oddly enough, "The Fate of Champions": a letter from my brother Jim training to be a pilot in New Zealand: my own guilt feelings about not joining up . . .

And more images yet, for in June 1940 I was transferred from Harefield to an emergency psychiatric hospital at Mill Hill in north London. It was full of neurotic young soldiers troubled by an anxiety illness that had baffled doctors since the American Civil War, called Da Costa's Syndrome. The illness fascinated me. I was still trying to pass my MRCP and probably, with my nail-biting phobia about this examination, was becoming as neurotic as any of the patients we were treating at Mill Hill. I remember one of the patients called Louis Wain who painted cats and later became famous. He was a chain-smoker. You could always tell the date by when Louis stopped smoking – cigarette rations ran out in the middle of the month. It was an unreal time. The crash was in September 1940 but before this – it must have been well before – came my final viva for the MRCP. I cannot remember now if I took the viva from Mill Hill or before, when I was still at Harefield, and it doesn't matter – except that in some way the viva is linked in my mind with the crash that followed. And the viva brings up the strongest image of all, a man in golden robes. He is the President of the Royal College of Physicians and he is sitting in his robes with gold bands on them. He is sitting in the old College of Physicians in Trafalgar Square. He's at the head of a long table with the five Censors, the senior examiners, round him. They are in black gowns, awe-inspiring. The President is saying as I enter the examination room, "Please stand before me . . ." And even as I write those words a chill runs down my spine and my knee starts bucking uncontrollably. Anyone seeing me on the tube that morning would have said I had already chucked it, as indeed I had. In my mind I had already failed the examination. Hope dies harder than we think.

338

I had come in early, hopelessly early by about an hour, and taken the tube. I was riding round and round on a Circle train, unable to bring myself to get off and take the right train that would bring me to Trafalgar Square at 9.30. The MRCP examination is in four stages – the paper, the clinical section, the path. or preliminary viva and the final viva. The first time I sat, in July 1939, I hadn't even passed the paper. The second time, I had failed the clinical stage. This was my third shot. I had somehow scraped through the clinical and the path. viva that followed, but in the path. viva I had been lucky – I was shown a microscope slide of a rare condition of a section of the brain and by a fluke had recognised it. Now came the final viva.

A sailor got in and sat next to me on the train, a young naval commander. He had a nose like a badly peeled onion and he smelled of gin. He did a double-take, recognising me, said nothing, then dropped a comment so flat and casual that I knew he had to be a New Zealander. He was. I sat on the edge of the seat unable to move or speak, holding the jumping knee. "Christ," he said, "you're twitchy." I don't remember his name. He began talking about some convoy he'd been on, making my hair stand up, some action in the North Sea sailing in and out of the minefields, and I thought, God, if he's been through all that, what am I worrying about? My worries went clean out of my head.

At the College we waited upstairs in a big sitting room like a club. In the square below I could see the statue of George IV sitting up on his horse. If I get through this morning, I thought, I'm going to saddle up and ride myself silly. There were about forty of us from an original batch of 200 waiting to be called into the Censors' room. Everyone lounged and avoided eye contact, but you could tell the New Zealanders by their superior tidiness. We had all had haircuts. It's like a race, I was thinking. But without the smell of wintergreen. I was watching the pigeons alight on the lime-encrusted mane of George IV's horse. Exactly like waiting for the start of a race.

A candidate came out, shaking his head. Another went in. As each candidate emerged a stillness settled and everyone shot him a starched glance. We were being called in by the Registrar singly in alphabetical order. As the apprehension grew, I suddenly realised what it was that running had given me, an enjoyment of heightened tension. I was actually enjoying the agony.

I heard my name called, then four more names called out, a Moloney among them. Ted Moloney was another Kiwi. We were five candidates being called in together. I looked at Ted. Ted looked at me. What did it mean?

"Gentlemen, please stand before me."

We stood at the end of a long table facing the President of the College in a high chair and the five Censors. The President adjusted his robes. He said, "I am glad to be able to say that with the paper and the clinical you have already sat, you have satisfied the examiners sufficiently. You are excused the final viva. Now would you please go with the Registrar . . ."

No handshakes, no smiles. Only the Registrar had a bright word as we followed him through to an office alongside the Censors' room. The Registrar congratulated us. Then he opened a metal box before him. "Gentlemen. That will be forty guineas each." We paid in cash, on the spot.

"That was a bit easy, wasn't it?" Ted said to me as we came out, blinking, into Trafalgar Square.

I was a MRCP!

Two memories crowd into my thoughts. One is of rushing round to Arthur Porritt's flat that evening still simmering, almost manic with joy, and bouncing up and down on his sofa among the cushions. The other is of attending a wedding in London a month or so later, at Notting Hill Gate, and being cold-shouldered by the New Zealanders at the reception afterwards.

The groom was an old friend. We had been at university together in New Zealand and had flatted together in London in 1937 and I had half-expected to be asked to be best man. But when I arrived, I realised why I wasn't. I was the only one not in uniform. I'm not going to soft-pedal on myself. The explanation is right in character. Flushed with my examination success, I had taken up riding in earnest and joined the Hunt set. Had bought (on borrowed money) a new outfit – tweed breeches, ratcatcher, patent-leather boots, bowler hat. I was in everything. Gala weekends at Lord Burghley's seat at Wakerley Manor, Lincs., Old Berkeley hunter trials at Great Westwood. The war in Europe was far away. I laughed when someone at the hospital said I was riding for a fall. My hospital work at Mill Hill was absorbing, my social calendar full. I was in over my neck, actually drowning, and the funny thing was I could see it happening, could see myself as in a distorting mirror – the poor boy from the sticks with upper-class pretensions playing at being the Englishman. I was completely out of my social depth and my class, neither fish nor fowl. I could see the distortion and I knew the mirror was going to crack. And I didn't give a damn.

At the wedding the groom, Bill Hawksworth, said to me: "I hear Jim's coming over."

"Yes." Brother Jim. My brother was the sickly one. Little Jim was seven years my junior, he was the weakling of the family. But everyone loved Jim. "Yes," I said. "He wants to be a pilot in the Air Force. Jim reckons he'll be in uniform before I will." I made a joke of it.

They were all New Zealanders at the wedding and at the reception afterwards – all the men were in uniform. I wore morning dress (hired) and a carnation in the buttonhole. I stuck out like a sore thumb.

It happened with the Bicester Hunt, north of Oxford. The night before it happened I had stayed with the Knoxes in Park Town. We sat up talking, mainly about Cynthia. I had cabled Cynthia: we had been corresponding non-stop: I had come up with, I thought, a brilliant plan for getting Cynthia back to England. But Nesta Knox was against. The Knoxes knew about Cynthia and quietly disapproved – they considered her, I think, pushy, which is probably why I had never brought Cynthia to meet the Knoxes when she was in England. Nesta Knox was certainly against Cynthia's return to England at this time, reminding me that *The Empress of Britain*, taking children to Canada, had just been sunk.

"But Mother," I said, "the war will be over in a month. The RAF's just shot down 170 German planes in one day."

And indeed next morning as I rode out with the Bicester pack, I looked up and there in the south was a plume of smoke falling out of a cloudless sky. We had left Stratton Audley Park at eight o'clock and were running out towards Marsh Gibbon and the Bombing Ground, putting the hounds into covers as we went. I remember one of the hunt servants, Albert Buckle, wheeling his mount in beside me to watch. Dusting his red coat with a gloved hand and staring quizzically up at the trail of black smoke plummeting to earth. "Ah, another Jerry," Albert said. Then he was cracking his whip and yelling to the hounds, "Kai back, kamai back . . .", and we were off again. We had already put up a fox within a mile of the Park, but we weren't hunting foxes that morning: we were going around the covers hunting out the cubs and spreading them so they weren't all in one area.

A mist was lifting. It was a perfect autumn day, quite luminous, with the leaves falling. We were jumping thorn fences, riding over farms – a lot of grass country but with very little cattle wire. There wasn't much wire. It was a depleted hunt, with most of the young men away at the war. A couple of women riders with sons or husbands at the front had looked at me askance when I arrived and paid my cap as a visitor. We seemed to be covering a colossal territory, the whippers-in being required to do in one day's work what is normally spread over two days or three. When we got to the Bombing Ground which is the wet country running vertically between Chardon and Edgecott I kept an eye peeled for ditches. Albert had warned me the fences would be stiff and that every one of them would carry a ditch, but I had a lively mount and was sailing the fences.

I remember a gallop when the riders swerved through a gate and I flew the fence instead, taking a short-cut, and then stopped to wait. Saying to myself, "What's got into me?" I was drenched in mud and spray from the horses' hooves, absolutely exhilarated.

We had already drawn Stratton Copse and Blackthorn Gorse and were somewhere at the back of Bicester working towards Grendon Underwood. I don't know how many miles we had come already. We kept starting and stopping. I was alone for a moment. They were to my right, spread out beside a copse – I could hear the familiar "Brr-rr-pp" of whip handles clapped on saddle leather which is the noise you make to frighten the cubs out. I ate a sandwich Nesta Knox had given me and looked up suddenly as three speckled blowflies – actually Spitfires – zoomed up out of the ground through a break in the copse drawing furrows of cotton over our heads. They were so close I could almost see the pilots.

Hurry up, Jim, I thought. Hurry up, junior, and get your

342

Wings. You'll miss the fun. As I thought this I heard the hounds baying and my horse stalled. The horse was fidgeting. I looked down and there at my feet was a fox, I suppose a vixen, slinking past in the wet, lifting her paws and shaking them delicately before putting them down in an inch of water, with two six-month-old cubs plopping along beside her. I did nothing. I was overcome by nausea. All the sounds had become strangely muted. Bloody Jim, I thought, holding on to the mane for support. I had always thought of my younger brother as a stay-at-home, bumbling, a bit slow, a bit of a failure. We had never been close, but at home I had mended his breeches besides mending his shoes – there was an affection there. Jim looked up to me. It suddenly hit me that he was going to beat me to it, the little bugger *would* be in uniform first. "I don't give a damn," I said, out loud, wheeling the horse. My ears popped. The baying had increased. I didn't see red, I saw brown. There were foxes, little ones, brown ones but lots of them. They were coming out from the trees through the bands of horsemen and running in all directions. Total confusion. "Chop, chop," I heard yelled. "Kai back, loa back!" The hounds were coming out behind them charging in circles, running six ways. And one bracket, breaking cover, was bearing down on me in full cry. They had seen the vixen. I couldn't hold the horse. I didn't want to. Where were the whippers-in? It wasn't my job to turn the hounds but somebody had to. I knew it was wrong. I went after the hounds and the vixen, spurring, yelling. Splashing. Oh, a lovely fence. The air pulsated with cries. I jumped one fence, another fence. Then a gate. The cries were fading, the hounds had stopped. I kept on. Cleared a brook under a screen of trees and a branch, whipping back, caught me in the mouth. That did it. I tasted blood. Forgot the hounds, the vixen, never saw them again – only fences. I was creasing the horse. Oh, a nailing good jumper! "Gubbins Hole – Ditches", I read posted up on a gate. Of course there were ditches, I was flying them. I could see a ditch looming a hundred yards ahead under a built-up fence, a beauty, the fields puddled and glinting with bog-water all around. My bowler had come off in the trees. Who needs a bowler? I was invulnerable, impervious to injury. I didn't give a damn. "I don't give a damn," I yelled, and went at the fence.

It was weird. I believe now that I actually lost consciousness in the air. As the horse rose, clearing the ditch and the fence together and I looked down and saw there was a ditch on the other side as well, just before I blacked out, I had a sharp vision, sharp and instantaneous, of Jim flying towards me out of the sky at the controls of a Spitfire. He was wearing goggles and an oxygen mask; the cockpit was full of smoke and he was struggling with the controls. "Bale out," I cried. "Bale out, you silly bugger. Why don't you bale out?"

"That's all I can remember, Topsy."

I had given Cynthia a shortened, less emotional account, omitting the Knoxes and the premonition about Jim.

"I must have landed on my head, I suppose."

"Don't you know? Sorry, that's a silly question."

"I think they carried me out on a gate. Somebody said that. Apparently they didn't find me for some time afterwards."

"You said something about smoke, seeing smoke. I don't get it."

"Fit of the mads, I'd say. I'm really a cautious bloke at heart."

"Don't be flippant. You weren't depressed beforehand, were you? I still don't get it. What caused it?"

"There was a ditch on the other side, Topsy – I didn't see it till too late. It was more of a moat."

"Water. Then you saw water, not smoke. But you saw smoke, you say?"

"Smoke, yes."

"Then what happened?"

"Nothing, darling. I woke up in hospital two days later."

25

On the desk in front of me is a silver christening mug given to me by Jim. He bought it in a pub after he came to England. I think he bought one for Dossie too, Cynthia's friend. Here

344

in Brooklyn I am surrounded in the study by mementoes and trophies, mostly from running. There are cups, goblets, gold and platinum watches, dress chains, medals and various shields presented to me by governments and sporting organisations – I like having them round me when I write, they help me to remember things. They are also a source of great pride. I've still got the cartridge that Bill Bonthron gave me, from the bullet that started our race at Princeton in 1933. I had it mounted as a paperweight. Every time I sit down at the desk I am reminded of old friends and the desk, given to me by the amateur athletic clubs of New Zealand, is also a memento. It is made of kauri inlaid with jade and other native woods. I think my brother may even have had a hand in that – he was good with timbers. It's Jim I'm still thinking of.

Alongside the mug Jim gave me is a photograph of him in flying uniform taken in London in 1943 or 1944. It is taken outside "Folly Lodge" which is what Cynthia and Dossie called the converted stables in Abercorn Place, St John's Wood, where they flatted together from 1942 to 1945 after they left the hospital in Oxford – this was after America entered the war. In the photograph Jim is holding a pipe and grinning and I start whenever I look at him. He has the same toothy grin and the same pointed ears as I have and his hair, woolly and parted in the middle, covers the head in frizzy waves. Seen from above he looks, as I still look, like a Bedlington terrier.

Cynthia must have taken the photograph after Jim was promoted to flying officer, shortly before his last mission. He had only been in England a few months. He failed to return from a raid over Germany, "missing, presumed dead on active service". We heard later that his plane had caught fire. He had been unable to bale out.

I'm not a prophet. I'm not telepathic. I don't think anyone in my family has ever been gifted with the faculty of second sight. Yet I seem to have the knack in moments of stress of being able to step outside myself and see into the future. It has happened time and again. But I wish I could see backwards as well as I can see forwards.

Cynthia wrote: "The years between my return to England in February 1942 and our marriage were really pretty deadly." She wrote this to my sister Olive after we came to live in New

York. I'm sure Cynthia is right. What was I frightened of? Why didn't I break out and marry her sooner? The plain fact is I had become "institutionalised" without realising. I couldn't see it. If you can't see the walls, how can you break out? I seem to have spent my whole life in institutions like schools and hospitals. From boarding school on. It's more complicated than that. Places like Oxford are said to be forcing grounds for intellect and character. They are supposed to "form" you. I reckon that they cement you. It is something that happens to Rhodes Scholars if you don't watch out: you get used to places and people doing the thinking for you. Yet I like institutions – they go forwards and backwards like rivers, they're continuous. I mean I like the sense of continuity. Aldershot – the army – another institution. I actually *like* institutions, I feel safe in them. Yet at school I was held up as a shining example of an "independent" sort of character. I'm puzzled by this contradiction in myself. And I am particularly puzzled about Aldershot. I was no soldier. When I saluted and brought my feet together, my puttees fell down on to my boots. Yet I was happy in that enclosed atmosphere. In that stable world, still mellow in my mind, a comradely spirit emerged. We were cocooned from the fighting, I and a few others like Alan Pennington – Alan was another Oxonian, another ex-Olympic athlete. What did we do? We encouraged soldiers softened by hospital to "regain their military militant spirit". And we turned to each other for company. Travel was difficult. I was happy pursuing my experiments on the knee. I had always set myself goals and after the crash at Bicester my medical goals began to loom larger than ever. Who knows? I might be there yet pursuing those experiments if Cynthia hadn't still been around determined to sort me out and make a man of me.

Cynthia's friend Dorothy Stevens was even more determined.

"Why don't you just marry the girl?" Dossie would say when I came up to Abercorn Place. Dossie was a bit older than Cynthia. "And don't give me that bull about not being ready for marriage."

"Well I'm not ready, Dossie."

"You were saying that four years ago. God, you make me mad."

We would have had supper – dried eggs and corned beef.

Cynthia would be out working on night shift. I would wash up and eat two or three soggy peppermint bullseyes from a jar in the kitchen, and then Dossie would come in and go for me. Sometimes Jim would be there. Jim would be mad at me too.

"You can't keep Cynthia waiting for ever," he would say very reasonably. Jim had a sweet tooth and after he arrived there were no more peppermint humbugs to eat in the kitchen. But Dossie and I went on arguing just the same.

"You'll lose her, Jack. Why don't you shape up?"

"I've told you, Dossie. I've set myself all these goals. Cynthia knows."

"What goals? Aren't you in love with her?"

"Of course I am. I've told Cynthia not to wait for me. She shouldn't wait. She should marry someone else."

"You're making her desperately unhappy. What goals for gosh sakes?"

"Medical goals. There's so *much* in medicine I don't know yet."

"Well don't look so pleased about it."

"Cynthia knows. I've told her it will take me another three years."

"Bunch of bull."

But I would get round Dossie and take her out to a pub. Or, if Dossie was doing the night shift, Cynthia and I would go to the pub for a drink and the kitchen scene at the flat with Dossie would be repeated with Cynthia in the pub. Then we'd go back to the flat, make up and go to bed with nothing resolved and next time I came up it would start all over again. I don't know how you would describe our courtship. Cynthia says "deadly" and Dossie says "stormy". I'll think of a name for it soon.

I should explain that Cynthia and Dossie were now working for the OSS, the American secret service. When America entered the war they had lost their jobs as volunteers in Oxford and then applied to the Embassy in London for work as secretaries. After months of waiting they had been hired as clerks – "code clerks", Cynthia said. "Filing and stuff", that was how she put it. I thought they were just secretaries. One night at the flat she woke me up talking in her sleep, blurting out that at that moment forty-seven spies of hers – or it might have been seventy-four – were being dropped into occupied

France. At this point she woke up. When I told Cynthia what she had just said, she began to sob uncontrollably. She had broken secrecy. Until then I had no idea that the work she was doing was so important and probably I was too dumb to realise the strain she was under at this time. Probably too the realisation that she was able to do something extremely valuable underlined my own feelings of inadequacy – I don't know. I mention it only because of something Cynthia said when the American Embassy first hired her. Cynthia and Dossie were sitting there whispering and giggling like a couple of teenagers. Cynthia was saying to her, "Dode, this beats the band." Oh my, Dossie giggled. Oh my.

"We've got a job, darling," Cynthia said to me. "We're going to be code clerks." "What's *that*?" I said. "You know, filing and stuff." And she turned to Dossie and said, "Dode. This is going to be like the halt leading the blind." Cynthia was killing herself laughing but at the time it sounded more like a definition of what it was going to be like being married to me.

Nobody told me when I was discharged from hospital after my crash in 1940 what the sequel might be. I was in the Acland Home in Oxford.

"You've made a wonderful recovery," the nurse said. "Mind you get well."

It wasn't until 1943, nearly three years later, at Aldershot that I noticed anything unusual was happening; and two years after that when Duke-Elder the famous eye surgeon took me into the London Clinic that I understood I had fractured the malar bone – that's the big facial bone that controls the alignment and if it is fractured or knocked down the eyes won't line up. In 1943 at Aldershot I had put a squad of instructors through the Harvard Step Test to check on pulse rates; and from there on to an obstacle course we called the Monkey Rack. I picked out three men at once. They all had wonky knees ("that most serious of training injuries", as I subsequently wrote in a medical paper). I pulled them off the rack. " 'Fighting fit', you are not, but 'Fit to Fight' you will be," I said, quoting the Corps motto, and I marched them off to my office for further tests. I wrote them up. One case was especially interesting and I spent several afternoons on it.

The major in charge said to me, "Fascinating. But do you know you have written up these notes on the wrong case?" I had, and I didn't know I was doing it.

I thought I must be going blind. Now I think differently. Now with hindsight I reckon I was losing the capacity for self-assessment – I no longer knew what I was capable of. But apart from the headaches I was getting I assumed I was perfectly all right.

There were other examples. Somebody rushed into my office one day and said a recruit had fallen off a ladder. "Oh," I said. "Is he dead?" Things like this were attributed to me, showing my insensitivity to the misfortune of others. I know at times I was getting excruciating pain behind the eyes and taking morphine to deaden the pain. I know too that morphine has curious effects, deadening not only the pain but also distancing the world around you. Was that the trouble? Afterwards I had no memory of what I said. It is like the time I'm supposed to have been rude to the general and tried to bite someone – I have no memory of it whatsoever. I keep saying it but really I am a mild sort of chap. But if I *did* blow a fuse in front of the general there was probably a reason.

I had just been discharged from the Acland. Immediately on discharge I had tried to get into a fighting unit, and they wouldn't have me. I was spitting inside. I went back to Mill Hill treating neurotic soldiers – *at least*, I thought, with my experience here, I shall be able to go in as a junior psychiatrist. That will be of some use to the war effort. But after a couple of months back at Mill Hill the work became too difficult and I ended up at Aldershot.

"In I go," I remember writing in February 1941 to C. K. Allen at Rhodes House, "with some misgivings as regards efficiency."

I don't want to labour this inefficiency business. It's too bloody boring. But – there again. Why "bloody" boring? I never used to swear when I was running. I only began to swear and fly into tantrums after the crash. I am even told that in the army I dropped my Oxford accent and reverted to the New Zealand twang. Again, I have no memory of it. At all events ninety per cent of the time, I'm convinced, I behaved in a perfectly decent respectable manner. It is the odd ten per cent –

349

"zones of unbalance" the textbook calls it — that began to bother me. Brain damage is a puzzling thing.

"How long was I out?" I said to the nurse in the Acland Home.

The nurse wouldn't say. She had radish-red lips, I remember that. From where I was lying, the iron bed-end stood up on top of my chest like a battlement. Then it receded into the distance. I seemed to be in the midst of a mass of Victoriana, including fifty-three portraits of the Prince Consort. Later, when I found myself propped up in Fowler's position, I saw there were only two Prince Consorts on the wall. Later still when the neuro-surgeon explained there might be a temporary diplopia (double vision), I realised there was probably only one Prince Consort on the wall in front of me. The double vision could be corrected by lenses, he said; the eye muscles would heal and realign themselves. I remembered that from my textbooks. I was restless and had a slight headache, that was all. The neuro-surgeon, Joe Pennybacker, didn't tell me how long I'd been out either. I worked it out later by the date, but I still don't know for sure. There are islands of partial consciousness when you wake or seem to wake, sometimes ravenously hungry — but in my case there was a distant rumbling of carriages and everything looked twilight brown. Then you lapse into coma again. You don't come to all at once. Sometimes if the pulse is right down, hard and slow, exploratory surgery of the brain is needed. When I was well enough to have visitors, Joe Pennybacker talked about it with me. We knew each other by reputation.

"Boy, you had me worried there for a moment," he said. "I was on the point of cutting your head open, did you know that?" I didn't know it, and when Joe told me what it was that had worried him I grinned. Then we burst out laughing. It could only have happened at Oxford. Here's this high-powered young American surgeon called Joseph Buford Pennybacker, a Virginian, and he's in a stew. I'm in a coma, Pennybacker is in a stew. Pennybacker comes out of the Acland in Oxford and goes for a walk. Crossing the street by the Radcliffe, he bumps into another medic, John Stallworthy. They pull off on to the footpath. Stallworthy says, "You're looking worried, Joe. What's the problem?" Pennybacker says, "Oh a concussion. Lovelock's been admitted. He's come in unconscious after a fall

350

and I think he's got cerebral bleeding because the pulse is right down. It's down to forty." "Oh that's all right," Stallworthy says, "that's his normal pulse." Pennybacker was amazed. It's a small world, Oxford. It's an even smaller world, New Zealand. Sometimes I think New Zealand and Oxford are one and the same place. How clever of John to cross the road at just that moment! He and I used to run together – he used to pace me on the old Dunedin domain. He was the one who nominated me for a Rhodes Scholarship.

"My God, I was relieved to hear him say that," Joe said to me.

I said, "Joe, you don't know a thing about athletes, do you?" He admitted it and we roared with laughter.

Joe was absolutely painstaking. He was one of Professor Cairns' boys, a pioneer in brain surgery, quite brilliant, and he discussed with me several cases he had had with sequels like aphasia, anosmia, or hemiplegia, but somehow sequels like delusions – the delusion for example that all the doors are closing behind and in front of you – and other weird states akin to petit mal when you become abusive and perform some idiot action of which you are entirely unaware afterwards, were not mentioned. Or maybe they were mentioned and I wasn't listening properly. I'm not blaming Joe. You can't foresee everything.

"Mind you get well now, Dr Lovelock," the nurse said. "You've made a miraculous recovery."

I thought so too. I got out with a fractured collar bone and diplopia, a bit of muzzy vision. The diplopia was loud and clear, but I considered I was lucky to be alive.

I had strong lenses fitted and for a long time the double vision seemed to be stable, even improving, and I can't even put a date on when the depressions started again, the ones which finally wore Cynthia down and led her to do what she did. Without the lenses I had double vision all the time. With them I had double vision only when I looked down or up and in the army the only problem I had – because I could hide everything else – had to do with saluting. To salute I had to duck down coming in a door to get the C.O. in focus – I'd give him a creepy three-finger salute, bending down low, before I straightened up again. "What the hell are you curtsying for?" the colonel said, the first time I did it. The Commanding Officer, Colonel

Bradley-Williams, never got used to it. I used to fox him coming in one day with the left eye opaque, and the next with the right one frosted over. But I had no alternative. It was the only way to relieve the pressure behind the eyes. I kept alternating patches of frosted glass between the eyes, trying to balance them up. I tried exercises once. At Hendon one of the chaps, Noel Oliver, spent a summer hitting me backhands on a tennis court, forcing me to look down to the left to return the ball, and it worked a treat, Noel said. It improved Noel's backhand no end. But it didn't do a thing for my vision.

"Don't the exercises help?" Cynthia said to me once. "I don't mean just playing tennis."

"I've tried exercises, Topsy."

"I don't believe you. There are dozens of exercises you could be doing." Cynthia had been to a medical library and brought back some books. She read out some things.

"Too boring," I said. "Too bloody boring – I know all that."

"No, you don't or you'd be doing it. Listen. 'Diplopia,' she read out, quoting from a textbook. 'There are many cases of diplopia — '"

"I know all that."

"Just listen. Don't keep interrupting. 'There are many cases of diplopia resulting from temporary damage to the oculo-motor nerves but which show no other evidence of permanent damage to the brain. These nerves are easily injured,' it says, 'and it is usually found that the diplopia will disappear after some months.' There."

"I know it by heart, Topsy."

"Then why isn't your sight getting any better?"

This was about 1943. It amazes me sometimes that I managed to continue functioning at all. At one stage when the headaches began, after I began seeing patterns in front of the eyes, I had to lecture some of the senior medical officers of London District and they were tough characters, many of them Guards men. But I got through. Mind you, most of them read newspapers or discussed hunt parties during the lectures and never listened to what I said. But at least they attended the classes.

On another occasion Cynthia said to me, "You've got to see a specialist, darling."

"I already have."

352

"I don't mean an army guy, I mean a regular specialist here in London."

"I will."

"You keep saying that but you don't do anything about it."

"Like our marriage," I said.

"Oh shut up. I'll start crying in a minute. All right. When are we getting married?"

"Soon."

"You don't want to do anything about that either."

"Some things just get lost, Topsy. I'm getting used to it. You can get used to anything if you have to," I said. "I'm all right as I am."

"Oh buster." Cynthia always said "oh buster" when she was infuriated or I was starting to get into a black mood. "By the way," she said, "you were talking in your sleep again. Stop tickling."

"Sorry. I thought you liked it."

We were lying in bed at Abercorn Place, half dozing, and watching the searchlights out of the window over towards Regent's Park. It was the summer of 1944.

"What was I saying in my sleep, Topsy?"

"Oh the usual thing. Look at them." She sat up. "You know, I thought I could get used to anything when this war started, kitbags, rations, no whisky. But I can't. Searchlights, look at them. Just look at them all!"

"What about the searchlights?"

"I thought they were nifty when the blackout started. They made me feel safe. Now I hate them."

The day before, a buzz bomb had landed on a West End hotel near Grosvenor Street where Cynthia worked. She had become increasingly nervy as the blackout went on. She tired easily, dreaded going into closed spaces like tunnels and wouldn't travel on the Underground any more. We spent a lot of time in bed, just talking.

"Promise me, darling, you'll see a specialist next time you come up?"

"I'm not going blind, if that's what you're thinking," I said. "What was I saying in my sleep?"

"You were thrashing about, calling out 'Come on, Jack!' You always do it."

353

"You mean I've done it before?"

"You were jabbing me with your knees. You're very bony, darling. 'Come on, Jack!' you said. Then you said, 'Come on, Major. Nobody's looking.' I don't know who you were talking to."

That was the other problem – running. I still had withdrawal symptoms. We didn't call them withdrawal symptoms then, and only a few wise old owls like Nurmi knew what it was about. Bill probably knew and Harold certainly knew, even Cunningham and Beccali knew – that's why they went on running – but Nurmi understood it better than anyone. Nurmi was the simple son of an ebony worker, he ran in his undershirt, but he knew about human beings. "Water which doesn't run goes sour," he said – I overheard him say that at Los Angeles. And it's the same with human beings. Nurmi knew – I didn't. It would come to me during a meal or in bed on the borderline between sleeping and waking. It would hit me in the stomach or in the ends of the fingers. I would drop whatever I was doing and go for a trot. Then it would be all right for a time. Sometimes the urge would be preceded by a sudden choking fit like an unexplained "spike" in a temperature chart. When I couldn't satisfy the craving to run, I would be plunged into depression. First restlessness, then depression. I can't describe the craving any more than I can describe the depressions – it was like an addiction. I felt guilty about it. I felt I should have my mind on higher things, I should be pursuing my medical goals, not sneaking off running. I thought it was something bad.

I think people were laughing at me. I am told I once walked out of a lecture I was giving, hitched a ride to Oxford and appeared at Iffley Road where I stripped off my uniform and began running around the track. I can believe it – I loved that old Iffley Road track – though I'm sure I would have used the dressing-room to change in. People were a bit surprised, I'm told. There was an athletic meeting going on at the time.

It was as if the body were printing out old messages that had been received long ago and never fully understood or deciphered, like a broken-down morse transmitter that suddenly begins to chatter of its own volition. What caused it? I didn't realise that we runners produce opiate substances in the body, sources of intense pleasure that we can never do without. I told you, early on at Oxford, that I made a disturbing discovery about myself. Well, it hit me at Aldershot. I knew that Nurmi as a young man had run round his home town of Turku in an army battledress with a rifle and kit on his back. But Nurmi was training then for the Olympics. I wasn't in training for anything any more.

I can remember times coming out of the lecture room at Aldershot with the major-instructor who was my immediate boss and marching with him along to the tea-room. The lecture room was alongside the gym and the tea-room opposite the gym, quite near my office, and just round the corner was a running track made of ash, rough old place. I would sip my tea in the tea-room and squint out of the window towards the track. After a couple of sips I would stand up. "Come on, Major. Let's go for a run." The major would put down his cup and look at me with a heavy expression. "Come on," I'd say. "Nobody's looking." We would sidle out on to the track in our battledress and boots and anklets and run two or three miles, then we'd come back and finish our tea. At first the major wouldn't come at all. He got used to it eventually.

I can still savour, sitting here in Brooklyn, the intense satisfaction I got from those runs with the major. Long after I have forgotten all other loves and pleasures I shall probably remember those days and days like them at Iffley – and I *still*, believe it or not, do it, even now. I will get up from a table sometimes halfway through a meal, take off my shoes and trot off, padding round the streets in my bare feet. Cynthia gets mad at me whenever I do this and her mother – Cynthia's mother lives and eats with us, she is a dear sweet cuddly person, but very proper – she gets madder still. This is a very proper neighbourhood we live in, you understand. Running, I have to admit it, has probably been the most important thing in my life; the driving force behind all my creative energies. But I couldn't see it in England in those days, couldn't admit it to myself. Can I yet?

One of the chaps at Aldershot, Alan Pennington, had a gramophone record. When I was depressed or couldn't satisfy the craving I would go into his room, find the record, make him drag out his raucous wind-up gramophone and put it on. "Put it on," I'd say. "Get out the old Victorla, Alan, and put it on." It was a BBC record of Harold Abrahams' Berlin commentaries –

Jesse Owens was on one side and I was on the other. It always roused me. "Listen to that, Alan. Harold's gone berserk. 'Come on, Jack!' he's saying. Hear that? 'Come on, Jack!' Listen to him! That almost cost Harold his job." The recording never failed to rouse me, but afterwards when it had stopped I would be overcome by a depression worse than the original one which had driven me to hear it. Then I would go up to London and unload the depression on to Cynthia. I wasn't fighting her, I seemed to be fighting some hump or monster on my back that wouldn't go away.

"What's eating you two?" Dossie would say, coming into the living room. Mug that I was, I didn't even have the gumption to go round the corner and get it out of my system. The Paddington Recreation Ground where I had spent so many happy afternoons with Bill was within spitting distance of Abercorn Place.

"What's eating him, Cynth?" I would be sitting there with Cynthia with the corners of my mouth down, saying nothing. "He's in a mood," she would say hopelessly. Cynthia never adjusted to my moods. How could she? All she could do was recognise them. One night when I arrived and we had planned to go out to dinner Cynthia opened the door, took one look at my face and fled into her room sobbing.

"You're ruining her life," Dossie said to me. "Why don't you just marry the girl? You're ruining her life!"

"In that case, Dossie. I'd better get out of it."

"Yes. I think perhaps you should."

Of course I never did. But it was things like this that finally drove Cynthia to do what she did and plump for the other man. For there was another man, the son of a peer as it happened.

26

I came up once on a night pass, unexpectedly, to find Cynthia just going out.

"Sorry, darling. You should have let me know."

"It's all right," I said. "I'll stay and talk to Dorothy." And then: "Who gave you the ring? It's new, isn't it?"

I couldn't see the ring properly but it seemed to sparkle with precious stones.

"Oh just a friend, an old friend. You've met him. David gave it to me ages ago."

"David Geddes? He's back, is he? On leave?"

"He's on leave. He's taking me to dinner."

The next time I came up, it was either the end of 1944 or early '45, she wasn't wearing the ring.

She had known David Geddes, the youngest son of Sir Auckland Geddes, at Cambridge where they had both read history. They shared a love of music and opera and I knew Cynthia sometimes spent weekends at Frensham, the Geddes home at Rolvenden, Kent, with Lord and Lady Geddes when David was away. At the time David Geddes was serving with a gunnery unit, I think in France. I had met him once – I have a memory of someone younger than me, medium height, floppy hair, a very pleasant cultured voice, and I believe we liked each other. And I knew there were other admirers, ex-Cambridge friends of Cynthia's and Canadian doctors who turned up at odd times – there was sometimes a party going on at the flat when I arrived. But David, I guessed, was special.

"Is David the one who gave you Jonathan?" I said. Jonathan was a porcelain fawn that Cynthia kept on her dressing table.

"You know it was David who gave Jonathan to me. He bought it in Copenhagen before the war. Why do you say that?"

"Just wondered, Topsy. I'd forgotten."

"Next thing you'll be saying, why don't I marry David?"

"Well, why don't you? I've said it before. You're very fond of Lady Geddes and he's much more dependable than I am."

"Don't push me," she said.

A bit later, early '45 – it was during the Allied advance on the Rhine – an orderly came into my office with a message to ring Cynthia in London. It was afternoon. I had been working with a group of Free French and Czechs due to be dropped into Germany and after lunch had gone to the surgery, my little office, where I was analysing and collating data from my various experiments. By now I had filled hundreds of loose-leaf folios, the result of testing scores of recruits, and was on the verge, I thought, of a discovery. I had almost succeeded in redesigning the human knee.

"You know what?" I had said to Cynthia just before this – I had been in London two nights earlier. "I've done it, I think I've done it. I've redesigned the bloody thing. The knee, Topsy! The knee!"

"Oh."

"If I'm right, it may be an important discovery, like Harvey's discovery of the circulation of the blood."

Cynthia wasn't a bit excited. She wasn't feeling very well.

"It's terrific, Topsy. Well, isn't it? The hip joint is all right and the shoulder joint is all right but the knee is hopeless, I've explained it before. It has to do with the hinging and the rotation of the bones. The bone must never be allowed to ossify. Now — "

"Darling, I've got a pain in the shoulder and a headache. And I've got a train to catch."

"But listen. It concerns us."

"How does it concern us?"

"I was thinking. If I'm right and my discovery is of real benefit to medical science, well it might mean after the war I can go into rehabilitation work with disabled people, injured athletes. We've talked about it before. I might become an orthopaedic surgeon."

"A surgeon?"

"Why not? I could study, get my exams. Then we could get married."

"A *surgeon* now? Do you know how long that will take? And I suppose you'll want to be a crack surgeon?"

"The best, Topsy. You know me."

"Oh for God's sakes. One minute you're in the dumps saying everything is futile, the next you're in a dream world. Darling, with your eyesight you can't *ever* become a surgeon. When will you stop trying to beat the world?"

"You don't think it's a good idea?"

"Oh, I'm through. Dode, you talk to him."

Dorothy was there, listening with half an ear. Cynthia was wearing a tweed costume and packing a case. There was a lumpy kitbag in the hall with a greatcoat on top of it – I think Dossie had a visitor. The blinds were down and one of the bulbs

358

covered by a napkin wasn't working. Dossie asked me to fix the broken bulb.

I said to Cynthia, "Don't you want to get married?"

"OK. Name a date. Name me a date, buster." She threw something in the case and said, "Just give me a date."

"Topsy, how can I? The war isn't over yet. You know it's a long-term plan I've got. We've been over all this before. But — "

"No more buts, darling. Just give me a date."

But I couldn't give her a date. She was starting to cry. Dossie said something about the train.

I fixed the bulb and said to Dorothy in the hall, "Where's she going anyway?"

"Frensham. She's going down for the weekend."

"She's been going there a lot lately, hasn't she?"

Dossie nodded. She was kind of poised, leaning against the banister rail in the hall. She lit a cigarette. "Yes, she has, Jack. And this time she might not come back."

I was preoccupied with my discovery and I suppose it didn't sink in. I may even have gone with Cynthia to the station. That was on the Friday night. And the message I had to ring Cynthia was on the Sunday afternoon. I rang the number – it was the flat. Dossie answered.

"She's not here. You've heard the news?"

"What news?"

"Oh brother." There was a giggle and a pause. Dossie said, "I think Cynth should tell you herself."

"What do you mean? Where is she?"

"Try Brown's Hotel."

I rang Brown's in Dover Street. Brown's Hotel was a haunt of Cynthia's. She had lived there for some months before moving to Abercorn Place. I couldn't get through. I went back to my office and tried again ten minutes later. The hotel said Cynthia hadn't been in. I rang the flat again. Dossie said, "Well I'm sorry. She must still be at Frensham then."

"What's going on?" I said. When Dossie wouldn't say, I banged the receiver down and stood there fuming. I had just got back to my office when the orderly reappeared. "Telephone, sir."

It was Cynthia.

"Where are you?"

"At Frensham, darling."

"What's going on?"

"Nothing much. I'm having a lovely time. I've just got engaged."

"You've what? Say that again."

"Engaged, darling. I'm getting married — "

"No, you're not."

" — to David Geddes."

"Oh no, you're *not*."

"Sorry, darling."

"Wait there," I said. "You just — " But she had rung off.

I had a car by this time, a clapped-out Austin, and must have driven down to Frensham. It was dark when I arrived. I don't remember the place very well. Cynthia had described to me an old English manor house of the Anglo-Norman period with several wings and a row of cottages beside an oast-house but all I could distinguish in the blackout was an elongated mass surrounded by trees at the end of a sweeping driveway. I rang the bell and debated what I would do if David Geddes came to the door and wouldn't let me in. My teeth were chattering. It was a winter's night. I carried a little cane and I gripped it. After some minutes Lady Geddes appeared. I introduced myself.

"But she's gone back to London," Lady Geddes said.

"Oh."

"Is something wrong, Major?"

"I'm sorry," I said "Cynthia rang me. It seems to be a mix-up. I thought she would wait for me.

"I'm sorry," I added stupidly.

"They went some little time ago."

"They?"

"I think Cynthia said something about Brown's Hotel." Lady Geddes was very kind and asked me in for a moment. I thanked her and left.

I'm going barmy, I thought. I drove back badly in the blackout. At one stage between Tonbridge and Sevenoaks I ran out of petrol and began pushing the car towards London. Eventually I flagged down an army vehicle and siphoned off some fuel. It was late when I reached London and finally found Cynthia. I was so agitated I just grabbed her like a bale of wool and said, "Marry me."

360

"Darling, don't. You're hurting me."

"Marry me," I said.

"But I've told you. I'm marrying David."

"I don't give a damn what you've told me. You're marrying *me*. Not him."

"Keep your voice down," she said.

Now where were we? Brown's? I'm muddled. It can't have been the flat because Dossie wasn't there. Yet I seem to remember that Mrs Bowyer, the char who did for them at the Place, was there. That can't be right, it was far too late at night. Mrs Bowyer would have gone home, anyway it was a Sunday. Cynthia was wearing the same double-breasted tweed costume. Her face was flushed and she had a drink beside her. It must have been Brown's Hotel. It was, because there was a colonel at the next table. Welch Fusiliers, and he tripped over a kitbag. The colonel had a soup-strainer moustache and a gammy leg. His batman had an enormous kitbag. The room was full of cigarette smoke and people, I suppose it was the house bar; I was wearing a greatcoat, pulling off my gloves and bending forward trying to get Cynthia in focus. Then I went down on one knee.

"Do get up, darling. People are looking."

"Marry me."

"I can't."

"You have to. I'll cut off my arm if you don't."

"Please don't."

"Don't what?"

"Cut off your arm."

"You mean you *will*? When?" I said.

"Jolly good show," the colonel said. Cynthia was nodding at me and smiling, I was holding her hand and getting up and at this point the colonel tripped over the kitbag and cannoned into me. He swore and whacked the kitbag with his stick. Then he apologised to Cynthia for swearing, grabbed my elbow and said, "Jolly good show, Major." I must have been shouting all the time. There was a party going on in one corner. The colonel insisted on buying us drinks to celebrate the engagement, pale ale. There wasn't anything stronger.

I won't swear to the accuracy of this account. Cynthia's version of how it happened is different. Dossie's is different

361

again. Dossie claims that after I rushed down to Frensham I brought Cynthia back with me and we had a champagne celebration at the flat. I dispute this. And so incidentally does David Geddes. David Geddes is quite emphatic on certain points and he has asked me to be discreet about the affair. As it happens there is nothing at all to be discreet about, but I can't avoid mentioning him altogether. I didn't plan it like that and I don't want to leave out the punchline. David Geddes says that to the best of his recollection I never at any time visited Frensham while he was there. He is absolutely right. That surely is the whole point. He wasn't there that weekend at all. There never was an engagement to David Geddes. Cynthia engineered the whole thing.

Dossie told me this later, before Cynthia did. All along I think Dossie was secretly plumping for David Geddes, but she hid it very well – Dossie is a great sport. Sucks to you, Lovelock, she said with a chuckle when she finally told me, although Dossie didn't use these words. What she said or rather wrote in her diary at the time was:

"Cynthia and Jack are actually going to be married. She is terribly happy and like her old swell self . . ." And, a few days later, on 19 March 1945, she wrote: "Jack too seems to have changed, so maybe . . . this will straighten him out."

Cynthia and I were married the same month. We were married at St Peter's Church in Vere Street on 26 March 1945. In the wedding photograph I have on the desk before me we are holding hands and grinning like a couple of kewpie dolls. Cynthia is wearing a spray of orchids and is radiant in white with big buttons on her costume. I don't look so bad myself without glasses, shined up in a major's uniform. My pebbled lenses are hidden for the photographers. Just a few friends came to the wedding like the Porritts and the Knoxes and Cynthia's old friends from Cambridge, the Nourses. Rusty Fraser was my best man. Dossie was the maid-of-honour. As we came out of the church and paused for photographs, I turned to Cynthia and said, "Topsy, this is absolutely wonderful. Why didn't we do it sooner?" That was the time Cynthia said she could have beaned me. That was when she gave me the look.

27

Now it is May 1949, four years later and four months on from my thirty-ninth birthday, a lovely crisp spring morning in Brooklyn, a Sunday. All along Marlborough Road the dogwood is in flower and the crab apple tree at the end of our garden is trailing arms of fruit everywhere. In the street the neighbours are gossiping or returning from church, their convertibles cruising past the squares of emerald grass in front of the houses and pulling off into driveways under the maple trees. My next-door neighbour is taking the shade on his porch, reading the paper; occasionally he glances up with a questioning look and I half-expect him to come down and cross the fence and invite me in. But he won't do that. I hardly know him and anyway these big colonial houses don't have fences. It is a very different scene from anything I could have imagined for myself on the day of our wedding. It seems to me that everything I have been describing to you has taken place in a dream and if I say that I am still somehow in the dream, still trying to tell it, it isn't because I like repeating myself – that is simply how it is. Life is a riddle and a wonder, whichever way you look at it.

Though it isn't difficult to say how we got here.

After we were married, I couldn't get demobbed. Then there were no jobs. Things seemed to happen very quickly. My eyesight deteriorated. It was discovered that not one operation but four would be needed. I finally got a job, then lost it. Our first child, Mary, was born and became very ill. Cynthia's father died. Cynthia was bereft. Her mother wouldn't leave New York and join us in London. Our landlord became difficult and we lost our London flat. All this happened in about a year. I'm sure that far worse things happened to other couples at the end of the war. I remember Cynthia saying to me one day, "What is this London anyway? It's not an address, it's just a place on a map." By then we were both starting to feel boxed in by the English. Probably our packing up and coming to the

States had very little to do with England and the English, it was just the situation at the end of the war. The thing is when you have lost your country and can't go home again, you've lost the sense of continuity – it's like being orphaned. I wasn't a New Zealander any more, still less was I an Englishman. What was I? I was a colonial misfit. Things are always getting lost in this life, I have discovered, and you'd better get used to it. But the thing is, I have learned – I have learned it from Cynthia – that you have to keep breaking out and *not* get boxed in: have to keep making a fresh start. That way there is hope. And that is what this place is to me, America. It's a fresh start.

Mind you, I still haven't managed to break out of hospitals. Yet I don't mind that: I'm happy where I am. If I pass the examinations and get my licence, the possibilities in front of me are endless. I work in a hospital in Manhattan down by the East River.

Cynthia is away for a few days with the children at our cottage in New England. It is three, three and a half hours from here. We bought the cottage last year when our youngest, Janet, was born and Cynthia lives from weekend to weekend so she can get away up there. The cottage is in a quite beautiful countryside – Winchester Center, Connecticut – and I'm thrilled. It is the first time I have owned anything that is bigger than a packing case. I can see them now, Cynthia with little Jan and Mary and Cynthia's mom, walking down through a farmer's field, down through the cow flops to the lake to go swimming. The roof leaks, but there are big picture windows looking out over the Massachusetts hills in one direction and over the lake in the other. I would be there too if I didn't have to study so much. I don't mind studying. I have been studying medicine for twenty years now, so I am quite used to it, and Ella is here if I need anything. Ella is the cleaning lady we inherited with the house. Our home in Brooklyn really belongs to Cynthia's mother and Ella comes with the house. Ella makes the best mashed potatoes in the world.

Actually in my sneaky way I quite like it when they're away. I can go out running with Addie.

When we first came to the States, I used to look for excuses to go out. "Isn't there something you'd like from the store, Topsy?" I would say when I got in from the hospital.

"Wouldn't your mom like an evening paper?" Off I would trot for the paper, but sometimes I would get round the corner into Church Avenue where the stores are and keep running and next thing, zoomph, I would find myself at Prospect Park way over by the cemetery on the other side of the parkway. The paper would have gone from my mind. "Can't you stop it?" Cynthia would say when I got back. "It really bugs Mom when you do that." I don't think Cynthia really minded the running, what bugged her was when I went out bare-footed and left my shoes lying about the floor and embarrassed her mother in front of the neighbours. I tried to explain that in New Zealand everyone grows up going bare-footed – it didn't cut much ice. I promised Cynthia I wouldn't do it again and now I am more circumspect.

When Addie comes by this evening we shall probably run through Flatbush and down past Brooklyn College towards Jamaica Bay: either that or we'll go for a spin on the Parade Ground or over to the park. Addie is a fresh-faced Brooklyn boy who runs evenings, he walks all day and runs all night. Addie is a serious runner and I'm helping him. I mentioned Addie before. He reminds me of an English boy I knew in London before the war, John Lockwood. John lived at Barnet in north London and every Sunday we used to run together on a local school track. Poor John. He was going up to Oxford and was desperate to get to the 1940 Olympics, but the war came and that was that. Addie is also in training for the next Olympics and just as desperate but I don't think he is going to make it either. In a way these two young men who have nothing in common except me are the story of my life. In London John Lockwood was known as "the man who runs with Lovelock". That was in 1937–8. Now I am known as "the man who runs with Addie". Addie is our local postman.

I can still run. I am not as fast as I once was and my sense of pace judgment isn't the same but I get a kick out of helping Addie and showing him things like finessing on a bend and an even bigger kick when I sometimes light up and let myself go, like last night. I came back last night feeling elevated and I can still taste the tingling from that run with Addie. I'm still elevated and I don't think this euphoric feeling has anything to do with drugs like morphine. I take a prescription containing morphine very occasionally when the pain behind the eyes becomes intense: that is a sort of frozen horror I don't like to talk about. I have had one or two giddy spells, blackouts. I don't take anything at all if I'm depressed.

During the war after my crash I took luminal for a time to help me sleep and, though I may have experimented with drugs as sleeping draughts from time to time, I have always controlled the doses carefully. I am terrified of becoming addicted to any drug, terrified of losing control. I have always taken a sleeping draught containing barbiturates, chloral, bromide, tincture of opium – a standard prescription – but it is possible, I suppose, there has been a cumulative effect in the body over the years, hence the bouts of restlessness I get which are so uncomfortable and so difficult for Cynthia to live with. I don't talk about these things with Cynthia – she has problems enough bringing up the children and looking after her mother and I know she has worries to do with her father's estate. I don't like to bother her with my problems.

The only thing I have noticed, because people mention it, is that my face has filled out. It's puffy. Oddly enough the last one who mentioned it to me was Glenn Cunningham. We had a reunion in New York the other day at the New York Athletic Club – Cunningham, Gene Venzke and San Romani were there. At first I didn't recognise Cunningham in a regular suit and tie. Luigi Beccali came too. Beccali lives in New York now; he is married and runs cross-country. Luigi threw his arms wide and embraced me, kissing me on both cheeks, then – it sounds crazy, I know – he asked after his vest. Most people who go to reunions talk about, what? Their kids, I suppose. Luigi and I discussed running vests. In 1936 after the race in Berlin we did a swap – I still have Luigi's blue vest with the green, red and white shield of Italy, and he has kept my black one with the New Zealand fernleaf. I told Luigi I played squash in his. I forget what he does with mine. We had a great time at the dinner reminiscing. And Cunningham said to me, "Jack, you look puffed out." Puffed out was what he said. I think he meant puffy.

But it's only the face.

It saddens me a little that I may be coming to the end of my story. I feel like the boy in the reformatory who says to the Governor on the day of his release, "Not yet. I quite like it here." It isn't just that I am starting to feel at home in New York – I feel in fact more at home in America after eighteen months than I felt in England after eighteen years. And it isn't just that I love Cynthia and the children, it is more of a family feeling. Cynthia's whole family has adopted me. They accept me totally and don't mind what I call "my silly side" when I say or do something just to shock people, like last summer when Cynthia's sister-in-law, Elizabeth, was pregnant and we were discussing names for the coming child – it was a serious discussion. Elizabeth said, "I'd like a girl really but if it's a boy what shall we call him?" "Cadwallader," I said. I remembered we had a boy at school in New Zealand called that. And I recited

Cadwallader, Cadwallader hath seen the hare
Or hath he swallowed her?

Things like that they don't mind a bit. Sometimes we will all get together up at the lake and have a blast on Gordon's gin, and maybe Dorothy will come over. Dossie lives in Nashua, New Hampshire, and is godmother to one of our children. We see a lot of Dossie still. It's a great big affectionate family feeling I'm talking about, with a sense of belonging and lots happening, in my experience something quite new. I am not quite used to it yet. I'm getting there. Maybe – maybe I won't go out with Addie tonight. Elizabeth has telephoned and asked me over for a meal. I go to Elizabeth's place a lot when Cynthia is away – it's only four or five blocks. Cynthia's brothers live here in Brooklyn. There are three brothers. One of the brothers married a children's doctor – that's Elizabeth – and Elizabeth and I have a lot in common, though I don't discuss my problems at the hospital with her. All the same, Elizabeth seems to know about it. She told Cynthia once she thinks I am too intense.

Probably she's right. I wish I wasn't so intense about my work and was less vain and had more self-confidence, and that I didn't have this feeling all the time that my colleagues at the hospital are laughing behind my back. On the other hand, I don't have footrot or halitosis and am not going bald. I have a lot to be thankful for. What really scares me, and here again you'll think it crazy, is the thought of what might happen, not

367

if I fail my examinations but if I *pass* them. What then? My boss at the hospital wants to promote me. I am in line for advancement – but will I be good enough? To do the job, I mean? That's what scares me. I had a dream about it the other night and I woke up sweating. I don't expect you to understand this.

Fear of failure, I know – it's the commonest thing on earth. But fear of success? It is an irregular condition. I doubt if there is even a name for it. But you see it has happened to me before. It happened in London in 1947.

It was an autumn evening in 1946 when Arthur Porritt telephoned, mid-November. We were living in Devonshire Place. I had taken Mary for a spin in the pram in Regent's Park – Mary was just eight weeks. I parked the pram in the hall and carried Mary upstairs. While I was bathing her, I said to Cynthia:

"Where do people get the idea that all doctors are equal?"

"Don't know, darling. What about New Zealand? You were going to write back to New Zealand."

"What's the point?" I had already written to New Zealand for a job since being demobbed. The replies were not encouraging. "They don't want me," I said. "Anyway it's like an admission of defeat going back there." I finished bathing Mary and put her to bed and tried to think what I should do next. I came into the kitchen where Cynthia was cooking. "What shall I do now?"

Depression is one thing. But to be depressed about one's own depression when it is over and done with, that's unforgivable. I had done a terrible thing. Shortly before this, after Mary was born, I had walked out. I almost broke Cynthia up. Cynthia had cabled Dossie, NEED YOU DESPERATELY, but Dossie was in Berlin at the time and the telegram didn't arrive for a week. By then I was back and things were all right again, more or less. It had been "more or less" now for weeks. And I couldn't understand why I was out of a job. Since being demobbed in January 1946, I had applied for several posts at London hospitals – and there *were* posts available. Only I wasn't getting them. I remember talking about it with another New Zealand doctor, "Rusty" Fraser – Rusty was best man at our wedding. Rusty was also having trouble, and we agreed that the people getting the jobs we had put in for were less qualified than we were.

"You know what it is, don't you?" I said to him. "Prejudice."

"It isn't just because we're colonials, Jack."

"Of course it is. We haven't been to the right schools. It's bloody prejudice, Rusty."

"No, no, Jack, not prejudice." Rusty was more philosophical. "It isn't prejudice on the part of the English. It's just habit."

I wasn't incompetent. I had glowing references. From the army, for example:

> This post was of tremendous importance . . . All the exercises and tables which were introduced for training soldiers for war, such as preliminary exercises for parachute jumping, rifle exercises, shell exercises for AA gunners and tank crews, skiing and hill-climbing exercises for mountain warfare training and many physiological tests were analysed and passed by him before being brought into general use . . . No doubt his work had indirectly a great deal to do with the fitness for war of British troops that took the field in the final stages of World War II.

That was what the Commandant of the Army Physical Training Corps at Aldershot, Colonel Bradley-Williams, wrote. I had equally good references from my medical chiefs at Mary's and of course Arthur Porritt was backing me. Arthur, KCMG, CBE, FRCS, Surgeon to H. M. the King, and still a relatively young man, was now near the top of the tree. Since the war ended the best I had managed was a temporary position for a few months as an ex-Service registrar; now I was unemployed. He had just kept going up.

"I don't know how you do it, Arthur," I would say to him. "You make it all seem so easy."

"Of course," he would say with a twinkle, "you are a bit labile, Jack." Even when he was criticising me, Arthur was so engaging and genial he made it sound like a compliment. I didn't know what labile meant until I looked it up – "liable to change". Arthur was generous about my shortcomings. I had taken to calling on him almost every day when I was depressed. I must have made his life a misery.

"Eyes coming right now?" he said to me on one occasion. "Getting better?"

"Oh much, Arthur." I had had one operation, in March, for muscle balancing, and was going regularly to the London Clinic for post-operative treatment. I was dreading a second operation, but I could actually see now out of the left eye. I had been so excited to have clear vision in one eye and so impatient to get back to Cynthia that on the day of my discharge from the clinic I had rushed on to a tube platform and gone to step off before the train came in. I sat down. I had to sit down on the platform feeling dizzy – all the warm colours on the ground came up to meet me. For some minutes I couldn't see anything at all. That was when I had the first blackout. I was still getting buzzing noises in the head and strange moments of disorientation waiting for buses and trains, but I didn't say anything about that.

"Oh much better," I said to Arthur. "The exercises at the clinic are helping."

Arthur said that a job was being mooted at St Bartholomew's Hospital and that I should apply for it. He had already talked to some of the people at Bart's. When I told Cynthia she said, "But you will apply for it?" "Oh yes," I said, "but really it's just a pipe dream of Arthur's. It's a responsible post. I won't get it." "Don't underrate yourself, darling." That was in September or October. I wasn't expecting anything.

I was standing in the kitchen after I had bathed Mary and put her down and said to Cynthia, "What shall I do now?"

"What about the porridge? Have you remembered to put the porridge in the oven?"

I prepared the porridge and put it into the oven for the morning. The telephone rang. It was Arthur.

"Congratulations," he said. "You've got it."

I put down the phone and hugged Cynthia. I had been appointed Director of Rehabilitation at St Bartholomew's Hospital at a salary of £2000 per annum. "Bully for you," Cynthia said. "That's real recognition at last." I thought so too. I was elated, though I didn't quite believe it until a letter

370

came on 16 November 1946 confirming the appointment and asking me to name a date to take up my duties.

"What is it exactly?" she said. "Do you know exactly what you'll be doing?"

"Physical medicine, Topsy, I told you. It's my speciality."

"Bones and joints, you said, and a few other things. What other things?"

"They want me to set up a new department."

"To handle what, exactly?"

"Physiotherapy, speech training, occupational therapy – there's no occupational therapy yet. Bring it all in together."

"Under one roof? Straight in? Bang, like that?"

"That's the general idea. It's an experiment. It will be the first department of its kind in Britain, Arthur says."

"You mean it's *brand* new? I didn't realise it was that new, darling. That's some assignment."

"It's a challenge."

"So what's the framework?"

"What do you mean?" I said.

"You'll have a team to help you, I suppose? To plan the thing?"

"I suppose so."

"And you'll be working in the wards with physios and orthopods – orthopaedic cases, like we had in the hospital in Oxford? Injury cases?"

"Oh more."

"All the arthritic diseases? Post-op cases too?"

"Mm."

"Congenital diseases?"

"It's right up my street, Topsy."

"Speech therapy too, you said?"

"Oh everything. The lot."

"And planning things? Reorganising?"

"Mm.

"What's wrong with that?" I said.

Cynthia didn't say anything. She was looking a bit startled.

There was a committee. Preliminary discussions were held – lots of discussions with the committee. There was already a small physiotherapy unit in existence at Bart's but at that time physical medicine had barely started in England and doctors

371

still had a blind faith in antiquated methods like imprisoning the limbs of polio victims in plaster. Some of the therapy in use seemed to me little more advanced than the ancient method of covering the body with hot sand. There was no pool therapy and the idea of replacing crippled or worn-out joints with artificial limbs was considered revolutionary. "Give us your ideas, Dr Lovelock," I was told. I set to. I drew up plans and made recommendations, advocating new equipment and techniques some of which we had pioneered in the army, some of which were my own invention based on original research like the knee experiments.

"You're not running into trouble, are you?" Cynthia said to me one night early in 1947.

"No, no, I'm just revising the plans. The committee considers they're not scientific enough."

"Which committee? I thought you were responsible only to the Governors?"

There were several committees.

"I'll get there," I said.

Had I known from the outset that I was ill-equipped to forge a team? That some of the orthopaedic staff who liked to order their own forms of treatment would resent an outsider coming in? That they would resist any radical change as a threat to their status?

As yet there was no accommodation for the new department. Accommodation had been promised by January 1947 but the weeks passed and nothing happened. Somehow my ideas, like an unsuccessful vaccination, weren't "taking".

"Don't let them gyp you, darling."

"Nobody's trying to gyp me," I said.

"Then why's it taking so long? Where's your new department? You've hardly begun."

"It will be all right," I said. But it wasn't all right. The truth was I was no administrator. The most I had ever administered before was the Junior Common Room at Oxford. I could see the deficiencies in the system and I knew exactly what was needed to remedy the situation, but somehow I was failing to organise it. Obstacles I hadn't foreseen would appear in my path overnight, as if by magic.

"I seem to be going in circles, Arthur." I discussed it with

Arthur many times. "Just persevere, old chap," he said. "Just persevere."

"The idea, Arthur – the simple idea that in a case of polio or rheumatoid arthritis we should be looking to the *whole* patient and trying to re-educate *all* the muscles is completely foreign to some of these people."

"You have to work with these people, Jack."

"I mean they're brilliant in their field, but that's all they can see – their own field, their own speciality. They ignore the rest of the patient. You know what I am in their opinion?"

"Jack — "

"Just a glorified masseur."

"Jack, you're worrying too much. Why not take a break?"

"Just a glorified masseur, Arthur."

"You're a specialist in physical medicine, one of the best. You'd be an acquisition to any hospital."

"Not in their opinion."

"Well in my opinion what you need is a few days' break."

That was it. I took some leave in February, stayed at home and at Easter I was still there. The longer I stayed at home, the more the problems multiplied themselves in my mind and the harder it became to go in and face them again. I wasn't sleeping and in the evenings I was so neurotic I withdrew from conversation altogether. "Are you sure," Cynthia said to me, "that it isn't the eyes letting you down?"

I didn't know what was wrong. I refused to admit that I wasn't coping. Then Cynthia's father became ill. She rushed over to New York taking Mary with her and it was then, while she was away, that it happened. I had gone back to the hospital, trying to pick up the threads again; I had reviewed a case on electric-shock treatment, recommending changes. One of the orthopaedic surgeons came to me and said, "Do you realise, Dr Lovelock, that you have written this up on the wrong patient?"

Oh no, I thought. Not again. "Oh, have I?" I said with a sheepish grin. I grinned and tried to brazen it out. "How silly of me." For some reason I added, "I thought I'd got over that."

He was silent for a moment. He said, "You mean? You mean that this sort of thing has happened before?"

Nothing was said. Nobody harangued me or was rude to me.

Not an impolite word was spoken. But I could feel it happening. Within the medical profession there is a conspiracy of silence about the incompetent physician. From then on any goodwill I enjoyed among the departments evaporated.

I turned up one evening at Arthur's flat and told him I couldn't do it. "I can't do it, Arthur. I can't seem to handle the thing, can't organise it somehow. I don't know where I'm going.

"I'm sorry," I said. "I've let you down."

Arthur tried to talk me round. We sat up half the night. "Much better," I said, "that I resign."

"But on what grounds, Jack? On what grounds?"

But the grounds were easy.

Clerk's Office
St Bartholomew's Hospital
London E.C.1.
28 July 1947

Dr J. E. Lovelock
34, Devonshire Place
W.1.

Dear Dr Lovelock,

Further to my letter of 7 July I now have to inform you that the General Court of Governors has accepted with deep regret your resignation from your office of Director of the Rehabilitation Department on account of your health.

The Governors desire me to express to you their appreciation of the services you have rendered to the Hospital during the short time you have held the office . . .

Yours sincerely,

C.C. Carmalt Wilson
Clerk to the Governors

28

Christmas 1949

So here I am. My third Christmas in New York (or very nearly, at any rate it is the end of the year) and nothing bad has happened. On the contrary it has been, as I predicted, a bumper year. I passed my State Boards! I sat the papers in the summer. I telegraphed to Dorothy – Dossie was in Boston about to undergo a horrible operation – "CHIN UP. WE'LL BOTH FLY THROUGH." She did and I did. My licence to practise came through a couple of months ago, September. It is too early yet to say if I can do great things with it, but at last I'm a qualified GP accredited to the State of New York. The worst that has happened is that I have caught a cold.

I am at home with a filthy cold. Little Jan is wrapped up like an Eskimo pretending to help Ella polish the front steps and Mary, who is now three, is bouncing around downstairs on Cynthia's grand piano. I am still working in hospitals. I'm thinking about one of the patients at the Hospital for Special Surgery where I work, a little boy who is crippled. A polio victim, one of the cases who came in after the recent epidemic. He's had surgery. His left leg is drawn back and the kneecap is rigid. I have grown very fond of him. I have been trying to stretch the ligaments so the knee will unbend and I think I have finally found a way to help him so that for the first time in his life he will be able to walk without crutches. It came to me last night in bed. I'm impatient to be there with him now. When Cynthia gets back (she is in Manhattan shopping) I'll get up and go in. It is an exciting time at the hospital. No more depressions!

Depressions are interesting, they are not all despair and gloom as people seem to think. I can look back on that episode at Bart's, that fiasco as Cynthia calls it, quite philosophically. After I told Arthur I couldn't accept the responsibility, couldn't handle it, I went to pieces. I went into the back of the cave and huddled there – I suppose you would call it a breakdown. But I remember how I snapped out of it. Hoddie rang me up, John Hodson: my old room-mate from Harefield who was riding with me when I crashed on the bridge. We had been out of touch for years. On the telephone I didn't know who Hoddie was – he told someone later that I was so distressed and incoherent that I was unable to form words properly or make them into sentences – and when I put down the telephone I still didn't know who it was I had been speaking to. But a few days later it came to me. "You know what?" I said to Cynthia. "That was Hoddie who rang last week, good old Hoddie. He said to me, 'Where's it gone, Jack? Where is that vivid encyclopaedic memory of yours?'"

Nobody had ever called my memory vivid or outstanding before and for some reason the recollection of what Hoddie had said on the telephone acted on me as a tonic. I cheered up at once. My self-confidence began to return, I could face up again to things, like more eye surgery, and when another job I applied for fell through I could shrug it off and think seriously about what Cynthia was saying. "What is this London anyhow?" she was saying to me. Damn right, I thought. It's only a place on a map. It's not a setting for a home and children. Six weeks later we were on the water sailing for New York.

We sailed from Southampton on 4 December 1947. Hoddie now thinks that my riding falls coming one on top of the other may have had a cumulative effect and that there may have been, after all, a cerebral haemorrhage. But, as he says, that is pure speculation. I don't want to speculate about it either.

What seems to happen in depression is that a hidden lever comes into play. It is like that extra dimension you sometimes get running, tick-tock. It is almost magical. It is a very narrow threshold, but suddenly you've crossed it, you're in it. It is all around you. It is a form of shielding where you notice everything that is going on (and *how* you notice!) and yet you remain isolated from the outside world. All you can do is give way and let it rip. It may sound silly to compare a depression to running, but in one way it isn't so silly – can you explain them?

They're both inexplicable.

Explain to me please, if you can, a birthmark.

Neither depression nor running can be explained. It has just occurred to me what I am. I am not ambidextrous. I am not bisexual. But I have both the inexplicables.

It's interesting. Not long ago Cynthia and I were out to lunch with an old school friend of Cynthia's in Ridgewood, New Jersey – just an informal lunch visit. And there was Peter, the little man of the house, waiting. Peter opened the door to us.

"Hullo, Uncle Jack."

"Hullo, Peter. Gosh," I said. "You're all dressed up."

"Ready, Uncle Jack?"

I had barely got in the door. Peter is five.

"You'd better be ready," the mother said. "When I told him who was coming, he said 'Gee. Big Company.' Peter's been waiting for you for hours."

"Ready, Uncle Jack?" Peter said. "I'm gonna race you. C'mon, ready? On your marks . . ."

He really meant it. I took off my shoes, Peter rolled up his sleeves, the mother blew the whistle and off we went. We started in the hall, went through the living room, through the sun porch, across the dining-room, round a table in the kitchen and ended up back in the hall. Peter had cleared the course in advance. Now you would think, wouldn't you, that if you have won a Gold Medal in Berlin against the world's best and you are challenged afterwards to a race by a five-year-old, you wouldn't mind losing? Now wouldn't you? Tick-tock, here we go again. Who won? I won. What's more, I had to win. I couldn't help myself.

It's interesting.

Who was it said that the kink we are born with stays with us till the day we die?

Cynthia says that I talked non-stop through the meal that day and told Peter things about Berlin she had never heard me say before. Next day, predictably, I was depressed, thoroughly out of sorts. But I think I was right to stop running when I did in 1936. Now I have reached a plateau of normality when I realise all I ever wanted was to become a doctor and have a home like anyone else. Yet obviously something is still missing. I can't help looking back. I sometimes wonder if all those people sitting in the stands realise the sense of joy the athlete gets, the sense of rapture and physical joy that comes through

377

competition. It's a quivering sensation. Ever watched an arrow shot into the blue? Seen it hit the target? The arrow goes on quivering. It's the quivering sensation that I miss.

The only time I've felt it lately was one day last June at Princeton. I was invited back to watch the Oxford-Cambridge track team compete at the Palmer Stadium in the same series of matches in which I had set up my world record in 1933. There was some talk of me being asked to start the mile event but in the end I wasn't asked. I was an inspector on the day, just one of the officials. However there was an Oxonian in the race from my old college, Exeter, fair-haired, leggy, very nervous at the start. He ran in a sort of fit, with passion. He won by 30 yards. Watching him, my heart missed a beat. It was like a kind of back-projection of myself the day I ran riot and came "off the cobbles" at Iffley Road in 1932, the day I broke my first record and Bill threw his bowler hat into the air. Afterwards I went up to the winner and introduced myself; there was something I wanted to tell him. He surprised me by saying we had met before and added that he had to acknowledge a debt to me, though I can't now remember what that debt was. And then I completely forgot what I had intended to say to him. I didn't say anything at all. I think he was disappointed.

Now I've remembered what it was I wanted to tell him. I wanted to say that if he went on running like that he would one day break the "sound barrier" of the four-minute mile. He'd be the first to do it. As I say, he was an Exonian like myself and, oddly enough, also a budding doctor. His name is Roger Bannister.

Cynthia is back from Manhattan laden with Christmas presents for the children. Douglas, Cynthia's brother, is here; and Dud's wife Elizabeth – they have come in for a minute. They've been shopping together. Cynthia has brought Mary half the instruments of a symphony orchestra made out of marzipan. At three Mary is already picking out notes on the piano; I think she's going to be a musician like my mother. I don't know what Jan will become. Janet is seventeen months and thoughtful. Her mouth goes up at the corners. Her grin, Elizabeth claims, is just like mine – it goes all the way. My mother has sent them each a little baby carriage from New Zealand.

"We'll put them under the tree when I get back from the hospital," I say to Cynthia. Cynthia makes a face but she doesn't try to stop me going in. I'm well wrapped up. Her brother insists on driving me to the subway station on Church Avenue. "I'll drop you," he says. "It's on our way."

We have two subway stations, Church Avenue and Beverley Road. Usually I walk round the corner to Beverley Road, it's a bit closer; but from Church Avenue there is an express to Times Square on 42nd Street and from there I take the shuttle to Grand Central. After that the hospital is only a few blocks. At Church Avenue Douglas wants to come down with me to the platform.

"What for?" I say.

"You shouldn't be going in at all, Jack, with that cold. It's starting to snow."

"It's only a cold, Dud. I'm not getting 'flu."

Cynthia's brother is funny like that; I mean, fussy. It's very nice of him. Of course, I ask for it – I said to him once, "One of these days, Dud, I shan't be able to see where I'm running," and he took me seriously. He's always grabbing me and pulling me back from the edges of platforms. "Don't stand so close," he says. Or: "Don't lean out. The train won't come any faster." He's right of course, but I am impatient in that way. Half the time I'm not aware I'm doing it.

27 December
"Next Christmas, Topsy, let's sneak off to Winchester Center. Have Christmas at the cottage."

"Darling, whatever for?"

"Just the four of us."

I am lying here in bed picturing it. Subway to Grand Central. Steam train to Waterbury. Past Goshen and Pie Hill and on to the cottage – the cottage is hidden away in woods on top of a hill, like a little Switzerland. There's a stone fireplace. We'll bank the fire up with logs and I'll make Cynthia a whisky sour, the way she likes it. The children asleep in their red cot beds. In the morning we'll look out through birch trees with the snow drifting down.

"I've always wanted to be snowbound, Topsy. *And* I won't be able to go in to the hospital. You'll love that."

379

"Darling, in winter the roof leaks. In winter it *floods*."

"Just the four of us," I say, "we can be invisible. Forget all about Christmas."

What's Christmas done to you? her look says as she goes out of the bedroom. But there you are – some people get high over Christmas, I just get flat. And now I have got 'flu. I should never have gone in on Saturday. I stayed up for Christmas Day, Sunday – Cynthia's family was here – then yesterday took to my bed. Now it is Tuesday. I should really be at the hospital but Cynthia won't hear of it – "There's nothing doing there over Christmas." How does she know? People here almost make you feel that going to work over a holiday period is some sort of un-American activity. OK, I've given in.

I don't think it is real 'flu but there is a disturbed taste in the mouth and my lips are dry. It may be this drug I'm trying, pale blue tabs, 50 mg, one of the new antihistamines we have got at the hospital. I don't think it is readily available yet. It is French, called Tripelennamine, and the trade name is just as long. The hospital pharmacist can't pronounce it either. It is supposed to dry out the mucus in the throat and stop the buzzing in the head. I'm trying it out. I was looking just now for something to read to the children when they come in – they like verse stories – but I haven't got the right glasses. Usually I know where everything is. I'm a bit fuddled. I have drawn the curtains. All I can think of in the way of verse is something by Noël Coward I copied out once in England, called *Lie in the Dark and Listen*; but it isn't suitable for children.

> *Lie in the dark and listen.*
> *It's clear tonight so they're flying high.*
> *Hundreds of them, thousands,*
> *Riding the moonlit sky.*
>
> *Lie in the dark and listen.*
> *They're going over in waves and waves . . .*

I'm listening. I can hear a band playing in the distance over by Beverley Road, "Away in a Manger". It's a very sweet sound, but sad. What do I have against Christmas? Nothing. But it makes me sad to hear it. There goes our local train passing at

380

the end of the garden, yet it sounds too tinny for the local. It is probably the noise in my ears. I dozed off a few minutes ago and now my head is clearer. When the children come in I shall make up something, or we'll play Hares and Frogs. I'll be a frog under the bedclothes. I'll go

> *Down to the brink the frogs went hopping*
> *Down to their watery grottoes plopping –*

and Jan and Mary will shriek with laughter. They're *so* energetic those two. They make me feel old just walking around. I got up just now to go to the bathroom and lurched. There seems to be a false sensation about my movements. I'm wearing a pair of tinted lenses while Cynthia and Ella are down there looking for the right ones.

"Is it the tortoise-shell frames you want?" Cynthia calls up.

There was a time after Duke-Elder operated in London when I experienced flashes of normal vision, but – I don't know. Lately it has got worse. The affected muscles which should have balanced up and stabilised seem to have forgotten how to perform their correct function. I keep telling Cynthia that one day I'll throw the damn lenses away, they're only props – they imprison the muscles. The eye muscles haven't got a chance. It's like the work I'm doing at the hospital with crippled children trying to get their iron braces and plaster casts off. How else do you rehabilitate the limbs? It is only common sense, isn't it? I want to read you something in a minute.

Cynthia has come in with a drink and brought me the right lenses for reading. "You know," I said, "I might go in tomorrow. If I feel better." "In where?" "To the hospital." "Oh buster," she said. That's telling me. She'd keep me in bed till the cows come home if she could. But I have to go in. I'll get round her yet.

I think the drug is helping.

I'm trying to figure it out. The eyes and the nervous system do the sensing and the mind is supposed to do the perceiving, that is how you see, isn't it? So if this new drug is working – it is certainly clearing the head – I should be getting heightened perception and better vision without the use of lenses? No go, so far. Everything looks muddy and opaque; it is like a perpetual twilight. *That* is what I wanted to read to you. That's exactly what Evelyn Montague said, writing about me in the *Manchester Guardian* thirteen years ago. He used the very same word. It's prophetic.

I have said that Evelyn Montague was the only one who understood my temperament, that flaw or contradictory genie which enabled me to give of my best only once in a season. He was the only one at Berlin who guessed that I had been programming myself for a supreme test, although he couldn't possibly have known I was planning to jump the field with a lap to go. Evelyn wrote about it afterwards. But more than that, he wrote about what it was like to be alive in that "golden age" of miling during the last days of peace and he put it better than anyone. The article was published on 5 October 1936, two days after my last race at Princeton when I lost to San Romani. It occurs to me that Evelyn may even have coined the expression, "golden age", for that time. So many people have said to me, "What was it like, that time?", and all I could think of to say to them was, very short, my dears, very lovely – but I can't conjure it up the way Evelyn can. It almost seems like a mythical time. Here's what Evelyn wrote.

After describing my eclipse by San Romani, he says:

So ends a great career, and with it an epoch. Up to 1932 the world had seen two consummate milers – W. G. George, running in peerless splendour in the eighties, and Nurmi. Since 1932 there have been four, Lovelock of New Zealand, Beccali of Italy, Cunningham and Bonthron of the United States. They have made the last four years a golden age of miling. Races were arranged between them to which half the world listened. They became household words among thousands of people who took no other interest in athletics. They demonstrated with supreme skill the art of running the most scientific of all races . . .

The golden age really began when Beccali beat Cunningham and Lovelock in the Olympic 1500 metres of 1932, but it was not fully realised until July 1933 when Lovelock beat Bonthron at Princeton and made a new world's record of 4 mins. 07.6 secs. for the mile. Two months later in Italy Beccali beat Lovelock and made a new record for the 1500 metres. In 1934 there was a series of five great races in America between Cunningham and Bonthron, at the end of which Cunningham held the still-unbeaten mile record of 4:06.8. Bonthron held the 1500 metres record and Bonthron had won three races to Cunningham's two. In July of that year Bonthron came to London and Lovelock beat him in a relatively slow mile by some of the most exquisite tactical running ever seen. In the following year (1935) Lovelock went to Princeton and beat Cunningham and Bonthron in the first* "mile of the century" and this year he beat Cunningham and Beccali in the Olympic 1500 metres, making a new world's record . . .

The art of these men, ever inciting each other to greater heights of achievement, reached its most complete and thrilling expression in the Olympic 1500 metres at Berlin. It seemed then, and it seems now to at least one spectator, that in that race he saw for the first time running that was perfect in all its elements – grace, skill, speed, judgment and courage. It was a supreme exposition by the three supreme performers, Lovelock, Cunningham and Beccali, who were first, second and third. It was their greatest triumph and, as one can see it now, it was their last, for San Romani was knocking at the door . . .

The golden age is over. Lovelock has finished; Bonthron has finished; Cunningham's powers are waning; Beccali with ten years' running and three Olympic Games behind him cannot last much longer. The new age starts with San Romani . . . But it will be a different age, for genius is individual and irreplaceable, and though we may see a greater runner than Lovelock, we shall never see one like him again. It should have ended in the sunshine of Berlin rather than this autumn twilight.

Evening: Dr Hansson from the hospital rang to ask how I was and he told Cynthia I shouldn't go in tomorrow. Kristian Hansson is my boss, he is in charge of the Rehabilitation Department. I wish he hadn't done that. Now she has every reason to keep me here. I said to Cynthia, "You'd put me in a straitjacket if you could." We laughed about it – but that, incidentally, is what

* Actually, the second. The first "mile of the century" was in 1934.

has happened at the hospital with the little boy there, the one with the rigid knee I was telling you about. When I got in on Saturday I found him confined to bed with a metal frame over it and the limb in iron braces. I have been working with him for weeks – I was about to put him in the pool for a new range-of-motion exercise I'd worked out. One of the ortho-paedic surgeons has changed the treatment without telling me.

They do it all the time, the orthopods. It's a constant running battle we have with them. I thought it would be better here after England, but it isn't; it's worse than it was in London at Bart's. These surgeons, they think they are gods. I want this little boy to walk, not spend the rest of his days on crutches!

Dr Hansson is sympathetic. He knows how frustrated I am. Dr Hansson pioneered physical medicine in New York and it doesn't seem to bother him that we are completely under the thumb of the orthopods – he seems to be able to cure patients almost by mesmerising them. Me, all I can do is think up ideas for improved therapy. I'm the ideas person. "Give me your ideas, Jack. Get them down on paper." Dr Hansson is encouraging me. He wants me to take over a department at another hospital on West 30th Street – he's lined up a responsible post for me. He wants me to start in the new year and that's another reason I have to go in tomorrow. I have to talk to him about it.

If I get a good night's sleep, I'll go in before Cynthia's awake. She won't know I've gone. I have taken another tablet, two actually.

Well, I'm here. I left home at 6.30 a.m. and arrived just after 7.30. I haven't seen Dr Hansson yet.

Of course, I woke Cynthia stumbling about looking for my glasses. I should have put a light on. "Where are you going?" she said. "What's the time?"

"Just in to the hospital." I said I had some research to do.

"How do you feel?"

"Terrible. But I have to go in."

"Don't be a mug, darling. Stay in bed."

I thought I wasn't going to make it out of the house. Luckily, she fell asleep again.

Some of the physiotherapists are still arriving. It has gone

384

eight o'clock. I have talked with Nurse Winter and been over the referral slips for the day. I've seen the little boy – I think he is going to be all right eventually. He's a game little kid. My eyelids feel heavy. I went into my office for a few minutes and sat down and I didn't even open the briefcase to get my papers out. The lid felt too heavy to raise. I wanted to draft some ideas for Dr Hansson but as soon as I sat down at the desk I began to get coloured stabs in front of my eyes like measles left on the retina. I have brought the wrong glasses anyway. I took an antihistamine before I left home and another one a few minutes ago, but they don't seem to be doing very much.

Now I am in the main office waiting for Ann Papura, the secretary, to come off the telephone.

"Ann?"

"Yep. Gee, you look bad, Doctor."

"Ann, tell me something. Is it foggy on the river?"

"No. The sun is coming. Going to be a beautiful day."

Then why is it so brown on the river? Everything looks brown and streaky. Ann's office is right on top of the East River.

"I must have the wrong glasses. Ann, is Dr Hansson in?"

"Sure. Doing his report for the Rehab. Committee. Say, you want to sit down?"

"Will he be long?"

"But you can just go right in, Doctor. You know that."

"It isn't urgent. I think I'm getting 'flu."

"You look to me like you've got it. Why don't you go hom?" It sounds cute the way Ann says it. "Hom." She's Hungarian.

"I have to call my wife. I said I would call my wife when I got in."

"I'll call her. You sit right down while I call Mrs Lovelock ... Mrs Lovelock? This is Ann Papura, Dr Hansson's secretary. Your husband's not looking so good. I think he should come hom. I'll put him on."

"Cynthia?"

"Darling, are you all right?"

"I've just got in. Feeling a bit dizzy, that's all. I think I'll come home."

"Promise?"

"I'll just sit here for a minute, then I'll get my coat."

"Please come home."

"Here's your coat, Dr Lovelock. Smock off – here, I help you. Overcoat on. Now do it up, it's cold outside." Ann's a sweetie. She is always helping people on and off with their coats.

"You want something more from your office? Here's your briefcase. Now go hom, Doctor. I'll tell Dr Hansson you're not so good."

"Go hom," she says. "Hom to bed. Hom, hom, hom."

The glasses are in my pocket. When I came out from the hospital on East 42nd I looked up and the Chrysler Building seemed to be falling on top of me, so I've put them away. I made two decisions coming in this morning and one of them was to think positively in future and not rely so much on artificial lenses: they're too confining, like splints. It's what I preach all the time with my patients – I've got to start practising what I preach with my own eyes. Get the splints off, start activating the muscles. The light hurts, but I'm walking slowly. So far I haven't bumped into anyone.

I had to sit down once on a shoe-shine crate before Grand Central. I leaned against the window of a delicatessen to get my bearings and the window wasn't there; next thing I was sitting on the crate and a boy was shining my shoes. Without lenses it's more tranquil yet disruptive somehow – things which are under your nose suddenly retreat into the distance. "Man, you're cool. Hey mister!" – the shoe-shine boy called after me. I must have walked on without paying him. People are moving past me in a sluggish stream and I keep thinking I must be hitting them, yet I don't, it is as if I am seeing them through the glass of a rounded pearly vault. The light's pearly.

I used to boast I could walk the three blocks from the hospital to Grand Central and make the transfer to the D train at Times Square without looking but it's more complicated than I thought. The steering muscles feel loose. The light is pearly even inside the station. I caused a jam getting down to the escalator – I forgot you need a token at the turnstile. Now it is easier. I'm on the D train heading downtown, it goes all the way to Brighton Beach, and all I have to do is remember to get out at Church Avenue after Prospect Park and change to the local. "West 34th Street . . . Washington Square, step right in! . . . Grand. Mind the closing doors!" The conductor is calling out the stops. You can hear him above the hissing and screeching when the train stops. They call it an express but we've stopped once between Washington Square and Broadway-Lafayette and now we have stopped again on the bridge. We've passed Grand. After Grand on Lower East Side the train crosses Manhattan Bridge and then goes underground, four more stops. I'm counting the stops.

We have stopped twice on Manhattan Bridge, this last time nearly five minutes. It could be only five seconds. I can't judge time. When the train stops the lights usually go out, so maybe everyone else is sitting in darkness. But I know the scene intimately. We are high over the East River with water on both sides, iron girders all round and motor traffic is flowing past in both directions. If you look back, there are the scrapers on Broadway and Wall Street. There's a cold blue sky (probably), white clouds, more clouds than sky I imagine, and the Stars and Stripes flying on a building ahead as the train dives off the bridge going underground. Brooklyn Bridge is on the right and if the train were moving, which it isn't, Brooklyn Bridge would appear coming towards you even though it is going away from you. It is an optical illusion of course. We're still sitting here.

How do I feel? Like the train. The train is vibrating and wheezing like an asthmatic. Now it has stopped wheezing and is emitting a high humming sound. I am sure that's the train humming. I keep falling asleep. Now it is moving again, swaying empty. The train feels empty. I have opened a window to let in the cold air, I have got one foot braced against the centre pole to keep awake and I'm holding the briefcase on my lap, gripping it with two hands so I won't forget it. People in my condition, I've read it somewhere, are said to long for indifference to pain: but there is no pain: no nausea: I had a headache but it's gone: this Tripelennamine is a *peculiar* drug, it dries you out like a clothes drier. I could eat a gallon of ice cream, I'm so dry.

I have remembered something after all these years, about Bill Bonthron. Before a race Bonny would always eat a gallon of ice cream, a whole gallon. I don't know how he did it.

"Step inside please. Watch those doors!"

We're racketing along – the rush hour must be over. I think a couple just got on. That was Atlantic Avenue. The other decision I made going in this morning was to tell Dr Hansson I don't want the post he has lined up for me. "I can't accept the responsibility, sir." That's what I have to tell him. "It's all too vague, sir. There's nothing concrete about it. I'm lost, sir, running a department on my own." I'm thinking of Cynthia – if I crack up again, what does she do? "I'd rather stay on as your assistant, Dr Hansson. It's safer. I don't expect you to understand this but, look, sir, if I can't do a job well, at full capacity, I'd rather not do it at all." My father was the same. Harold Abrahams wouldn't agree with me – it was Harold Abrahams who said to me that history doesn't repeat itself. But Harold, old boy, I think you're wrong.

There should be a perfect solution to these problems, in life as in running. I can't seem to find one. I can't even count the stations properly. I almost got out just now, one stop too soon. That was Prospect Park. These last two sections after Seventh Avenue are downhill and the train goes very fast. We're screaming along. It's like going down the back at Iffley Road. In fact, when you step out at Church Avenue, the first thing you see looking up to the skyline is a tower, a square church tower rising through the foliage of trees exactly like the tower of St John the Evangelist at Iffley Road. I always think of that when I get to Church Avenue. It's a nice little station. The subway is below street level but you are above ground. The train has stopped. We're here.

I've remembered to bring the briefcase. Looking up, I can see the faintest of faint traceries where the leaves are, like spiders crawling over a sky seen through speckled glass. I can't see the tower. There's a saw whining. Now it has stopped. The train has gone on. It is very quiet. I can hear the points clicking over.

It must be about 9.30 a.m. I am groping along the platform to where the local for Beverley Road will come out of the tunnel. Groping is an exaggeration – it's not so difficult. I can feel the pillars. There are numbered pillars spaced out on the platform, they run from 11 to 1. I reckon I am beside the third pillar. When I get to the first pillar I am at the mouth of the tunnel where the steps lead up to an exit. If I wasn't feeling so dizzy I would climb the steps and walk along Church Avenue to

Marlborough Road. It is only a few minutes. There aren't so many locals after nine o'clock. I don't seem to be able to make the effort to climb the steps.

Another express has gone through.

The express trains go on to Brighton Beach and Coney Island. I can hear a girl crooning down the platform. Otherwise it seems deserted; the rush must be over. Some people have come down the steps, tap, tap. The heel-taps echo like the points clicking over. The points sound like crockery vibrating. There go the points again. My own feet don't make a sound but all the other sounds are immense, spaced out; they're unreal. The worse your eyesight, the more your hearing intensifies; big sounds, little sounds are lying side by side and I seem to be floating through an hour-glass. I know it is a false sensation, like the voices rustling inside my ears. That's only an old newspaper blowing about in the tunnel. The tunnel has a kink in it. There is a series of small tunnels arched over and the last one where the train straightens to come on to the platform has a kink in it. The trains come in fast, creating a wind, and there is usually an old newspaper blowing about when they've gone. I am beside the first pillar now, leaning out. Above my head is a sign telling me not to – DO NOT LEAN OVER THE ED — The rest is rubbed out. But I've stood under this sign dozens of times.

In London the sign says "Mind the Gap" and in Berlin they call out "Zurückbleiben!" Here there is no gap and the trains are grey-coloured with cowcatchers in front. In London the trains are red. The last time I saw my brother Jim he was getting on to a train in London to rejoin his squadron. Dear God, I wish I hadn't had to see him go! Jim hated getting on to that train. In Berlin the S-Bahn trains have a nickname – there are two lights high up, one over each ear. They're called Ladybugs. Here the lights are low down over the cowcatcher and close together, and orange – I can see a light winking back in the tunnel. Another express has gone through, but on the other side, going back to town.

It is either a light coming or sunlight glinting on the rails. I keep getting stabs of normal vision. I think my eyes have grown closer together, but I am cold, ice cold. The lower part of my body is completely cold. This one is the local.

I know it is questionable to stand so close to the edge but it's also attractive; I mean exciting. When I was growing up in New Zealand I used to play a game with my brother standing on the edge of a swimming pool – we used to see who could lean out furthest without overbalancing into the water. Jim called it baling out. There comes a point when you are leaning right out teetering when you can't stop yourself and at this point it is actually easier to bale out than in. That is probably what people mean when they talk of a point of no return. But Jim and I got very good at it – we could beat the other kids hollow. It's the same here. There is a point when you know to step back. You see both lights together low down, orange. I can see them now. That means the train is straightening to come out of the kink. After that you see the motorman, the driver, but oh boy, don't wait that long; if you can see the driver it's too long. So you don't wait that long.

I'm stepping back. I am holding the briefcase and stepping back. I'm cold and sweating but not falling and I can read the lights. The lights are expanding in front of my eyes. I can hear the wind. Everything is increasing in volume – hear the wind? Hear the voices rustling? That is Jim's voice. Jim is calling, Cynthia is calling, Harold is calling, Walter and Bill and Sydney Wooderson are calling. What's Jim saying? I can see the driver! He is wearing spectacles but I don't believe it. Something is happening beyond belief. I can see the eyes. The eyes, the eyes. And the eyes are *inside* the spectacles! I can SEE. I've got cosmic vision, clear vision at last.

Jim?

Where's he gone? Time to bale out.

There's a wind rushing past. I can't hear the points clicking over.

EPILOGUE

What is there left for man to desire, except divinity?
Ancient Greek exhortation to athletes

EPILOGUE

Three documents:

Extract, 29 December 1949
New York Times

. . . The accident occurred at 9:30 a.m. at the Church Avenue
station of the Brighton BMT line. Dr Lovelock's wife said he
had telephoned her from the Hospital for Special Surgery, 321
East Forty-second Street, that he was feeling ill, and was
returning to their home at 203 Marlborough Road, Brooklyn.

Mrs Lovelock said her husband had been suffering from
influenza and had gone to the hospital early to do some
research work. She said he had poor eyesight and had
undergone surgery for this in England before coming to this
country two years ago. His glasses were found in a pocket.

Identification was delayed . . . The police sent the body to
the morgue and reported only the death of an unidentified
man.

Later a briefcase and papers were found scattered on the
tracks. These contained Dr Lovelock's name and address.
Then a brother-in-law, W.G. James, made the identification.

The family and authorities agreed that Dr Lovelock probably had suffered a spell of dizziness after leaving an express
train from Manhattan and while waiting for the local that killed
him. This local would have take him to Beverley Road station
near his home.

Dr Lovelock fell to the track at the end of the platform nearest the approaching train. The motorman, Patrick Hayden, saw him fall and quickly put on the brakes, but two cars ran over the body . . .

Extract, 6 January 1950
Fowler Hamilton, Attorney, 52 Wall Street, New York
to
Gilmore Stott, The Rhodes Scholarship Trust
                                        Princeton, New Jersey

Dear Mr Stott:
  In response to your letter of January 4, 1950, I have been able to obtain the following information from the Medical Examiner of King's County upon a confidential basis.
  Inquests are no longer held by New York City authorities. If the cause of death is unknown, the body is sent to the Medical Examiner for an autopsy and the Police Department conducts a separate investigation. In this case the cause of death was given as "fell or jumped in front of train".
  The Medical Examiner conducted an autopsy on Dr Lovelock's body and found absolutely no traces of alcohol. Examination of witnesses disclosed that Dr Lovelock was at the time of his death returning home from the hospital because he had felt ill. There was a finding that he had had trouble with his eyes. The conclusion of the Medical Examiner is as follows: "Probable accidental fall in front of train" . . .
  I might add that no further investigation by either the Medical Examiner or the Police Department is presently intended.
  I trust this answers the questions that Dr Allen had in mind.

Extract, 17 January 1950
Dr C.K. Allen, Office of the Warden
                                        Rhodes House, Oxford
to
Gilmore Stott, The Rhodes Scholarship Trust
                                        Princeton, New Jersey, USA

Dear Gil,
  Many thanks for the further information . . . We are terribly sorry for his wife. She and only a few others of his intimates

knew what a gallant fight Jack Lovelock had put up all his life against a severe inherited handicap. So far as our press is concerned, I have never known such a spontaneous outburst of obviously affectionate appreciation of any celebrated athlete.

APPENDIX

The following is a transcription of Harold Abrahams' live commentary on the final of the 1500 metres broadcast from Berlin on 6 August 1936 by the BBC domestic and Empire services:

They're just about to start. Pistol. They're off. An American in the lead.

Lovelock is now sixth. American leading, I can't see who it is but it's an American leading. But I think Beccali second. Coming round the corner, the first corner of the 1500 metres – they've probably gone about 150 metres. American still leading, Beccali second. Lovelock running – fifth, with Cornes about eighth or ninth. Doesn't look to me to be particularly fast, but we'll tell when we get the time for the first 300 metres.

Coming down the straight . . . I'll tell you who's leading in a moment. No, it's the German Böttcher that's leading with Cornes second and Beccali third. I'm so sorry. Lovelock is fifth. Cunningham has just come up to Lovelock's shoulder. They've covered about 300 metres, they're going round the first corner for the second time – Lovelock fifth, Cornes leading and Böttcher second. Beccali's running just behind Cornes. They're just getting to the end of the first 400 metres, approximately a quarter of a mile, with Cornes still leading. The time for the first 400 metres was 61.4 seconds. Probably won't be the official time . . .

They're all bunched together, with Edwards of Canada last but one.

Cornes is still leading – no, the German. I think Cunningham is going up into the lead! Cunningham's in the lead now, just coming into the straight for the second time. Cunningham leads with – Cornes has dropped back.

397

Cunningham's leading, the German second and Lovelock and Beccali third and fourth. God, it's going to be a race by the time they get to the last lap.

Cunningham leading, coming into the straight for the second time with half a mile to go – Cunningham, the German (either Schaumburg or Böttcher, I can't see his number), with Beccali fourth and Lovelock – Cornes fifth.

Now Ny the Swede is coming up into the lead, just at the end of 700 metres. The Swede Ny at Cunningham's shoulder. Cunningham leading, Schaumburg, the Swede Ny, Lovelock fourth and Beccali fifth. Nearly completing the half-mile with Cunningham still leading. Lovelock third. Lovelock's running *beautifully*. He's got a perfect position. Cunningham leading at 800 metres with Ny second and Lovelock third. Those three are going a bit away from the rest of the field. The time for the 800 metres I missed. I'm sorry. Excitement.

Cunningham leading still, with Ny second on his outside, Lovelock third, Beccali fourth. Cornes I think is fifth or sixth. Cornes fifth. Coming round into the straight for the third time – you'll hear the bell in about 30 seconds, Cunningham still leading, Lovelock just behind him – just the same position he had in America two years ago. Let's hope the result is going to be the same. Cunningham is – no, Ny is now leading, slightly ahead. No, Cunningham and Ny are *level*.

They're coming up to the bell. Cunningham, Ny, Lovelock, Beccali, Cornes. And Lovelock's just running *perfectly* now. Come on, Jack! Ny leading, Cunningham second, Lovelock third, three-quarters of a mile to go. No, that's wrong. A quarter of a mile to go. Ny is setting the pace hard as Cunningham follows on his heels. Lovelock's third. Ny leads by about two met – No, Lovelock's gone up into second position, Cunningham third. Three hundred metres to go. Lovelock LE-A-A-A-A-DS!

Three hundred metres to go, Lovelock! Cunningham's gone up into second position. Lovelock out on his own – about four yards ahead. Cunningham leading – no, no, Lovelock leads by three yards. Beccali third. Come on, Cunningh – Jack! Edwards coming up into fourth position.

Lovelock leads by about four yards, Cunningham fighting hard. Beccali's coming up to his shoulder. Lovelock *leads*! Love-lock! Love-lock! Cunningham second, Beccali third. Come on, Jack! A hundred yards to go! Come on, *Jack*!! My *God*, he's done it. Jack, come onnn! Lovelock wins. Five yards, six yards, he wins. He's won. Hooray!

Race Final of Olympic 1500 m at Berlin on the mile still left. v. fit but v. keyed up.

Drew 11 in field of 12 and at the start moved out fast but kept really well out down the long back straight. Moved in a bit at the far bend & lay about the middle of the field c Jenny Cunningham leading. The pace was steady but not excessive, my first lap being 61½. In the second Glenn Cunningham, moved up c Eric Ny & Schaumburg and for over the pace. I lay behind a little. In the third lap Cunningham kept up the lead c the rest of the field starting to flag a little. I still lay behind him and I delegated how long I should stay for though the pace was fairly good it was not excessive. Though the half was 2·5 as I roughly noted by the Stadium clock, the pace in the third lap, run in 61 → 3·6 was easier to me than the first half! At the bell Ny came up but Cunningham took the lead again down the top bend, just before entering the back straight I felt the tension of the field relax and realised, unconsciously perhaps, that everyone was taking a breather ready for a hard last 200. So at the 300 m mark I struck home passed Cunningham and ran c a 5 yard break before he awoke. Then it became

$S.M.H. Inject ~ 1,500,000.$